The Complete Forester Trilogy
A Triad in Three Acts

THE COMPLETE FORESTER TRILOGY

A TRIAD IN THREE ACTS

Blaine D. Arden

Part of the *TALES OF THE FOREST* series

A Triad in Three Acts
Copyright The Forester © 2011, Lost and Found © 2013,
Full Circle © 2016 Blaine D. Arden
ISBN: 978-90-822966-9-3
Paperback edition

Cover Art by Simoné. www.dreamarian.com
Edited by KJ Charles
Proofread by Tami Veldura
Scene divider silhouettes by zhaolifang at Vecteezy.com

This is a work of fiction. Names, characters, places, and incidents are either the products of the author's imagination or used in a fictitious manner. Any resemblance to actual persons, living or dead, events, or locales is entirely coincidental.

First Edition, August 2016

Cayendi Press
Zutphen
The Netherlands
CPress@cayendi.nl

Also available in ebook
ISBN: 978-90-822966-8-6

TO KEES AND OUR KIDS

FOR THEIR FAITH, LOVE, AND SUPPORT

AND FOR FOLLOWING THEIR OWN PATHS, PUDDLES AND ALL

TABLE OF CONTENTS

Act One
The Forester

Chapter One

THE COLD BREEZE whipping around my head, the constantly moving shadows, the absence of sound in the early morning sunlight: the forest was mourning the loss of one of its children.

Cyine lay in the frosty grass, her pink dress torn, her milky wings grey and broken. Her skin was pale, almost bluish. Her long, red curls lay in disarray around her head, but her eyes were, thankfully, closed. Despite the icy weather, she was barefoot and cloakless.

I bowed my head and folded my wings as I uttered a prayer to Ma'terra to watch over her. We dated once, Cyine and I, many turns ago when we were barely more than striplings, before I realised I preferred flat chests and stubble. Shaking my head, I watched Brem, my wingless apprentice, sweeping the ground around her for evidence, a soft mist rising where his magic touched the earth. Now was not the time for memories.

I knelt next to Cyine, the frozen ground hard under my knees, and spread my hands over her head and stomach. A soft vibration built up beneath my hands, and finger-shaped imprints appeared around Cyine's neck. Strangled, then. But who would do something like that to a kind and generous elf like her? As our tribe's truth seeker, it was my job to find out.

"Master Kelnaht?"

I turned around at the soft lilting voice of the guide, a cloud elf like Cyine and me, who stood among a small gathering of our tribe, just outside the area Brem was sweeping. He had removed his hood and tilted his head, a silent request for permission to enter the area. I nodded to him.

The guide moved towards us, wings spread and hands cupped in his familiar ritual posture as he chanted words of prayer. Those large wings only made his waifish figure seem more fragile. He knelt gracefully on the other side of Cyine's body, seeming unconcerned by the cold. He stretched his arms out and turned his hands over as he placed them above her heart and eyes. "Will you join me, Master?"

I nodded again.

The guide's voice sounded crisp, clear, and melodious in the quiet forest as he sang the Prayer of the Dead. My voice was deeper and muddier than his, but I was certain Ma'terra would forgive my lack of harmony. As the prayer progressed, my hands started to warm and tingle. Vibrations bounced between our hands and Cyine's lifeless body.

A puff of white smoke rose from her mouth and drifted higher and higher until we could see no difference between Cyine's essence and the clouds above the trees. We let our voices fade, and the guide moved his hands on top of mine as he sang the last notes alone.

I sighed, still staring at the sky. I would have loved to talk to Cyine, but we were not permitted to agitate the dead in any way or form. We were not allowed to trap them where they could not be free. The evidence would have to speak for itself. Evidence I had yet to find.

"Master Kelnaht?"

I tore my gaze away from the sky and faced the guide.

"Can we take her now?"

"Brem? Are you done?" I asked, without looking at my apprentice.

"Almost, Master. If they stick to that side, it'll be all right. I'm done checking that part."

"No more than one elf to help you," I told the guide. I pointed to the areas Brem had covered with goshe leaves to preserve the evidence. "And be careful where you step."

The guide rose and motioned for Olden, the tribe's most senior healer, to come forward. "Thank you, Master Kelnaht. I will lay her out in my safehold."

It was hard to tell him not to prepare Cyine for her journey, but I needed to examine her further. The guide would make certain no one would touch her until I had examined her.

I didn't help them pick Cyine up. I couldn't risk touching her, couldn't risk spending energy when there was still so much to do. So, I watched the guide and Olden wrap her in a cloth and pick her up, watched them carry her out of the clearing and disappear between the trees to take her home for the last time.

When they were gone, Brem joined me. I could feel his power surrounding him. Brem would one day be a much stronger truth seeker than I could ever be.

"Are we going to arrest him?"

I blinked. Brem pointed towards the other side of the clearing at the forester's dwelling. My heart pounded as I studied the old, pregnant-looking tree the forester lived in. A knee-high set of stairs led to the entrance. There was a filmy shanna leaf window on either side of the door, and two more were set into the tree above it. The forester had done a beautiful job in creating his dwelling.

A tiny flicker drew my attention to one of the windows, and my heart skipped a beat. Was that movement inside? Of course, I didn't need to see the forester to know what he looked like. The mere mention of him brought his long, thick, grey braided hair to mind, his dark clothes, his tall, wiry form, and his eyes—a blue so bright I found it piercing, despite the blank expression. Always that same blank expression.

The forester, a wingless tree elf like Brem, tended to our trees, protected them from abuse, shaped them into our homes, and encouraged them to grow. He was said to be covered in vine tattoos from head to toe, which he had done when he was apprenticed to the last forester, many turns ago. I had only caught glimpses of the beautiful green vines adorning his face and neck, but I longed to see it all, longed to touch...

I shivered at my sinful thoughts and pushed them down. Despite my continuous attempts to free my mind from him, he had claimed a place in my heart that should have never been his, could never be his. He was forbidden. He was shunned.

"You know we cannot. Not without permission from the elders," I finally answered.

Only one elf was allowed to talk to the forester, and that was the guide. But as our spiritual pathfinder, our confessor and confidant, he would not—could not—discuss their conversations. Not even with the elders, and certainly not with me. No, aside from the fact that I didn't think the forester would do such a thing, I would have to rely solely on the evidence we found to solve this case.

"But Healer Olden says he must have done it."

"Healer Olden knows better. His claim is not the proof the elders need."

With a sigh, I cast one last look at the forester's dwelling and turned back to inspect Brem's work. We were far from done here.

THE GUIDE WAITED for me outside his safehold—a meditation room—his wings folded and hood pulled forward. "We have taken care not to touch her," he said, raising his eyes to meet mine.

The guide's grey eyes showed a sadness I felt as well. Cyine was a cherished female, ten days away from vowing herself to Kadil, a young winged herder. I had seen them sit together at the centre a couple of times; he doted on her, and her eyes lit up when he smiled at her. Had the guide already spoken to Kadil or Cyine's parents? Or was he waiting until I had examined her?

"I need to wash first." Wash off the debris from examining the clearing and cleanse my mind of sinful thoughts before I could even think to examine Cyine's death.

The guide bowed his head and led me into a small chamber with a bowl and pitcher. He handed me a towel and left me to wash up.

I held my hands under the water until I could no longer feel the cold. Only then did I take a bit of the herbal mixture the guide had placed beside the bowl and scrub them clean. I closed my eyes, splashed my face, and said a quick prayer to Ma'terra to guide me through my task and forgive me my misplaced desires. A couple of deep breaths and a quick dry later, I felt ready to face one of the tasks I dreaded most in my work.

Cyine had been placed on a low bed, her wings so carefully laid out, I could barely see the breaks. She seemed even more pale in this well-lit, serene room. Though the guide and I had freed her spirit, I could not help but see Cyine's smile when I looked at her face. She was supposed to be an empty shell, just her mortal vessel, but to me, she was my first kiss, and I couldn't look away.

The guide coughed, and I looked up at him. "Do you need my help?" His question was a mere formality. His attendance was a fact, and he hated not being useful. He needed to know he was tending his elves the best he could, even after they departed.

"If you could help me remove her clothing."

The guide nodded, and we set to work. We cut the dress open on the front, carefully pulled it over her arms, and laid it on the floor. She wasn't wearing underwear, but barring some scratches, her body seemed unblemished, and I couldn't help but be relieved. A soft sigh from the guide told me he felt the same way.

My hands were still cold from washing. I rubbed them together and placed them over her body. I took a deep breath and focussed all my energy on my hands. From the corner of my eye, I noticed the guide turning away, and I couldn't blame him. *I* didn't much want to know what my examination would turn up. But it was my job, and one I was good at.

The vibrations started out softly, centred beneath my hands, slowly spreading out until it became difficult to keep my hands still. I had never grown used to how a body felt beneath my hands when I examined it. Even when I closed my eyes, I could feel every bump, sense every curve. I didn't open my eyes until my hands stopped trembling.

The guide's sigh of relief wasn't as soft this time. The marks on Cyine indicated she had been dragged across the ground, and her murderer must have grabbed her by her arms to stop her from clawing at them, but she hadn't been beaten or violated sexually. She had tried to fend her attacker off, that much was clear from the way her fingers had coloured, showing bruise-like imprints.

I carefully scraped her fingernails to collect anything she might have gathered under them, and examined the band of finger-shaped imprints around her neck. Wrapping the evidence in goshe leaves, I asked for Brem to be summoned. He was a better artist than I was, and the print needed to be perfect.

The guide called out to his novice to fetch him. "Can we put her dress in order?" he asked, eyes averted.

I shook my head. "You can cover her with a cloth, but we'll need to examine the dress as well. As soon as Brem has copied the marks on her neck, we can roll her over, remove her dress, and I can examine her back."

The guide took good care to cover her so that only her neck was still exposed. I leaned back against the wall and closed my eyes, letting the guide's murmurs wash over me as I waited for Brem.

TIRED AS I was after spending all day scouring the clearing for evidence and examining Cyine's body, I wasn't to be granted any rest yet. Someone knocked on my door just as I finished washing up and changing my clothes. I regretted opening the door as soon as I saw Ianys standing outside, but managed not to slam it closed.

"What do you want?" I asked, not caring how hostile I sounded.

After all this time, Ianys couldn't even look at me as he stood there, fidgeting with his tunic, eyes lowered to the ground.

Ianys was as gorgeous as ever. Cropped brown hair, sticking up at all sides as if he had just risen from sleep, that made me want to run my hands… I swallowed and lowered my gaze to his chest. His muscles were visible through his tight tunic. He was a broad tree elf, more muscular than when we had been together, but as a smith that was to be expected; working the bellows was hefty exercise in itself. I pushed down the memory of watching him work when we had been together.

In all the turns since he had left me, betrayed me, he had barely spoken two words to me. Instead, I had to watch from afar as he vowed himself to another, only to lose her to illness after their daughter was born. I could only stand by and watch how hard he worked at being a good father, how he finally became a full-fledged smith. He'd never once approached me, but the hope lingering inside me could never be buried deep enough. How could I still want him? After eight turns, I should know better.

"I don't have time for this, Ianys. I am tired and I—"

"I need to talk to you."

"Can't it wait till morning?"

I had to bite my lip to keep from reacting when he finally looked up. His eyes, green as fresh grass and filled with turmoil, drew me in the way they had always done. I'd loved him once. I shook my head. Who was I fooling? I had never stopped.

Holding the door open, I stepped aside to let him in, staying in the small hallway until I managed to compose myself.

"He didn't do it, Kel."

Whatever anyone had or hadn't done was the furthest thing from my mind when Ianys called me by that name. I clenched my fists and turned my back to him, hoping he couldn't see how it affected me. "You have no right to call me that."

A long silence followed. I tried to school my features, but I was too drained. Instead, I kept my back to him and waited for him to break the silence. I heard him sigh.

"I heard they accuse him of killing Cyine, but he didn't do it," Ianys finally said.

"Who?" What could Ianys know about the murder?

"Taruif."

I froze. My first instinct was to tell Ianys he shouldn't be saying that name, shouldn't even think it, but there was something in Ianys' voice that made me stop. Something of a memory from long ago, when I didn't know how Ianys had betrayed me, and we lay together in the dark, and he would whisper my name in that same way.

It could not be true. But when I finally turned around and looked at him, it was all too clear in Ianys' face. The one I loved —had loved—and the one I desired, joined in illicit relations.

I should arrest Ianys, should send him to face the elders and have him punished, shunned, shut out for his transgression. But then I pictured Atèn, his daughter, looking at me with those same green eyes, and I knew I could not rob her of a father as well.

"He didn't do it, Kelnaht. He couldn't have done it, for I—"

I shook my head and held my hand up to stop him. "Don't tell me, Ianys. I beg of you, do not confess to this...this abomination."

It hurt me to say it, having the same feelings myself, but if he told me, I could not help him. Being caught talking to the forester was bad enough, though I had the right to pardon him for that, a first offence. But confessing to lying with a shunned, that would have to be reported to the elders; it was my duty. I would not be able to save him then.

"He saw someone outside, Kelnaht. He didn't see Cyine, but he noticed someone out in the dark, in that clearing." His eyes begged me to understand, begged me to help him, but I was rooted to the floor.

I knew that the forester—I could not allow myself to think

of him by name—hadn't killed Cyine, even if the evidence was still inconclusive. I had no doubt in my mind, no matter how loud Olden proclaimed him guilty. And here Ianys was, confirming my belief in his innocence and giving me the best and worst witness I could ever have. No matter whether I believed Ianys or not, I could never use this information. The forester was out of bounds.

"Kel, please, help us. Help him. I could have been out walking when I stumbled across the clearing. You know I don't always sleep well."

I didn't want him to bring our history up. I didn't want him to tell me about the forester. I wanted him gone, wanted him to go back to his daughter and go back to not being part of my life. But I found myself unable to turn him out. "You would perjure yourself, would risk losing your daughter?"

"No! No one but you knows the truth."

I laughed at that, flinching at how harsh it sounded. "I am the truth seeker, Ianys. I seek the truth; I do not bury lies."

"I *was* in the forest."

"But you didn't see what he saw. One mistake and you will be shunned, just like him."

Ianys flinched then. He shook his head. "There has to be a way."

"Get him to talk to the guide."

"Anything the guide hears during those conversations is confidential. He can't reveal anything Taruif tells him."

"Please." The word left my mouth before I could stop it. I couldn't handle him speaking that name with such devotion. Not when I ached to be able to myself. "Remember who you are talking to, Ianys. Do not incriminate yourself any further." I leaned back against the wall, trying to stay upright, and closed my eyes. "Go home, Ianys. I need to... I need to think."

I swatted away the hand touching my cheek and waited for the door to close. Gasping and fighting back tears, I slid to the floor.

Chapter Two

Lying in my bed, images of my past with Ianys, of my desires for him and the forester, of Atèn and Cyine swirled around in my head, not giving me a moment's rest. Yet, when Brem knocked on my door in the morning, I jerked awake, so I must have slept at least a little, even if I felt like I hadn't slept all night. Not even the strongest tea seemed to clear my head.

Brem had his own key to the workshop. By the time I made it down there, he had already laid out most of the evidence and stood with his hands hovering over one of the items, trying to read it. I watched him work, pride filling my heart. Never before had a tree elf shown an aptitude for truth seeking, but Brem did, though I suspected his mother's cloud elf lineage had something to do with that. Brem had been my apprentice for almost two turns now and, despite his occasional clumsiness, he was very gifted and learned quickly.

"Good morning, Master. I have made you breakfast."

I sighed. Brem knew my habits only too well. Breakfast was the last thing on my mind, but I needed to eat if I intended to work today. Powers did not flow well on an empty stomach. "Thank you, Brem." I sat down at the table and looked at the sandwich. "How are you faring with the evidence?"

"Slowly, Master. Frost and dampness make it difficult to read. Plenty of smudges on her dress, including some blood from her scratches. But nothing that leads to who did it."

I nodded and took a careful bite. My stomach stayed steady. As much as I understood Brem's complaints, there was nothing to be done. I had left a small fire smouldering in the workshop during the night, but I couldn't risk burning it any higher as it would dry out the evidence, causing important elements to evaporate. And too much smoke would have contaminated it all. Better wet evidence than no evidence.

"I do hope we'll have solved this before Solstice, Master."

The Solstice Circle. I closed my eyes. The gathering of the unvowed in search of a mate. Every turn I went, and every turn I returned home alone. Ianys never came to the Circle. The forester did, despite his status, but no one would dare approach him. It was painful to see him slighted turn after turn after turn, yet he would still go. At times, I wished I had the courage to walk up to him and claim him as mine.

Images of Ianys and the forester drifted to the surface, and with a sigh, I pushed away the plate, only half the sandwich eaten, and rose. Maybe I should skip the Solstice Circle this turn. It wasn't as if I wanted anyone else.

Standing across from Brem, I cleansed my hands and studied the evidence. A piece of leather lying on soggy grass and soil in a dish caught my attention.

"I've not been able to get a clear reading from that, Master. I'm afraid it is just too wet."

I raised my hands, rubbed them against each other, and spread them above the leather. Vibrations rose more quickly than I expected; the food, little as it had been, had helped. The piece was too small to discern any colour changes, but I could definitely sense something coming from it. I breathed in and out as I closed my eyes and focussed on that tiny thread. Blood. There was blood on the leather, or had been. It had mostly been absorbed by the soil by now. It couldn't be Cyine's; her wounds were too insignificant to bleed like that. So, it had to be the murderer's.

Digging deeper gave me nothing else. The blood was too diluted, and the leather sliver itself was useless as evidence unless we found the torn glove or shoe or maybe cloak it came from. I shoved it aside.

For the next couple of hours, we examined every bit of evidence we had found. Most turned out to be useless, left at the clearing well before Cyine was murdered. All we really had in the end were the piece of leather and the marks of fingers around Cyine's neck.

I took Brem's drawing of the finger marks and studied it. It was as detailed and complete as I expected his work to be. He had even included a tiny mole on Cyine's neck. "What do you think, Brem? Gloves?"

"That was what I thought when I drew it, Master."

I took the paper and rolled it up. "See if you can put your hands around it."

"It needs to be a bit tighter, Master." Brem picked up a small piece of paper. "I took the liberty of measuring Mistress Cyine's neck."

"Quick thinking, Brem. Well done." I rolled the paper up tighter.

Brem checked the measurements, and wrapped his hands around it. Brem's hands were smaller, and his fingers thinner than the ones on paper. And bare. "Did you bring your gloves?"

Brem nodded and put them on. His hands were still smaller, though it was difficult to say with the paper moving and sliding the way it did.

"If you give me a little time, I can make a sturdier copy that we can glue to a thick branch, Master."

I didn't try to hide my pride. If the elders still had any doubts Brem would make a fine truth seeker one day, his quick thinking would surely convince them. I would make certain to mention it in my next report to them.

BREM HAD JUST finished gluing the paper onto the branch, when a loud knocking on the door interrupted us. Brem nearly dropped the branch. I shook my head at him and turned towards the door.

The guide greeted me with a solemn face. "We have been summoned by the elders."

I turned to Brem. "Let no one in," I warned him as I grabbed my cloak and gloves. It took some doing to drape the cloak so my wings would slide through the slits, but the guide showed no haste. He didn't seem at all happy to have been summoned, and neither was I.

"Were they not satisfied with my report?" I asked as we walked to the oldest oak in the forest.

"They seemed content enough when I reported to them yesterday, and told them you would see them after you finished your examination of the evidence. I don't know what this is about."

"How are her parents holding up?"

"They're devastated, and so are Master Kadil and his family. He insisted on seeing her, but I managed to convince him not to. He will want to see her when you're finished, though."

"Of course. Though you might have to ask for a dress to cover her."

"Already did." Of course he had. Dignity was important to him. Always had been. "I also told them you might need to speak with them."

"That's good. I'll be as brief as possible."

"I know you will, Kelnaht."

A true sign of the friendship we shared for the guide to speak my name in public without the proper address attached. Granted, there was no one around, but it was a welcome gesture. If only I could return it, but his name existed solely within the walls of his dwelling, where no one but he resided.

We reached the ancient oak, and I looked up at the platform just underneath the wealth of leaves at the top of the tree. Elders' Court was one of few higher dwellings still in use. Many chose lower dwellings nowadays, not wanting to climb stairs or fly down to talk to their neighbours. I loved how my own dwelling spread over three spacious levels, with my workshop on the lowest level. Knowing the forester had created it that way for me warmed my heart.

"Ready to go up?" the guide asked.

I nodded and spread my wings, shivering as the chill hit them. The guide seemed steadfast as ever and, not for the first time, I wondered how cold did not touch him the way it did everyone else. We lifted off and flew up towards Elders' Court's platform, landing just inside of it. I was quick to fold my wings, but the chill had reached my spine already, and I shivered anew.

The guide hadn't even finished knocking when we were allowed into the warmth of the court. We took off our cloaks and gloves, hanging them on the railing to one side of the door, and crossed the room to the dais where the five elders sat watching us. We bowed and sat only when one of them gestured us to.

Elder Garren inclined his head. "We understand suspicion rests on the forester." I opened my mouth to protest, but Elder Garren held up his hand. "We know no evidence supports this suspicion. Yet, we know your hands are tied in this matter, and we have decided to grant you leniency."

Grant me leniency? I glanced at the guide, but he seemed as puzzled as I was.

"You are allowed to question the forester about this case, and this case only," Elder Garren continued. "In the presence of the guide, of course."

I barely managed to stop my jaw from dropping. I had permission to talk to the forester about this case. I thought of Ianys and his plea to let him perjure himself. I didn't think either had talked to the guide yet, and now they wouldn't have to. Well, the guide would have to be there when I talked to the forester, but still. I could ask the forester what he had seen, could bring the evidence to him and have his hands checked against Brem's tree branch model of the fingers that had circled Cyine's neck. Maybe I could examine his gloves, his cloak, his shoes, and see if there was a piece missing.

I rose and bowed. "Thank you for this leniency. I will not squander it."

For the first time, I was allowed to talk to a shunned, to the forester, without risking punishment, even if it was only about the case. My knees wobbled, and I turned about stiffly, hoping no one would notice. I had no doubt the guide knew what was going through my mind. I never mentioned the forester in our talks, but the guide didn't learn all about his elves just from talking to us.

I felt his hand at my elbow, steadying me as I stumbled. He led me towards the rail and handed me my cloak. One last perfunctory bow later, we stood on the platform again, wings spread out in the chill.

The guide nodded at me as we descended and landed side by side in the snow below. I folded my wings and drew my cloak more tightly around me, hoping it would chase the chills away soon.

"When are you free?" I asked him when we reached my workshop.

"Call on me when you are ready to leave." He turned, walked a few paces, and turned back. He opened his mouth, but closed it again when a couple of children ran past. "Call on me, and I'll let you know if I am free."

"I will. Thank you."

Thank the elders for giving me this opportunity. I muttered a quick prayer to Ma'terra as I tried to remember if I still had something left of that valerian root I bought moons ago to dull my nerves. It wouldn't do me any good to be unable to utter a word when I questioned the forester.

I STOOD WATCHING Ianys hammering on a piece of metal. Every now and then he held it up or reheated it, repeating the process until he was satisfied and finally thrust it into a bucket of water. He was so absorbed in his work, that he didn't even notice me.

"Master Ianys."

He turned as if bitten, eyes wide as he saw me. "You thought on it?" he asked.

I shook my head and held up the tree branch model Brem made. "I'm here in official capacity. I need to see your hands, gloves, cloak, and shoes."

"My shoes?"

It was a good thing Ianys' forge was on the outside of the village and no one was around to hear us speak. "You were in the forest at the time of the murder, Ianys."

"But—"

"Just show me what I asked you for."

Ianys shook his head and sighed, but he opened a cupboard and handed me his cloak and gloves. He sat on a small stool. "Do you want me to take my shoes off?"

I held up the familiar soft leather cloak lined with a dark green fabric and only barely resisted the urge to smell it. I didn't need the distraction. "No. You can keep them on. For now."

His cloak wasn't ripped anywhere. I grabbed the piece of leather. Not even the same colour. I put the cloak down and studied the gloves. Same colour as the cloak. Not that I expected a match, but I needed to rule it out before I visited the forester. "Lift your foot, please."

Foot in the air, Ianys looked at me as I examined the shoe. "You look good."

I froze at the unexpected desire in his voice. I should have sent Brem. No, I couldn't have. Brem would have asked questions, would have wanted to know why I thought Ianys a person of interest. Ignoring Ianys' words, or at least pretending to ignore them, I checked out the other shoe. No tears, not even the same leather. Relief flooded my mind. I hadn't realised how much I'd worried, despite knowing Ianys had an alibi, and no reason to murder Cyine.

Only one more thing to check. I held up the model and

asked Ianys to put his gloves on and wrap his hands around it.

"What does this mean?" Ianys asked as he did what I told him to do. "What is that?"

It was easy to see that Ianys hands were larger than those on the model. "It means that you are not the murderer."

Ianys' eyes widened in hurt. "You thought—"

I hastened to reassure him. "I never suspected you, but I needed to check because of what you told me."

"And you can tell from that thing that I didn't do it?"

"Yes."

"Does that mean you're going to—" He stopped himself and shook his head. "I apologise."

He didn't need to know, it was not his business. But it was, and he did. It was in his eyes, in the way he held his body. Hating that I could still read him so well, I deliberately turned away from him to compose myself. He wasn't mine anymore. "No. I will not let you perjure yourself. I've been granted leniency by the elders. I'm allowed to talk to Ta—the forester." It was too much to hope Ianys wouldn't notice my mistake, but he didn't remark on it.

His eyes lit up at that. "That's good. These things you checked with me, they'll clear him as well."

There it was again, that tone in his voice. It was more than I could bear, and I left the forge without a word, and before he could ask more.

I HAD BARELY replaced the evidence on the table when Brem came running into the workshop, out of breath and looking harried.

"Master. You need to come with me to the guide's safehold."

"Is the guide giving you a hard time?"

"No, Master. I've found..." Brem swallowed and closed his eyes for a moment. "I've found disturbing evidence."

I frowned. "Evidence?"

"Yes, Master."

Had Brem found evidence I missed? I grabbed my cloak and followed Brem to the guide's safehold. He rushed me through the cleansing ritual, and within moments, the three of us were kneeling over Cyine's body. Still, Brem hadn't told us what he'd found. All he would say was that he'd sensed something he hadn't been prepared for and wasn't certain if he'd read it correctly.

All three of us spread our hands over Cyine's body, stomach, heart, and head. It didn't take long for our powers to combine as the vibrations built up beneath our hands. The guide's power was unlike ours. It felt different, like a ribbon of light between our dull vibrations, yet it completed our circle, our stream.

As soon as Brem moved his hand across Cyine's stomach, I sensed what he had sensed and understood what had upset him. Cyine was with child—had been with child—and the child's essence had been released to the light before Cyine was found dead. I doubted Cyine had done that.

I didn't dare look up to see the guide's reaction. The stuttering of his power was hard enough to bear. He who guided us through life and death was a strong elf, however fragile he might look, but this useless shedding of life undid him every single time. Despite this, the guide stayed with us as I had Brem delve deeper to try and find out as much as he could, softly singing the Prayer of the Dead. Still, I wasn't surprised when he excused himself as soon as Brem was done, his face as ashen as his hair.

Brem and I repeated the cleansing ritual and sat outside the safehold on a low bench. The ground had been cleared of snow, wiped to the edges, forming a low border around us.

"The life was new, barely a moon and a half. Its essence was released after Mistress Cyine died."

I swallowed. Maybe Cyine hadn't known she was with child. The idea was comforting, but whoever killed her had obviously known. "Are you certain?"

"Yes, though it was hard to read since there were no traces

of the child's essence left behind." Brem paused and took a deep breath. "Mistress Cyine was thoroughly scrubbed clean of any evidence, barring the thickening of the uterus I sensed earlier, and the lingering traces I found after we merged our energies."

"Why remove the child?"

"Because whoever killed Mistress Cyine didn't want anyone to know about the pregnancy." The guide's voice sounded even softer than normal, as if he'd been crying.

Brem and I turned our heads, but he wasn't coming out of the safehold. He came down the path next to it, hood pulled over his eyes and his hands folded in the sleeves. Where had he disappeared to?

"They released the child's essence. Tried to erase its existence. They didn't count on Apprentice Brem's gift."

The guide was right about that. I hadn't sensed the thickening of the uterus when I examined Cyine, but Brem had, even if he needed our powers to confirm his find.

"Or mine," the guide continued. "I flew high above the trees, hoping to find the child among the essences dwelling there. And I did. A boy. Such a tiny presence, but his ancestry clear. I'd have recognised him even if he hadn't been clinging to his mother's essence. Master Kadil is his father."

He once told me he found their presence soothing. Did he still feel that way now? "Did Master Kadil mention anything about expecting a child? Or Mistress Cyine's parents?"

"No. No, I don't think they knew."

"Do you think Mistress Cyine knew?"

"I don't know. Mistress Cyine mentioned she would like to try, but that was at least three moons ago. Master Kadil's sister had just given birth then."

"Master? About Master Kadil..." Brem sounded hesitant.

He was supposed to visit Kadil with his tree branch model. I didn't blame him for having second thoughts. "Best get that over with. But nothing about the pregnancy."

"But he didn't do it."

Neither had Ianys, but I couldn't say that out loud. "It would rule out his involvement. You know we need to, if only to prevent rumours."

Brem sighed. "Yes, Master." He pushed himself to his feet and walked away.

"So, need I know why you visited Master Ianys this morning?"

"Nothing I care to talk about, Guide. But rest assured, Ianys is not a suspect."

"Ah. So noted." He sat next to me.

He knew. The guide knew about Ianys and the forester. I should have known. The guide knew all our secrets, probably even those we didn't tell him. I hadn't expected him knowing about their affair to hurt.

"Kelnaht—"

"No."

The guide rose and rested his hand on my head. "Your path is muddy, Kelnaht, but don't think avoiding the puddles will make it easier to travel."

He said puddles. I envisioned lakes, deep, treacherous lakes, and I was drowning.

Chapter Three

T HE VALERIAN ROOT seemed to be working as the guide and I walked towards the forester's dwelling. I felt strangely detached and dulled, as though my head was wrapped in multiple layers of cloth. Yet, my mind was clear, and I felt better prepared to question the forester. I wasn't nervous by nature, but after five turns of desiring the forester, of dreaming of him, it was a bit daunting to finally talk to him.

The guide kept looking at me sideways as we walked side by side, but he didn't ask, didn't offer unsolicited advice. Yesterday's offering still lingered close to the surface.

We passed the murder scene, bedecked with a new layer of snow that crunched under our feet, making it look as if Cyine had never lain there. The guide stared straight ahead, but I heard him mutter a prayer. Finding out Cyine's unborn child had been murdered as well had shaken him. It had shaken all of us. The elders had pressed us to hasten our investigation.

After speaking to the forester, I hoped to exclude one more suspect. But most of all, I hoped the forester's witness report would lead us closer to who murdered Cyine and released her son's essence. Her unborn son.

The guide hadn't told Kadil yet, and I wished we could get away with not telling him at all. Neither Kadil nor Cyine's parents needed the added pain.

The forest was quiet in these parts, but contrary to when we found Cyine, I could hear birds chirping in faraway trees. The forester's dwelling seemed rather lonely here at the edge of our grounds, a brisk walk away from the village itself. I knew he had chosen to live here, but it seemed so isolated. As isolated as the forester himself was.

The guide knocked, and when the forester opened the door, he shot the guide a smile, a genuine smile, until he noticed me. His face immediately moulded itself into the blank expression I knew so well.

"Guide, Master Kelnaht. Please, come in."

His voice was deeper than I had imagined, deeper than mine even. A dark timbre that vibrated through my core. So much for the valerian root working. I inclined my head and followed them inside. I'd been given permission to talk to him, not to use his name, so I was a bit lost as to what to call him.

Standing in the door opening of the living room, I froze. I don't know what had made me expect old wooden furniture, cosy but dark, but this was nothing like that. Though the floor was dark, the furniture was all light wood, sleek. The walls as well, and not a single decoration adorned them. A side table across the room seemed to hold all the decorations: small paintings and wooden carvings. I liked the clean and calming mood this room seemed to reflect.

"I made goraf tea," the forester said from behind me.

I only barely kept from jumping, though suppressing the shudder that passed through me was more difficult. I sat down in a chair next to the guide and put my bag on the floor so the forester would be forced to sit opposite us, on the other side of a low table.

The forester poured the tea and sat down, looking straight at me. I couldn't resist staring at the beautiful green vines disappearing below the neckline of his tunic. When the forester swallowed, the motion made it seem like the vines were alive, moving. What would it be like to kiss him there?

The guide's voice dragged my thoughts away from the forester's neck. "Master Taruif. As you've been informed, the elders have granted Master Kelnaht permission to ask you questions about the murder of Mistress Cyine. The elders request you answer all questions to the best of your knowledge."

"Of course, Guide. I have nothing to hide."

Nothing but an illicit affair with Ianys, that was. I pushed my irritation down. His relationship with Ianys had nothing to do with the investigation.

"Good." The guide turned to me. "I will be present at all times, and if I feel you're overstepping boundaries, I will end the conversation."

"Of course, Guide."

"Good. Well, then you can begin."

I opened my bag and took out the tree branch model and wrapped piece of leather. "I'd like to see your cloak, gloves, and shoes."

It seemed the forester already knew what I was going to ask, because he grabbed the items from the floor next to him and handed them to me. As expected, they didn't match the piece of leather. His cloak was made of dark, almost black leather, the same colour as his tunics, and, not surprisingly, his gloves and shoes. The cloak was heavy, thick beneath my fingers, and a dark woody scent reached my nose. I compared it to the piece of leather, but, even from a distance, the difference in colour was plain to see, and I handed them back with a muttered, "Thank you."

I held up the model as I rose. "Please, put your gloves on and wrap your hands around this, your fingers on the drawn marks."

The forester frowned, but didn't hesitate. He stood and placed his gloved fingers on the marks, wriggling them around a bit to get them in the right position. My heart almost stopped as they seemed to overlap perfectly. Until I took a closer look. His fingers might be the right length, but they were thinner than the marks. I had the guide take a look as well, since I couldn't afford any mistakes.

"No match. Right?" the guide asked as he pointed at the fingers and the marks beneath them. "Not the same thickness."

I nodded and turned to the forester. "You're not a match, not a suspect."

The forester stared into my eyes and inclined his head. "Thank you."

After putting the model and piece of leather back into the bag, I sat down again and grabbed my tea, enjoying the sweet scent of the goraf leaves as I raised it to my lips. I needed this. Even if it was just to give myself some time. The forester's eyes, however, were still locked on mine. I averted my gaze, afraid of what my eyes might show him.

I finished my tea and sat straighter, trying hard to ignore the forester staring at me. "Did you see anything suspicious outside this dwelling on the night of the murder?"

"I did. But only briefly, I'm afraid. I didn't see poor Mistress Cyine lying on the ground, and I didn't recognise the elf, but he was stocky, wide, wingless."

His voice wasn't any less distracting than his appearance, his staring, had been. "Are you sure about that?"

"His cloak hung too sleek for someone hiding his wings underneath."

"What makes you certain it was a male?"

"None of our females have that build."

He could be right about that. At least, none of the females I knew fit that description. "Where did you see him?"

"Just along the trees. He stuck as close to them as possible, but the moon was bright last night. Unfortunately, his head was hidden by his hood and he faced away from me. I thought he'd been out hunting."

"Why?"

"He carried something in a large, lumpy looking bag. My guess was rabbits."

My guess was Cyine's shoes, and maybe even her cloak, though he might have been a hunter carrying game. "You didn't see Mistress Cyine in the clearing?"

"No. When I saw him, the clearing was empty."

"So, you saw this elf before Mistress Cyine was murdered?"

The forester shrugged. "I couldn't say. I didn't realise what had happened until I came downstairs for breakfast the next morning and you were already investigating."

After what Ianys told me, I had expected more. The elf the forester had seen might not even be the one we were looking for. Still, if I did a trace scan where the forester had seen him walking, I would know soon enough. I hoped.

I WALKED THE same stretch of land for the fourth time. All I had to do was imagine the forester's voice and stubbled jaw, picture the vines moving as he swallowed, as he talked, and my concentration was lost. Again. I needed to get my head together, but I couldn't put him out of my mind.

It was his voice telling me what the suspect looked like, his hands slipping inside his gloves… And there I went again. I walked back to the tree I'd started with and took a deep breath. Maybe I should just give up and have Brem investigate this part later.

No. This was my job, I was good at it, and I wasn't going to walk home with my tail between my legs just because the object of my desire was so close. I grabbed my small bag with cleaning herbs out of the inside pocket of my cloak and rubbed a small measure into my gloveless and cold fingers for, hopefully, the last time.

I kept rubbing my hands together until they tingled with warmth, then moved them away from each other and turned them palms down. I focussed on my hands, on the ground beneath me, the ground I hoped held the clues I was looking for. Even just a small clue would be helpful, something to connect the elf the forester saw with Cyine's murderer. Anything.

The ground beneath the snow was cold, unyielding. It didn't give up anything without pressure. I prodded as deep and as far as I could, little trails of snow melting beneath me from the warmth of the energy flowing from my hands. Step by step, I advanced along the trees until, finally, I had to admit defeat. There was nothing here. Nothing but the useless indentations of smudged footsteps. Their depth indicated that whoever walked here had been carrying something heavy, but whether that meant Cyine's murderer or a hunter, I couldn't say.

I flew home, but not before taking one last look at the forester's dwelling and remembering how that deep voice had made me shiver.

Brem greeted me with news that Kadil wasn't a match. Not that I'd expected him to be, but it was good to have him ruled out. Brem had discovered something interesting. Olden was Cyine's healer. Cyine's, but not Kadil's. And Olden had come to visit Kadil just when Brem was leaving.

"He had this odd expression in his eyes, Master. Haunted, I'd say. And he appeared to be wearing new gloves."

New gloves? Of course, having new gloves didn't automatically make him the murderer, but the timing made it suspect. With a start, it dawned on me that Olden could easily fit the forester's description. He was a stocky elf, about the guide's height, but much rounder and sturdier, and he was Cyine's healer.

I needed to interview him. Soon. But, considering how dark it was outside, not today. I excused Brem and let him go home for dinner with his family while I cleaned the workshop.

Olden was a respected healer in our village. He had helped deliver Atèn, helped deliver me, and healed my father when he had been struck by a falling branch once. Why would Olden kill Cyine and her unborn child?

I grabbed my cloak, leaving my wings underneath it since I didn't plan on flying, and went outside. Maybe the guide was still up. But just as I turned onto the path towards the guide's safehold, Ianys disappeared into the forest.

All thoughts of the guide and Olden disappeared when I realised where he was going, and without a moment's thought, I wormed my wings through the slits in my cloak and followed

Ianys to the forester's dwelling.

Ianys glanced behind him every couple of steps, but only until he was far enough into the forest that he couldn't be seen from the village. I hid from view as I tracked him, staying close to the trees, hovering in the air just outside his direct line of sight, hoping Ianys wouldn't think to look up.

It was madness, this need to follow him, but I couldn't bring myself to turn around. Not while I followed him through the forest, not when he entered the forester's dwelling, and not when I noticed movement behind the bedroom window. I didn't even hesitate to fly up to a branch sticking out to the side of the window and look in.

The forester was shirtless. I couldn't look away from the vines trailing down the left side of his chest and strong abdomen, alongside a light dousing of hairs. He was beautiful with his long, grey hair hanging loose. I ached to run my hands through it.

Ianys, standing with his back to me, undressed as the forester watched him, the tips of his ears red as he blushed. Ianys always blushed so prettily. I could just imagine his expression, part arousal, part anticipation, and part love. Ianys exposed his broad, muscular back, and I grabbed the tree tighter to keep from falling down. Aside from his obvious strength, I loved the control Ianys possessed when he moved.

His muscles contracted, tensed as he reached for his trousers and pushed them down his arse. My mouth went dry. I should go. I knew I should go, but I wanted to stay, wanted to keep watching them. They were gorgeous together, the elves I desired. They fit.

When Ianys finished undressing, he moved closer to the forester. How could I keep calling him that when I watched them like this? Taruif. His name was Taruif. I convinced myself it was all right to use it here, where he lived, where no one could hear me, see me.

Taruif trailed a hand down Ianys' chest, then pulled Ianys against him and kissed him. I wished they would turn just a bit, because all I could see was their heads moving. I couldn't see their expressions, only the way Ianys' hand snaked up across Taruif's shoulder, trailing up his neck until he grabbed a handful of Taruif's hair.

I must have closed my eyes for a moment, because the next moment, Ianys and Taruif lay side by side on the bed, naked and touching, caressing and kissing. I only barely kept from moaning as Ianys kissed a path down Taruif's chest, his abdomen, his cock. Taruif pushed himself up on his elbows, eyes heavy with desire, and his gaze met mine through the window.

Biting back a gasp, I jumped up, flying as high as I could go. The cold did nothing to stave off my arousal. What was I doing, spying on them? Why was I watching them?

As I flew home, I prayed to Ma'terra that Taruif's eyes meeting mine had been my imagination.

The shock of what I'd done didn't keep me from climbing underneath my blankets and bringing myself off to the image of Taruif and Ianys making love, the way they fit together, the desire in their eyes.

When I finally came, I couldn't help but wish I'd been part of it, part of them.

Chapter Four

I slept fitfully, lost in dreams, and torn between desire and guilt. By the time I made it downstairs, Brem was already sweeping the floor.

"I made breakfast, Master."

Of course he had. I nodded at him and sat down, gobbling up the bean stew he had served me.

"Shall I pick up Healer Olden, Master?"

Only then did I remember that I hadn't visited the guide as I had planned. Despite not being awake enough to deal with this, I told Brem to go ahead, but to inform the guide first. No doubt the guide would be here before Brem returned with Olden.

As soon as Brem left, I ran up the stairs to the bathroom, rubbed my hands together, and placed them against the reservoir to heat the rainwater for a quick shower. I needed to focus on this interview, not get lost in what would never be. Dried, dressed, and back downstairs, I set up the room for the interview. I put chairs on both sides of one end of my work table and placed the evidence, including Cyine's dress, on the other end, in sight but out of reach. Then I made myself some strong tea and settled into my chair.

I started when the door banged open and the guide entered the workshop.

"What is this rubbish about suspecting Healer Olden?"

"No rubbish, Guide. Healer Olden fits the description, and

he was Mistress Cyine's healer. He may have known about the pregnancy."

The guide shook his head. "No. Not Healer Olden. He's still mourning the loss of Mistress Esaye."

That stopped me. The guide sounded so certain. Mistress Esaye, Olden's vowed, had been a generous elf, just like Cyine. Giving and friendly and never too busy to talk or help out. She had died about five turns back after a terrible illness. Olden had tried so hard to save her, but it had been too late.

I knew all that. So, why was it that all that ran through my mind were the similarities between Mistress Esaye and Cyine? "That doesn't rule it out, Guide. You know that. I have to talk to him, have to check his hands, his gloves—"

"I'll attend the interview, but I refuse to believe he is capable of killing anyone."

I thought better than to mention Olden was certainly capable of hitting other elves when he disagreed with them. It didn't happen often, but every once in a while he'd be spending the night in a cell because of it, something which had gotten worse after Mistress Esaye died.

The guide declined the tea and sat down with his back to me. I had downed two cups of the vile stuff by the time Brem finally returned. Without Olden. I frowned.

"He's not at home, Master," Brem said, sounding out of breath. "Or in his infirmary."

"He's disappeared?"

"It seems so, Master. His neighbour said she hasn't seen him since he went to the infirmary yesterday morning."

"But he wasn't at the infirmary?"

"No, Master, and neither his bed nor the one in his office looked slept in."

Had he run? Or had something happened to him? "Brem, alert the elders. We need to find him."

Brem nodded and went back out.

I turned to the guide, who frowned at me. "What's the first place we should look?"

The guide seemed to think for a moment. Stalling for time, I suspected, since he didn't think Olden could have murdered Cyine. "He loved fishing. Loves fishing. He usually treks all the way to the Ageir River to catch some trout."

"Thank you, Guide. I know that wasn't easy." I rose and grabbed my cloak, but the guide's voice stopped me from leaving.

"I'm going with you."

I knew protesting would only waste my time. "As long as you stay close to me." Whether he was hurt or on the run, I wasn't going to risk Olden talking to the guide first, making everything he said confidential.

The guide smiled, though his eyes stayed grim and determined. "Of course, Master Kelnaht."

Despite our differences in height, the guide had no problem following my fast and steady pace towards the ancient oak, even if he was gliding more than running. Then it dawned on me how to keep the guide out of harm's way. The two of us could circle above the trees while others searched the ground. Provided the elders agreed on the urgency, and there were others to help us.

I needn't have worried. When we arrived at the ancient oak, it seemed Elder Layt had already assembled a large group of elves who all seemed ready to leave.

Brem came to me as soon as he saw us. "Elder Layt told them Healer Olden is missing and may be hurt, and that he could be unpredictable."

"He *is* unpredictable," the guide said, sounding like it pained him to admit it. It was clear he believed that Olden had run.

I squeezed the guide's shoulder. "We'll find him, and then we'll see what really happened."

We walked towards Elder Layt and bowed in greeting. He studied us for a moment. "Keep these elves safe, Master Kelnaht."

"Of course, Elder Layt."

"With Ma'terra's blessing, find Healer Olden quickly."

I bowed and waited until he had retreated up the stairs. It

didn't take long to divide the volunteers into groups and organise the search. While the guide and I flew up with a few other cloud elves, Brem led the villagers towards the river. Behind us, I could see Elder Layt watching us.

The guide was silent as we hovered, his eyes on the group who followed Brem, searching the ground for a sign that Olden had walked there. We stayed close to the group, keeping in their line of sight as we scoured between the trees, hoping to find Olden. I tried to get a reading from the ground, but the distance was too great, and I gave up, using my eyes instead.

We didn't see anything for many hundreds of yards ahead, not even when we finally spotted the Ageir River, water glistening in the sun light. A sudden cry from below stopped us. I turned around and studied the group. There seemed to be a struggle among them, and I cursed. That had to be Olden. The guide and I dove down as one, straight into the group as if we'd planned it. The rest of the flyers kept hovering above us, ready to intervene.

Most of the ground group made way for us, except the ones struggling with Olden. Brem was among them, holding Olden's left arm while Raden, a sturdy farmer, held his right arm. At the very last moment, the guide and I slowed down and landed in front of them. Brem had managed to wrap some rope around one of Olden's wrists but couldn't seem to bind the other. Olden was struggling too hard.

The guide took a step forward, raised his arms, and muttered a prayer. Instantly, Olden stopped moving.

"What did you do?"

The guide smiled that same sad smile. "Calmed him."

I raised an eyebrow. "Useful trick," I told him as I helped Brem bind Olden's wrists together.

The guide shrugged.

Olden seemed confused. He barely appeared aware his vowed had died, let alone Cyine. He didn't seem to remember Mistress Esaye's name, just kept calling out for his vowed and ignoring my questions. There was no use continuing with Olden in such a state, so, despite my earlier intention, I had to allow the guide to talk to him alone, if only to try and calm him while Brem fetched Healer Muros, once Olden's apprentice. Between them they should be able to figure out what was wrong with Olden.

I sat on the hard bench just outside the cell as they spoke, growing tired of waiting. Every now and then, I got up and looked through the gap in the door. Just the two of them talking, whispering, until Muros arrived. It bothered me that the guide would not be allowed to reveal what they talked about, but I was certain I could at least rely on his observations. I yawned and closed my eyes, leaning awkwardly against the wall. I hoped the guide and Muros would come out soon. I needed to catch up on my sleep.

I jumped when the guide tapped me on my shoulder. I blinked to clear my vision, stretched, and hoisted myself up. "And?"

"Healer Olden isn't himself."

"I gathered that. But, was he like that before the murder, or did the murder do this to him?"

"I'm glad you're not asking me what he said."

"Your integrity will never be in question, as far as I'm concerned."

"Good. Then you won't mind me telling you it's going to take time for him to remember what happened."

Just as I feared. "Is he fit to stay here until he does?" I didn't intend to let him go, but if the guide had doubts about his recovery here, I'd have to do something about that.

Healer Muros stepped out of the cells, looking as weary as I felt. "As much as I want to say he isn't, he is. He'll need care and supervision, though."

We arranged for the guide's novice to watch Olden, and then I walked the guide home. He repaid me with a smile. "Talk to me tomorrow, Kelnaht. Release your burden."

"I'll try."

The guide inclined his head, but I heard the sigh as he turned away from me, followed by a muttered prayer.

I flew home, looking forward to crawling underneath my blankets. Morning would arrive early enough.

"Kelnaht. We need to talk."

I froze as Ianys stepped out from the shadows of my tree. Not now. "I'm tired, Ianys. Go home."

"No. I'm staying, and you're going to listen to me."

Letting him into my workshop seemed the only possible solution. I didn't want to wake up the village because Ianys was yelling at me. And he was going to yell: his body language and his voice were very clear on that. I grabbed what was left of the strong tea. It was cold, but it would at least keep me awake a bit longer. It was bitter as well, and I cringed at the taste. "What do you want, Ianys?"

"You spied on us."

Remembering the forester's face as he saw me, I saw no use denying it, but Ianys seemed to think my silence meant just that.

"Did you think a talented forester like Taruif wouldn't register your touch? On his own dwelling?"

"Stop saying his name," I bit out, ignoring the shiver that passed through me at the thought of the forester not just seeing me, but sensing me as they were making love. "Do you *want* me to arrest you?"

That seemed to give him pause. "We're having a private conversation."

"He is shunned. *'No one shall here after speak his name but the guide.'* You're not the guide, and I am the truth seeker. Do not speak his name again." I didn't want to have to arrest him, but I had no choice if he didn't stop.

"I demand to know why you were spying on us," Ianys said, but his voice had lost its strength.

I just looked at him. What I wanted to say, he didn't want to hear. If he did, he wouldn't have left me all those turns ago.

"Coals! Kel. Are you so bent on ruining us?"

My hands were around Ianys' neck before he could move, and I growled, "You gave up the right to call me that when you left me for that trull."

Whether it was the way Ianys closed his eyes or how all the anger seemed to drain out of him, despite my calling his vowed a whore, I didn't know, but I pushed him back until he hit the wall and kissed him. A dark, ravaging kiss, all frustration, anger, teeth, and scratchy stubble, my hands still around his neck. A muddled thought that I should slow down, or stop, was drowned out by the familiar taste of his lips, the scent of burning iron that surrounded him. I couldn't stop. I had missed this, had missed him, so much.

Ianys grabbed my hips and pulled me close, and I finally let go of his neck, burying my hands in his hair instead. I pushed my hips into his, and Ianys groaned into my mouth. He was as hard as I was, which only encouraged me. I might never get this chance again. I had to make the most of it.

Ianys pulled me closer and moved with me, against me, turning me on faster than my fantasies of him ever had. Not wanting it to end too soon, I grabbed his hand and dragged him up the stairs and into my bedroom. Ianys seemed out of breath as he lay back, but his seductive smile was all the acquiescence I needed.

My clothes fell to the floor as I ripped them off. He watched me, and I knelt over him to undo the laces of his trousers, pulling them down slowly, savouring the sight of his cock and the dark tufts of hair surrounding it. Not to mention his strong thighs and calves.

My fingers trembled as I took his boots off. I left his tunic for last, half expecting him to take it off himself, but Ianys merely stared at me as I helped him out of his tunic. It made me feel uncomfortable, bashful almost. It had been so long. Ianys wrapped his arms around me, pulled me down on top of him, and kissed me.

Ianys' kiss was as aggressive as mine had been. He claimed

my mouth completely, holding my body still when I tried to slide my cock against his. I struggled to gain more contact, but his grip was too strong. His way of assuring himself I wasn't going anywhere. Still, he was mindful of my wings, making certain his arms went underneath them and not over.

I needed to take control back. I moved one of my hands to his side, slowly, careful not to alert him, and stroked lightly with just one finger. Ianys bucked beneath me, giving me the chance to pull myself away from his grip. Still kissing, I aligned our cocks and pushed into him. It felt so good settling into a once familiar rhythm, no matter how everything had changed for us. It was selfish holding on to that, I knew, but the way Ianys bucked up against me told me he wanted this just as much.

Our movements became frantic, our breath erratic, stuttering, our moans louder and our kisses sloppier. None of that mattered as we raced to completion. Ianys ran his thumbs across the most sensitive parts of my folded wings. I groaned and dug my nails into his shoulders. He moved his hands to my hips, squeezing tight as he bucked up again. I knew I'd have finger-shaped bruises later, but I didn't care. All I cared about was feeling his body tense just as I came all over him, and I collapsed on top of him feeling more satisfied than I had been in a long time.

Chapter Five

THE SOUND OF rustling woke me up, and I turned to see Ianys sitting on the edge of the bed, his back towards me. "Sneaking out?" I asked, too groggy to keep from sounding bitter.

Ianys shook his head, but didn't look at me. It fuelled my anger, and I clenched my fists to keep from lashing out. He stayed silent for too long, and I couldn't bear having him here any longer.

"Just go, Ianys."

That made him turn. "No. We talk first."

"I don't want to hear it."

Ianys moved across the bed and lay down next to me before I could roll away from him. He clamped a hand on my wrist and looked down into my face. "I never meant to hurt you."

"You should have thought about that when you left me. You could have told me the truth. I didn't even know you were seeing her."

"I didn't know how to tell you. You said you didn't mind not having children. I couldn't seem to make you see how much I did want them. And you don't like females that way."

"I wouldn't have minded you finding a mate to have children with. I wouldn't have had to sleep with her. We could have made it work."

"I know, and I'm sorry. I should have talked to you then, but

I didn't think I could walk away if I tried to explain."

I closed my eyes and clamped my lips shut to keep from shouting he shouldn't have left in the first place, shouldn't have sneaked out while I lay sleeping.

"Please believe me, Kel. I *tried* to convince Naia we could form a triad, but she couldn't stand to share me with you." Ianys swallowed and shook his head. "She threatened to leave and take our unborn child with her. I couldn't lose them, Kel. I love them as much as I loved you. I wanted for us all to be together, but I couldn't give up my child to be with you."

It seemed so trivial, hearing it now when I had needed so much to hear it then, to know, to understand. The sadness in Ianys' eyes could not make up for the pain he'd caused me all those turns ago.

"When she..." Ianys closed his eyes. "She made me promise not to let you raise Atèn. She said her parents would take her from me. I..." Ianys opened his eyes again. "I had to promise."

Promises were binding. Whether sang in private or amongst others, Ma'terra bore witness. To break a promise was to call punishment and shame upon oneself.

It was hard to believe Naia had forced Ianys to choose between lover and child because she couldn't bear to share him with me. Even harder to admit that Ianys had had no choice but to leave me the way he had. He would never have been strong enough to keep his promise if he stayed till morning. It didn't make me feel any better, didn't excuse his behaviour that night, but it, at the very least, made me understand. And if I had not been as bitter, had not felt as slighted, then, maybe, I might have seen what Ianys was going through.

"It was wrong to keep my relationship with her from you. You have every right to be angry. I just... Atèn is precious to me. I don't want to risk losing her."

With Naia deceased, her parents would be within their rights to raise Atèn in Ianys' stead if he broke his promise, forbid him any contact with his daughter. Ianys would be devastated. I understood that, but it didn't explain his affair with Taruif, with the forester, and anger welled up in me.

"So you're sleeping with the shunned instead," I bit out as I rolled away from him. I didn't get far with Ianys still holding onto my wrist.

Ianys yanked me back. "I love him," he said, "Like I loved her, loved you."

Loved, past tense. I turned away, but he grabbed my chin.

"No. Don't do that. Don't close yourself off. I love you, Kel. I never stopped loving you."

I wanted to hate Naia for making Ianys choose, but she was dead and deserved better, even if she had been wrong. Ianys, on the other hand, had stopped making sense. "So what makes him worth the risk?" It felt like I was begging for scraps, but I needed to know.

"That's not..." Ianys frowned. "Is that what you think? That he's worth more than you?"

"What am I supposed to think? You left me and avoided me because of a promise to your vowed, but you're risking your daughter to fuck around with the forester." I had no doubt he could hear the jealousy in my voice.

Ianys rested his forehead against mine. "Oh, Kel. It isn't like that. We were never supposed to be more than a casual fuck, but—"

"No." I shook my head. "Please." I couldn't stand to hear him talk about Taruif like that.

"I know," Ianys whispered. "It's in your eyes, Kel, even if you'll never let yourself admit it."

"He is forbidden."

"He is perfect—"

I struck out and hit him hard enough to make him let go of my wrist. I jumped off the bed. "Go!"

Ianys lay back, breathing harshly in and out. "You really need to let me finish my sentences."

"Go!"

"No. Not until you listen to me."

"Listen to what? I've had quite enough of you telling me

you're sorry, you love me, but it's him you're risking losing your daughter for."

"If he invited you to his dwelling, would you accept?"

I froze. "It's not allowed." But…I wanted to.

"All you have to do is say yes."

I sank onto the bed and shook my head. "I can't."

"But you want to."

I bowed my head and prayed to Ma'terra for understanding. For the first time, I acknowledged my feelings to someone else. I nodded my head, more like a quick jerk, but I knew Ianys would understand.

Ianys moved behind me, wrapped his arms around me, and pulled me against him. I leaned my head back and closed my eyes. A strange sort of peace settled over me as Ianys moved us to lie down. I rolled into him and nestled into his strong arms until I lay with my back against his chest.

Ianys betrayed me, left me for a female who was already pregnant, and I never knew. But here and now, it was obvious he still loved me, still wanted to be with me. With me *and* Taruif. It could never work, but it was good to pretend. Who cared about rules and impossibilities in the middle of the night?

IT WAS TOO much. Ianys confessing he still loved me, Olden unable to confess because he couldn't remember, and my inability to avoid running into Taruif everywhere I went. No. I cursed. The forester. He was the forester. The one I kept seeing everywhere.

Right now he stood across the path to my dwelling, tending to the saplings that were now reaching his hips. His slender hips that I could just imagine grabbing as I…

The forester turned his head, and I pushed the thought down as his gaze caught mine. An intense gaze rooted me to the ground. I barely remembered where I was going as he looked at me. The piercing blue of his eyes looked like the sky on a clear and sunny day. I felt like spreading my wings and flying. The mere thought of soaring through the crisp air made them twitch in anticipation.

He seemed as frozen as I was. The air between us seemed to stand still. We were all there was, just the two of us, nothing else. Until someone crossed our path, and the enchantment was broken. I lowered my gaze, and when I looked up again, the forester was gone.

"Master!" Brem yelled as he ran towards me. "Master, we found it."

"Found what?" I asked, slipping my hands into the pockets of my cloak. I frowned when my fingers touched something that hadn't been in there before. Flat like folded paper. I didn't dare take it out while Brem was watching me.

Brem held up a large, soggy bag, dripping with mud. "It was buried at the edge of the forest, next to the path leading to Healer Olden's dwelling."

Finally, something that might help us solve Cyine's murder.

We went into the workshop. While Brem put the soggy bag onto the table, I turned my back to him and fished the item out of my cloak. It *was* a folded piece of paper. My heart nearly stopped as I unfolded it and read the forester's invitation. I brushed his signature with my thumb, and pushed it back into my pocket. This was neither the time nor the place.

Brem had emptied the bag. Cyine's shoes, her cloak, and a pair of gloves. I picked up the gloves. One of them was torn at the edge. I grabbed the sliver of leather and fitted the pieces together. Perfect match.

"There was something else in it, Master," Brem said as he pushed a soggy notebook across the table.

The only thing legible was the name scribbled on the bottom of the cover. Olden. The notebook itself was too wet to even try to open. "Hang it on a wire. It needs to dry," I told Brem, though I doubted we'd be able to read it even then.

Brem nodded and I frowned.

"Whatever is going on with Healer Olden must have started after he buried these."

"Why?" Brem asked.

"Why would Healer Olden bury them if he couldn't remember?"

"I..." Brem closed his mouth when there was a knock on the door. He opened the door and let the guide in.

"Good morning, Guide. What brings you here?"

The guide bowed and took off his hood. "Healer Olden woke up much more lucid. I think it's time you questioned him."

"We tried that—"

"You're the truth seeker, Master Kelnaht. Use your powers."

I shook my head. "He's not fit enough."

The guide held up a piece of paper. "I already received permission from the elders."

"No. I might damage him if I go in with him in this state. I can't."

Moving closer, the guide whispered, "I cannot be certain his condition is true."

"What?"

"We've been observing him, Novice Darver and I, and Healer Olden...sometimes he says things that don't seem right. As if he has his memory back."

Using my powers on Olden, I could read the truth, but not in the state he was in. Suspects needed to be fit and informed. How could I do this? Yet the guide had the elders' permission. I sighed. That would have to do. "All right." I grabbed my cloak, not feeling as confident as I sounded. "I'm ready."

We walked to the cells. Olden was sitting on his bed, looking weary and unshaven. Tired, too.

"Good morning, Healer Olden," the guide greeted him, "Master Kelnaht is here to question you."

"About my vowed?"

"No, about Mistress Cyine's death. You remember Mistress Cyine?"

"Yes, Guide," Olden smiled. "She is always very kind."

Until he killed her, ran through my mind. I dreaded digging into his head, dreaded the muddled mess I would find there. I kept my back to Olden as I washed my hands and rubbed them with herbs. I kept rubbing them as I sat down opposite him, activating my energy flow. Without looking at him, I moved my hands apart and turned them palm forward, keeping them slightly relaxed until I was ready. Only then did I stretch my fingers and direct my energy towards Olden.

Olden flinched, his eyes wide. I knew what he felt. Master Lerrund, the last truth seeker, had done it to me when I was still his apprentice. It had felt as if something burrowed its way into my body. It had only lasted an instant, until the right strand was found. Then, it had felt like something was being pulled out of my body. I shuddered at the memory.

I aimed high, needing to know his thoughts, his motivations. He was muddled, but it seemed *off*, just as the guide had sensed. Olden didn't seem to be faking, but throughout his addled thoughts, there were fully formed sentiments that seemed lucid, but strangely at odds with his muddled ones. It didn't make sense.

Hatred. I sensed hatred, but towards whom? And why? Those answers were difficult to find. With too many strands to follow, I'd get lost. There had to be something more, something that would prove Olden's guilt or innocence.

Mistress Esaye. Olden kept mumbling about his vowed, though he never mentioned her name. She was obviously still near to his heart, maybe there was a clue in that. I closed my eyes and focussed on Mistress Esaye, on everything Olden remembered about her. How he loved her, how he missed her.

I froze when I found something that didn't seem true. There were two sets of memories of his vowed. That couldn't be. I followed one of them. Yes, this was Mistress Esaye, at the end of her life, when the disease had all but claimed her mind. Leaving that strand alone, I focussed on the other strand, entering it at a random point, only to be confronted with a picture of Cyine, smiling and carefree and much younger.

I closed the connection and sat back. When the guide wanted to ask me something, I shook my head and stood up. He followed me outside.

"You found something."

I nodded. "An image of Mistress Cyine. I need to delve in again, but..."

The guide put a hand on my shoulder. "It never gets easier, but you need to get through this."

"I know." I took deep breaths, in and out, and tried to centre myself as best as I could. I needed to not see her as my first kiss right now.

"That's right. Keep breathing." The guide squeezed my shoulder. "Do you think you can go on?"

I nodded. "Let's go back in."

I washed and cleansed my hands, and rubbed the herbs in as I sat down. Olden seemed a bit more awake, more wary, tracking my every move.

The strand was easy to find now I knew what I was looking for. I grabbed hold of it and dove in, ignoring Cyine's smile. It was jarring and creepy to discover Olden truly saw Cyine as his vowed. I would almost say he loved her, but what I sensed seemed more like obsession.

And then I found the proof I needed.

I STOOD IN the middle of the infirmary. I knew it wasn't really me —it was Olden's point of view—but it felt like it was me. It was disorienting and unsettling, to say the least.

Olden was angry, raging. Cyine was pregnant, and it wasn't his child. She looked a little scared because Olden was shouting at her. That was strange. I could hear Cyine, but not Olden.

I had no idea what he yelled at her, but I could clearly sense he hated her for not telling him, hated her for going behind his back to that young herder. She didn't belong to him, she belonged to Olden.

I wanted to close my eyes as I, Olden, hit her and grabbed her arms, screaming at her while she started crying, started begging Olden to let her go. Olden didn't, and I couldn't.

I couldn't look away, couldn't stop what was happening. I couldn't handle this, but as painful as it was, I had no choice but to see this through.

I—Olden—wrapped his hands around her neck and choked her, still screaming. Olden just went on and on, though I couldn't hear any of it. I could only feel his anger. Cyine was his, and he would never let her go. Would never allow her to carry the herder's child.

But as he robbed her of her last breath, she was still begging for her life and the life of her child. Her son, although she didn't know it was a boy, and Olden wasn't going to tell her. Finally, she went limp and I—Olden—let her drop to the floor.

I needed a drink.

I let go of the strand and only barely resisted the urge to push energy through Olden to stop his heart. My hands were never meant to kill. I couldn't kill. Yet, I had never wanted it as much as I did now.

Arms wrapped around me, and I felt myself being dragged out of the room.

"He did it," I whispered.

"I know," the guide whispered back, "You spoke as you delved in. Even Olden seemed taken aback by what he heard."

I didn't care. I couldn't care. Not after seeing him, *feeling* him choke the life out of Cyine. It would be a long time before I would be able to forget the image of Cyine begging for her life. Although, thanks to Taruif's note, I knew exactly where I could go to try and forget.

Olden no longer looked weary when I glanced into the cell. He seemed harried and angry. I knew he would try to talk his way out of it all, but it wouldn't help him. I had found the truth, had spoken the truth, and the elders would convict him. Olden deserved whatever punishment he received. I would suggest banning and the harnessing of his powers. It was a cruel punishment and meant he would never again find work as a healer, but he deserved nothing less. He killed Cyine and her son.

I nodded at the guide. It was time to involve the elders.

Olden's eyes narrowed as the guide left. "The trull deserved it," he bit out.

I grabbed the door to keep from going in and striking him.

Olden tried to stand, but though we hadn't bound his hands, we made certain he wouldn't be able to get up. I hoped the chair would topple, but I didn't want to explain to the elders why I hadn't helped him up again.

"She had no right to go and get knocked up by that herder. She was mine!" he yelled at me as I locked the door and went to get some air.

Outside I could still hear him scream, but I kept walking until I couldn't hear it anymore.

Chapter Six

T HE DOOR OPENED immediately when I knocked, and, without a word, the forester let me in and led me up to his bedroom. No, not the forester. Taruif. His name was Taruif.

Ianys sat on the bed, dressed only in his trousers. His eyes lit up when he saw me. "He told me you'd come," Ianys said as he rose to greet me. "I wasn't so sure."

"Neither was I," I whispered, stepping into his embrace and kissing him as if it was the most natural thing to do.

I shuddered when fingers brushed along the ridges of my wings and trailed the edges, followed by Taruif's deep voice. "I always admired your wings. So graceful when you open them before taking flight."

My wings were no different than anyone else's, but the fact he noticed mine, noticed me, warmed me. I opened them just a bit, giving Taruif access to the more sensitive parts while Ianys brushed his lips against mine again.

I'd never done this, been with more than one lover at the same time, but it felt good to stand between these two. I brushed my hands across Ianys' stubbly chest, his shoulders, and grabbed hold of his hair as he deepened the kiss, shuddering against him as Taruif's touches became bolder, lighter, more teasing. I moaned into Ianys' mouth and felt my knees buckle. Taruif's arm snaked around me, and I was pulled against his naked chest, carefully, mindful of my wings. When had Taruif undressed himself?

I didn't want Ianys to stop kissing me, but I had a sudden desire to watch Taruif, to see his vines, to trace them down to...

Taruif stepped back, giving me the space to refold my wings and do as I was imagining. I ran my tongue across Ianys' lips one more time and turned around. Taruif was beautiful, all sleek, lean muscle and wiry, hidden strength, and not an ounce of fat. A narrow waist and the most beautiful trail of vine leaves from his neck to... My breath hitched at the sight of the leaves this close to his cock. One seemed to disappear below it as the vines curled along the inside of his leg, all the way down to his ankle.

Fingers brushed my skin underneath my tunic, rucking it up as they trailed across my stomach and up to my chest.

"He is beautiful, isn't he?" Ianys whispered in my ear.

"Yes." I gasped as he rubbed my nipples at the same time as Taruif raised his head and looked at me with his piercing blue eyes. Taruif's lips parted as he caught my expression. He seemed shocked and pleased at the same time. No blank expression at all. I had never seen emotion so clear in his face, and I couldn't help but smile. "You are beautiful." I had to say it. How could I not? He deserved to have it mentioned.

Taruif seemed almost bashful now, a slight red blush adorning his cheeks as he smiled, too. He *was* beautiful, more than I could have ever imagined.

Ianys lifted the back of my tunic over my folded wings and grabbed the hem. I raised my hands to let him take it off. He dropped it to the floor and pulled me back against him. "He couldn't stop talking about inviting you to complete us."

My jaw dropped. I had a hard time imagining Taruif as talkative as that. But I didn't really know him, did I? How could I?

Taruif stepped closer and reached out, placing one hand flat against my sternum. "I knew you belonged to us even before Ianys first told me about you."

I swallowed away the jealousy at their bond, their closeness. Swallowed against the emotion of knowing they were together when I was dreaming of them, separately. "I…" I couldn't say a word, couldn't express what I was feeling, but as Taruif brushed his lips against mine, I found that words weren't needed at all.

Taruif's lips were warm, softer than Ianys' but no less forceful as he ran his tongue across my lower lip, demanding instant access. I parted my lips, and his tongue slipped inside, brushing against my teeth, my tongue. He stepped closer, pushed his body against mine, and I felt overwhelmed by the warmth of his skin against mine. It should have felt claustrophobic, being pressed between the two, but all I could do was sigh into Taruif's mouth as I revelled in their presence.

Ianys trailed his hands across my sides and down the insides of my arms until he reached my hands and entwined his fingers with mine. "We've wanted this for a while, but I didn't think you would ever be here with us."

Neither did I. Not outside my dreams. And even in my dreams I never thought I'd be with both of them at the same time. Now, with Taruif's tongue caressing the inside of my mouth and both of them pressed against me, it seemed like I'd always been here. And I wanted more.

I pushed my hips into Taruif's, enjoying his gasp, his shudder. He nipped at my lower lip with his teeth, and it was my turn to shudder.

Ianys' hands left mine, and he stepped away, but before I could turn my head, Taruif pulled me closer to him, trailing his lips down my jaw, nipping, kissing his way down my neck. Hands wormed their way between us, pulling the strings of my trousers loose and pushing them down.

The first touch of cock to cock sent shivers down my spine, and then Ianys' cock nestled against my arse. I was glad he was quick enough to catch me when my knees finally buckled.

"Let's move this to the bed," he said, more to Taruif than me.

I soon found myself lying between them. Ianys at my back, trailing paths with his fingers across the edges of my folded wings, my sides, my hip. Tantalising little touches that kept me moving into Taruif's body, pushing our cocks together, trying to create friction.

From somewhere behind him, Taruif grabbed a small jar of oil. He dipped his long fingers into it and oiled both our cocks.

Ianys grabbed the jar from Taruif and barely a moment later, his hand moved in between us, grabbing both our cocks. I gasped as he started moving his hand up and down. Not jacking: teasing, moving too slow to bring us off.

I watched Taruif's face, watched the myriad of emotions in his eyes. More emotion in one look than I had ever seen him show before. Although he was going slow, I could feel I wouldn't last long. I tried to tell Ianys to stop, because the last thing I wanted was to finish this too soon, but Taruif silenced me with a kiss. A sloppy, uncoordinated kiss as we were both gasping and shivering and running out of breath.

Almost as an afterthought I reached behind me, but I shouldn't have worried about Ianys being left behind. He was dripping with oil as I found Taruif's hand working him faster than Ianys was working us. I put my hand over Taruif's, as best as it fit in this awkward position, and together we jacked him off while he did us.

Our movements became jerky and fumbling as we lost any sense of rhythm. Ianys' hand slipped away as he came with a shout, and Taruif and I kissed and rutted together until we, too, came. Ianys' lips brushed my neck as Taruif's brushed my lips. I shuddered in the aftermath, gasping for air, and with no intention of ever moving again.

I WOKE UP with only one body plastered against mine. One with luscious, grey hair splayed all around him. His braid must have come undone at some point.

"Good morning." Taruif's deep voice rumbled past my ear. He reached out and cupped my cheek.

"Good morning." I turned my head and kissed the palm of

his hand.

"Ianys had to leave early, and you were still deeply asleep. He hung a note on your door so you won't be disturbed."

I raised an eyebrow. "Brem would have been in the workshop already, I'm sure. He's always there when I wake up."

Taruif shrugged. "Ianys will find a way."

I hoped he would. I wasn't looking forward to being asked where I had been when I came in late, and I wasn't ready to leave just yet. I moved towards Taruif and pulled him against my body. "I wish I could stay here all day, but I expect to be summoned by the elders any time now."

"Healer Olden confessed?"

I shrugged and hoped he would drop it. Talking to him was an experience in itself; I wasn't ready to add talking about work. I just wanted to hold him for a little longer before I needed to leave.

Taruif nodded and brushed his lips against mine. Up close, there was nothing blank about his expression. I could barely imagine how he pulled it off, to seem so closed off towards our tribe. So many questions. Though there was only one that ruled them all. Could I do this? Could I be with them in secret, sneaking around to be with them, pretending I was single?

The guide would know with one look, of course. He'd told me my path was muddy. There was no easy path to choose, and I needed to make my own way.

This was new and exciting and good. It felt so good to lie with them. But I was the truth seeker, Taruif was shunned, and Ianys had made a promise to his dying vowed. Put together, it was impossible.

Impossible didn't beat the relaxed smile on Taruif's face. No one but us would ever see him like that. They all just saw the shunned forester with the ever-present blank expression, tending to our trees, the way I'd seen him when I was younger.

"I can hear you thinking."

"Interesting power."

"Kelnaht." Taruif sighed. "I know you have questions. You

can ask them."

I shook my head. "Not now." It would ruin this, would ruin everything. I needed to think for that, on my own. Right now, I didn't want to leave. I kissed Taruif and banned all thoughts from my head. Here and now was all that mattered.

I HAD NO time to think when I arrived home. I'd barely finished my shower when the guide knocked at my door.

"The elders request your presence."

It wasn't a surprise. I grabbed my cloak and followed the guide. "Do we need to bring Healer Olden?"

"No, the elders had him picked up earlier. They've been questioning him."

It was to be expected. The guide would have told them about me probing his mind, and they needed to check Olden for lasting effects. Nothing for me to worry about. Olden had been fine when I left.

Olden was indeed with the elders, bound to a chair to the side, staring at us with an angry glint in his eyes. We bowed before the elders and sat in the chairs when Elder Morenn motioned us to do so.

"We have reached a decision on Master Olden's fate. Master Olden will be banned, and his powers harnessed, as you have suggested. He will also be stripped of his healer's title, branded, and flown a ten days' journey south with provisions and clothing. No utilities but a bowl and spoon. He will not be allowed to return here in this lifetime."

The guide uttered a sigh of relief, followed by a short prayer to Ma'terra. At least Olden's essence would be allowed to return to where he belonged. Only a few elves had ever been denied that comfort.

"We will need volunteers to take Master Olden to the drop point, Guide. I'm sure you'll find suitable flyers."

"Of course, Elder Garren. When will he be transported?"

"After the new turn. The season of celebration is upon us, and we don't want anyone prohibited from attending. Master Olden will stay in his cell until then."

"I'll have that list ready before the new turn."

The elders inclined their heads, dismissing us, and we bowed and made our way to the platform. We flew down in silence, and I followed the guide into his safehold without prompting. There was no better time to talk to him.

We washed our hands, rubbed herbs into them, and entered the safehold where Cyine still lay on the low bed surrounded by flowers given by the tribe. Her burial would have to wait until after Solstice as well. Not because the elders had decreed it, but because Kadil wished it. The guide's magic would keep her intact for as long as Kadil needed to come to terms with her passing and the loss of his son.

I sat down and accepted the laros juice the guide always poured me when I visited. He knew it reminded me of picking laros berries with my father when I was a wee elf. While bright red and very sweet when ripe, the muddy red of the juice meant the berries had been dried, ground, boiled in water, and left to cool. I took a sip. The hint of tanginess did nothing to ruin my memories. Meanwhile, the guide looked at me expectedly. I had neglected our talks for too long.

It was easy to talk about the usual things like work and Brem, but when it came to what I really wanted to talk about, I clammed up. Solstice was tomorrow night, and I knew I needed to go. I hoped Taruif would not be there, but Taruif was a traditional elf, and he always attended the Solstice Circle, even though no one would choose him. I couldn't let him go through that. Not now that we had found each other. All three of us. Our triad. Although Ianys could never break his promise to Naia, so I knew he would not be at the Circle.

"Kelnaht. Look at me."

I did, bracing myself for whatever he was going to say.

"Solstice is a time, not a place."

It wasn't as cryptic as I expected, but would Taruif see it the same way? There was only one way to find out. "Thank you, Guide."

"You will be good for each other. Good for young Atèn, too, one day."

One day. The guide made it sound as if there would come a time we wouldn't have to hide our relationship. I shook my head. "Ianys cannot break his promise." And Taruif was shunned.

"There is always a way, Kelnaht."

I saw none.

Chapter Seven

AFTER MY TALK with the guide, I needed some time to myself. To think about Taruif and Ianys and Solstice. About muddy paths, puddles, drowning, and the guide's latest offering that Solstice was a time and not a place.

These thoughts kept running through my head the next couple of days, right until Solstice morning. I knew what I wanted to do. I wanted to be with Taruif, wanted to be with Ianys, thinking about a nice, large tree with space for all of us, even Atèn someday. But I knew that was nothing more than wishful thinking. It could never happen.

Ianys couldn't risk losing his daughter, and Taruif would never ask us to risk shunning to live openly with him. As every turn before, Taruif would attend the Solstice Circle in the full knowledge that nobody would claim him. But I couldn't let him suffer through that again.

It was the easiest decision I had ever made.

I had no family left to shame, and Brem could handle being the truth seeker. He wasn't quite ready, but he was learning so fast, there was no doubt in my mind he would grow into his task and be a better truth seeker than I ever was.

Those last three days before Solstice, I worked through my days and spent my nights walking around my dwelling. Saying goodbye. Promising my beloved oak that Brem would take good care of it. I refrained from talking to the guide, but I would visit him again. After Solstice. After my sentence was passed.

I resisted visiting Ianys as well. I didn't think I could handle him telling me he didn't want me to risk it. No, Ianys would visit us in his own time, and maybe, just maybe, he would be free to join us one day.

I started at the knock on my door. I wasn't expecting anyone, didn't want to see anyone. That didn't keep me from opening the door. I half expected to see the guide with some last-moment advice, but it was Ianys who leaned against the doorpost, an anxious expression in his eyes.

"Can I come in?"

I moved aside and let him in.

"I just spoke to the guide, and I need you to know."

"Ianys, what you talk about with the guide is your business."

"No." Ianys shook his head. "This is about you as well." He grabbed my hand. "About us. There is an us, right?"

"Yes. Yes." No matter what was going to happen, there would always be an us.

Ianys smiled and relaxed a bit. "Oh, good. That will make this so much easier."

"Make what easier?"

"I need you to attend Solstice tonight. I need you to choose Taruif."

"I—"

"No," Ianys interrupted me. "Don't say anything yet. Not until I've told you what you need to know."

Then tell me, I almost shouted.

"The guide petitioned the elders for Taruif's sentence to be changed."

My jaw dropped. "What?"

"Taruif is not to know yet. It may take a couple of moons for the elders to answer the petition."

"What would the change mean?"

"The guide proposes reducing his shunning from forty turns to twenty."

Twenty turns. I tried to remember how long it had been

since Taruif was shunned. It had to be close to that, right?

"Five moons," Ianys answered for me. "That's all that would be left for him, Kel. Five moons."

"If the elders allow it."

"Yes. But the guide is optimistic about that."

"Why?"

"He found a stripling with a knack for foresting."

And that stripling would need a mentor. Taruif had been the only forester for a long time now. The elders might just consider it.

Ianys pulled me against him and brushed his lips across my forehead. "Please, Kel. Please don't let him leave the Solstice Circle alone."

"*Solstice is a time, not a place.*" The guide's words echoed through me, and I knew what I needed to do. I looked into Ianys' eyes. "Whether he has five moons or twenty turns left, I will claim him as mine tonight. Only—"

Ianys kissed me, and I sighed into his mouth. I still couldn't believe that we were together again. Not the same—we could never be the same—but when he kissed me, it felt just as right as it had then. He was mine. I was his. We were Taruif's. And one day, one day we would all be together.

"I'm not going to claim him at the Circle, Ianys. I was going to, but I can't risk being shunned in case the petition is granted. My shunning would only hold Taruif back. He wouldn't leave me to be free."

Ianys' eyes went wide. "You were going to give up everything for him?"

I placed my hand over his heart, fingers spread. "For us, Ianys. For us all." But not now. Not if we had the slightest chance of this working out. I would still claim him, just not at the Circle, not in public.

Resting his forehead against mine, Ianys closed his eyes. His voice was nowhere near as melodious as the guide's, but his Promise Song sounded beautiful to my ears. He couldn't claim me without breaking his promise to Naia. Instead he promised me his love, promised to claim me when he'd be free to do so. It was more than I could have hoped for.

"*There is always a way, Kelnaht,*" I could hear the guide tell me.

Ianys' promise was that way, and it was all I needed.

THE FIRE BURNED bright as I approached the Solstice Circle, and plenty of elves were already seated around it. All single, all waiting to meet their mate tonight. Some would go home alone, some would pair up. I planned to belong to the latter group, if Taruif accepted me.

I circled the fire, showing myself a participant, and sat down on one of the low benches surrounding the fire. Elves came and elves went, some joined to stare at the fire, some even looked my way, but I ignored them all. I stared at the fire, rehearsing my proposal, and waited for Taruif to arrive.

I sensed him walking into the Circle even before I saw him. He looked gorgeous with his braided grey hair and his dark green tunic and trousers. Around his wrists, he wore bands of braided black leather, and a larger one around his neck. He was beautiful.

A thrill of arousal shot through me when he looked my way. I smiled, just lifting the corner of my mouth. Hoping he would see it in this twilight.

Taruif circled the fire the way I had earlier. No one looked at him. No one but me. Taruif didn't sit down inside the Circle. He stepped outside of it and leaned against a tree.

I sat in the Circle for a long time, throwing glances at Taruif every now and then, making certain he was still there, waiting for enough time to have passed for me to give up and leave. I didn't know if Taruif caught my glances. I never lingered long enough to check.

Finally, I'd had enough. I rose and stepped out of the Circle. Holding a folded note, I made my way towards Taruif. I had to be close enough to hand him the note, but looking as if I was just passing him.

I'd contemplated the easier choice, waiting until Taruif gave up and left, but I couldn't do it. I couldn't let him think I was not going to claim him. He deserved more.

When I reached Taruif, I passed him on his right side, slipped the note into his cloak pocket, and walked on, leaving him standing there. With my heart pounding, wondering if he understood, I walked until I'd reached the path to his dwelling and stepped into the shadow of a mayeng tree, waiting for him to pass.

He took his time following me, long enough for me to worry whether he had misunderstood my gesture, until I finally heard a rustling sound coming closer. It had to be him.

I ran through my proposal one more time and took deep breaths. My hands were trembling as I held them up, and I feared my voice would give out at the first word. Still, I stepped out from the shade when Taruif approached me. "My path is muddy, filled with puddles to lure me away from my goal. Will you ease my travels and keep me safe?"

Taruif stood still, too still, his expression blank as ever. But, when I looked closer, his hands trembled as badly as mine did, and he was biting his lip. He bowed his head as he spoke, "A long time ago, I made the mistake of doing everything to please my vowed. He wanted a dwelling high in the trees, and I built it for him. He wanted a bridge between the treetops, and I built it for him. He always wanted more, more height, more danger, and I would do everything for him. Yet none of that made him happy. One day, he asked me to let him go…and I did. He stood on the highest bridge as I made it disappear, and I never saw him happier than when he started falling."

I had heard the story, as far as the falling out of a tree was concerned. This was so much more complicated than the mistake we thought the forester had made. He had done what his vowed had asked him to. I couldn't imagine how much pain that must have caused Taruif. I opened my mouth, but nothing I said would do him any good, so I shut it again and waited.

Taruif raised his head and looked at me, his piercing blue eyes revealing a mix of sadness, resignation, and hope. "I will gladly keep you safe from luring puddles," he said, his voice a quiet rumble. He swallowed. "But I will not drown for you."

It was a serious offer, but I couldn't help but smile. "I will never expect you to endanger yourself." I didn't care I was deviating from the vows I'd memorised. He needed to hear it, needed to know he would be safe with me. I grabbed his hands. "I will keep you safe, will clear your path of mud and weeds, for as long as you need me to."

Taruif took a shuddering breath, and another one. "I accept," he whispered as he pushed me into the mayeng tree and kissed me.

Act Two
Lost and Found

"Y OUR PATH *is muddy, Kelnaht, but don't think avoiding the puddles will make it easier to travel,*" the guide, our spiritual adviser and path finder, had told me a turn ago in that soft, lilting voice of his, right before I vowed myself to Taruif, our shunned forester.

The guide said puddles. I envisioned lakes, deep treacherous lakes, and I was drowning.

No one was allowed to talk to a shunned, let alone have a relationship with one. But I did, in secret. I wanted to claim him in public, but the possibility of Taruif's forty-turn sentence being reduced kept me from approaching him openly at the Solstice Circle. I had claimed him, nonetheless, in private.

Ianys, my first love and our tribe's smith, completed our triad. He risked losing his daughter if anyone found out about the three of us—not only because of Taruif, but of the promise he had made to his deceased vowed to not let me raise their daughter.

We spent all turn sneaking around, stealing moments, longing for more. We did nothing but step into puddle after puddle, waiting for the one that would be out of our depth.

It was more and more difficult to hold on to hope, and yet all I needed to survive another day was to gaze into Taruif's eyes and have Ianys' arms around me.

If this was drowning, it wasn't so bad.

Chapter Eight

"U stion!"
I was glad I wore my trousers tucked into my high boots, as the mud sucked at them with every step. It had been raining off and on for the past half moon. The leaves of the few evergreen oaks and parulm trees scattered throughout the forest dripped water, and twilight threw the woodland into a cold and eerie darkness. Cloak wrapped tightly around me and wings folded, I tried to ignore the drizzling chill brushing my fingers as I held my hands out in front of me. I scanned for Ustion's footsteps, my energy flowing freely despite the cold.

"Ustion!"

Step by step, I circled the area to the left of the hunters' cave at the foot of Moors Mountain, while my apprentice, Brem, did the same on the right side of the cave. Even with the floating lanterns hovering above us, I could find little trace of Ustion. There was plenty in the cave, and just outside, but the farther I moved away from the cave, the less I discovered. At this point, I'd be thrilled to pick up even the tiniest trace that would tell me where Ustion had walked off to. I muttered a prayer to Ma'terra, hoping something would turn up soon. Deeper into the forest, the search party bellowed every couple of paces.

"Ustion!"

Ustion, son of Ashyu and soon-to-be carpenter's apprentice, had been staying with his father's hunting group when he disappeared. It was the hunters' tradition to take their older children with them once a turn for a break in routine. According to the hunters, Ustion had been doing fine—couldn't shoot a rabbit even if it stood still, but made the best arrows—until three nights ago, when he and Ashyu had argued, and Ustion had walked away to blow off some steam. When he hadn't returned that evening, Ashyu had assumed he'd gone home to sulk. At sixteen turns, Ustion was old enough to find his way back through the forest, but when the hunting group returned to the village earlier today, he hadn't been home. He hadn't been anywhere in the village.

"Ustion!"

Three nights was a long time for a stripling like him to be missing.

"Do you think we'll find him soon, Master Kelnaht?"

Ashyu, a tall tree elf built like an oak, looked old in the flickering light of the lanterns. Lines were etched into his face, lines of worry, lines of regret. He'd been mumbling prayers since we started our search, staying close to Brem and me as we searched for traces. Every time we paused or bent down, he held his breath. His expression when we found nothing was heartbreaking.

"I hope so," was all I could answer. Truth was, I had no idea. The lack of traces was alarming, the nearing darkness even more so. I hadn't expected the search to take this long. We weren't prepared to spend the night in the forest, and once the night creatures awoke, the fire would be needed for protection more than light. The sooner we found Ustion, the sooner we could all go home. I hoped Taruif wasn't waiting up for me.

"Ustion!"

Grabbing some herbs from my pouch, I sprinkled them over my cold hands and rubbed them together to cleanse and protect them from the worst of the chill. When my hands started tingling, I took a deep breath, muttered a prayer to Ma'terra to guide us in our search, and renewed my focus. Hands extended, I felt my way through the rubble and the mud, moving farther and farther away from the cave. Every now and then, Brem and I met up in the middle, but we had nothing new to tell each other. Neither of us could find anything, and we were both reaching the limit of our powers.

"Ustion!"

In the end, I had no choice but to call it a night. We could barely see our hands in front of us, the wind had become fierce and close to freezing, and Brem and I needed to stop before we ran out of energy.

"No! You have to... You can't…" Standing amidst his hunting group, Ashyu panted as he stamped his feet into the mud and swung his fists. "I'm *not* leaving. You have to find him. Now!"

I took a deep breath. "Look at your friends, Master Ashyu. You've all just returned from a quarter moon hunting trip. They need a good night's rest." I gestured at Brem and myself. "*We* need a good night's rest to replenish our energy. We'll restart our search in the morning and gather as many elves as we can to combine our energies. We *will* find your son."

Ashyu sagged against a tree, disappointment and pain clear in his expression. Two of his group had to help him regain his balance before they could lead him back to the village. We walked in silence. I couldn't stop myself from scanning the ground every couple of paces with what little energy I had left. Next to me, Brem did the same. A desperate act, or idle hope, maybe, but we'd never lost anyone in the forest before, and we weren't planning on doing so now.

When I entered the village, Ianys stood waiting in the shadow of my dwelling, keeping out of sight until the last door in the village had closed. As soon as I reached him, his strong arms enveloped me, and I sagged against him. His warm lips against mine brought a relief I couldn't express in words. Ianys knew me well. He wrapped his cloak around me, took my cold and wet hands in his, and led me to Taruif's dwelling.

WAKING IN TARUIF'S embrace made things seem a little brighter. The rhythm of his heartbeat and the fading light of the moon coming in through the shanna leaf window soothed me. It would be even better if Ianys were here, but he didn't dare spend too many nights with us for fear his deceased vowed's parents would find out.

Taruif's hands trailed up my side. His warm chest pressed against my back and his breath ghosted across my neck, my jaw. I shivered and pushed against him. Chuckling, he wrapped his arm around my waist and kissed me behind my ear. "Good morning, my Kel."

Almost a turn together, and this was the first time he'd called me that. I smiled and turned around in his embrace. Ianys had started calling me Kel many turns ago, after we first got together. It made me feel as special then as it did now. I lifted my head and kissed Taruif good morning.

He smiled into the kiss. "How long before you need to go?"

"We start searching for Ustion again at daybreak." I traced the outlines of the vine tattoo that covered Taruif's body from neck to stomach. "I'd rather not talk about it right now."

Taruif tucked my head under his chin. "Hmm. Did I tell you about Master Erwald's dogs?"

"No. What about them?"

"They keep trying to eat the saplings I planted this spring. I have to respell them every other day, because the bloody beasts drain the shields. The elders told Master Erwald to leash them, but they happily chew through the rope to get at the saplings. The guide said he'd suggest some sort of fencing to keep the pests away from them."

"I doubt the guide said pests."

Taruif harrumphed and tickled my side. I shrieked and tried to push him away, but he grabbed me tight, trapping my hand between our bodies. He kissed me, hard and demanding, and rubbed his cock against mine. If only we had more time, but the day was what it was, and we were used to taking what we could get. We settled into a rhythm just short of frantic, rubbing against each other, kissing, grabbing, panting. Taruif biting my earlobe as he trailed his fingers across the sensitive part of my wings was my undoing, and I came with a hoarse shout, a mere moment before he moaned his release into my ear.

We lay together, catching our breath. If only I could stay longer. We saw too little of each other. The previous night, I'd fallen asleep the moment Ianys and Taruif had wrapped me in their warmth. I hadn't even woken when Ianys left.

Taruif's piercing blue eyes bored into me, studied me. I tried for a smile and failed.

"You will find him, Kel," he whispered.

Pulling Taruif against me for a deliberately slow kiss, I tried not to let the day ahead ruin my mood. I wanted to enjoy these stolen moments for as long as I could. "We'll be combing the forest all day," I said against his mouth. "If we haven't found him by nightfall, we'll spend the night in the forest and start again the next day." And the next, and the next, until we found him.

Taruif brushed his hands along the edges of my wings. "I know. I'll be here when you come back."

We needed to find Ustion before another cold night passed. He'd already been missing for four nights. He might be a clever stripling, but there was no telling how long he could survive on his own, and in this weather. We had to find him as soon as possible. I took a deep breath, brushed my lips against Taruif's, and hoisted myself out of bed.

Taruif's hand caressed my hip. "I hung your cloak next to the hearth, but the rest needs to be washed."

With a nod, I opened the wardrobe, grabbed my spare set of clothes, and walked into the bathroom. I was glad I'd left some here; it saved me having to sneak into my dwelling in my muddy ones. My dwelling. Not my home. I couldn't quite remember when I started considering this my home, but mine now seemed cold and empty when I spent the night there.

Soon, we hoped, Taruif's sentence would be reduced, and we'd be free to be together, officially. But for now, we had to be careful.

A quick wash later, I returned to the bedroom with a damp towel for Taruif. He raised an eyebrow, but took it anyway, and wiped himself clean. "I am capable of washing myself, you know?"

I shrugged and pulled him off the bed and flush against me. "I like taking care of you."

Taruif wrapped his arms around me and sighed. "Don't stay away too long."

Closing my eyes for a moment, I soaked up Taruif's warmth and, once again, prayed to Ma'terra that we would find Ustion soon.

SOON WAS CLEARLY not going to happen. We searched the forest with at least twenty elves to support us, combining energies to increase our abilities—Brem's and mine—as we went deeper and deeper into the forest. The group included Ianys. I'd protested against his presence in private, afraid the closeness would pose too much of a distraction, but Ianys had waved it off and joined us anyway. I couldn't deny that his energy would be a real help in boosting mine.

Yet our efforts yielded no results. No trace of Ustion anywhere. At the end of the day, darkness forced us to find shelter in a cave long before we needed to tap into our reserves.

Conversations were hushed in the cold, damp air of the cave. Brem sat by the fire playing knobbles with some of the other elves, but they weren't half as loud as normal. I lay down and pulled my blankets up to my chin to ward off the chill. A large shadow moved into my corner, and before I could even open my mouth, Ianys dumped his sleeping gear next to mine.

"Brem could come to sleep any time," I warned him, but Ianys didn't seem to care. He wrapped himself in his blankets and lay down next to me.

"Doesn't matter where I sleep." His green eyes were bright

with exhaustion, and his brown, messy hair clung to his sweaty face. "We're chatting, not touching. Nothing suspicious."

It sounded like Ianys had tried to convince himself of that before he joined me.

"Besides, it's too warm on the other side. There were six in my corner, and only two in this one."

Made sense. Brem and I had been given a quiet corner to ourselves, since we'd used up more energy than any of the others. I turned my head at a frustrated groan from near the fire. No doubt, Brem was winning; he had a wicked mind.

Not too long now, and he would be passing his truth seeker's test. I'd already sent messengers to a number of other tribes, inquiring if any were in need of a truth seeker. I'd also asked them to scout for possible new apprentices, since none had been discovered among our own tribe yet.

I had no doubt Brem would come back to us one day—after I retired, perhaps—but two truth seekers in one tribe only led to strife.

I smiled at Ianys and tilted my head. "So, now that you made it into my corner, what is it you came for?"

"Taruif's sentence," Ianys whispered.

I resisted the urge to sigh. "What about it?"

"Aren't you curious why they're taking so long? Halving it would have left him five moons, and that was over six moons ago. This should be finished by now. Why haven't they summoned him yet?"

His guess was as good as mine. "I know the elders talked to Master Banhin to see if he had objections to the reduced sentence, but I don't know more than that." Master Banhin was the father of Taruif's deceased vowed, Fuzan. I didn't know if he'd objected.

"Oh. Oh, right. Makes sense. I didn't know they still consulted the victim's family when it happened so long ago."

It had been twenty turns, and all that time, Taruif had lived on the edge of our village, shunned, not allowed to talk to anyone except the guide. Sentenced for causing Fuzan's death by making a tree-bridge disappear beneath his feet. A desperate request from a tree elf whose lack of wings made him intensely unhappy.

Taruif rarely talked about it. I'd been the first person he'd told, and he'd never mentioned it to Ianys until one morning this past summer. He'd dragged us far into the forest to show us where it happened, to ask us to join him in his remembrance prayer. Afterwards, confused and upset, Ianys told me he didn't mind I already knew. "I'm glad he felt he could confide in you," he said, and we never spoke of it again.

I reached out and grabbed Ianys' hand. "It's not just down to Master Banhin. Don't forget that young Merel's parents want her to become Taruif's apprentice. She's only fourteen turns, and they don't want her to leave the tribe yet. That means there are elves on Taruif's side." Who was I trying to convince? "The elders will let Taruif know when they're ready."

"I worry about him, Kel. I don't like keeping this from him. He should know, should..."

"We've discussed this. He'd only fret if he knew, and it would hurt him too deeply if the elders reject the petition."

Ianys put his warm, rough hand against my cheek. "Why do you always have to be the voice of reason?"

"Because you're the impulsive one." At least, he used to be spontaneous, before his life became complicated.

Rekindling our relationship had been tough in the beginning. Despite our love for each other, Naia stood between us. Or, rather, Naia's manipulation of him. It hadn't been easy for me to overlook his lying to me about her, but I couldn't begrudge him going after what he wanted. And Ianys had always wanted children.

However, I couldn't forgive Naia so easily for making him choose between us. If that wasn't enough, she had made him promise that he wouldn't let me raise their daughter, keeping him from seeking out a relationship with me after her death. She had passed away barely a turn after Atèn was born, but I couldn't forgive her for keeping Ianys from me with that impossible promise, not when he so clearly loved me still.

Ianys must have seen something in my eyes, because he looked away and swallowed. The elves sitting at the fire were paying no attention to us at all, and I leaned forward and pressed a quick kiss to his cheek. "I remember, Ianys." I would never forget the touch of his forehead against mine as he sang his promise to me, in secret. With it he had sworn to claim me once he was free to do so openly. It was the only way he could without breaking his promise to Naia.

With a sigh, he turned back to me and squeezed my hand. No words were needed.

I understood Ianys' worries all too well. It was hard, sneaking around, making certain no one caught us entering his dwelling or going back out again. Ianys rarely dared spend a whole night, and I often found myself creeping through the village in the early morning to return to my dwelling before Brem arrived for work. And we'd been waiting so long already, without being able to tell Taruif.

Still, Taruif made it all worth it. Taruif and Ianys both.

Mother sometimes talked about belonging to a triad for a while, long before I was born, long before she'd met Father. I never thought I'd be part of one, never thought I could love anyone but Ianys. And then I fell for Taruif, and slowly every piece fitted into place. I belonged with both of them. We couldn't be anything other than a triad.

"Do you think we'll find Ustion tomorrow?"

"We *have* to." But I wasn't so sure. Aside from the initial results, we'd discovered no further traces to tell us where Ustion was or even which direction he'd walked off to. It was almost as if Ustion had disappeared into thin air.

I yawned and closed my eyes. Ianys mumbled something that sounded like "Rest well", but I was already drifting off.

Chapter Nine

Among the tracks of the night creatures roaming the grounds while we slept, I found a flicker, a tiny trace of Ustion's energy hidden under the muddy leaves. This was the first day after the heavy rainfall, and the leaves had dried enough to brush aside. They bared a piece of fabric stuck in the mud at the edge of the path.

Rubbing herbs into my hands for a quick cleansing, I breathed deeply in and out to centre myself until my hands tingled with warmth. I picked up the piece of fabric and studied it. A strand of long, blond hair was wrapped around it. Not just wrapped, but knotted, as if someone wanted to make certain it wouldn't become separated from the fabric.

Ianys took Ustion's hairbrush out of the bag and held it up while I scanned the stray hairs caught in it. They matched the hair I'd found. The fabric also contained traces of him. I had Ianys mark the spot by ramming a stick into the ground as I noted the find in a small notebook. Then, I wrapped the fabric in large, durable goshe leaves and stowed it in the bag Ianys carried for me.

The first trace of Ustion since the cave, and it filled me with hope and doubt at the same time. I couldn't be sure Ustion had left it behind. It could have been someone else. Still, this was the only lead I had for now, and we had to go on. Despite the uncertainty, it gave me hope we were closer to finding Ustion.

We progressed slowly as I scanned the ground for more traces, more hints of where Ustion might be. The hands of the elves merging their energy with mine were warm on my shoulders. The warmth travelled through me as their energy boosted my own. As the top layer of the ground dried out, I could penetrate deeper into the earth to look for traces, could scan beyond the path into the first line of trees, and go longer without a break. But though my energy went further, it didn't bring me more results.

Much later, with Ianys walking next to me holding a lantern, I was losing hope again. Brem and his team were visible across a clearing to the left of us. They hadn't found any trace of Ustion at all. We were moving farther and farther away from the village, yet we were no closer to finding him. No hidden dwellings, no sign of fires or footprints. And it was getting dark.

The lack of footsteps, on and off the paths, bothered me. Even if someone had carried Ustion—incapacitated or voluntarily—there still would have been impressions to find, despite the rainfall, but there were none. Could he have been carried by a cloud elf? But we weren't exactly built to carry a heavy burden while flying. We could only manage it for small distances.

I turned around to ask Ashyu where Ustion would likely hide in this part of the forest, only to remember I'd sent him home. The lack of results had agitated him more and more as the day progressed, and his endless cursing and complaining severely hampered our search.

Brem's cry of, "I found something!" reached me at the same time as the sound of wings flapping above me. The guide's novice, Darver, descended between the treetops.

"Please, don't tell me the elders want a report, now?" I asked him as he landed in front of me.

Darver shook his head and grabbed at me. His black curls hung in disarray around his face, framing a grave expression. "Come quick!" He tried to catch his breath, "Master Ashyu's attacking Master Jannes. He's trying to throttle him!"

So much for hoping Ashyu would calm down. Even from a distance, he managed to disrupt the search for his own son. I ran towards Brem, who was already making his way over. "I'm needed in the village. Keep at it until your energy levels run low. Bag and mark everything you find. If I'm not back before nightfall, make camp and continue at first light."

"Yes, Master."

With a nod towards the elves, I took flight and followed Darver back to the village. We landed outside Jannes' workshop, a large open area strewn with cut trees, stacked planks, and sawdust. Angry shouts came from the other side of a stack of planks. Jannes' apprentice, a young elf named Perron, sat next to a small, teary-eyed stripling with eyes wide in fear and long blond locks dancing as she sobbed.

I turned to Darver. "What is she doing here?"

"That's young Merel, Master Ashyu's youngest. She came to warn us."

Merel? Taruif's apprentice-to-be was Ashyu's daughter? "Take her home, Novice Darver. She shouldn't be here right now."

"Yes, Master." He reached to take Merel's hand. Merel wiped her eyes and took his hand, though it was easy to see she'd rather stay.

When I rounded the stack of planks, Ashyu stood bent over Jannes—a stocky, bald tree elf, and one of our tribe's carpenters —holding a knife to his throat. A number of elves stood behind both of them, unmoving, but poised to interfere, if they could catch Ashyu unaware. One of them nursed a bleeding arm.

"Where did you take him?" Ashyu screamed at Jannes, pressing the blunt side of the knife deeper into Jannes' skin. "You foul-breathed boar. Where? Tell me where my son is! Tell me!"

The guide stood to the side, his hands forming a bowl. Like the others, he seemed to be waiting for a safe moment to use his skills to subdue Ashyu. I waited until the guide acknowledged my presence, and then announced myself, loudly.

Through all his yelling, Ashyu hadn't even noticed my arrival, and he turned his head towards me in surprise. It was the moment the guide had been waiting for. He moved in, muttered something, and touched Ashyu. As Ashyu wobbled on his feet, the elves behind Jannes shot forward and pulled him out of Ashyu's reach. Ashyu sank to the ground, dropping the knife, which the guide kicked away as he shuffled out of reach. The elves behind Ashyu moved to grab him, but the guide shook his head.

"Leave him be. He'll be out for a while."

They nodded but lingered close to Ashyu as I approached the guide. "How do you mean, out for a while? What did you do?"

"A calming spell wouldn't have sufficed, Master Kelnaht, he was far too angry. I sent him to sleep, instead."

Seemed Ma'terra hadn't considered truth seekers, when she handed out those talents. Maybe the guide could teach me how to do it, and save me energy, and bruises.

I turned to Jannes. He sat on his heels, coughing and spitting, trying to get his breathing under control, as he kept one hand pressed against his neck and his eyes fixed on Ashyu. I knelt down in front of him and waited for him to catch his breath.

"He just came at me," Jannes said, stuttering, voice scratchy. "Just ran in here, grabbed me by my throat, and pushed me against a tree. I tried to ask him what was wrong, but...he wouldn't let me talk, wouldn't let me go. He just—" Jannes coughed. "He was so angry, but he wouldn't tell me what happened." He looked up at me. "Did they find Ustion? Is he hurt? Is that why Ashyu's so angry?"

Something I would have liked to know myself. I wanted to interview Jannes, but the bruises around his throat needed to be looked at first. I rose. "Why don't you get checked out at the infirmary, and I'll do my best to find the answers."

Jannes grabbed my hand and nodded as I pulled him to his feet. "Thank you."

I gave him a short nod and pointed to the elf closest to us.

"Go with him. Both of you report to the cells for questioning as soon as you're done at the infirmary."

Both elves nodded. Jannes whispered something to Perron in passing. He nodded to his mentor and approached me. "Master says I'm to show you around the workshop."

"In a moment," I said and turned to the remaining elves. I grabbed my pencil and notebook out of my cloak and took their statements. They'd all arrived after the fight had begun, leaving me with little information of use, and I sent them to help the guide carry Ashyu to the cells.

Perron led me through the workshop and its surroundings, explaining what they used every space for, while I scanned them. I couldn't believe how many traces of Ustion I found, until Perron explained that Ustion, as carpenter's apprentice-to-be, had been helping them out with some orders. He even handed me Ustion's experience sheet, as he called it, showing me exactly when Ustion had been here. There was no indication why Ashyu thought Jannes had taken Ustion, though.

Done with the search, I flew to the cells. With nothing to do until Ashyu woke up or Jannes returned from the infirmary, I settled down on a chair in the hall and waited.

By the time Jannes arrived, Ashyu had come to. The guide and I sat next to each other with Ashyu slumped in the chair across from us. Jannes sat waiting for us to interview him in the next cell.

"What was that about, Master Ashyu?"

"He hurt my son. It had to have been him. They say he hasn't been home for a couple of days." Ashyu banged his hand on the table. "And he's out to acquire my son as his apprentice."

Considering Ustion had already been working with Jannes, I'd say Jannes had pretty much succeeded in that. "But?"

"I want him to serve his apprenticeship with Master Zulryn."

Ah, rivalry. As far as I knew, Zulryn and Jannes weren't enemies, despite competing for the same work. They weren't exactly friends, either, but there was plenty to do in the village to keep both carpenters busy. "Was that what your fight with Ustion was about?"

"What?"

"The fight, Master Ashyu. You told me you and Ustion fought before he walked off. Was that about the apprenticeship?"

Ashyu blinked, opened his mouth, closed it again, and rubbed his fingers across his forehead. "Yes. Ustion wanted to apprentice with Master Jannes, but I told him I wouldn't allow it. We had words."

"Why not allow it?"

Ashyu shook his head. "Master Jannes and I, we don't get along."

"Doesn't constitute a reason to abduct Ustion. And you know it. You can't go around attacking elves and accusing them of taking your son because you don't get along."

Ashyu opened his mouth, but I shook my head and placed the experience sheet in front of him. "Ustion has been working at Master Jannes' workshop off and on for almost a moon, now."

That seemed to deflate Ashyu. He grabbed the sheet and stared at it, shaking his head as he leaned back.

"Is there any other reason why you think Master Jannes could have taken Ustion?"

"No. Just... I heard he hadn't been home, and Yerriny had been crying, and I..." Ashyu looked at his hands as he flexed his fingers. "I was angry."

And Jannes was a convenient target. "I'm locking you in here for the night at least, so you can get your head screwed on straight again."

Ashyu clenched his fists. "But..." The guide put a hand on one of Ashyu's fists and shook his head. Ashyu swallowed. "I understand, Master Kelnaht."

"Good." I rose and asked the guide if he was coming, not surprised when he declined. Ashyu clearly needed someone to confide in. I locked the door and left them to talk while I fetched Darver to sit in on my interview with Jannes.

The carpenter looked better already, despite the bruises around his throat. "Where were you the past couple of days, Master Jannes?" I asked.

"Checking on some old trees I know won't last this winter."

"Where?"

"Towards the Ageir River. I returned late this morning."

The opposite direction to where Ustion had been headed. If Jannes could prove he was there when Ustion disappeared, I could rule him out as a suspect.

Jannes put his hands on the table. A bandage around his left arm peeked out from under his sleeve. I pointed at it. "What's that?" Had Ashyu done that? Or had he fought with Ustion? Ustion didn't seem like the sort to not fight back.

"Tripped over a tree stump and fell into some velorum bushes."

Velorum bushes didn't grow in the forest, only in open fields where plenty of sunlight could reach them, like the area bordering the Ageir River. "Show me the wound."

Jannes' eyes opened wide, as if he only now realised he might be a suspect. He looked from me to Darver. "You don't think..."

What I thought didn't matter, and Darver was experienced enough to not comment. Only proof could rule him out. "I need to see the wound, Master Jannes."

Jannes swallowed and started to unwrap the bandage. "Of course, Master."

The tears were too severe to be nail scratches. Most were scabbed over, starting to heal already, but one of the wounds was open and blood welled up as I prodded the skin next to it. Darver grabbed a clean piece of fabric from the linen cupboard in the hall and dabbed it up.

"One of the nurses took a sliver of thorn out of that one this morning."

I would check with the infirmary later: the nurse could no

doubt tell me how old the wound was as well. The wounds did look like they'd been caused by a thorn from the velorum bushes. It seemed Jannes had spoken the truth.

"I didn't do anything, Master Kelnaht. I like young Ustion. He's a talented carpenter, and I'd love to teach him what I know. He's worked with us a couple of times to see my style. I know he's done the same with Master Zulryn."

Just as Perron had said. Most striplings tested out future mentors, if they had a choice.

"He said he felt a little more at home with my style."

"Master Ashyu says you and he don't get along." I wrapped the bloody fabrics in goshe leaves to be filed as evidence and scanned Jannes' wound. Though it had been cleaned out, it still showed traces of the velorum bushes he'd fallen into. The proof I needed.

"No we don't," Jannes said as Darver rebandaged his arm. "We used to be friends when we were striplings, you see, until we fell in love with the same elf. Neither of us shares well, and it came to a fight. He won, yet Ivy chose me. After a suitable amount of grovelling on my part, of course. Still, Ashyu has never forgiven me for that, even though it was Ivy's decision."

I could sympathise with Ashyu. I doubted I would ever forgive Naia for the fact that Ianys chose her over me. I straightened in my seat and gritted my teeth. This was not the time. I still had a stripling to find.

I let Jannes go with a warning not to leave the village during the investigation, thanked Darver for his presence, sent him back to the safehold—the guide's meditation room—and checked up on Ashyu and the guide. Ashyu stayed sullenly silent until I told him Jannes had nothing to do with Ustion's disappearance. At that point he ranted and raged, and the guide and I left him to it.

I sat on the bench outside to wait for Yerriny, Ashyu's vowed, to arrive, with Ashyu still screaming in the background. Maybe Yerriny would be able to calm him down.

"Such a long time to hold a grudge, especially after vowing

himself to someone else and starting a family," I remarked to the guide.

"Master Jannes is merely a convenient target for his frustration, his helplessness at not being able to find young Ustion. He has a tendency to act before he thinks."

"I'd noticed that." With Ashyu's screaming, it was hard not to.

"He *will* calm down," the guide said as he sat beside me, gazing out on the village. "It'll take a while, but he'll remember what he has done and he'll feel ashamed of his behaviour."

Sounded like this wasn't the first time something like this happened. "I know I shouldn't ask you directly, but—" A shake of the guide's head shut me up immediately.

"No, you may not ask."

"I'm sorry, Guide. I..." I didn't have to tell him I was frustrated. No doubt he was, too.

He closed his eyes for a moment. "But I will give you this: like Master Ashyu, I know of no one with a grudge against young Ustion."

"Thank you." He didn't have to tell me that. Of course, if there were, he wouldn't be allowed to tell me, just as he wasn't allowed to tell the elders of my involvement with Taruif. He could advise us, warn us against missteps, but in general he simply wanted to make us think before we decided which path to choose. I admired the guide for his loyalty to all his subjects. It couldn't be easy, knowing all he did and keeping it to himself.

"Master Ashyu is proud of young Merel's foresting talent. Did you know?"

"No." I barely knew Ashyu. Still, it raised my opinion of him, albeit minimally.

"You should see their garden. It's filled with flowers and herbs young Merel has grown this past turn."

Ever since her talent had been discovered, I guessed. She had to be practicing. We all did when we discovered our talents, whether or not we had a mentor yet.

"Any word on when—?" I meant the reduction of Taruif's

sentence, but I couldn't make myself say it here, out in the open.

The guide rubbed his temples. "None at all. Elder Rynth does *not* appreciate me asking after it every time we meet. She told me it was still under advisement."

That didn't sound hopeful. He had done his best to convince the elders to consider it all those moons ago, and all we could do was wait until they finally made a decision, however long that might take.

Spotting Yerriny walking up to us, I rose and dusted off my tunic. She looked at me with wet, dull eyes as she greeted me. If only I had better news for her. She merely nodded when I told her Ashyu would spend the night in his cell, yet the moment I let her in, she flung herself into Ashyu's arms.

"You don't mind staying?" I asked the guide. "I'd best check whether the search party has returned yet, and see if Brem found anything useful."

"With me as guard, they can at least talk freely."

Ashyu had wrapped his arms around his vowed. He was talking to her, his voice low and kind. I nodded.

The guide rested his hand on my shoulder. "When flood runs dry, stones stop sinking, Kelnaht. Remember that."

I was sure I'd figure out what he meant at some point, but as I stumbled along the path, it made no sense to me at all. The guide was like that at times, cryptic and vague, but he was never wrong. I shivered and drew my cloak tight around me to fend off the cold breeze. I could barely keep my eyes open or stop yawning, but I couldn't go to bed before I had news from Brem. And suddenly, Ianys was by my side, grabbing my arm and turning me onto the path to my dwelling.

"What are—?"

Ianys put his fingers to my lips. "Sshh. You don't need to find Apprentice Brem. I'll tell you what you need to know." He supported me until we were inside my dwelling, and tucked me into my bed without giving me the chance to protest or ask questions. When he crawled in bed with me, he wrapped me against his broad, muscular body and whispered all I wanted to know about the search, bleak as it was. As his voice faded, and I basked in his warmth, my heart went out for Ustion, spending another night alone in the forest.

CHAPTER TEN

WHEN I WOKE up in the middle of the night, Ianys was gone, but he'd left a note saying he'd gone to see Taruif and would be back in the morning, after visiting Atèn. I buried my head in his pillow, savouring his scent. Our relationship, the sneaking around, wasn't easy on me, but I could only imagine how hard it was on Ianys. For him, seeing me was as unsafe as seeing Taruif. We both risked shunning, but Ianys also stood to lose his daughter if he broke his promise to Naia. He hadn't broken it, since I wasn't raising Atèn. But if word got back to Naia's parents that Ianys was in a relationship with me, they'd have a good case to argue that he intended to break his promise.

After a surprisingly restful night, morning still came too soon, and before I knew it, I found myself sitting at a table in my workshop, eating hot porridge Ianys had made.

"Apprentice Brem found one more piece of fabric," Ianys told me. "On the edge of a path, like the other one, and again with a strand of hair wrapped around it." He pointed to the goshe leaves on the large worktable. "He said to tell you the fabric looked torn, not cut."

I studied Ianys' face. So strange to have him sitting carefree in my workshop. "Does anyone know you're here?"

"Those who saw me arrive on horseback last night, I suppose." He put his hand over mine and smiled. "Don't worry. I'm here on business, Kel. No one'll ask questions about that."

True. Which was probably why he'd volunteered to play messenger. I turned my hand under his and grabbed it, yet I couldn't stop myself from glancing at the door.

Ianys shot me an apologetic smile as he pulled his hand free. "We followed the path for as long as we could, but found no other traces before reaching our resting place. Apprentice Brem wanted to get his findings to you, so you could examine them this morning."

It was good to have him here. If only I could ditch the research and drag him back to bed. I finished my porridge and put the bowl into the sink. Time to get to work. "Are you sure Brem isn't expecting me yet?" It didn't feel right for him to be doing my job.

"He said he could manage until you finish examining the evidence."

Of course he could. "What about you. Aren't you going back?"

Ianys nodded. "But I'm not expected back until late evening." He swallowed. "All this… I need to spend some time with Atèn, after class."

Meaning he did not need to go home yet. "Well, if you're here, you can help me." I sprinkled cleaning herbs over our hands, and we both rubbed them in. I stared at his hands, imagining them on my body, and shook myself. "Focus on your work," I muttered to myself. How could I stand here thinking about Ianys naked with a stripling missing?

We stood shoulder to shoulder as I carefully took both pieces of fabric out of their goshe leaves. Ianys moved the leaves aside, so I could place them on my worktable. I removed the hairs from the fabric, spread the pieces out, and left them to dry.

"Dyed pattern. Traditional style." Not the sort of style a stripling like Ustion would wear, unless his mother dyed her own fabric, but Yerriny wasn't a dyer or a seamstress. "Not many wear those anymore," I said more for Ianys' benefit than mine. "Though it could have been a sheet or towel." Hard to say from such small pieces. Some of the older elves still wore traditional style dyed tunics, but not all. I'd never seen Taruif wearing them.

I nearly dropped the hair I'd picked up when Ianys wrapped his arms around me from behind and leaned his chin on my shoulder. "I love seeing you work. Always have."

A hint of pain coloured his voice, but I tried to ignore it. I turned my head and kissed him on his stubbled cheek. "It's good to have you here." If only I could have him here without all the secrecy.

Still holding the hair, I wormed out of his embrace. I couldn't afford the distraction, as tempting as he was. "Mind going over to the cell and bringing Ashyu here? I need him to tell me whether this cloth could be Ustion's. You'll have to ask the guide to open the doors for you." Only the elders, the guide, Darver, Brem, or I could lock up and open the cells. "That's assuming Ashyu's calmed down. If not, you'd best fetch Yerriny." Though I'd rather put up with Ashyu's temper than cause Yerriny more anguish.

Ianys tucked a stray hair behind my ear. "I could do with some air. Something to distract me from wanting to nail you to your work table." He stepped back and walked away.

It was hard not to turn around to watch him until he disappeared, but I kept my eyes on my worktable, even if I couldn't focus on my work. Only when the door closed did I place the blond hair on a thoroughly cleansed piece of black slate. I rubbed my hands until the energy started flowing, and muttered a short prayer to Ma'terra to help me find the answers. To help me find Ustion. I drew my hands apart shaped like upturned bowls and held them over the hair. I already knew it was Ustion's, but I scanned it again to be certain I hadn't made a mistake.

I took a deep breath and scanned the hair bit by bit, marking its shape, its condition, searching for foreign traces. I stopped halfway and frowned. There was a knot in the hair, a double one. That didn't happen on its own. Someone had knotted it. I released the tension in my hands, grabbed the other strand of hair, and repeated the process. Same double knot. Definitely knotted on purpose, most likely to make certain the hair would be found with the fabric. Ustion was dropping breadcrumbs for us.

If only we'd found more of them, maybe we would know which way to look. I'd have to ask Ianys if Brem had said anything about the distance between the locations where the pieces were found. I wrote down everything I read from the hair, useful or not, and did the same with the fabric.

Ianys dragged Ashyu into my workshop sometime after I finished scanning the fabric. I even had time to clean my bowl and make tea, strong tea, for all of us. Ashyu immediately went for my worktable, reaching out for the fabric. "Is that—?"

"Don't touch it!" I hurried over and grabbed his hand. "You'll contaminate the evidence."

Ashyu stepped back, abashed. "I'm sorry."

My heart pounded, and I accepted his apology, glad I had stopped him in time. I hadn't found a trace of the owner—not from evidence left soaking in the mud for who knew how long— but I had found some traces of suspicious materials soaked into the fabric on both pieces. Mixed together, they formed a numbing agent used by animal healers. Not that I'd tell Ashyu that, not after his outburst the previous day. I didn't want him going after someone else.

Though it was too muddy to see the colours clearly, Ashyu studied the pattern of what appeared to be grey and blue fabric as if it could answer all his questions.

"Does Ustion own a tunic with this design on it?"

He shook his head. "He's never worn anything looking like this. He wears a lot of green, not blue."

So, not his tunic, if it was a tunic at all.

THOUGH WE BOTH wished he could have stayed longer, Ianys left shortly after Ashyu. A kiss and a quick rutting later, that was. I couldn't wipe the grin off my face, even if I'd wanted to. No doubt the cold from the upcoming flight would take care of that before I met up with the search party.

Sliding my wings through the slits of my cloak, and wrapping it tightly around me, I left my dwelling. Taruif was working on a tree close by. I drank in the sight of him at work. He had his eyes closed as his hands roamed across the bark of an oeral tree. Though his face was the normal unreadable mask, one corner of his mouth turned up a smidge. Before, I wouldn't have noticed, but I'd come to know him well this past turn, knew all his expressions, his moods...

My heart stuttered as he glanced my way. Torn between duty and feelings, I turned off the path and walked around the tree, making sure I couldn't be seen by anyone passing. Hiding didn't feel right, but that was how it was. I couldn't touch him while his hands were pressed against the bark—it would muddle his readings—so I watched him work, enjoying that little smile, his focused expression, the way his long, grey braid swung when he nodded to himself, and the movement in the vine tattoo disappearing below his neckline as he swallowed.

I didn't apologise for not being with him the previous night. But when he paused in his work and looked up at me, his blue eyes warm and longing, I cursed myself for being so tired, and Ianys for not taking me to sleep at Taruif's. "I'll be there tonight," I whispered. "I'll fly back to do research." Even if the flight would take hours. And if there wouldn't be anything to research, I'd make up an excuse. Brem was perfectly capable of leading the elves on his own.

"Focus on finding Ustion. I can wait."

He could and he would, but I didn't want him to, because I knew he'd be lying awake wondering, even if he would never admit to it. After being alone for so long, he couldn't always believe we were with him to stay. We needed to show him we were, as often as we could, until he believed it. Putting my hand over his, not touching, but close enough for him to feel my warmth, I promised to be by as soon as I could manage. Taruif nodded and turned his attention back to the tree, but he kept the hand underneath mine still for as long as I covered it. Eventually, though, I had to go.

As I FLEW over the forest to the meeting point, staying clear of the dense foliage of the evergreen oaks and parulm trees, I took the opportunity to check the distance between the locations where the fabric was found. It took less time than expected to reach both places. My stomach clenched at how little progress we'd made. It would take most of a moon to search the whole forest. We'd have to find Ustion well before that.

With the distance we'd travelled in the past few days in mind, I flew to where my calculations led me to believe the search party would be. Turned out, I miscalculated by a hundred yards, and didn't find them until halfway around the Cabaj Pond. I hadn't spotted any markers along the way and assumed Brem hadn't found new traces. Yet the moment I landed, he bent over, prodding at something at the edge of the path. When he straightened up, he held up a piece of fabric, complete with a strand of blond hair wound around it.

We secluded ourselves from our helpers to confer, and while Brem wrapped it in goshe leaves, I compared the distance between here and the second find to the distance between the first and second finds. If you were following the paths, the distances matched. Brem's eyes shone with enthusiasm when I told him.

"We could test it out. Master Ellon and Mistress Vroni could fly the same distance in different directions."

Having just finished a long flight, I wasn't looking forward to taking off without resting first, but I had plenty of energy left, and I wasn't letting two random cloud elves do my job. I glanced at the flyers Brem pointed out. "They're not truth seekers; they might destroy evidence by accident."

"I'll tell them what to do. You need some rest, Master."

I shook my head. "I can do it."

"There are too many directions to choose from. If I thought it was doable from the ground, I'd go. But flying is quicker."

True. "Which is why it has to be me." It was my job.

Brem ran his hand through his hair. "If you won't listen to me, Master, will you at least let them help you?"

I didn't want to, but once we sat down to discuss where to search, it became clear Brem was right. I couldn't do this on my own in the time we had until darkness fell. Ellon and Vroni were glad to be of help. They listened intently as Brem explained what we expected of them. He handed them markers while I made sure they understood they weren't to touch the evidence. All they had to do was find and mark the location, and let Brem know. Of course, since they didn't have our abilities, they couldn't scan the ground, but they knew what to search for. By now, everyone in the group did.

We drew a rough map in the mud, indicating our discoveries and the possible directions to go next, and divided the routes amongst the three of us. After Ellon and Vroni took flight, Brem held me back, insisting I sit down and have a cup of tea to warm up first. I suspected he only did it to give me a moment to catch my breath. Sometimes, he reminded me of my mother.

Despite the rest, my wings were more sensitive to the cold than usual. I shivered with every breeze, and my speed wasn't good. The first place I landed held nothing of interest, and neither did the second. It took me longer to reach the third destination, with fatigue setting in, but even before I landed, I knew I'd find something. The earth was as muddy as the rest of the forest, but I still spotted footprints as I descended. Close up, it looked as though parts of the footprints had been washed away in the rain. But from above, the line had seemed too clean, too sharp to be natural. I guessed someone had tried to sweep away their tracks with a branch.

Studying the footprints, I found a piece of fabric next to the clearest of them, stuck in the mud, half hidden by fallen leaves. Thanking Ma'terra for the end of the rainfall and preserving this evidence, I performed a quick cleansing, dug out the fabric and wrapped it in goshe leaves.

As I examined the partial prints, the guide's saying came back to me. *"When flood runs dry, stones stop sinking."* I had no idea how he did it, but he was right, again. The footprints and the line in the mud would have been hidden from sight had it still been raining, or even washed away.

I didn't carry anything that would allow me to make a cast of the prints, so I secured them by covering them with goshe leaves I pinned to the ground with sticks. Not allowing myself any mistakes, I checked the fourth destination, even knowing I wouldn't find anything there.

When I returned to the meeting point, Brem, Ellon and Vroni were waiting for me. Their faces told me all I needed to know, but I asked them, "Nothing on your routes?" to be certain.

Brem shook his head, and then narrowed his eyes. "Something on your side, though, Master. Am I right?"

"More fabric and hairs." I showed him the wrapped goshe leaves. "And partial footprints."

My findings were met with enthusiasm, and we settled down to have some buttered bread and apples as Brem and I discussed how to proceed. The success of our experiment made it easier to plan the next step in our search and calculate the new destinations. I had to admit I appreciated Ellon and Vroni's help, because there was no way I could cover all those distances on my own. Cloud elves weren't built to fly all day. It was said that our ancestors did nothing but fly. But once we met the tree elves, formed an alliance, and settled down with them, cloud elves flew less and less. Our bodies were no longer used to so much flying, and especially not in this cold.

After dinner, we sent all the other elves back to the village with one of the carts; the four of us should be able to manage, now we knew where to search. As Brem loaded the cart, I remembered Ianys' intention of rejoining us and told the group to keep an eye out for him.

We took the cart to where I had found the partial footprints. As soon as we arrived, Brem set about making the cast for the shoe print while Ellon, Vroni, and I took off in our various directions. By the time we found the next location—no print, just a piece of fabric and strand of hair—I knew exactly where we were going to end up. Raden's farm.

Raden was a sturdy, straightforward, pig farmer. He would have access to the numbing agent I'd found on the fabric.

We spread out in different directions again, but didn't find new evidence anywhere in the vicinity of the farm, or in the other directions, either. I took a gamble and flew towards the farm, just in time to see Raden's son Vlem near one of the sheds, his back turned to me, pouring a clear liquid out of a canister onto a muddy patch. Why was he pouring it out? Could it be the numbing agent?

Landing behind him, I laid a hand on his shoulder. "Put it down, young Master Vlem."

Vlem, a wiry tree elf with bright red curls, jumped and dropped the canister. Liquid gushed out onto the already soggy ground. I grabbed the canister and righted it. "Turn around."

He raised his hands and faced me, revealing a nasty bruise on his cheek.

Chapter Eleven

T HE CANISTER TURNED out to only contain water. But Vlem still acted suspicious. He refused to tell us how he got the bruise, refused to tell us where he was when Ustion disappeared or answer even a single question. What was he hiding? And why?

We searched the farm, Brem and I, every nook and cranny, from the house to the fields on the far ends of the property. Raden, who'd come running out of the house when we secured Vlem to the cart, hovered close by, asking questions we had no time to answer. Unfortunately, we found nothing. No fabric, nothing but pig prints in the fields, and no Ustion. We found no fresh traces of Ustion in the fields, but we did find traces of him in the house.

Raden said it wasn't unusual for Ustion to visit them. "He and Vlem are friends," he explained, "though Ustion hasn't been round for a while."

Something I could have known if I'd had more time to interview Ustion's family. But I'd been relying on my powers to solve the case and assumed I'd have time for that later.

Raden looked none too happy when we took Vlem to the cells for interrogation, and he insisted on coming with us. Considering Vlem's wide eyes and trembling hands, I understood, but as long as Vlem kept refusing to tell me where he was when Ustion went missing, he left me no choice.

Once I'd locked Vlem up, I took Raden outside with me.

"Look, Master Raden—"

Raden interrupted me with a shake of his head. "I saw him coming out of the forest with that bruise on his cheek a couple of days ago. He's been moping around since then, and I have no idea why."

"Did he say where he'd been?"

"Just out walking, he said. I didn't buy it then, don't buy it now. But..." He sighed. "I don't think he's got anything to do with Ustion's disappearance." Raden repeated that the boys were friends, good friends, as far as he knew. "Like I said, Ustion hasn't visited lately, and Vlem hasn't mentioned his name once." Raden threw his hands up.

I put a hand on his shoulder. "Why don't you take a seat in the last cell while I interview Vlem? I'll talk to you after." Assuming talking would be enough. Because if Vlem kept his silence, I might have to take more drastic measures, and delving into a suspect's mind was something I only used if all else failed.

Raden nodded. "Please, Master Kelnaht, be easy on him. He's just a stripling."

I gritted my teeth. I'd seen plenty of mischievous striplings, but those who deliberately hurt another in anything but a fair fight were few and far between. Still, I couldn't promise Raden anything. I turned away from him without answering and made my way into the cell, where the guide was already seated across from Vlem.

"Well, young Vlem." I sat next to the guide. "It seems you've got yourself into quite a mess here. Refusing to tell us why you were in the forest when young Ustion went missing. Refusing to tell us where you got that bruise." Vlem showed no reaction at all. "Come on, Vlem, we already know you weren't pouring out numbing agent in your—"

"What?" Vlem's head shot up, yet he didn't look at me or the guide. "That's what you thought I was doing?" He clenched his jaw, eyes wild, with a spark of something I couldn't quite decipher. "Father would kill me if I contaminated his land with stuff like that. I was watering and heating the mud pits." Vlem lowered his gaze and drew circles on the table with his fingers. "Father's pretty strict about helping out at the farm despite my talents lying elsewhere."

"Like I said, we know you weren't pouring out numbing agent. We know there was only water in the canister." Time to find out what Vlem was doing in the forest that he didn't want to talk about. "But the timing of your little trip places you in the forest when young Ustion disappeared. So, unless you tell us where you were, I'm arresting you for abducting him."

He ran a trembling hand through his hair. "But I didn't abduct him. We're friends."

"Friends who haven't seen each other for a while, your father says."

Vlem blushed. "We...er...Ustion..." He shook his head. "I was taking a walk. That's all."

And he clammed up again, no matter what I asked, or how I asked it. This wasn't going well.

I turned to the guide, who studied Vlem's face with a frown. Vlem was still avoiding looking at the guide. I leaned over and whispered, "I'm going to step outside for a moment. Talk to him. I want some answers when I get back, or I'll have to go in." Even saying it made me shudder. It was the nastiest part of my job, entering an elf's mind, searching for the information I needed inside them instead of getting it out of them by asking questions. The guide's eyes took on that sad expression I knew so well, but he nodded nonetheless.

"Make certain he knows the rules." I had told Vlem the rules when we took him here, but with some elves, especially the young ones, it bore repeating. I walked outside and leaned back against the wall. It was getting dark. Raden joined me and asked me if Vlem had told us where he'd been yet.

"Nothing yet. I'm giving the guide a chance to talk some sense into that stubborn son of yours."

Raden closed his eyes and swallowed. "I told him what happens to elves who try to keep things from a truth seeker when he was a wee elf. He'd broken his brother's toy and refused to say a word." Raden picked up a twig. "My eldest had been so proud of that wagon. He made it himself, you know. He wouldn't let Vlem play with it, and one morning when we came in from feeding the pigs, we found Vlem stomping all over it, screaming and raging." Raden looked at me. "He never misbehaved again, after our talk, and we never had to caution him again. Not for that, at least. He could be quite a handful."

I could imagine. "He said his talent is not in farming."

"No. It's in weaving." Raden didn't sound thrilled about it. "None of the weavers have room for another apprentice. Vlem'll have to wait until they've passed their tests, or find a mentor with a different tribe."

The disdain in Raden's voice made it clear what his opinion was. "You don't want him to leave."

"No. He's young enough. He can wait a turn or two."

I wouldn't be surprised if Vlem preferred to find his own way, even if it meant travelling to other tribes. Before I could ask Raden more, the guide called me back inside. Sitting next to the guide, wrapped in his arms, Vlem had tears in his eyes.

"Tell him, young Vlem. Tell Master Kelnaht what you did."

It was far past midnight when I finally let myself into Taruif's dwelling. It would be a short night, too. We'd be heading out again before dawn, and Brem had left a note that he'd be in long before that to go over his findings with me.

I stifled a yawn as I took my boots off in the dark and walked up the stairs and into the bedroom. Taruif looked up from the book he was reading and smiled at me, inviting me into bed. Smiling back, I quickly shed my clothes, but instead of lying down next to him, I stood at the foot of the bed and spread out my wings as far as I could, to release some of the tension in my back. I hadn't had a moment to properly unfold them after all that flying. There was barely enough room, but spreading them outside in the frosty air, with my back as tense as it was, wouldn't do me any good.

"Any word from Ianys?" I asked as I fluttered my wings in the warmth of the room.

Taruif put his book on the night table. "He passed me a note, earlier. Atèn was a bit feverish. He didn't want to leave her."

I could easily picture Ianys reading a story while she slept next to him. It made me smile, despite missing him. A twinge in my back muscles turned my smile into a grimace. Taruif rose and motioned for me to fold my wings. I enjoyed the view as I did, watching muscles twitch beneath his tattoo, wanting to touch him, lick him...

He moved behind me and pushed me onto the bed. His hands were warm against my back, and I sighed in bliss. Sighs turned into moans as he worked the knots out of my muscles. By the time Taruif finished, I lay practically boneless on the bed, with Taruif's fingers trailing the edges of my wings. I rolled onto my side, pulling Taruif flush against me and brushed my lips against his. "Thank you," I whispered, not wanting to break the serene silence. "I needed that."

"You need to take it easy tomorrow."

"I know. No flying in the cold." I hoped it wouldn't be necessary, now that we had a lead, at last. It was a meagre one, but Vlem had at least seen Ustion after he'd disappeared.

Vlem had been sobbing after admitting he had met up with Ustion on the edge of the forest near the farm, the day Ustion left the hunters' cave. It had been a last attempt by each boy to convince the other to change his mind. Ustion had begged Vlem to stay in the village, while Vlem had tried to convince Ustion to go with him, to explore and visit other tribes. Vlem wanted to travel, wanted to see more of the world, but Ustion wouldn't hear of it. He didn't want to leave his family. They had argued, fought, and when Vlem had realised Ustion could not be swayed, he'd run off into the forest, leaving Ustion standing by himself.

That the boys were new lovers as well as best friends seemed to come as a surprise to both sets of parents, but it explained why they hadn't seen much of each other lately. It must have been painful for both, neither willing to give in to the other, but hoping the other would see it his way.

For me, it meant restarting the investigation anew. It looked more and more as if Ustion had been abducted close to the farm, not near the caves. Although that still didn't explain the lack of traces there.

Taruif trailing kisses along my jaw took me out of my thoughts. "Time to let go of work, Kel."

"But—"

"Whatever it is can wait until morning."

I surrendered myself. He was right, of course, and I apologised for letting my mind drift while I had a gorgeous elf in my arms. Running my hand lightly down Taruif's arm, his side, circling his hip, I revelled in the way he shivered and moved into the touch. Part of me wanted to just rut against him, bringing us both off quickly, but another part of me wanted to take my time. I might be tired, but as Taruif claimed my mouth in a searing kiss, I knew taking it slow would be the right thing.

The kiss ended with both of us out of breath. Taruif moved in to kiss me again, but I shook my head and prodded him until he lay on his back. I straddled him, trapping him beneath me. I enjoyed the hitch of his breath, the ripple in his stomach, the hardening of his cock. He pushed up against me, but I shoved him back down. I tore the band binding my hair loose and let my hair fall down across his face, his chin, and his chest as I leaned down to kiss his neck where his vine tattoo met the space behind his ear. I kissed my way down his vines, from neck to stomach, dragging my hair across his body, teasing him with it to make his breath hitch, to make him whine. Which he did, freely, in low, deep moans that turned into groans when I dipped my tongue into his navel and licked my way down across his cock to his balls.

Taruif's muscles tensed as he pushed himself into my touch, and I nipped his balls with my teeth in reply. Taruif only groaned louder. With a smile, I licked him up and down repeatedly, then paying the same attention to his balls, sweeping my hair across his cock. The sounds he made urged me on, and I whipped my hair against his length by shaking my head left and right until he started trembling. Only then did I close my mouth over his cock.

Taruif gasped, grabbing at my head, shoulders, the bedding. I pinned his hips before he could push his body up to force himself deeper into me, and sucked and licked him at leisure until he finally burst. He barely gave me time to swallow. He grabbed my wrists and pulled me up until we were face to face, my body covering his.

"Thank you," he whispered against my lips. "I needed that."

I was still smiling when he kissed me.

"...AND THEN I had to wait until the squirrels moved their nuts to their new home, three trees back from the one I was working on..."

With my head resting on his shoulder, I listened to Taruif, tracing the vines up and down his chest in the flickering candle light. Taruif had chosen his dwelling well. Isolated, yet at the right side of this clearing to catch the early morning sun. Such a pity we could not stay in bed until dawn, when my own dwelling would still be shaded by its neighbours, leaving me plenty of darkness to sneak in or out.

"Time to go," Taruif said.

I silenced him with a kiss, even though he was right. I had to be at the workshop before Brem showed up to discuss his findings with me.

"Remember, no flying for you today," he said when I finally let go of him and hoisted myself out of bed.

Impossible. I had a search to organise, again. "I can't—"

"I know, but try to."

My heart warmed at his words. I liked him taking care of me

as much as I did taking care of him. If only I didn't have to leave. With a sigh, I started hunting for my trousers. "I don't know if I'll be back tonight."

"I know that, too." Taruif rose elegantly, retrieved my trousers from under the foot of the bed, and handed them to me, making me look like a fool, stumbling around the room trying to find them when he knew where they were all along. He helped me dress and even bound my hair for me. If he had been trying to make it hard for me to leave, he would have succeeded, but Taruif didn't do it on purpose. If anything, he tried to enjoy my presence for as long as he could. I kissed him again, revelling in the feel of his naked body against my clothed one.

"Find Ustion and bring him back," Taruif whispered against my mouth.

"I will." I would. I *had* to.

I didn't look back when I walked out the door, knowing he'd be watching me through the window, and I made it to my dwelling just in time. Brem arrived soon after me, when I'd just put breakfast on.

"I've been thinking, Master," Brem began as he shed his cloak, "about the distances between the fabric locations."

He wasn't the only one. Thoughts of a cloud elf abducting Ustion, carrying him through the air, hadn't been far from my mind.

"I ran an experiment last night." He placed two sheets of paper on the table in front of me. I studied the first one, a crudely drawn map of the forest noting the fabric locations. Based on what Vlem had told us, the location nearest to Raden's farm was our first location, not the last. Our search had been the wrong way around. Of course, now we knew, we could fix it. The other sheet held a series of lines and numbers. What had Brem been doing?

"This number—" Brem pointed "—is how much Ustion weighed, according to his family. The lines show distances."

I saw where he was going with this now. I pointed at the numbers near the lines. "Distance and time?"

Brem nodded. "I asked some cloud elves to carry a trunk of Ustion's weight, courtesy of Master Jannes, and fly as far as they could with it."

Trunks were more easily carried than a body, either unconscious or struggling, and some elves were stronger than others, but the distances wouldn't be far off. "That makes a cloud elf abducting Ustion seem more and more likely."

"It's the only thing that explains the lack of footprints."

"But what about the lack of footprints around the cave?" I asked Brem, though I did have some idea now.

"Either the abductor did it, to keep the hunters from following Ustion. Or Ustion used some sort of cloth to wipe those clean himself. An extra tunic, a blanket, I'm not sure. But that's the only thing I could think of, since no one knew he was meeting Vlem that night."

As a stripling's attempt to keep his father from knowing where he was going, it made sense. And that might well have been the fabric he used to drop us hints, since all we knew about that fabric was that it wasn't from Ustion's clothes.

Brem and I tried to map out the course the abductor could have taken. As with all the locations so far, there were many possibilities, but some of the directions seemed more plausible than others. We'd try those first.

While I cleared away my breakfast—the porridge had gone cold by the time I remembered to eat it—Brem packed our bags with the map, a new supply of goshe leaves, and every tool we thought we could use along the way.

Chapter Twelve

S ITTING IN ONE of the two carts we managed to acquire, bent over Brem's map, a cold breeze reminded me of Taruif's request to not fly today. We both knew I couldn't promise him that, but with the number of cloud elves the elders had gathered to help us, I wouldn't have to fly much. I wasn't for taking so many inexperienced elves, but Brem assured me the elders had personally chosen them, and they all understood the rules. Besides, we didn't have much of a choice; Ustion had been missing for seven nights now. We needed all the help we could get.

We assigned routes to the cloud elves, sending out no more than four at the same time, while Brem and I stayed with the tree elves who'd volunteered to drive the carts and cook our meals. I wasn't going up unless they needed me, to give my wings some respite. They were still sore, and the frosty air didn't help. I pulled my cloak tight around me. At least it was still dry.

The first place was easily found, and we took the carts as close to that location as possible. No prints, though, only a piece of fabric with a hair knotted around it. While I performed some scans, Brem sent the next batch of cloud elves up. They didn't have the same success, however. After sixteen flights, sixteen directions, we had found no more fabric, no prints, no clues at all.

Brem and I studied the map and discussed the possibilities,

argued even. We'd made a mistake, but where? Had it been wrong of me to disregard the area surrounding the cave that Ashyu's hunting group had used? I'd been certain the abductor would avoid going near it, but there were more caves in that direction...

Caves. That was it. The abductor could have taken Ustion into a cave. They had to sleep somewhere. And, fool as I was, I hadn't merely discounted that particular cave, I'd discounted them all. Or, rather, not instructed the volunteers to look inside nearby caves.

We studied the map, and came up with four caves that needed to be checked. After we sent volunteers to those caves, Brem and I started calculating new directions. Brem did more than I, since I couldn't stop watching the sky, willing one of them to come back with good news. My hope was sorely tested when three of the volunteers returned without results. Only one was left, Vroni.

She didn't return before dusk set in, but she brought the good news we'd been hoping for.

"The entrance of the cave was swept clean. No footprints anywhere." She sat down in the cart. "I didn't dare enter the cave at first, afraid someone might still be in there, but I didn't want to return without being sure I'd found the right place." She ran a shaky hand through her hair, but her voice was steady. "I found fabric and an abandoned fire. No one's been in that cave for hours, at least. The ashes were cold."

"Good job. Thank you, Mistress Vroni." I handed her a cup of tea and a blanket and looked at the sky. "We might make it before it gets too dark," I told Brem. "If we can process the evidence quickly, we can set up camp there."

Brem nodded and hopped off the cart to tell the drivers where we wanted to go.

It took some manoeuvring to reach the caves because not all the paths were wide enough for the carts, but we got there in the end. The drivers started building a fire while Brem and I followed Vroni into the cave. Everything was as she said. The ashes were cold, and in the midst of them lay the hair-wrapped fabric.

"I found the fabric when I prodded the ashes to see if it still sparked," Vroni explained. "I hope that didn't contaminate the evidence."

I shook my head while I sprinkled herbs onto my hands. "If you didn't touch it with your hands, it'll be fine."

Vroni smiled in the flickering light of the lantern.

Despite the ashes clinging to it, the fabric was neither burnt nor singed. If anything, it looked as if it had been buried among the ashes on purpose. Fabric was all we found, though, so Brem and I didn't need a lot of time to wrap things up.

We gathered around the fire for the soup and bread the drivers had prepared for us. Brem answered many a question as we ate, but I found myself thinking of Ustion. I wanted to compliment him for doing such a good job leaving clues for us. I hoped he'd been careful. But, on the other hand, it seemed too clever, too easy. A stripling of barely sixteen turns old who knew enough about a truth seeker's job to leave behind a hair, so we could identify him? What if he'd set this all up by himself to misdirect us? But why would he do that? To leave? No. He didn't even want Vlem to leave the village. That couldn't be it.

Why then? To get away from his father? Ashyu might have a temper, and a clear view of where Ustion should apprentice, but it still seemed excessive. Of course, so did erasing his footsteps to meet Vlem. I sighed and shook my head as I dug into my soup. I didn't want to believe him capable of such deception, and unless proven otherwise, I'd give him the benefit of the doubt. I just wanted him found. Tomorrow, if possible. And then all my questions would be answered.

IT COST US most of the next day, but we found two more pieces of fabric. We started out before first light and gradually made our way through the forest until we reached the fields leading towards the Ageir River. From there, we found ourselves circling back to the village. Only two routes remained for the next clue, assuming we'd find one. It was my turn this time, and Riak, a wiry old tanner, flew the second route. Because he didn't seem to feel the cold as much as I did, I gave him the route in the shade of the trees, while I flew across the open field, enjoying the warmth of the sun on my wings.

The carts stayed within our line of sight, ready to assist us should we find Ustion and his abductor. They avoided the existing path and almost hugged the trees to avoid being spotted. We didn't want to spook the abductor, but we didn't want to give them a chance to flee, either.

For the past hour, I'd had a feeling we were close. I couldn't explain it, but I couldn't shake it, either. Even less so when I found the next piece of fabric, bloodied, almost four hundred yards past the calculated distance, in the middle of the field. The blood had dried, but scanning it convinced me it wasn't more than a day old. So, we *were* close. Question was, how close?

"Found something, Master?"

I nearly jumped at finding Riak standing next to me. "Yes." I signalled for Brem to join me and sprinkled herbs over my hands.

"Anything I can do?"

Rubbing my hands together, I nodded. "Keep an eye out for any suspicious movement."

Riak nodded. "You think someone's watching us?"

"I don't know. But if anyone is, I want to know." Here in the open, we were far too visible.

Brem arrived, out of breath from running, took one look at the fabric in the grass, and cleansed his hands. While he scanned the area around us, I scanned the blood. Any hope of finding out who was with Ustion faded when the blood turned out to be Ustion's and not his abductor's. And with it, my hope of Ustion coming out of this ordeal unscathed also faded. All I could hope for now was that he wasn't hurt too badly.

Brem found more traces of blood as well as footprints leading towards the forest. About halfway to the trees, the footprints stopped suddenly. Ustion had most likely tried to run after he'd been hurt, but had been caught again. Judging from the footprints, it had taken his abductor quite a while before he caught up. We took our time scanning all the blood, even the tiniest spatters, in the hope that Ustion had managed to hurt his abductor as well. No luck: all the blood we found traced back to Ustion. But even though the footprints stopped, we found tiny spatters of blood every couple of yards, leading us into the forest.

After securing all the evidence, and filling our growling stomachs with sandwiches the drivers prepared while we were working, Brem and I led the group into the forest. We scanned the ground and overhanging branches for more traces of blood. The traces were harder to find and follow here, and many times we strayed in the wrong direction and had to backtrack to the last drops found. The elves in the cart followed us as well as they could along the slightly muddy paths while the hunt for traces sent Brem and me zigzagging through the trees.

When darkness fell, two of our companions aided us with lanterns. Time to decide whether we'd continue or whether we'd try to find a place to spend the night. We were about a day from the village at this point, but there were no caves here, which meant sleeping in the carts and keeping a fire burning to keep the night creatures away. After a short discussion—none of our companions wanted to quit—we kept going until both Brem and I came close to tapping into our last reserves and had no choice but to stop.

As we bedded down, we studied Brem's map once more. He drew in our route through the forest. It dawned on me what our possible destination could be as I tried to predict the continuation of said route. If we kept going in this direction, we'd end up near Taruif's dwelling.

With the elders reviewing his sentence, the last thing he needed was to be suspected of a crime...again.

About a turn ago a female I dated when I was barely more than a stripling had been found dead, and Taruif had been suspected of murdering her. He hadn't done it, but some of the villagers had been only too ready to believe he had, even if the evidence showed otherwise. They needed no other reason for accusing him than that Taruif was shunned.

I knew I could easily prove Taruif had nothing to do with Ustion's abduction, not least because he couldn't fly, but thought it wiser to keep my mouth shut when none of the others seemed to have noticed where we were heading. I fell asleep believing Taruif might escape a false accusation this time.

BREM AND I heard a strange, rhythmic knocking when we neared Taruif's dwelling sometime the next afternoon. We'd lost track of the blood a while back, but had kept on a steady path, intent on taking our companions home before we continued our search. Looking up, we could see the branches of a tree shudder, some fifty yards down the path. I took flight, knowing exactly what tree it was, while Brem yelled instructions at the drivers.

I was glad no one could see me as I reached the small platform high up in the tree that served as Taruif's shed. He'd built it in memory of Fuzan, and only visited rarely. "Ustion is here!" I called to Brem and the others. I wasn't surprised.

He had a nasty head wound and was bound, blindfolded, and gagged. But alive. I clamped my hands around the nearest branch and took deep breaths to calm myself down. Ustion screamed into the gag as he kicked against the edge of the platform where it leaned on one of the branches. Very much alive. Though, with the way he squirmed, it was a miracle he hadn't fallen off. He stilled as I landed.

"Sshh, calm down." I eased the blindfold over the wound. "I've got you."

Ustion started talking the moment I removed the gag, but he

barely got a word out as he began to cough. He tried over and over in between bouts of coughing that didn't let up. By the time Brem landed with a flask of water, Ustion had fainted in my arms, and all I'd understood was "forest".

I instructed Brem to scan the scene and secure any evidence, and flew down to the approaching carts with Ustion in my arms. He felt lighter than Ashyu had told Brem. Had his abductor even fed him? Wrapping him in blankets, I had the cart drive us to the infirmary, and sent one of our companions to locate the guide and tell him to meet me there.

Ustion didn't regain consciousness while Healer Muros—the tribe's senior and only fully-trained healer since Healer Olden had been banished for killing a much-loved elf last winter— scanned, cleaned, and healed him. Under Muros' grumbling supervision, I performed scans of my own but learned nothing conclusive. Nothing but bruises and scrapes, not to mention the signs of malnourishment and utter exhaustion. Ustion's clothes didn't show any traces of anyone either. Whoever had been carrying him must have worn gloves.

After finishing all examinations, I sat in a chair next to Ustion's bed and listened to Brem's report of his findings at the platform. I couldn't stop glancing at the door. The guide had yet to arrive. He'd never kept me waiting this long before.

"Nothing that leads us to anyone but Ustion and the forester."

I opened my mouth, but Brem wasn't done. "Yet the forester's traces were old, buried under fallen leaves and sand. The platform doesn't show any signs of anyone else having been on that platform recently. It's as if Ustion was literally dropped there."

Which could explain some of the bruising. The abductor hadn't taken any chances. But he *had* known about the platform. Or had he merely stumbled across it as he planned to take Ustion back into the village? "Anything on the ground?"

Brem shook his head. "Nothing but traces from the forester leading into his toolshed."

Muros entered the room. "Excuse me, Master Kelnaht. Young Ustion's family have arrived."

"Let them in."

"Immediately, Master."

Dragging our chairs to the corner of the room, Brem and I moved out of the way in order to give Ashyu, Yerriny, and Merel as much privacy as we could while still staying in the room. Their eyes were red-rimmed as they approached the bed. Merel sat down on the edge of the bed and latched on to one of Ustion's hands. Ashyu and Yerriny moved around the other side of the bed, caressing the unblemished side of Ustion's face, talking softly to each other.

"Have you seen the guide?" I asked Brem, keeping my voice low as to not to disturb them.

"Oh, Novice Darver didn't tell you?"

"I haven't seen him. Tell me what?"

"The elders summoned the guide earlier today. The lights were still on at Elders' Court when I passed."

That was bad timing.

"And that's not all. He told me the forester was summoned as well."

That woke me up. Summoned? Today? Of all days? Suddenly, all I wanted was to see Taruif. If only I could be there for him when he received the news. Being summoned must mean good news. They wouldn't bother summoning him if they weren't going to reduce his sentence, surely. Did Ianys know? He must. A summoning didn't often go unnoticed. And once one elf knew, the whole tribe knew.

"Shall I take first watch?"

Pulling myself out of my thoughts, I shook my head. As much as I wanted to be there for Taruif when he returned from Elders' Court, I still had a case to solve. One that, however indirectly, involved him. Something told me that the abductor dropping Ustion on that platform hadn't been a coincidence. "I'll take first watch." Brem needed more sleep than I did to replenish his energy, being an apprentice.

At least, that was what I told myself. It had nothing to do with me wanting to be here when the guide finally came back from the summoning, nothing to do with wanting news about Taruif.

Brem left, and I leaned back, absentmindedly listening to Ustion's family murmuring to each other as I glanced at the door, willing the guide to arrive.

Every time Muros came in to check up on Ustion, he had to reassure the worrying family that Ustion really *was* merely in a healing sleep and would wake up when he was ready. Pallets were provided for Merel—who kept nodding off and nearly fell off the bed once—and Yerriny, while Ashyu settled down in a chair next to Ustion's bed, grabbing the hand his daughter hadn't wanted to release. Ashyu glanced my way a couple of times, always with a little nod, but he said nothing. I didn't expect him to.

Chapter Thirteen

A LIGHT TOUCH to my arm woke me. I had no idea how long I had slept, but it was still dark out. I'd rested my eyes for a bit. I'd never meant to doze off. Across the room, Ashyu snored softly, still sitting on his chair at Ustion's side.

"Did Ustion wake up?" I asked before realising it wasn't Muros who'd woken me, but the guide.

Taruif. If the guide was here, Taruif had to be home. Or… Hoisting myself upright, I pushed away the thought of Taruif's sentence not being reduced. I didn't know what to ask the guide first, and when I opened my mouth, no sound came out.

"They reduced his sentence. Master Taruif's free. The elders will announce it to the tribe a day from now," the guide whispered as he laid his hand on top of mine.

Taruif, a free man. Free to talk to whomever he wanted, free to be with whomever he wanted, with us. There could *be* an us now, openly. We didn't have to hide anymore.

I rose. I needed to go to him, needed to see him. Then I sat down again. I was stuck here in the infirmary. If only I could leave the guide here in my stead, until Brem took over, then I could go. But no, of course I couldn't do that. I'd have to wait for Brem.

Brem walked in the door not long after, when the guide and I were softly speaking of the coming Solstice Circle. Dark shadows beneath his eyes belied his insistence he'd slept long enough, but I wasn't going to send him back to bed. Not this time. The guide squeezed my hand as I wished them good night. I smiled, promised Brem to return mid-morning, and walked out of the infirmary and into the cold outside. My leg muscles protested as I set off at a run towards Taruif's dwelling, but after all the flying I'd done the past few days, and hadn't yet recovered from, running was the fastest way to get there.

Even before I reached the clearing, I could hear noises coming from the tree. Ianys was cursing, and he wasn't being subtle about it. As soon as he saw me, he came running at me, hair in disarray, cheeks red, and cloak half undone.

He grabbed my arms. "Kel. I'm so glad you're here. You have to help me. He won't let me in. He did something to his blasted tree, and it won't let me in."

Nothing seemed out of the ordinary about Taruif's dwelling, but when I tried the door, it wouldn't open. "Have you tried knocking?" I asked.

Ianys glared at me. "Of course I have. I knocked when I couldn't get in. I called out to him, too, but he doesn't answer."

I tried the door again, but it wouldn't budge. It was as if Taruif had sealed his home.

"They did reduce his sentence, didn't they?"

Ianys didn't know? "Yes. Yes, they did. The guide didn't tell you?"

"I didn't wait for the guide. I saw Taruif leave Elders' Court, and followed him home." Ianys grabbed my arm, and I turned to look at him. "He's really free, then?" There was a desperate edge to his voice I hadn't heard for a while, not since he came to beg me to help Taruif after Cyine had been killed.

I reached out and cupped his cheek. "Yes, he's really free."

"So why won't he let us in?"

To that I had no answer, no answer at all. Only one other thing I could do. I opened my wings and slid them through the slits in my cloak, shivering as the cold touched them. Flying up to the branch near the bedroom, I remembered the last time I'd done that, when I'd watched Ianys and Taruif making love. That wasn't the scene I'd see now. Not with Ianys pacing below, waiting for me to return.

Taruif sat on his bed, elbows on his knees and head in his hands, only a small candle burning behind him on the night table. He seemed...broken. I expected him to be relieved, to celebrate the end of his isolation, but his posture told me otherwise. He looked utterly lost.

Below me, Ianys knocked on the door again, calling out Taruif's name. In the bedroom, Taruif flinched. My heart constricted. I wanted to reach out, wanted to take him into my arms, but for me to do that, he'd have to let us in. Ianys called my name in a loud whisper, but as I turned towards him, there was movement inside, and my gaze caught Taruif's. The sadness in his eyes overwhelmed me, the way he shook his head at me, even more so. We wanted so much to be there for him, but all he seemed to want was to be left alone. At least for now. And we'd have to accept that.

"I love you," I said through the window. "*We* love you." I didn't know what I was trying to accomplish, but I couldn't leave him without letting him know.

Taruif sank back onto the bed and closed his eyes. He didn't look at me again, and when Ianys' whispers became insistent, I descended and folded my wings.

"We should have told him about the guide's petition to have his sentence reduced, shouldn't we?" Ianys sagged against me, and it took all of my strength to keep from falling over. "Why won't he let us in?"

Though he weighed considerably more than I did, I still managed to drag him out of the clearing, and propped us up against a tree. The tree was chilly and rough against my back, despite Ianys' arms caught in between me and the tree. "I don't know." I could only guess what Taruif was thinking, how he was feeling. I could only imagine how shocked he must have been, being released from his isolation after over twenty turns of being shunned. He needed to process it, and that would take time. I tried to tell Ianys how Taruif had looked, sitting on his bed, but I had no words. None but *lost*.

We couldn't have told him about the petition, of course, not while there was a chance the elders wouldn't grant it. Taruif would have been truly devastated then. I didn't need to tell Ianys that. He knew. At least, he would if he calmed down for a moment, if he stopped to think, stopped mumbling that we should have told him.

I had to get him away from here. Could I risk taking him back to my dwelling? Or should I drop him off at his forge? "Where is Atèn?"

That seemed to sober Ianys up. He sighed into my cloak. "With my parents."

How could I forget? This was the night Ianys usually spent with Taruif. His family thought he spent those at the forge, and he did, after waking up in the early morning so he could sneak out unseen.

Ianys tightened his grip on me and buried his head in the crook of my neck. "Can I go home with you?"

How could I refuse?

WE BARELY SLEPT. Either of us. We talked and clung to each other and talked some more. About us, about Taruif, when he would see us, and about our future. The way Ianys deliberately didn't mention Atèn made me want to scream at him, but I didn't. I couldn't, because I understood, even though I didn't agree.

"*You will be good for each other. Good for Atèn, too, one day,*" the guide had told me last turn. He'd also insisted, "*There is always a way.*"

Ianys had already shown that by promising himself to me, but it was clear he thought that was all he could ever do. He didn't believe he could have us and Atèn without breaking his promise to Naia. Maybe it *was* easier for me to find hope in the guide's words. I opened my mouth to try and convince him, but the look in his eyes stopped me. I couldn't add to his misery, so instead, I kissed him.

We didn't make love. Not as such. There was nothing gentle about the way we rutted against each other. It was need, with a hint of desperation that left us both satisfied as well as undone.

As we lay panting afterwards, watching each other, legs entwined and hands clasped between us, Ianys kissed my forehead. "It doesn't feel right with Taruif not with us."

I squeezed his hands and closed my eyes, feeling the same. Taruif might not have let us in, but our thoughts as we dozed off were with him with every breath we took.

It was still dark out when I woke. Through bleary eyes, I watched Ianys in his sleep. It wouldn't be long before he had to go. The lines on his forehead betrayed how tense he was, how worried he had been, that he couldn't even fully relax in his sleep. Lightly rubbing my thumb across the lines, I smoothed them all out, slowly, quietly, until Ianys uttered a soft sigh. I trailed my thumb across his stubbled jaw until I reached the corner of his mouth, feeling the slight smile form beneath it.

Knowing he still had a little time, I rose and prepared some tea to keep him warm at the forge. He could make his own tea there, but it was the least I could do for him.

"What are you doing up so early?"

I turned. Ianys stood behind me in his tunic and thick socks, holding his trousers in one hand, boots in the other. I checked his forehead—no lines—and smiled at him. "Making you tea."

He padded over to my counter and sniffed. "Goraf tea? I didn't know you had any."

"I never used to, but Taruif's fondness for it is contagious." The mere scent of it made me think of him and smile.

"I have some at the forge as well," Ianys confessed, and leaned his scratchy chin on my shoulder. "Do you think he'll want to see us today?"

If only I had an answer that would satisfy Ianys. But all I could do was shake my head and say, "I hope so." Even just a glimpse of him before I was sucked back into solving Ustion's abduction would suffice.

Ustion. We had him back, but we still had no idea who had taken him, or why. Now that I was awake, I might as well make it over to the infirmary early. After a good breakfast, at least.

"Do you think the door will be open if I walk to Taruif's come lunchtime?" Ianys asked.

"I don't think so." I didn't intend to stop Ianys from trying, but Taruif's expression the previous night had told me he needed space. I told Ianys so. "Let him come to us in his own time."

"And if he doesn't?"

"Give him two days, three maybe. If he hasn't come to us by then, we'll go to him."

Ianys let out a long, shuddering breath and moved away. I poured the tea into a mug for him to take with him while he dressed himself, pushing the cork lid on tightly so he wouldn't spill any. I didn't watch him leave, though I couldn't help listening for the sound of the door closing. Instead, I puttered around in my kitchen to make myself breakfast. Fried eggs were what I really wanted, with mushrooms and tomatoes, but I was too lazy to even bother, so I heated some milk and made myself porridge...again.

THE GUIDE WAS coming out of the infirmary doors when I arrived. I blinked at him. "Did you stay all night?"

"Apprentice Brem wanted to talk."

As should I, his expression said. He looked tired, but as I was about to wave him off, I realised Brem wasn't expecting me yet. And I really did need to talk. "All right," I said. "Lead the way."

The guide raised an eyebrow and motioned me inside the infirmary. He led me to a small room with shelves filled with corked containers and two small stools. I hoped he hadn't been in this room all night.

"I sometimes talk to visitors in here. It grants a bit of privacy, but leaves them close enough should their loved ones need them. I talked to Brem in Ustion's room. His family were fast asleep, and Ashyu snored loud enough to mask our conversation."

"He hasn't woken up at all, has he?"

"Young Ustion? No. Still deep in healing sleep. Healer Muros checked frequently. He thinks he might wake up sometime in the morning, if his progress is as steady as it has been during the night."

"Good. Good." I sat down and took my cloak and gloves off. "Taruif wouldn't let us in."

The guide frowned, but said nothing.

"I know I can't ask what happened, but you were with him most of the day. Maybe you can...talk to him, see what's bothering him."

"What makes you think he'll let me in, but not his vowed?"

His vowed. I was now officially Taruif's vowed. It didn't matter the claim had been made when we weren't allowed. I'd claimed him, and that was what counted. We still had to inform the elders, but that was a mere formality.

The guide watched me, his eyes open, friendly, waiting for an answer.

"Because you're his confidant. You're the one he's always been able to talk to."

"Do you know he spoke to me far less this past turn?"

"I had no idea." I didn't even know how often they'd talked before I met him.

"Twice a moon, sometimes thrice."

Seemed a reasonable amount. If I didn't count the small talks we had after or during a case—nothing more than stolen moments here and there—I probably talked to the guide as much as Taruif had.

"He talked to me twice every quarter moon before that. Every other day, when he was really struggling."

As much as that? I thought, and could have slapped myself for it. The guide had been the only one Taruif had been allowed to talk to for almost twenty turns. If I had no one else around me, wouldn't I talk to the guide more? Going a quarter moon without speaking to anyone...

"I never..." I swallowed. "I took his silence for granted."

"But he isn't silent with you, is he?"

I smiled. "No." He could be, but even when silent, he said so much. There wasn't a moment he wasn't touching me, caressing me, smiling at me. At times, he talked more than Ianys did. Ianys was the chatty one—at least, that's what I'd assumed—but Taruif talked up a real storm sometimes, as if... as if he was catching up.

I did slap my hand against my forehead, then. I knew this, had wondered about it again and again, yet it had never really sunk in.

"Taruif was never silent by choice. But it's been so long most elves have forgotten who he was. Before." The guide put a hand on mine and smiled. "Foresters nurture, Kelnaht, and not just trees."

We saw evidence of that every day. The blank mask Taruif wore when he was outside, working in plain sight. The tiny smile when it was just us. His deep resonating voice as he told us about his day, about his trees, prompting us to tell him about our days. The way he enjoyed Ianys talking about Atèn. The way he prepared meals and goraf tea for us. He liked taking care of us, just as he'd taken care of Fuzan, even to the extent of letting Fuzan go when he begged Taruif to let him fall.

I glanced at my hand beneath the guide's. "We need to show him we're his, still."

The guide nodded.

"I told Ianys we needed to give him time."

"He will need time, yes. And he might not open his door to you today, or tomorrow. But he needs to know you'll be there for him, regardless."

He needed to know our love wouldn't disappear because he closed the door. I almost snorted: that sounded like something the guide would have said, albeit more vaguely and cryptically. I squeezed the guide's hand. "Thank you."

"Be patient, Kelnaht."

"I will be, Guide. *We* will be."

"Is Master Ianys at his forge?"

I nodded. "He wants to visit Taruif during lunch."

"I'd best walk past the forge before bedding down, then." The guide rose and opened the door. "If you need anything, Novice Darver will gladly assist you. I expect to be unavailable until midday, at least."

Barring emergencies, he meant. Darver wouldn't hesitate to rouse the guide for those. Darver would make a good guide himself, one day, but that day was still far into the future. A guide remained a guide until their passing. Our guide still had many turns to go, and Darver was not even twenty turns yet.

"I'll make an effort not to force him to rouse you before midday, Guide," I said as we rose and left the cramped space.

"Very much appreciated, Master Kelnaht."

We clasped each other's arms for a moment, and I waited until he disappeared through the infirmary doors before turning towards the room where Ustion lay.

Chapter Fourteen

A NURSE, SENT by Brem, summoned me after dinner. Ustion had finally woken up and was asking for me. Later would have suited me better. I'd been examining evidence since Brem took over watching Ustion mid-afternoon. This had left me with no time to check on Ianys or Taruif, from whom I'd heard nothing all day. I rubbed my fingers across my forehead. It would be close to midnight before I'd be able to pay either of them a visit.

Ustion was sitting up when I entered the darkened room. He looked a lot like Merel, with his long, blond hair framing his gaunt face. He waved me over when he saw me, seemingly eager to talk to me, but I motioned to Brem. I wanted to speak with him first. Ustion nodded and turned back to talk to his family, his voice soft, and a bit raw with overuse.

Brem rose and stretched, stifling a yawn. "Healer Muros says he's fine. He'll need to rest for another couple of days until his headaches have faded, but he's fit enough to talk."

"Anything else I need to know?"

"Neither Master Ashyu nor Mistress Yerriny has demanded to be present when you interview Ustion. They've been talking for a while, but I heard nothing of importance. He seems very protective of his sister, though."

Good to know. "Let the guide know Ustion is awake. I left some things unfinished at the workshop. Do what you can, but don't stay too late. We can finish in the morning if need be."

"Yes, Master," he said with a yawn. He wouldn't last much longer, I expected.

Once Brem left the room, I asked Ashyu and Yerriny to leave, so the guide—as soon as he arrived—and I could talk to Ustion alone. They rose as one, but Merel didn't move. She just glared at me. Yerriny whispered something in her ear, and, with great reluctance, Merel got up and walked out of the infirmary, still glowering.

Yerriny shook her head at her daughter and threw me an apologetic smile. "I'm sorry, Master Kelnaht. She feels she's all grown up, now she's been assigned a mentor."

I could understand that. Being apprenticed could happen at any age for a stripling, depending on when their powers showed and were strong enough to be trained. Merel was one of the younger ones. "Thank you. I'll try not to keep Ustion too long."

"Take as long as you need, Master."

The guide arrived not long after Ustion's parents left, looking well-rested. Ustion hadn't wanted to wait for him, until I told him the elders wouldn't accept my report if the guide or Darver wasn't present during the interview. Now, Ustion glanced at me, and when I nodded, he took a breath, and told his story.

"Vlem had just run off when I heard a noise coming from the other side of the field. I thought maybe one of the pigs had broken out. It happens sometimes. They're stubborn beasts, you know. I ran towards the trees, hoping to catch it before it could get far. Someone grabbed me, pressed something foul-smelling against my face... and the next thing I remember is waking up on a blanket, bound and blindfolded, with fabric pushed into my mouth."

"Do you have any idea who took you?"

Ustion shook his head. "He barely spoke, and when he did, I didn't recognise his voice."

"But it was a male?"

That seemed to startle Ustion. "Yes... at least, I think so. His voice seemed too deep to be a female. And he held me kind of tight, but didn't have any..." He blushed and moved his hands in front of his chest, forming cups.

No breasts. I smiled at him. "Good point. What can you tell me about where you were?"

"It had to be a cave. It was damp and cold, and I could hear the wind howling, but barely felt it. At first, I thought I was back with Dad's hunting group. I couldn't understand why they bound me. Until I heard him mumble."

Good observational skills. "Did you sense anyone following you?"

"No. No one. I heard night critters rustling through the leaves, but that was all."

"No wings flapping?"

Again a frown. "You mean did I hear him fly before he caught me? I'm not sure. I can't remember hearing wings, aside from a bird or two."

"What made you leave pieces of cloth behind?"

"Someone told me truth seekers could find out who we are by scanning a strand of hair. He bound my hands in front of me, I think with strips of the blanket I used to erase my footsteps when I left the cave to meet Vlem. At least until I was far enough away. It's not that easy erasing footprints with a blanket." He shrugged. "The blanket felt like mine, it was an old ratty one I'd taken with me from home. He carried me as he flew, you know, and every time he landed, he put me down on the ground so he could rest. Being blindfolded, I couldn't see him, but I thought if I laid my head on my hands, he couldn't see me pull out my hair. Knotting the hair was the tricky bit, but I tried just wrapping it around the fabric, and it kept slipping off." He grinned at me. "I guess I'm lucky my hair's so long. Anyway, as soon as I managed, I pushed the fabric into the mud."

"You did well, young Ustion," the guide said.

Ustion seemed uncertain as he glanced at me, so I nodded my agreement. He had done well, even if erasing his tracks at the cave had led us the wrong way. "Do you know how long you were in the cave?"

Ustion shook his head. "I tried to keep track of time, but it was hard. I don't know how long I was out when he took me, and I don't know whether it was morning, afternoon, or evening when I first woke. He gave me water, but barely any food. A dry piece of bread once or twice. I slept when I was able."

"Do you know why he took you?"

"No," Ustion said, but he wasn't looking at me as he did so. He was staring out of the window.

There was something he wasn't telling me. I didn't push him, but kept it in mind as I asked him to describe, with as much detail as possible, anything he'd noticed about his abductor. Maybe if I gave Ustion some time to think, he'd tell me what he knew.

Ustion closed his eyes, moving his hands as if he was reliving something. He mentioned the roughness of the fabric against his cheek as the abductor had carried him. "It didn't feel like a cloak." He didn't think his abductor had been much taller than he was, though he wasn't on his feet enough to be sure. "But he wasn't broad-shouldered. His shoulders dug into my ribs and stomach quite a bit."

That was consistent with some of the bruising Muros had found. The abductor had to be strong, with all the carrying he'd done. Ustion didn't say much else. It was time to convince him to tell me what he was trying not to. I pondered the abductor's motivation, out loud, and Ustion glanced out the window again, avoiding my gaze. "Ustion, if there's anything else you know, you need to tell me. It's the only way we can catch whoever did this to you."

Ustion shook his head and closed his eyes as he fidgeted with his hands. I gave him a moment. At last, when I finally thought he wasn't going to say anything, he opened his eyes and turned to me. "He thought I was Merel."

"Merel?" Did that mean the abductor would be going after Merel now?

Ustion put a hand on my arm. "I'm not saying it right. He

thought I was the forester's apprentice, or apprentice-to-be. And I let him believe I was."

"You told him?"

Ustion shook his head. "When he talked, he was mumbling to himself mostly, though I couldn't understand half of what he was saying. He kept mentioning the forester, and having his apprentice, and stopping something. But..." He wrung his hands. "Look. I know I'm not supposed to know about the forester's sentence being reduced so Merel can be his apprentice, but I couldn't help hearing Mum and Dad talk about it. They were so proud of Merel, so glad they wouldn't have to send her away for her apprenticeship. So, when I heard him mumbling, I knew he thought I was the apprentice, and if having me meant he'd leave Merel alone, I wasn't going to tell him the truth."

"Did he let you go because of Merel?"

"No, no. He didn't find out. I'm not sure why he left me there. All he did was mumble about stopping it."

Stopping what? Stopping... I wanted to slap myself when it dawned on me. He'd wanted to stop the elders reducing Taruif's sentence. But why try to frame Taruif for Ustion's abduction? Why keep Ustion for days with all the risk of him being found? He could have petitioned the elders. Or maybe he had, I'd have to ask them.

The elders were announcing Taruif's new status tomorrow. I couldn't even begin to imagine what the abductor would do when he heard his plan had failed.

WHEN I ARRIVED at Taruif's, Ianys was sitting on the steps, leaning against the door.

"He's being stubborn," Ianys told me as he got up and brushed the sand from his trousers. "Door's still locked, and he hasn't said a word." He grabbed my hand, dragged me behind Taruif's dwelling, and kissed me. The combination of his cold lips and warm breath made me shiver. I sank against him as he wrapped his arms around me. "But I haven't let him get to me, Kel," he whispered against my lips. "Not this time. I told him I wasn't going to let him get away with it, 'cause he's mine." Ianys closed his mouth and looked at me with a sheepish expression. "Ours. Sorry."

I shook my head. "Yours, mine, ours, it's all the same. What matters is he knows we're here for him."

"I hope he figures that out sooner rather than later. It's far too cold out here."

Ianys was right about that, but we would both do it, over and over, until Taruif let us in again. Right now, it was my turn. "Go. Before your family send out a search party for you. I'm sure Atèn is waiting for you to tell her a bedtime story."

"She came by the forge earlier with my mother." His expression softened into a dreamy smile. "She loves watching the bellows work without me touching them."

It was a smith's power. Ianys would start working them manually, but once the fire was in full swing, he'd keep the bellows working with his magic. Atèn wasn't the only one who could watch him at it all day. I'd done the same plenty of times, many turns ago, when Ianys and I were both apprentices.

Ianys drew me close and kissed me again. "I wish I could stay." He let go of me. "I hope he talks to you."

I doubted it, even though it would be good for Taruif to talk to us before the announcement. "Come on. Go. Or Atèn will be fast asleep."

Ianys scrubbed his hand over his face and took a hesitant step back. After a deep breath, he reached out, squeezed my shoulder, and turned around to grab his satchel. I waited until he crossed the clearing, then flew up to my favourite branch. Wrapping a blanket around me, I settled down to watch over Taruif until he went to sleep.

The guide knew where I was, should anyone need me. Though he'd promised to see the elders with my request for an audience post haste, I doubted they would summon me before morning. A morning that promised to be busy. When I'd checked in at the workshop, Brem, having ignored my advice, had still been working on identifying the coarse threads we'd found on Ustion's clothing. As much as I wanted to know, I'd pushed him out the door and locked it behind him to make sure he went home. He needed the sleep. And working while exhausted never led to good results. We'd have to finish it in the morning.

I glanced through the window, but Taruif wasn't in his bedroom, even though the candle on the night table was burning. I placed one gloved hand against the bark, knowing he would feel my presence, despite the glove. "I'm here," I whispered as I leaned my head against the bark as well. "I'll always be here for you."

Shivering in the cold breeze, I pulled my cloak and blanket tightly around me. If only I could get in. Not because it was warmer, but to see Taruif's face. To try and read him, to hold him, and to keep him safe from whoever abducted Ustion. Because the abductor wasn't going to rest until he got his way.

I DREAMED I was falling. I flailed my arms about, trying to grab on to the branches I passed as I went down. Even as the ground rushed up to meet me, it didn't occur to me to open my wings. I closed my eyes, bracing myself against the fall, but nothing happened. When I opened my eyes, there was a ceiling above me. Taruif's ceiling, Taruif's bedroom. No Taruif, though.

The bedding was soft against my skin. Skin? How did I get here? And where were my clothes? I sat up, dragging the bedding with me, wrapping it around me as I stood. The wood chilled my bare feet as I made my way down the stairs. My left ankle was throbbing by the time I reached the hallway, but I ignored it. I had to get home and see if Brem had solved the riddle of the coarse fabric, had to see the guide about the audience with the elders, had to—

I froze in the doorway. Taruif stood at the stove making tea, naked. The mouth-watering smell of bread and butter came from a tray on the counter next to him. He looked gorgeous, the lines of his body almost relaxed. Part of me wanted to let him know I was there; part of me tried to keep from making a sound. He heard me anyway and turned around.

We started at each other, awkwardly, silently, for a long time. I didn't know what to say. I didn't even know how I got here. Last I knew, I was sitting on a branch outside his window, waiting for him to come up.

"I..." Eloquent, Kelnaht, very eloquent.

"You fell."

I frowned. I had? That couldn't be right; I'd never fallen out of a tree before. Of course, I'd never actually fallen asleep in a tree before, either. It would be the only explanation for not remembering. Holding up the blanket, I wriggled this way and that, feeling the pull of sore muscles all over. And my left ankle was bruised. No wonder it was throbbing.

"Your foot got caught when you fell. I needed a ladder to get you down. I was worried you knocked your head because you wouldn't wake up."

I moved my head from left to right and back. My neck seemed a bit stiff, but my head felt fine. "How?"

"The guide had Healer Muros check you out."

Because no one knew Taruif was free, yet. "Thank you." Though I meant him letting me in. He could have dropped me at the guide's safehold.

Taruif shrugged, keeping an eye on his stove, and we fell silent. I stared at him, trying to decide what to do. He turned to me as I shuffled towards him, step by step. Gazing into his eyes, I gave him plenty of time to stop me. He stayed still, worrying his bottom lip. I'd almost reached him when his kettle whistled. I let out a shaky breath and took a step back.

Taruif waved his hand to stop the heating spell. The kettle still whistled as Taruif wrapped his arms around me and buried his head in my neck. "I can do this now. We don't have to hide it anymore," he said, his breath sending shivers down my spine. He didn't sound exactly happy. "I'm sorry."

"I wish I could've been there for you. And I know Ianys wanted to be there, too."

"When they told me I was free..." Taruif went quiet, his arms tight around me. "I visited my mother yesterday morning. She... I..." Taruif shook his head, bouncing it against my shoulder. "She gave me every letter she wrote to me while I was shunned but wasn't allowed to send. I've read them all. I wished I had something to give her, but I never wrote. I never... It was easier not to think about her."

It had been like that for me when my parents died, too, and, to a lesser degree, during my separation from Ianys. It wasn't the same. I could never truly grasp what Taruif had gone through these past twenty turns. Not even allowed to talk to his mother. I'd lost my parents many turns ago, but I'd been with them until the end.

I held on to Taruif as he sobbed, one hand cradling his head, the other wrapped around him; it was all I could do to show him I had him. Time passed slowly as we stood there, holding on to each other. If only Ianys were here, then we'd be complete.

It didn't escape me that *I* now stood in the way of Ianys' future with Taruif.

Chapter Fifteen

I HAD BARELY made it into my workshop when Brem arrived with a message from the elders. I went to see them immediately. The elders were reluctant to share the letters they received about the reduction of Taruif's sentence, but, in the end, I managed to convince them to hand them to me.

When I returned from my audience with the elders, Brem had finally identified the coarse threads, though was nowhere near to finding the abductor. He gathered a list of elves owning a cloak or tunic made from that specific sort of coarse fabric, but it had quite a large number of names. Some names were easy to check out, and just as easy to eliminate, but that still left many elves we needed to verify alibis for. Easier to go through the letters the elders gave me and check them against the names on the list.

There weren't many letters, since only the elves involved or related to either Taruif or Fuzan had been notified of the elders' intent, yet, a couple of their writers appeared on Brem's list. My heart beat faster with every letter that expressed a positive attitude towards the reduction of Taruif's sentence. It warmed me that there were far more of those than there were letters petitioning to keep the sentence as it was.

One of the letters against freeing Taruif stood out. A petition from an elf named Sorse. It was harshly worded and betrayed great anger about what Taruif had done, even now, over twenty turns later. Sorse's letter led me to believe he'd been a friend of Fuzan's. Judging from the tone, though, not a friend of Taruif's. Or if he had been, that friendship had clearly ended when Fuzan died.

The tone of the letter was enough to prompt me to pay Sorse a visit, but when Brem and I reached his dwelling, he wasn't home. As truth seeker, I didn't have to ask permission to enter while on a case. We went inside and found a meticulously cleaned dwelling, barely even a speck of dust. Scans turned up nothing out of the ordinary. No sign of Ustion having been here, or anything related to him.

No sign of Ustion outside, either.

"Big footprints here," Brem said as he disappeared around the tree.

I grabbed the partial footprint we'd found near Raden's farm from my bag, and joined him.

Brem took it from me and placed it next to one of the footprints. "It matches. I think we've got him, Master."

It did. Right to the small crack in the leather under the ball of the foot. Finally! I was beginning to think we were never going to find out who the abductor was. "But where is Sorse?"

We interviewed his closest neighbours, but none of them knew anything useful. All they could tell me was Sorse was a grumpy cloud elf who kept mostly to himself, and that they hadn't seen him for a while. They'd all seen his sister come by earlier in the morning to clean; something she did about once a quarter moon. One neighbour went out of his way to tell us what a nice elf Sorse's sister was. None of them had any idea where he might be, though they knew him to hike into the woods at times. To look for inspiration, they thought.

Sorse was a bone carver. Hunters and farmers delivered the bones to his dwelling, one neighbour said. He didn't offer them something to drink for their effort, didn't even open the door. They merely dumped the sacks on the doorstep. Sorse did go into the village to deliver his goods, but as far as the neighbours were aware, only once a moon.

Asking around the village garnered the same answers over and over, even among the elves who used Sorse's goods: the last time most of them had seen him had been close to half a moon ago. But they didn't expect him to deliver new goods until the beginning of the new moon, so there was nothing out of the ordinary there, either.

Sorse's sister turned out to be a hunter called Jarda. Her bleary-eyed vowed opened the door, juggling a fussy wee elf on his hip.

"She's on a hunting trip. The group left mid-morning." He didn't have much good to say about Sorse. "She coddles him. I keep telling her to let him clean his own dwelling." He let the wee elf have his finger to suckle on and shrugged. "But he's her brother, she says. She has to take care of him."

We didn't have time to go after a hunting group, with the announcement declaring Taruif a free elf coming up. Brem and I headed to the Elders' Court tree, where most of the tribe was already gathered, waiting for the elders to appear. Our official job here was crowd control, and it gave us the perfect opportunity to scan the area and question elves in our search for Sorse. No sign of him anywhere. Had he heard about the announcement? No one had seen him in a while, but that didn't mean he wasn't in the village.

The crowd went quiet as, one by one, the elders descended the stairs. I scanned the crowd one last time, then focussed on the figure following the elders. Taruif wore a hooded cloak, hiding his face from the crowd. He would stay hooded until the elders announced his new status. We talked about it during breakfast, Taruif and I. He didn't want the attention, but it was tradition for the elders to publicly welcome a reintegrated member of the tribe.

Ianys stood with his family, almost bouncing on his feet, bursting with anticipation. Our eyes met, and I wanted to stand with him, but I respected his promise and kept my distance, though I made certain he could see me as we waited for the elders and Taruif to appear.

As eager as I was to find Sorse and solve Ustion's abduction, I couldn't help but be relieved he wasn't here to ruin Taruif's moment.

FOR THE FIRST time in over twenty turns, Taruif had dinner with his mother, in the village centre, amidst the tribe. Ianys sat with his family not far away, and I had joined the guide at the next table, making sure I could see both of them. Many elves walked past in silence, putting their hand on Taruif's shoulder to welcome him back into the tribe. It was beautiful and painful to watch at the same time. If there were elves who didn't agree with the elders' decision, none were close enough to worry about.

Suddenly, the whole tribe fell silent as Banhin, Fuzan's father, approached Taruif. He, too, laid his hand briefly on Taruif's shoulder before sitting down next to him. Taruif seemed anxious, but as Banhin whispered to him, his expression became more neutral, and the tribe picked up their own conversations again.

"Don't leave him out here too long, Kelnaht." The guide's voice came from next to me, loud enough for me to hear, but too soft for others to overhear. "Take him home as soon as dinner ends."

"What about his mother?"

"She'll understand."

The guide would know. I caught Ianys' eyes—it wasn't just me Taruif would need tonight—and let out a breath when he nodded. I dug into my food and ignored the chatter around me. All I could think of was taking Taruif home a free man. Granted, he'd been free since the moment the elders spoke their verdict at his summoning, but now, after the Elders' public announcement, it was official in the eyes of the tribe. Official and accepted.

Pushing my empty plate away from me, I rose. My heart beat

in my throat, and although I'd drunk plenty, my mouth felt dry. Yet, I couldn't help but smile as I walked up to Taruif, laid my hand on his shoulder like the elves before me, and let it linger. I was more than aware the tribe followed my every move, but that didn't stop me from bending down and introducing myself to Taruif's mother, using my name rather than my title. Introducing myself as Taruif's vowed.

Taruif tensed beneath my hand as murmurs went through the crowd. I squeezed his shoulder, focusing his attention back to his mother, whose eyes narrowed, but only for as long as it took for her frown to turn into a smile. Taruif kissed his mother on her cheek, and excused himself from dinner. My hand slipped off his shoulder as he rose, and I stepped back to give him room to move. He swallowed, unsure and aware all eyes were on him. I held out my hand. Taruif took it with only a moment of hesitation and followed me towards his dwelling.

"Take him home," the guide had said, and here I was, taking Taruif home a free man. Home and free. Those words lingered in my mind as we walked through the forest and the clearing in silence until we reached our destination. I looked at the tree Taruif had so lovingly turned into his home during his isolation. Would Taruif want to stay here? Or would he want a dwelling closer to the centre of the village? Was it wrong for me to hope he wanted to stay here with me?

As I followed Taruif up the stairs, my mind drifted to openly claiming him at the Solstice Circle, even if my heart clenched for Ianys. Ianys could wait, he'd said, no matter how many times I reminded him his claim on Taruif preceded mine. He insisted he could wait until he could claim both his elves openly. If only that didn't mean until Atèn was of age.

I'd already undressed Taruif and was taking off my own trousers when Ianys entered the bedroom, clothes in hand and a beaming smile on his face. He dropped them, wormed himself between us, and kissed Taruif possessively, even though he was still grinning.

"Congratulations, love," he whispered against Taruif's lips.

I kissed Ianys between his shoulder blades and squeezed his shoulders. Taruif's quiet, "Thank you," was swallowed up by another aggressive kiss. Their kiss turned into a battle with neither showing any intent of letting the other best him. I enjoyed their fight for dominance as I caressed Ianys' back and arse. Ianys, despite never letting up on his kiss with Taruif, kept moving his body into my hands, making it clear he wanted more. I wasn't going to give it to him. This was Taruif's night.

When Ianys finally caught on, he gave in to Taruif, who wasted no time in manhandling him onto the bed, still kissing. Their bodies moved against each other for a moment, and heat pooled in my belly at seeing my lovers enjoying each other. It didn't happen nearly often enough, and it was a treat to watch. I loved Taruif taking control of Ianys. And not because it meant Taruif's arse would be all mine.

I rid myself of the last of my clothing and moved towards the bed. Grabbing the flask of oil from the night table, I knelt between Taruif's legs while trapping Ianys' stretched legs beneath me. Taruif stopped kissing Ianys and looked at me over his shoulder, his eyes dark with desire. He nodded at me and went back to kissing Ianys. Taking some of the oil, I wriggled my hand between their bodies and slicked both their cocks. Ianys jerked on the bed, but between Taruif on top of him and me trapping his legs, he was pinned down. The sounds Ianys made told me he liked what I did.

I trailed my hands—one slippery, one dry—up Taruif's thighs and across his arse until I reached his hips. Taruif shuddered and jerked forward, pushing his cock against Ianys. Ianys protested—no doubt complaining about the way we pinned him to the bed—but the loud, mostly incoherent sounds were swallowed by Taruif's kiss. Grinning, I settled into a comfortable position, careful not to crush Ianys' legs. Taruif groaned and shivered as I rubbed his cheeks, spread them, and dipped my tongue into his crease. For a moment, I didn't move, letting Taruif's warmth and scent envelop me. Then I slowly swept my tongue down until just behind his balls and licked my way back up again.

I licked and teased and circled Taruif's opening, smiling at the way he writhed, rubbing against Ianys, who wriggled as much as he could manage in his trapped position. Only when both were moaning uncontrollably did I push my tongue inside, breaching Taruif's opening with the short, shallow little thrusts he liked so much. Taruif shuddered and let out a long, low growl. The time for teasing had definitely passed, but I couldn't stop yet.

Ianys moved his hand towards their cocks. I slapped it away; it was far too early for that, no matter what Ianys might think. Ianys growled into Taruif's mouth, but stopped when I straightened up after a parting kiss to Taruif's opening. He ran his hands along Taruif's sides towards his arse cheeks, massaging and pinching them while I slicked myself up. I slowly sank into Taruif, more or less trapping Ianys' hands under me as I draped myself over Taruif's back. Ianys didn't try to reclaim them.

For a moment, none of us moved. I kissed Taruif between his shoulder blades and waited for something—a sign, a sound—to tell me he wanted me to move. Ianys, unsurprisingly, broke before Taruif did and whispered harsh words against Taruif's mouth. Taruif pulled away from Ianys' lips and turned his head, but our positions didn't allow us to kiss. Instead, I ran my left thumb across his lips and smiled when he nodded. I could swear Ianys muttered, "Finally," when I started pulling out.

We settled into a slow, languid rhythm not even Ianys protested against. Ianys wasn't very patient—although we had shown him, time and time again, how much fun patience could be—but he hadn't pulled his hands away yet. He was too busy kissing Taruif, though they weren't so much kissing as panting into each other's mouths. Taruif's legs trembled against mine, and Ianys' legs brushed my thighs as he pushed up against Taruif, rubbing their cocks together every time I sank into Taruif's body.

Going slowly suddenly lost its appeal, and I straightened up and started moving faster, smiling as Ianys lost his rhythm. I wasn't going to last much longer, and I expected Ianys to pull his hands free any moment now, but he didn't. Instead, he kept them right where they were, between my hips and Taruif's arse, as his legs tensed and pushed against mine. Ianys came, keening, and his hands slipped away from Taruif's arse when I stopped moving.

Taruif leaned his forehead against Ianys' and pushed back against me impatiently. I smiled and picked up speed again, wanting to get him off before I followed them both. It didn't take long. Taruif's whole body shook as he came. He clamped down on my cock, and any control I had rushed out of me. My mind whited out with pleasure. The sound of heavy panting surrounded me, us, mixed with the smell of sex. I kissed Taruif's neck as I sagged onto his back. Ianys protested having to bear our combined weight, but he didn't push us off.

As I closed my eyes, Ianys put his hands on my shoulders and pulled us even tighter together. No need for words. Not right now.

JARDA'S VOWED DIDN'T know where her hunting group had gone, but Ashyu had no problem pointing us to the correct location.

A tall, slender cloud elf with eyes the same dark brown as her cloak walked towards me when I asked for Mistress Jarda. She put away her bow and inclined her head in greeting, a worried expression in her eyes. "Something's happened to my brother, to Sorse, hasn't it?"

"What makes you think that, Mistress Jarda?"

"I haven't seen him in days, and his house was a mess when I got there yesterday morning."

It was hard not to show any reaction on my face as she said that. She'd cleaned a possible crime scene, and I had to dig my nails into my hand to keep from telling her what I thought of that. She'd had no idea it was a crime scene. "Mess, how?" I asked as calmly as I could.

"Like he left in a hurry. His blankets were missing, as was most of his provision. He'd left all his doors open, even the front door, and there was sugar on his kitchen floor. Sorse has never not cleaned a spillage before. Left his dishes in the sink often enough, not even bothering spelling them clean, but he can't stand spillage."

I tried to imagine the situation she described. It seemed possible Sorse had been frantically packing to leave town. Or maybe he'd been angry, or... It was no use speculating.

"He didn't do anything stupid, did he?"

"I don't know, yet. What can you tell me about Sorse's behaviour that was out of the ordinary, aside from messing up his house?"

Jarda leaned back against a tree, almost squashing her folded wings. I cringed, but she merely shrugged. "He's been obsessed with some rumour he'd heard. Something about the forester being freed from his sentence. He's always been obsessed with that." She looked at me. "He was a friend of the elf the forester killed."

I couldn't gauge whether or not she would take the news of Taruif's free status well or not. "Sorse didn't want T—the forester to go free?" I almost made the mistake of calling him Taruif.

"Oh, no. Never. He wanted him to suffer for taking Fuzan's life."

And you? I wanted to ask, but I couldn't take the risk she'd shut down if she knew why I wanted to find Sorse.

"If it were up to me," she continued, "the forester would have never been punished so harshly. I knew Fuzan. And as much as Sorse liked him, was smitten with him, there was something not right about him. He..." She shook her head and looked down as she muttered a quick apology to Ma'terra. "I shouldn't speak ill of the dead."

It was hard to keep my expression blank. "I've been told

Fuzan could be reckless. Is that what you mean?"

Jarda bit her lip. "Yes. He was dangerous, always wanting to go further than anyone, higher, faster." She swallowed. "Sorse loved him, you know? Loved him so much, he couldn't stand Fuzan choosing the forester over him. But I don't think Fuzan ever felt for Sorse what Sorse felt for him, no matter what my brother thought."

So, Sorse thought Fuzan had loved him at one point. And Sorse blamed Taruif for killing Fuzan, as so many others had. Only, Sorse had obviously never wanted to consider that Fuzan had *craved* death. "Do you have any idea where Sorse might be?"

She narrowed her eyes at me. "Why do you need to know?"

"We think he might have some information regarding the disappearance of a stripling more than ten days ago."

"Ashyu's son? Sorse wouldn't know anything about that. He tends to avoid children. It's why he never visits me at home."

"We have to follow every lead, Mistress Jarda. *Do* you know where he might be?"

Leaning lightly on her bow, she looked at me for a moment. Her sharp expression made me want to fidget or turn my head, but I stayed still. She deflated. "No. Well..." She seemed to think. "There are a couple of places he tends to go when he's restless or too angry to focus on his work, but he's never stayed away this long."

Jarda told me Sorse's favourite hiding places, making me promise to tell her when we found him, and warning me to be gentle with him. "He's...different."

I was thinking *volatile*, but I doubted she'd see it that way. I wished her happy hunting and took flight.

Would Taruif know who Sorse was? Did he know Sorse had loved Fuzan? Maybe I should pay Taruif a visit before going after Sorse.

Chapter Sixteen

Taruif *did* know Sorse, remembered him as a dreamy stripling, always following Fuzan around like a smitten puppy. *"Dreamy, but a bit daft,"* were his exact words. I made sure Taruif, Merel, who would be with Taruif today, and Ustion were guarded; Ashyu needed but a moment to find volunteers amongst his hunting group. Taruif didn't want to believe the stripling he had known all those turns ago capable of abducting Ustion, but he accepted the guards for Merel's safety.

In any event, I had fewer elves to worry about when Brem and I left to check out Sorse's hiding places, which took us the better part of the day.

The one at the lake was hidden, but Jarda's directions were clear. Inspecting and scanning it confirmed what both Brem and I thought at first glance. Sorse hadn't been here. There was plenty of food, blankets, and enough wood to survive for a while, but the musty smell lingering around the cave made it clear he hadn't been here recently.

Finding the second hiding place took us a lot longer. No matter how we searched, how we followed Jarda's instructions, we passed by it numerous times before we finally found a cave entrance no bigger than a crawling space. Hard to believe Sorse could have dragged Ustion in here, but the inside told us he'd done just that. Two old pallets, blankets strewn everywhere, remnants of a fire, and torn pieces of the fabric Ustion had used to leave us clues. Though small, the cave was at a perfect distance between Raden's farm and the location of the fabric and hair dropped nearest to it.

We had no doubt that most of the blankets and provisions had been recently brought here from Sorse's dwelling. They didn't have that musty smell some of the more tattered blankets carried. Scanning the cave yielded plenty of evidence that Ustion had been here, too. This had to be where Ustion had been taken right after he had been abducted.

After finishing inside, we went back outside to search for traces, footprints, anything leading us to Sorse. I should have known it wouldn't be easy. Nothing about this case had been. Once again, we could find no trail to speak of.

Noticing something dark lying in the bushes, I bent down. A shoe. Had Sorse left his shoes here?

No. I had a pretty clear image of the footprints from around Sorse's dwelling in my head, and this shoe didn't fit that print, so it had to be someone else's. I almost laughed when I found a short hair knotted into the laces. Not Ustion's hair, wrong colour. Probably Sorse's, then, and therefore the shoe might well be Ustion's. I'd have to compliment the boy on his inventiveness and perseverance. Without scanning it—I wasn't going to waste energy on a certain outcome when we had plenty still to do—I wrapped the shoe in goshe leaves and put it into my bag.

Brem found the other shoe, farther away, but with no hidden surprises, and that concluded our search here. Neither of us had any idea where Sorse might have gone next. We tried a couple of obvious routes, but when we hadn't found the slightest trace some two hours later, we had to abandon the search. If only Jarda could have given us more than these two hiding places. Where had Sorse gone?

I received my answer when we arrived back at the village, tired and laden with bags of evidence leading us to nothing we didn't already know or suspect. There was a commotion at Elders' Court. The elders stood on the stairs, surrounded by elves chattering over each other, Taruif's mother at their head.

But before I could walk up to the elders, Ianys called out to me, hidden in the shadow of the next tree. I told Brem to find out what was going on, and made my way over to Ianys.

"He's taken Taruif. The one you warned him about."

Sorse. "Where?"

Ianys shook his head and opened his mouth to speak, but closed it again as he glanced at the elves gathered around the elders.

"Give me a moment," I said, not waiting for an answer as I strode towards the group.

Brem approached me. "The hunter guarding Master Taruif and young Merel was knocked unconscious and is not awake yet, but Master Taruif has been taken. Young Merel was unharmed." He added that not one of the elves gathered here had a clear description of the abductor, but he assumed it had been Sorse.

I nodded. Brem wanted to say more, but I raised my hand to stop him. He could report to me later, after I'd spoken to Ianys. "Ready a search party; make sure plenty of cloud elves are in the group."

"Yes, Master."

I slipped behind the nearest tree and made my way to Ianys. I squeezed his shoulders. "We don't have much time. Do you know what happened?"

"Young Merel didn't see Taruif get taken or the guard being knocked out. Something to do with their presence making her nervous when Taruif told her to grow a seedling. So they retreated behind a tree and let her work in peace. She heard a scream, but was too scared to look and came running here instead."

At least Sorse had left Merel alone. "How long ago?"

"An hour. A seamstress heard the scream, but when they found young Merel, and later the guard, Taruif was already gone. I've been trying..." Ianys paused, clenching his fists. "I suggested a search party, but it took a while for the elders to gather everyone."

Which would save Brem a lot of time. Ianys' muscles trembled beneath my fingers, and his expression was wild, riled up, like he was trying not to scream. "I know you want to join the search party, but only if you're calm enough to listen to me. I can't use you if you're going to lose control."

Raising his hands to my face, Ianys shook his head, anger and desperation fighting for dominance in his eyes. "You can't ask that of me, Kel."

"I have to. Can't you see?" I needed level-headed elves to follow my every command. "Sorse is dangerous, out of control. And if I can't rely on you to do what I tell you..." I swallowed and squeezed Ianys' knees. "I love you, but I can't risk losing you both."

Ianys pulled me to him and kissed me, hard and rough. I felt his anger and desperation in the way he held me, the way he shook. They were feelings I couldn't allow myself right now, yet I clung to him for all it was worth. When he finally let me go, I bade him to go home. "Be with Atèn. She'll distract you. I promise I'll bring our Taruif back to us."

"Catch the twice-blasted dross," he all but spat.

I had every intention of doing that.

THOUGH BREM AND I had just returned from inspecting Sorse's hiding places, I sent two teams to stake them out. They weren't to engage with Sorse if they spotted him, but to send word to Brem, who'd be stationed somewhere in between. My team—including Riak, Ellon, and Vroni—took flight, following the footprints leading from Taruif's dwelling into the forest. Sorse might have been strong enough to carry Ustion while flying, but he hadn't seemed to manage the same with Taruif. No large gaps between the prints, yet the indentations became shallower as we followed them, as if he had become used to Taruif's weight. Or maybe Taruif had been struggling more during that first stretch.

I immediately pushed that thought away and replaced it with the reminder Sorse had over an hour on us. Whether on foot or in the air, a lot could happen in an hour.

We kept low to the ground, eyes on the footprints below us, though one or two elves looked ahead to warn us for branches. Tricky flying, not least because I focused on the footprints and scanned the ground at the same time, despite the warnings. I'd already been struck in the shoulder by a branch once, and only narrowly avoided another one.

Suddenly, the footprints stopped, and so did we. Had Sorse managed to lift Taruif after all? There were several directions we could go, and we tried all of them. I was still scanning when I was called back.

Riak had found the trail. Two deep prints where Sorse must have landed, clearly struggling with carrying Taruif. He hadn't made it far, flying. A couple of footprints led us to a narrow path through some evergreens, and then nothing again.

We went through the same pattern a number of times, though each time the distance seemed shorter. At first, it seemed as if we were headed in the direction of Sorse's smallest hiding place, but before we reached it, the trail veered off in a direction I recognised with a start. Sorse had taken Taruif to where Fuzan had died.

When we reached the high trees where Taruif had built Fuzan the tree-bridge, silence met us. Yet, I could almost feel Taruif's presence. He had to be here. I rubbed my hands with herbs while sending one elf to find Brem. The rest of the group, I instructed to quietly scatter and search for footprints, broken branches, anything that would tell us where Sorse and Taruif were.

I stayed close to the trees, scanning the ground, the trunks, the lower branches, one by one, until I found a hair caught by a branch. No deliberate action this time, but the hair *was* Taruif's. Sorse had taken him up the tree. I peered up through the branches, hoping to catch a glimpse. Nothing. I silently cursed the age-old evergreens for being such perfect hiding places. How he had managed it, I had no idea, but it seemed there was only one way for me to go. Up.

Several of the others wanted to join me, but we didn't know where in the tree Sorse had Taruif, or whether Taruif was even conscious. If Sorse spotted one of us, he only had to push Taruif out of the tree, and no one would be there to catch him. I couldn't risk it. If something went wrong, I needed them below. It was silly, thinking they'd be able to catch Taruif, but I needed to believe they could.

How long before Brem arrived? Should I wait? Could I *risk* waiting?

I gazed up the trunk. Taruif was up there, somewhere, conscious or unconscious, probably bound, maybe wounded. I had promised Ianys I would bring him home. No, I wasn't going to wait. I left instructions for Brem with Riak, took a deep breath, and moved closer to the trunk. Despite the cold, I took my cloak off; it would only be in the way.

Inch by inch, I scaled the tree, half climbing, half flying where possible. I made slow progress, lingering on every other branch to peer up and reassess the situation. How high was this tree? I couldn't remember if Taruif had mentioned it. Height wasn't a measurement I could work with. I had to, though, had no choice but to keep at it until I reached my goal.

By the time the ground disappeared in a sea of branches, I had still caught no glimpse of either Sorse or Taruif. Breathing heavily, my neck aching from the strain of constantly looking up, I did hear a voice. At first, I thought it came from the elves below. But they wouldn't ignore my warning to be quiet, would they?

I climbed another couple of branches, and the voice became louder. Another few branches, and I could even make out the words.

Sorse's voice was grating, and sounded like loud, angry whispering. "Is this how you did it?" A slap, followed by a groan. "Don't lie to me! You lured him with that bridge, didn't you? You lured him, drugged him, and dragged him up here to kill him."

Another groan, longer this time. It sounded off, uncontrolled, as if Taruif could barely breathe. I made it to the next branch when the sound of another slap reached me.

"Liar!"

The tree shook. I clung to the trunk and sent a prayer to Ma'terra to keep us all safe, to keep Taruif safe.

Sorse cursed. "Oh, no! You go when I say you go."

Then don't shake the bloody tree! I wanted to scream at him. I climbed on, branch by branch, listening to Sorse rant, and Taruif's groans fading into breathless moans. He was definitely having trouble breathing. I stopped when I smelled something off, a nasty sour smell I couldn't place. The smell became stronger the higher I got, and just as I caught sight of the bottom of a boot, I finally recognised it. It was the numbing agent Sorse had used to drug Ustion.

I could make it up there in one swoop, one push. My wings wouldn't have much space, and Sorse would certainly hear me, but I knew I could make it before he could react. I had to.

My eyes on the boot, I hoisted myself up to stand on the branch, one leg braced against the trunk, and readied myself, flexing my fingers, letting my energy gather in my palms. One last prayer for Taruif to be safe, and I threw myself up, opening my wings barely halfway, flapping them once, twice. The boot moved away, but I managed to clamp down on the ankle above it just in time, pushing energy into it as I whispered a binding spell. He thrashed once before freezing, before his ankle stiffened beneath my palms. I hung for a moment, catching my breath. One down.

Hoisting myself up on the branch next to the one Sorse now sat frozen on, I caught sight of Taruif, or rather an immobilised bundle of cloth, hanging awkwardly over a branch. My heart nearly stopped. Grabbing my branch tightly, I reached out and put a hand on the bundle.

"He deserves to die," Sorse screamed.

Pity the spell didn't freeze his voice, too. I refused to look at him. Sorse's anger was palpable as an icy wind. I didn't need to see it written on his face. So much anger.

The bundle of cloth didn't move at my touch. My stomach turned, and I shivered. Taruif had to be alive. He had to be. Ianys would kill me if I let anything happen to Taruif now. I'd promised him. I'd promised Ianys to bring Taruif home.

Heart pounding in my throat, I performed a quick scan. The same numbing agent Sorse had used on Ustion, but a larger dose, a much larger dose. Too much. I needed to get him to the infirmary as soon as possible.

Taruif was heavier than I was, but the only way to get him down was to carry him. Surely, Brem had arrived by now? There was enough space under the branch to spread my wings, enough of a gap in the foliage to make it through. I took deep breaths as I cleansed my hands and rubbed them together. Lowering myself from my branch, I spread my wings and hovered next to the bundle Taruif lay wrapped in. I only had one chance at this.

I grabbed the cloth, wrapped it around my hands, and whispered the binding spell, diverting the energy to bind the cloth to me, not to the tree. Before I could change my mind, I picked Taruif up, cloth and all and flapped my wings for all I was worth. My wings burned with the effort needed to defy gravity. I'd never flown with such a heavy load, nothing beyond a bag or two. Calling out every couple of breaths, I tried to warn the elves below of my coming. I still descended too fast, and I flapped my wings with all my might as I tried to slow us down. It wasn't enough. I couldn't...

Landing was softer than I expected. Taruif's body on mine wasn't, and my ribs screamed. I caught a glimpse of a cart to my right, and released what little breath I had. Brem had arrived.

I cried out when my hands were dragged upward and quickly muttered the spell to release the binding. With Taruif's weight off me, I could breathe again. Deep, painful breaths. "Take him to the infirmary," I ordered, my mouth dry, my voice hoarse. "Sorse used too much numbing agent on him."

A horse appeared next to me, and Taruif was draped across its back. I didn't know the elf riding it, and I didn't care. He took off at a frightening speed, and I closed my eyes, catching my breath, my strength, and prayed to Ma'terra it wasn't too late.

Chapter Seventeen

Taruif's face was lax, and he looked terribly pale. He was sleeping, a healing sleep, but it seemed as though he was barely breathing. I leaned my head on Taruif's bed. I couldn't stay long. My wings and back were sore and screaming for rest, my chest showed a nice bruise where Taruif had fallen on me, even after healing, and the cold of the day had seeped into my bones. But I didn't want to leave while Taruif was still sleeping. I needed him to wake up, to hear him say he was all right. Needed him to know I was here. I couldn't bear him waking up alone.

A shadow fell over me, but where I expected the guide, I found Ianys standing in the shadow of the room.

"I couldn't stay away any longer. No one saw me enter."

I opened my mouth to tell him he didn't have to sneak around, since Taruif was a free elf now, but then it dawned on me he meant me, not Taruif. "Ianys. Your promise to Naia doesn't mean we can't be friends."

"But we haven't been friends for so long; it would look suspicious." He turned away from me. "I meant what I said, Kelnaht. It's hard to be around you and…and not touch you, not…stare. It's hard to pretend not to care."

"I hate that I'm keeping you from him."

"Don't even think about it." Ianys' face was close enough to kiss when I glanced at him. To his credit, Ianys didn't flinch away when I pressed my lips against his; instead, he sighed into the kiss. Leaning his forehead against mine, he said, "I don't want you to feel guilty about this. You're good for him."

"*We're* good for him."

"Yes. And I'll be by as often as I can manage." Ianys kissed my forehead and moved to the other side of the bed. It was hard to ignore the sadness in his voice. "Now. Tell me. How's he doing? The guide promised he'd be fine. He wasn't hurt?"

"No wounds." And the slaps I'd heard had all landed on the cloths swaddling him. He didn't even have a bruise. "The scream Merel heard was most likely Sorse letting out his anger. Or his triumph. I don't know. Taruif isn't hurt."

"But he was drugged."

I nodded. "Yes. Healer Muros has flushed most of it out of his system, and the healing sleep will take care of the rest."

"He's too pale."

"Aftereffects of the numbing agent. He might even stay drowsy for a day or two after he wakes up. Healer Muros said it was merely the body coping. He assured me what's left isn't strong enough to do him any harm." I blinked. I was answering these questions the way I answered questions from the family of a victim, with a strange sort of distance. Was I always like this when working on a case? I put my hand over Taruif's and hung my head. These were my vowed and my promised, my lovers. Or maybe I was just too tired to feel.

"I wish we were home," Ianys whispered.

I moved my other hand across the bed to cover Ianys'. "So do I. Soon. Healer Muros says he sees no reason why Taruif won't wake up soon. He might even be able to go home in the morning."

Ianys nodded. He turned his hand, squeezed mine, and pulled his out from underneath as he leaned back in his chair. "You're staying?"

"For a little while. I can't stay all night. I'm cold, my wings ache, and I've got a retrieval to do."

"Can't your apprentice do that?"

"Brem..." I started, and then closed my mouth again. Ianys

had a point. There was nothing else to do right now. "Yes. He could."

"Good. I'll let Healer Muros know you'll need another bed in here, and that back of yours checked out. And I'll send Apprentice Brem to you."

"Ianys—"

"I'll come back before light and sit with you both. I'll get you clean clothes as well."

"Thank you." It wasn't what I wanted to say, but short of begging him to stay, it was all I could utter.

I tensed at the thin smile he threw me as he rose and walked out of the room. If only I could take his worries away.

SORSE HAD SCREAMED while Brem and a couple of cloud elves freed him from the tree and transported him to the cells. He hadn't stopped screaming until he fell asleep there, long after midnight. Despite the thick walls and the distance to the village proper, Brem assumed by now the whole village knew what Sorse thought of Taruif.

Brem yawned. "Sorry. I tried until after midnight to interview him, but he was...difficult. I thought you might want to try before we think of going into his mind."

I nodded. I only wanted to do that as a last resort. "And then you ran the tests to compare the numbing agent, didn't you?"

"Only until it was time to release Novice Darver from his watch. How did you know?"

"Aside from the lack of sleep? The scent still clings to you." Not something I wanted to smell ever again. "Go. Send a messenger to Jarda's hunting group to tell her we found her brother. Make sure he knows she's to return at once. Then, have a nap and finish things at the workshop."

"Yes, Master." He turned to walk away.

"And Brem?"

He stopped.

"Please change your clothes."

A snort. "Yes, Master."

I shook my head at him, took a deep breath, and prepared myself to interview Sorse while I waited for the guide to arrive. Instead it was Darver who appeared, looking bleary-eyed after his short night.

"The guide was summoned by the elders," he said as he straightened his tunic. "They've requested your presence as well."

They'd have to wait until I was done here. Sorse didn't look at us, didn't look up at all when we walked into the cell and sat across from him. He just kept muttering words I could barely understand. This must have been what Ustion told me about.

Sorse's dirty-blond short hair stuck up in all directions, his forehead splotched with redness. Lack of sleep? Anger? I couldn't tell. His wings weren't folded but hung lax off his hunched shoulders. He had large hands, which surprised me; bone carving was a delicate job.

"How did you find out who the apprentice was to be, Sorse?"

I wasn't going to tell him he'd grabbed the wrong stripling, wanting him to feel accomplished in at least that...for as long as it suited me.

Sorse muttered something, but didn't lift his head. I asked him again, louder and with more force behind my words. Still nothing but muttering.

"Sorse," I said sharply, in an attempt to grab his attention. "If you don't answer my questions, I'll have to go look for the answers myself. And you know what that means, don't you?"

He stopped muttering, stopped moving, but said nothing and kept looking at the table in front of him. Did he understand? I gave him a few more moments, and finally, he looked up at us, at me, his cheeks hollow, and his eyes spitting fire.

"Heard the father boasting about his little forester. Saw him puttering about in their perfect garden."

Him? Sorse had probably seen Merel, but from behind, with

their long blond hair, she and Ustion looked very much alike. "But why abduct the new apprentice? Why not take the forester himself?"

"Not allowed, was I? No talking, no touching the shunned," he bit out. "Taking him was useless. No one would listen."

"What did you think would happen if you took the apprentice?"

"Stop *him* from getting free." Sorse narrowed his eyes and clenched his fists. He shook them at me before banging them on the table repeatedly. "He's a murderer! He should never go free! *Never!*" He resumed his muttering to the rhythm of his banging fists. He didn't volunteer more information. It seemed he was done talking to me. But, I knew enough, for now. Time to report to the elders.

We left Sorse alone with his muttering, which we could even hear outside, and I understood what Brem meant. I could only imagine how loud his screaming had been.

Darver sank onto the bench.

"Don't mind his muttering. It's when he becomes quiet you need to check if he's all right."

"Of course, Master Kelnaht."

I left Darver sitting on the bench and flew to Elders' Court. Despite Muros treating my wings and back, I was still sore. Even so, flying beat walking up those endless stairs. As I entered the Court, the elders were all seated in their usual chairs and immediately beckoned me to approach them. There was no sign of the guide.

None of the elders interrupted me when I reported the events of the day and relayed my short conversation with Sorse.

"He wished to stop us freeing Taruif by abducting his future apprentice?"

"Yes, Elder Layt. Only, he mistook young Ustion for the apprentice, as I've reported earlier."

"Yes, yes. Interesting young elf. A carpenter's apprentice, isn't he?"

"Yes, Elder Layt."

"Mmm. Yes. And Master Sorse is locked in a cell?"

"Yes. I will attempt to talk to him again when Mistress Jarda returns from the forest, though I doubt he'll say more than he has already."

The elders turned to each other and whispered to and fro, while I waited for them to issue me their orders. They did a lot of head shaking and nodding. What were they discussing for so long?

Finally, they turned back to me. "We want to know why Master Sorse was so against Master Taruif getting his freedom back," Elder Morenn said. "Calling Master Taruif a murderer is hardly new, but his petition wasn't detailed about the reason. Get it out of him."

They meant literally. Not something I looked forward to, and I'd do my best to avoid having to do it. I bowed and excused myself, agreeing to report back the next day before dinner. That would at least give me some time to dig deeper, without having to dig into Sorse's brain.

JARDA STOOD IN front of me, shoulders drawn up, elbows tucked to her sides, a dazed look in her eyes as she shook her head. Darver had already gone inside. And in his cell, Sorse was muttering to himself.

"I tried to get him to let it go, but he couldn't."

"About Master Fuzan?" I asked.

"Yes. I thought he'd gotten over it for a while. No outbursts, no disappearances, or fewer of them, anyway, no muttering about wishing the forester had died instead of Fuzan." She looked at me. "I thought he'd moved on, finally. But I was wrong, wasn't I?"

I wasn't sure I had the answer to that. "Maybe not moved on, but resigned himself to it. Hearing about a possible apprentice and reducing the sentence might have pushed him over the edge."

"What now?" she asked.

"The elders want me to assess him."

"Is there no other possibility?"

"The guide, Novice Darver, Apprentice Brem and I, we've all tried talking to him, but he doesn't react to any of us. He answered maybe one or two general questions. But nothing beyond wanting the forester dead."

Jarda flinched. "I'm sorry, Master Kelnaht. I only just heard he is your vowed. Is that why you had Apprentice Brem fetch me? You want me to talk to him?"

"Yes. It's his last chance. If he talks to you about it, then maybe I can assess him without going into his mind."

Jarda closed her eyes. "I'll try."

And she did. After a short conversation with Darver, she went into the cell wearing a smile that almost looked convincing, and sat across her brother. Sorse didn't glance up when she began talking softly about the hunt, her family, and the children. It wasn't until she started talking about their past, about things she knew he liked, that he stopped muttering. He still wouldn't face her, but he was listening now. It was something, at least.

Jarda kept talking, kept looking at him, kept smiling.

"He hurt Fuzan," Sorse suddenly said, his voice sounding so different from when I spoke to him. He sounded almost childlike, even looked like it, sitting there wrapping his arms around himself. "I was making wings for him, but he hurt Fuzan before I finished them."

Jarda's expression faltered. Wings for Fuzan. It sounded like a wee elf's wish, creating wings for a tree elf. Obviously, she hadn't known. I doubted Taruif had known, either.

"He hurt Fuzan." Sorse's voice sounded louder now, less childlike. "He doesn't deserve to live because he hurt Fuzan." He slammed his hands on the table, making Jarda lean back.

I stood with my hand on the doorknob, but seeing Jarda's reaction, Sorse immediately ceased.

"I won't hurt you. You're my sister. I love you."

"I love you, too, sweetie."

"I loved Fuzan. I was going to give him wings."

I swallowed, torn between wanting to strangle him for hurting Taruif and feeling sorry for him.

Jarda stayed with Sorse for quite a while, trying to get him to talk about the wings, but Sorse was done talking. He wasn't muttering as such, but he had clearly withdrawn into himself again. Finally, tears in her eyes, Jarda gave up and came out of the cell to join Darver and me. "He never told me about the wings. All he ever told me was that he hated the forester for killing Fuzan, for taking away his loved one. He never mentioned the wings." She wiped her eyes. "Do you think he kept them?"

I shrugged. "We found nothing in his dwelling or either of the caves that looked like wings."

"Is it strange that I want to find them?"

"That's more a question for the guide or Novice Darver than for me, but I don't think so."

She turned to Darver, clearly looking for some sort of closure, for some sort of answer to questions she wasn't even aware of. Answers I could not give her.

THE QUESTION KEEPING me busy through most of the day was what punishment to suggest to the elders. The offense certainly warranted either shunning or banishing. Shunning didn't seem like much of a punishment for Sorse; he pretty much kept to himself anyway. Allowing him to stay in the village wouldn't be fair to either Taruif or Ustion and his family.

Banishment posed its own problem. Was Sorse mentally capable of caring for himself? Though Jarda said Sorse's dwelling was always clean, she also said he tended to leave dishes unwashed. I doubted she had an accurate view of his eating habits, since we found a large part of his inventory in his hiding places. His body looked fit, but his cheeks were hollow. How could we be certain? And the state he was in now? I shook my head. No telling how stable he was.

It shouldn't be this hard finding a suitable punishment. He'd attacked Taruif in more ways than one. Why my hesitation? Because Sorse had looked so pitiful? Because he'd sounded so childlike? That shouldn't influence my decision, should it?

I grabbed my cloak. Maybe the guide could give me some advice. But before I visited the guide, I dropped into the infirmary to see Taruif. Contrary to Muros' assumption, he hadn't woken before either Ianys or I had to leave. When I had left, his mother was sitting with him, telling him family stories.

Taruif was sitting on the edge of the bed when I entered his room, dressed and looking ready to go. He smiled as I walked up to him and kissed him, but the smile didn't reach his eyes. Despite that, my heart skipped a bit seeing his face had returned to his normal colour.

"You're up."

"Yes. Healer Muros said there was no trace of the numbing agent left, though he did say I might feel sleepy for a couple of days."

"That's what he told me yesterday. Were you going anywhere?"

Taruif shook his head. Then he smiled, a genuine warm smile. "Ianys was here. He brought me lunch. He was a bit twitchy, though."

If Ianys were here, I'd kiss him. I hoped it meant he might give the 'appearance of friendship' thing a chance. "That's good. That's very good."

"I want to wake up tomorrow and celebrate Atèn coming of age." He clasped the edge of the bed until his knuckles went white.

"At least your thoughts are innocent," I said as I sat next to him. "I keep wanting to call back Naia's essence and have her rescind that stupid promise."

Taruif leaned his head on my shoulder. "She stole him from you."

"Like Sorse thinks you stole Fuzan from him," I burst out.

"Yes," Taruif said with a hint of sadness in his voice.

"I'm sorry." I kissed the top of his head. "It's not the same."

"Fuzan thought it was funny, you know, Sorse following him around like a lovesick puppy. I kept telling Fuzan to let him down gently, but..." His breath hitched. "Fuzan liked being admired. He didn't understand he was hurting Sorse."

"He said Fuzan loved him."

"It doesn't surprise me he thought that. No wonder he hates me."

"Sorse's pain is not your fault."

Taruif wrapped his arms around me. Should I tell him about the wings Sorse was making for Fuzan? I closed my eyes. I couldn't. Taruif already suffered enough. He couldn't start wondering if Fuzan would have wanted to live if Sorse had given him the wings. Besides, I couldn't even be certain the wings existed or would work.

"Merel stopped by after Ianys left." Taruif yawned.

"How was she?"

"She can't wait to begin training."

"That's good."

"She's too chatty. I can't follow half of what she says." Taruif wrinkled his nose. "She kept telling me I made her nervous."

I snorted then. "Taruif. She's not even fifteen turns, and she's used to you lurking around the village, working but not speaking to anyone. She's bound to be nervous on her first day. Once she gets to know you, it'll get better."

"What if it doesn't? What if I keep making her nervous? What if I snap at her for talking too much?"

"I don't think that'll happen, but if it does, you talk to the guide, and he'll help you solve it. Right?" Taruif nodded against my chest. "Good. Now, does being dressed mean I can take you home?"

"Yes. You have excellent timing. I was about to look for my

boots."

I found them under the bed on the other side. Taruif grumbled a bit as I put them on for him, but when I looked up, the gleam in his eye told me he liked seeing me on my knees. I rose and kissed him, hard. "Later," I promised him as I stepped back so he could get up.

As we walked across the centre, Ustion sat at a table with his family. He smiled at me, and I smiled back, but I couldn't stop the sigh from forming. I still had a decision to make concerning Sorse.

CHAPTER EIGHTEEN

T HAT DECISION WAS taken from me even before I managed to talk it over with the guide. Walking to the guide's safehold after taking Taruif home and having a quick 'meal' with him, I passed the cells. The outer door was wide open. I sprinted towards it and found Darver passed out in the corridor. A quick scan confirmed my suspicion: numbing agent. Not much, thank Ma'terra, just enough to take him out.

But if I'd expected Sorse's cell to be empty, I was wrong. Head leaning on the table, arms hanging awkwardly down his sides, Sorse sat slumped in his chair, and the cell door was closed. A sour scent reached my nose, making me gag, and I pressed my sleeve against my face to keep the smell away. A cloth lay on the table in front of Sorse. How did he get hold of the numbing agent? I put my fingers against Sorse's clammy neck, avoiding looking at his unseeing eyes. No pulse. Sorse was dead.

A sudden sob made me jump.

Jarda sat on the floor in a corner of the cell, knees drawn up, crying into her hands. "I *had* to, Master Kelnaht. I *had* to. It's like he's a child again. And when I came back with the cloth, he just sat there, muttering about wings and helping Fuzan fly. I…"

She must have come back soon after I left, because the numbing agent didn't kill instantly. And she must have given Sorse an even higher dose than the one Sorse had given Taruif, to make sure we'd be too late to revive him.

Jarda stared at me, sobbing silently now. Where had she found the numbing agent? We hadn't yet discovered where Sorse had got it from, but it hadn't been at his dwelling. Looking into Jarda's tear-streaked face, the answer came to me immediately. Jarda was a hunter. Apprentices made mistakes that couldn't always be fixed by another shot. They used the numbing agent to calm the wounded animal down. Sorse had no doubt stolen the agent from Jarda, and now she had used it to kill him.

I helped Jarda up on her feet, arrested her, walked her into the next cell, and locked her in.

Twenty turns of shunning was what I *should* suggest, for murder. It was what Taruif had received, if I counted his reduction. But was it murder? I'd had my doubts about Sorse surviving banishment, but Jarda might have been terrified. He was her brother, and she loved him. Like Taruif, Jarda only wanted to help a loved one. Twenty turns for that?

No. I could never suggest that much to the elders. Five turns of shunning, eight, maximum. She didn't deserve more, just as Taruif never had, despite what he'd thought himself.

A strange numbness settled into me as I carried Darver to the infirmary. A numbness that lasted through telling the guide and the elders what happened. My voice sounded as if it was filtered through cotton, and the edges of my vision blurred, but there was no rest for me yet.

By the time I finished my report to the elders, a messenger had come to fetch me. Darver had woken up. Within moments, the guide, the elders, and I stood gathered around his bed to listen to his statement.

"She told me you'd given her permission to visit her brother. I told her you hadn't given word to me, Master Kelnaht, and I know better than to let anyone in without express permission." Darver coughed and took a sip of water before continuing. "She waved a cloth under my nose. I thought it was strange, but then I started feeling light-headed, and the next thing I remember is waking up here. Healer Muros said she drugged me with numbing agent."

I nodded. "She did." I was glad he'd gotten just a sniff. If she'd pressed a cloth that soaked against his nose... Darver was a lucky elf.

Darver rubbed his hands across his face. "I'm sorry, Master Kelnaht, for not being prepared."

"Nonsense," I said. "What happened is not your fault."

"But..."

"Darver," the guide interjected. "When Master Kelnaht says it's not your fault, you nod and say thank you."

Darver nodded immediately and said, "Thank you, Master Kelnaht."

I almost burst into laughter at his prompt reaction, but a warning glance from the guide stopped me.

"You did well, Novice Darver," Elder Morenn said before turning to me. "Please, Master Kelnaht, follow us to Elders' Court, so we can decide what to do with Mistress Jarda."

I couldn't wait to be done and go home.

By the time I finally made it to Taruif's, both Taruif and Ianys were already in bed, snuggled up together, asleep. Tired as I was, I didn't immediately undress. Instead, I leaned against the windowsill and watched them. The room was warmer than I'd expected—a heating spell no doubt—and they'd forgone a blanket. Ianys lay spooned against Taruif, arms wrapped tightly around him, their legs entwined. They'd left room for me on Taruif's side. I could easily worm myself against him, moving one of Ianys' hands to my hip. And I would. Just...not yet.

Time stood still as I watched my elves. Taruif's face seemed relaxed in sleep, peaceful. Ianys softly snored into Taruif's hair, yet Taruif never moved a muscle. I grinned. After a turn of hearing it regularly, Taruif and I were used to it. At times, it even helped us sleep.

"Will you please get into bed before you collapse?"

I blinked. I could have sworn I'd heard Ianys snore. And yet, it was Ianys who was looking at me with a reproachful expression in his eyes.

"As much as I love the way you look at us, I really don't want to get up and carry you to bed. Get in. Now."

I tried pretending to be put out, but I couldn't stop myself from smiling. I dropped my trousers and pulled my tunic over my head, letting it land on top of the trousers. I'd pick them up in the morning. Taruif would be grousing about it, but I didn't care right now. I climbed in next to Taruif, nestled into him, and closed my eyes.

"Half the tribe already heard what happened," Ianys said as he rested his warm hand on my hip. "I'm so sorry, Kel."

All I could do was nod. If I opened my mouth now, I wouldn't be able to stop the tears from falling. Ianys seemed to understand and rubbed slow circles on my hip with his thumb.

"What will happen to his sister?" Taruif asked.

I opened my eyes to find him gazing at me sleepily. "Shunned for seven turns."

Taruif's eyes widened.

Ianys lifted his head and looked at me "Your doing?"

"I suggested five to eight, and the guide helped me convince them." Had I made a mistake? Did Taruif think she deserved more?

Taruif leaned forward and brushed his lips against mine. "I'm glad the elders saw it your way."

I wanted to explain, wanted to make sure he understood my reasoning, but Ianys pinched my hip before I had the chance. A small shake of his head kept me silent. "Go to sleep, truth seeker. You can present your case tomorrow."

"But..."

"You did well, Kel. I understand. Go to sleep," Taruif insisted and kissed me again, tender and slow.

I tried to relax and closed my eyes, expecting Taruif and

Ianys to go to sleep as well. What I got was Ianys asking after Taruif's mother and Taruif telling him about the letter she gave him when he woke up. She'd written it the night before, the habit too ingrained to stop because he was free now.

I drifted off with Taruif's voice enveloping me like a safety blanket.

A DISPIRITED MOOD settled over the tribe after Jarda's shunning was announced. The shock was palpable throughout the village. Not even the first snowfall could lift our spirits.

The previous night, Taruif had taken Ianys and me to the platform where Ustion had been found. He'd set a basket on the platform containing a myriad of evergreen plants in greens and purples. Purple had been Fuzan's favourite colour. Taruif had burnt a thick letter—six pages, if I'd counted correctly, written to Fuzan during the mourning period—while we chanted the Prayer of the Dead and sang a song celebrating our lost ones.

As if realising I was thinking about him, Taruif glanced up from his work and smiled at me.

I sat on a low bench in front of Taruif's dwelling—our dwelling. I couldn't get used to saying it. Taruif and Merel were clearing snow off the smaller plants. With the snowfall, the smaller growths had to be protected, and Taruif took Merel on his daily walks around the village to make sure the shields held and the snow hadn't caused any unexpected damage.

Merel was still talkative, but after following Taruif around for almost a quarter moon now, there was barely any sign of nervousness left. Taruif complained about her non-stop talking every night, but he sounded almost fond. This apprenticeship was doing wonders for him. His freedom was doing wonders for him.

Less so for Ianys. He did his best to approach Taruif and me in public, under the guise of striking up a friendship—or rekindling one, in my case—but the expression in his eyes told me how difficult it was for him not to greet us with a kiss or a hug, how hard it was to keep the conversations from becoming intimate. He'd only managed to come by once recently, the previous night, disappearing shortly after we were asleep, or thought we were asleep. He was pulling away from us, and I didn't know what to do about it.

Pushing myself off the bench, I waded through the soft layer of snow across the clearing. I hugged Taruif, told Merel to be good, and walked towards the guide's safehold. This past quarter moon, I'd visited the safehold at least once a day. Our conversations weren't long, but even the shortest conversation helped me understand.

I wasn't the only one. Taruif visited the safehold daily as well. Not that Taruif hadn't talked to me—to both of us. He had, until deep in the night sometimes. What he struggled with was how the tribe treated him. They greeted him and made small talk as if he'd never been shunned. The sudden change overwhelmed him, and he didn't always remember he could greet them back.

I checked in with Brem, but he was doing fine. Once spring announced itself, I'd let him take his test. What a difference a turn could make. Last turn, I'd been ready to have him take over for me when I decided to claim Taruif at the Solstice Circle, before Ianys told me about the guide's petition. This turn, I was looking forward to sending him out into the world, to find his own place in life. He was ready for it.

A couple of striplings snickered as I ducked, narrowly avoiding being pelted by a snowball. It was good to see the young ones playing and laughing again. I could just hear the guide say something about the joy of the young lifting the spirits of the old. With Solstice coming in two days, I took it as a good sign.

The guide sat in the middle of the room, cross-legged, looking like he'd been expecting me. He smiled as I entered and motioned to the small chamber where the bowl and pitcher for cleansing were. I went in and performed my cleansing ritual, taking my time, rubbing the herbs in until my hands were tingling, before finally joining him. He reached behind him and offered me a glass of laros juice. I took a sip, enjoying the sweet, slightly tangy taste.

"You seem more relaxed than you were yesterday, but there's a tension in you that seems to worsen each day, too." The guide burned a candle. "You're worried about Master Ianys."

I nodded.

"He has to set his own path, Kelnaht."

I nodded again. I knew. It wasn't the first time the guide had told me this, but it didn't make it any easier to see Ianys suffer. "You say he has to set his own path, yet he sacrificed his chance—"

"To stop you from retreating."

"It was my path to set," I retorted.

"To leave your vowed?"

He had me there. I wouldn't have, couldn't have. "Ianys is part of us."

"Yes."

"Naia should never have forced him to make that promise," I burst out without thinking. The guide shook his head, narrowing his eyes at me. "I apologise."

With a small nod, the guide lit another candle. "I understand your feelings, Kelnaht, but keep her essence in mind. She deserves her rest. Tell me about the Solstice Circle."

"Nothing to tell. Taruif probably won't be planning to go, but I'll drag him if I have to." And I would, because it didn't matter if we were vowed already; he deserved a public claiming.

"You could just tell him?"

"And ruin the surprise?"

The guide burned another candle. "Mistress Jarda moved into Master Sorse's dwelling."

"She's strong." She'd been silent when I last saw her, but resilience had shone in her eyes as she puttered around the grounds of Sorse's dwelling—her dwelling now. She'd shown that same strength when her vowed and children visited her for the last time, despite plenty of tears flowing on all sides. "And she has you to comfort her."

"That she does. How are you sleeping?"

I shrugged. "I lie awake more than I sleep." Sleeping meant dreaming of running into the cell, choking on the smell of numbing agent as Sorse's dead eyes haunted me. "But Taruif's presence is soothing." And so was Ianys', when he was with us.

"Healer—"

"You know I'm not going to do that. I'll be fine." And I *would* be. It just wouldn't be tomorrow or the day after.

Waiting for Taruif to arrive, I sat on a bench in the Solstice Circle, staring into the fire. I couldn't help looking up at every snap of a branch, every rustle of leaves, every voice ringing out in a greeting. I hadn't seen Taruif all day. He'd already been outside doing his rounds when I woke up, and when I made my way to my workshop, he was nowhere to be seen. Though it wasn't a busy day, by the time Brem and I went to have lunch, Taruif and Merel were just disappearing into the forest on the other side of the village. And tonight... Tonight I'd left for the circle before Taruif had even arrived home. My heart pounded in my throat. What if he wasn't coming?

To keep myself from looking up at every arrival, I focused on my conversation with Brem. Even though he'd be leaving the village after his test—no doubt he would pass—he gladly accepted my offer of moving in to the dwelling above my workshop. I'd already moved most of my possessions to Taruif's dwelling, our dwelling, so I gave him permission to move in whenever he wanted.

A branch snapped behind me, and before I could stop myself, I'd already turned my head. Taruif stepped out of the shadows and looked straight at me, the corner of his mouth turned up in a barely visible smile that took my breath away. My heart skipped a beat. Taruif was dressed in his favourite dark green tunic and trousers, just like last turn, cloak loosely hanging off his shoulders. He even wore the same braided black leather bands around his wrists and neck. Gorgeous didn't even begin to describe him.

It was hard not to invite him to sit with me the moment he arrived, hard to watch him circle the fire to show himself a participant. As hard as it had been not to see Ianys at the fire, turn after turn, while I'd been waiting for him to change his mind. My stomach clenched. Ianys would not be at the circle tonight, either. The guide was right. Ianys had to set his own path. If only there was an easy solution.

A rhythmic tapping on my leg distracted me from my thoughts before I could start to wallow in them. I turned my head and smiled at Taruif, who held out his hands. Taking them, I let him pull me to my feet. This was it. Last turn's speech was still fresh in my mind, and I opened my mouth to repeat it, in public this time, but Taruif beat me to it.

"My path is muddy, filled with puddles to lure me away from my goal. Will you ease my travels and keep me safe?"

For a moment, I didn't know what to say. I hadn't expected him to repeat my own words back to me. Silence fell around the circle, and I was certain everyone was watching us. All day, I'd been worried he wouldn't come, but he had, and was claiming me with the same words I had claimed him with last turn. I should have been relieved, but instead I was shaking and struggling to find the words. Taruif smiled patiently as I gathered my wits.

I swallowed and took a deep breath before finally replying, "I will keep you safe, will clear your path of mud and weeds, for as long as you need me to."

His smile widened then, though he had an uneasy glint in his eyes when everyone started cheering for us. He leaned closer, his mouth but a hairs-breadth from my ear. "That is all I ask," he whispered as he trailed his lips along my jaw line and kissed me in front of our tribe for the first time.

We didn't linger, didn't stay to watch other claimings. Instead, we left as soon as our kiss ended and walked home, hand in hand, shoulder to shoulder. The soft sounds of a promise song reached my ears when we were halfway across the clearing. Sitting on the steps in front of the door, Ianys sat, cloak tightly wrapped around him. He looked at Taruif as he sang. His voice wobbled when Taruif stopped.

Taruif turned to me, silently asking me if I had known. I shook my head. I had no idea Ianys was planning this. The opposite. I'd been convinced he was pulling away from us.

"Go to him," I told Taruif, giving him a little push, but Taruif shook his head and wouldn't budge.

He grabbed my hand again, and together we walked across the remaining half of the clearing until we reached our mate and our home.

INTERLUDE

"WILL YOU JOIN me for a short flight?" the guide had asked when he'd shown up at our door at the break of dawn with a lantern.

Now, an hour later, we landed halfway up a mountain on a small ledge. I was still folding my sore wings when the guide, holding his lantern out in front of him, disappeared into a low opening. The chamber we entered wasn't as dark as I expected it to be; there were a number of crevices letting in daylight.

The guide walked to the middle of the chamber and waited for me in front of a raised area. Spread out on top of it laid a framework of the finest cut bones knotted together with a thin oiled string, adorned with finely sewn-together shanna leaves. My jaw dropped as I took in the perfect craftsmanship. So much love had been poured into this project. I itched to inspect the wings, check the bindings, the weight. When Sorse had muttered about making Fuzan wings, I never could have imagined such a beautiful structure. He must have studied cloud elves extensively.

"I don't know what to do with them," the guide said.

"How did you know they were here?"

"Master Sorse talked about a hideaway no one could climb up to, once. I told him he shouldn't hide himself away so much, but he insisted he couldn't let *anyone* know where it was." The guide shook his head. "Another time, he mentioned a mountain that looked like a sleeping bear. After he'd mentioned the wings, I had to check. I flew around the forest for an hour every day. I finally found this cave yesterday."

I ran my hands across the shanna leaves. Despite looking thin and fragile, shanna leaves were some of the sturdiest leaves in the forest. They didn't rip or tear easily, though they could be cut and shaped quite well. The fine structure of veins was what made the leaves so strong. They could withstand many a storm.

"Do you think they could work?" the guide asked.

I had no idea why he thought I could answer that question. "I'm a truth seeker, Guide. You'd be better off asking the carpenters." Or a bone carver.

"None of them are cloud elves."

"*You* are a cloud elf," I retorted, still not understanding why he asked me.

"Exactly. We're both cloud elves. I don't want anyone else to know, Kelnaht, not until we know they work."

"You'd need a tree elf to test them." It was out of my mouth before I could stop myself. Was I really thinking of helping the guide test these wings? Sorse had hurt Taruif, intended to kill him. How could I even consider it? "We should leave them be."

"Master Fuzan wasn't the only elf plagued by such a longing."

I didn't know what to say. It was difficult to imagine anyone wanting something so badly. But that wasn't true, was it? Last turn, I would have given up my life to be with Taruif. How was that different from wanting to fly so desperately?

I gently lifted a corner of the framework; it was even lighter than I'd imagined. From the way the bones were attached to the leaves, it was clear the wings were placed upside down. Thin belts were attached at several points, to be fixed around the arms, wrists, chest, and waist. They would fit neither of us. "We need a tree elf, Guide. There is no other way to test them."

The guide was silent for a moment. He frowned, studying the wings. Finally, he looked up and nodded. "So, you think it might be possible?"

In the end it didn't matter *who* had made the wings. Especially if it could soothe some elf's desperate yearning.

"Do you know, Guide..." I rubbed the smooth, perfectly carved bone. "I think it's worth a try."

ACT THREE
FULL CIRCLE

WILL KEEP you safe, will clear your path of mud and weeds, for as long as you need me to. That was the promise I had made Taruif, our shunned forester, when I claimed him in secret a turn and a half ago.

This past winter, I had almost failed to keep my promise and nearly lost both Taruif and Ianys, my first love, who completed our triad. Taruif had almost been the victim of an elf's plot to stop the elders reducing his forty-turn sentence. Meanwhile, because Ianys had promised his deceased vowed not to let me raise their daughter, we could not be seen as lovers. Sneaking around and stealing moments became almost too hard for him to bear. It was a heavy winter.

But the plotter was caught, Taruif was now a free elf, and we had renewed our vows, our claiming, proud and openly at the Solstice Circle. The heavy winter made way for a light, breezy spring in which Ianys, though he still had to be cautious, made an effort to rekindle our friendship in public, despite the burden he carried.

We spent many moons on a path cleared of mud and weeds, stepping into the occasional puddle but not thinking of drowning for even a moment. Simply being able to greet Ianys as we did all elves, or talk to him in public, even just in passing, brought us the hope we needed to hold on.

CHAPTER NINETEEN

T HE WARMTH OF the sun on my face and chest, a steaming cup of goraf tea in my hands, Taruif's arms wrapped around me, and Ianys splashing about in the water below us—this day could only be better if I was in the pond too. But I needed to wait for the water to warm before I could join Ianys.

After the freezing weather this past winter, and flying more than was good for me while I tried to find a missing stripling, my wings were still a bit sore and sensitive to cold, even to a cool pond that was usually so refreshing.

"Ianys will let us know when it's warm enough." Taruif kissed my neck, shooting little sparks of desire through me. "And then we can both join him."

Grass tickled my bare feet and birds chirped in the trees surrounding the small pond. It was a perfect day for a swim. My waiting time would have crawled past, had I not been wrapped in Taruif's arms. I tilted my head to give him better access to my neck.

It had taken us half the morning to get to this hidden pond, but the long trip had been worth it. Both Taruif and I had been overjoyed when Ianys agreed to join us. One whole day for the three of us, away from spying eyes.

"What have you planned to shut Merel up with tomorrow?" Merel was the chatty kind, and after having spent over twenty turns speaking to nobody but the guide, Taruif tired of it quickly. He'd become good at quieting her with boring, repetitive tasks in the five moons she'd been his apprentice.

Taruif leaned his chin on my shoulder. "We'll be checking dead trees near Cabaj Pond."

He meant she'd be checking them, and he'd be correcting her. Luckily, Merel enjoyed any work Taruif threw at her, however boring it was. She was a perfect match for him in will. "Shall I see you for lunch?"

"Doubtful. We'll be taking lunch with us."

I faced him and kissed his cheek. "In that case, I'll be keeping your mother company for lunch tomorrow."

Taruif's smile lit up his entire face. "She'll like that."

Not a day went by where Taruif didn't visit his mother, even if it was only to wish her a good day, or tend to her plants.

Ianys was waving. Taruif nodded toward him and took my mug. "Seems the water is warm enough now."

One last peck and I wasted no time in getting up, dropping my trousers, and jumping into the pond, making sure to keep my wings tightly folded. They'd become damp regardless, but this would keep them from getting drenched.

Ianys appeared in front of me, treading water, a frown on his face. "The water is warm enough, isn't it?"

I nodded.

"Are you sure?" He ran a wet hand across my arm. "You're shivering."

Goose pimples appeared where he touched me. "Because of the breeze. The water is lovely." Nothing like a heated shower, but lovely even so.

"You'll get out when you get cold, right?"

It was hard not to roll my eyes at him. "Motherhood suits you."

That earned me a thump on my shoulder and a splash of water in my face for good measure. I laughed and swam after him as he backed away. We horsed around, chasing each other across the pond, splashing when we couldn't reach, grabbing when we could. And laughing. We couldn't stop laughing.

Taruif got right in the middle of us when he joined in, and for the better part of an hour we splashed, dunked, jumped each other, and swam until we were tired. Only then did we get out of the water, wrinkly skin and all, to dry out and warm up lying on the grass.

At least, that was the plan. Instead we ended up in a heap of naked bodies and entangled limbs as we kissed and hugged each other in the warmth of the sun. Taruif and Ianys were careful to keep me on top to dry out my damp wings, and I lazily sprawled across them, wings spread, and hands entwined with my mates. I could have easily fallen asleep like that. But then Ianys rolled away from us.

Despite being far away from the village, he seemed uncomfortable with being out in the open, naked and exposed. "As much as I'd love to continue," he said as he rose to his haunches, "let's go to the cave."

There was a small hidden cave we'd inspected as soon as we'd arrived, in which we'd stashed our food. Taruif, who could have spent hours lying in the sun, heaved a sigh as I pushed myself up, but said nothing as he followed us to the entrance.

Barely inside, Ianys pulled me to him and kissed me, hard. I smiled into his kiss, knowing what he wanted. "You didn't forget the oil, did you?" I asked when he let me go.

He gestured toward a satchel on the ground next to our food basket. Taruif went off to grab it.

"You want to do this standing up? Or do you—"

Ianys shut me up with another kiss, and walked me backwards until my shoulders touched the wall of the cave. My shoulders, not my wings. I blinked, and Ianys smiled.

"There's a crevice behind you. Is it wide enough for your wings?"

I nodded. Nothing pinched them, and the rock was smoother and warmer than expected. The whole wall was wet with warm water that trickled down my back. It had to come from a sun-warmed stream outside the cave.

"Good," was all Ianys said before he nipped my jaw, sank

down on his knees, and took me into his mouth.

I closed my eyes and shuddered. I stretched my arms and found a small ledge to hold onto as he licked and teased me until I gasped. The shock of cold, slippery fingers brushing my anus made me shiver and cry out. My whole body thrummed and when fingers breached me at the same time Ianys swallowed me down, my scream echoed through the cave.

My sounds were stifled by a mouth descending on mine at an awkward angle. It was Taruif, tasting of spiced goraf. He deepened the kiss, just as Ianys pushed his fingers in farther, making me tremble harder and yearn for more.

He slowed his teasing to light licks and scratching nails up and down my inner thighs. I drove my hips forward in desperation, but Ianys merely chuckled and let go of me altogether. I wanted to scream for him to get back to it, but couldn't. Not with Taruif keeping my mouth busy.

And then Taruif shivered and groaned and moved his hips closer to mine. He was hard and leaking, and I knew exactly what Ianys was doing. My breath hitched at the delicious friction of Taruif's cock against mine as he writhed on Ianys' tongue. I opened my eyes. Taruif was nothing less than gorgeous in his pleasure.

Taruif's moans became strangled, urgent, and he tore his mouth from mine to catch a breath. I released the wall with one hand, trailed it down the beautiful green vines adorning Taruif's left side until I met Ianys' wrist, and squeezed. Using my hand as support, Ianys rose from his knees and pressed himself against Taruif's back for a moment.

He stared into my eyes. "Still comfortable?" he asked, before kissing Taruif's shoulder.

"I'm fine." I was. My wings were safe in their crevice, my arms weren't tired yet, the wall was warm, and I couldn't wait for them to get on with it.

Ianys nodded and kissed Taruif's shoulder again. He grabbed Taruif and manoeuvred them both until he could press his body against mine. "Hold on, this is going to be fun." He brushed his lips across mine as he nestled between my legs. He put his hands under my arse to lift me up and slowly pushed himself inside me.

Hanging on to the ledge above me, I gasped into his mouth. He went slow, tantalisingly slow, and I wished he'd hurry up. I wanted him deep, wanted him fast, wanted Taruif to join us. Taruif stood behind Ianys, watching us through half-lidded eyes. I smiled at him, but it turned into a gasp when Ianys pushed fully into me with a shudder, and Taruif disappeared from my sight.

Ianys' movements became jerky and shallow after his first few thrusts—I could easily imagine Taruif teasing him with his fingers. When I tilted my hips, his thrusts became smoother, deeper. I let my head fall back, groaning and panting as he brushed my prostate.

Taruif rose and leaned against Ianys' back, pushing me into the rock as he kissed my cheek, and whispered, "Don't come yet."

He pressed into Ianys, and we all froze for a moment, waiting for Ianys to adapt, until he uttered a needy sound, and Taruif started moving.

Our cries, moans, and gasps echoed through the cave. There was no rhythm to our motions, no synchronisation in our thrusts, no elegance, only need, lust. I couldn't close my eyes, because I enjoyed watching theirs too much. Everything had its own sensation, whether pushing in, pulling out, or needy, shallow jabs. Shivers wracked my body at their gasps, and their shudders caused me to moan. There was no difference between my pleasure and theirs as it rose and rose.

When Ianys' breath hitched, I leaned in and claimed his lips in a searing kiss, while Taruif nibbled on his neck. Settled deep in me, Ianys came first, his thrusts fierce and chaotic at once, driving me over the edge with him. We were both soaring, and yet Taruif was still moving.

I had no idea how Ianys managed to hold me up when I could feel his legs trembling. My forehead rested against his, and we breathed in sync. Taruif set a brutal rhythm, chasing his own release, driving Ianys—though softening—into me with every thrust. He came with a shout and sank against Ianys, who did his best to save me from bearing all their weight.

"I think..." Ianys' voice was barely more than a whisper. "I like this cave."

We chuckled, awash in tiny aftershocks, savouring the moment with stuttering breaths and messy kisses.

SATED, SMILING, AND bathed—twice—we made our way back to the village in the glow of the evening sun. Several times, I found myself glancing over my shoulder. I hadn't wanted to leave, but duty called, or would, sooner or later.

Ianys walked several paces in front of us. Even though we were openly friends now, he couldn't help keeping himself at a distance. I clenched my hands by my sides and accepted Taruif's arm around me. Ianys' sense of propriety made me want to scream sometimes. It wasn't for appearance's sake, even though it had all the signs of that. No, Ianys created the distance because he was afraid he couldn't stop himself from touching us if he came too close. If only he didn't have to.

An uncanny silence greeted us as we entered the village. With the summer bug—a harmless flu amongst children brought on by warm weather insects—going around, it wasn't unexpected to see few children playing outside, but no one seated on the benches in the centre talked or smiled. We were met with nothing but sad, silent, and even tear-streaked faces.

"What happened?" I asked the elf closest to me. He was a wiry cloud elf who looked vaguely familiar, and when he turned his head I recognised him as Ellon, one of the elves who had helped me find a missing stripling this winter. His clothes were covered in flour.

"Young Ninge was found unconscious this morning."

Next to me, Ianys gasped. When I faced him he had a

trembling hand clasped over his mouth and his face had paled. "But he was free of his fever two days ago. He was playing outside." His voice sounded strangled. "Is it...is it the summer bug again?"

Ellon gave a sad shrug and nodded at the infirmary. "We know nothing yet. His mothers are in there with the Healers, the guide and Novice Darver. We've been waiting for news all afternoon."

"I need to check on Atèn," Ianys burst out. "She and Ninge often play together." He ran off before either Taruif or I could offer him words of support.

I wanted to run after him, but Taruif's shaking hand on my shoulder kept me rooted. "No use in worrying before we know more, Kelnaht."

He was right. Atèn had been all right before we'd left in the morning, and Ianys would tell us if something was amiss, even if it was just a cough. Though it was hard to see Ianys distraught.

The summer bug did seem early this turn. I couldn't remember children ever falling ill with it this long before Solstice.

"Master Kelnaht?"

I faced Ellon, who was watching me with a thoughtful expression in his eyes.

"I've heard you play a mean game of knobbles. None of us have any intention of leaving until we've had some news at least. Would you mind indulging us?" He indicated the elf across from him, a robust female with puffy eyes, red cheeks, flour in her black hair, and her hands tangled in her apron. "Kore is Ninge's aunt." He motioned me to lean closer before whispering, "And she needs a distraction that doesn't involve baking right now."

Kore narrowed her eyes at us, and both their expressions told me there was more to that story, but Ellon ignored her glare and gave her a sweet smile instead.

"I'm afraid you have me mixed up with my former apprentice, but I can hold my own." I turned to Taruif.

"I wouldn't mind a game myself," he said as he sat down next to Ellon and reached for the knobble stones in the centre of the table.

Ellon mouthed a "thank you" to us. "I'll get you some tea." He rose before we could protest and all but skipped toward the cauldron steaming in the middle of the centre. The flour clinging to his clothes and wings spread around like dust sparkling in the sunlight.

Kore followed Ellon's movements with the barest hint of a smile. She accepted a handful of knobble stones from Taruif. "What he's too polite to mention is I went out of my mind when I heard the news, and my apprentices are still cleaning up my mess. The guide said they couldn't allow us into the infirmary until they knew what caused Ninge—" Kore blinked back her tears and shook her head. "I... I keep expecting someone to come out and tell us he is gone."

It was that bad? I sat on the end of the bench next to Taruif and reached across to put my hand over hers. I wanted to tell her Ninge would be all right, that Muros was an excellent healer, but without knowing what was ailing the child, there was nothing I *could* say.

Ellon returned with the tea and sat down next to Kore, wrapping his long, slender arms around her. Kore sighed and sniffed, resting her head on his shoulder. "Ninge's always such a lively child, you know. Drives my bakers mad the way he manages to nick buns from right underneath their noses."

The melancholy in her voice shot right through me, and I couldn't help but think of Atèn. What if something happened to her? Taruif put his hand over mine as if he knew what I was thinking. It was still shaking. No doubt he was thinking the same.

Kore kissed Ellon's cheek and focussed her attention on her tea. Ellon kept his arm around her until Taruif shoved some knobble stones his way.

Knobble stones came in different shapes, and every one bore a different set of symbols on each side. I never considered myself a decent player, but playing with Brem had improved my skills.

He could always remember the symbols on each and every one of them after the first couple of throws.

Ellon threw five of his stones, and we studied the symbols facing up. Kore was next, throwing all hers, picking and choosing between them in order to match the symbols on Ellon's stones. The rules were simple. Players had to match symbols in as few throws as possible, discarding a stone with every throw and losing points for the stones they couldn't match. It was a tactical game, but a fun one.

The game served to distract not only Kore, but her parents and the rest of poor Ninge's family as well. They watched us play, or began their own games. Though, every couple of throws, at least one elf would turn their head towards the infirmary. And more than once someone muttered that Sami and Ocer, Ninge's mothers, should have their families with them.

Everyone rose as one when the infirmary door finally opened and the guide and Novice Darver appeared. Ellon supported Kore, whose face turned as pale as the flour in her hair. Sami and Ocer's parents didn't look much better. Novice Darver nodded at us and walked off while the guide approached Kore and clasped her hands in his. His smile was full of compassion, his voice warm as he said, "Young Ninge is still unconscious. The healers don't know what's wrong with him yet, but he seems stable for now. You can all go in now. But only for a little while."

Something in the guide's expression stopped me from asking questions until everyone had gone into the infirmary and the centre was cleared. I motioned him to sit down. The guide stared at his hands as he did, and I covered his with mine.

"How bad is it?" Though the guide was stronger than his waifish figure suggested, he was at his most vulnerable when a child was harmed—whether by elf hands, accident, or sickness—and an unconscious child was no different.

"Healer Muros can't find a cause for young Ninge's coma."

"But it's not the summer bug?"

The guide shook his head. "Both young Ninge and his little

brother shed their fevers about three days ago. They'd been among the first to fall ill, and among the first to heal." The guide closed his eyes. "Mistress Sami and Mistress Ocer found young Ninge unconscious in bed and with a high fever this morning, but all he'd complained about last night was a slight headache. They thought he'd overdone the playing after having been ill." The guide's hand shook beneath mine. "Healer Muros hasn't managed to bring his temperature down yet."

And the guide must have been fretting all day. "You need to rest."

The guide shook his head. "No. I'm all right. I can rest later. I can't leave Darver to do my duty, Master Kelnaht. They need me."

For the guide, his elves always came first. I rose and urged him to rise as well. "If you won't sleep, maybe some quiet time at your safehold will do."

"But—"

"You're not going to be of use to anyone if you don't at least replenish your energy, Guide."

There was nothing he could say to refute that, and with a sigh he let me lead him towards his safehold—his meditation room.

Chapter Twenty

T HERE WAS NO change in Ninge's situation, the next morning. The villagers were quiet, few children were out playing, and Ninge's family were once again sitting in the centre, waiting for news.

Inside the infirmary the healers fought hard to keep Ninge with us. The healers and the guide were also fielding questions from concerned elves whose children were still sick with the summer bug. Questions they had no answers to. And despite being far too tired, the guide didn't want to hear about taking a rest.

Taruif and I hadn't had an easy night of it. We'd heard no news from Ianys. He hadn't dropped by, and I hadn't seen him at the centre since I arrived, either. I was more than a little worried. So, when I caught sight of smoke rising from the forge's chimney halfway through the morning, I left the guide in Novice Darver's capable hands, and made my way across the village for a visit.

Ianys was working the bellows. His smile when he noticed me was wan, and he kept pumping until he'd fed enough energy into them that they worked on their own. I was about to wrap my arms around him, until a pitiful cough alerted me to another presence. I let my arms drop as I stepped back and turned towards the sound.

On a cot in the back of the forge Atèn lay huddled beneath

the blankets, her eyes closed, but her mouth open. She was pale and had the unhealthy blush of fever.

"She fell ill around lunch, yesterday."

I wanted to hug him, but refrained. Instead I gave his shoulder a quick squeeze. "Oh, Ianys. I'm so sorry."

He shrugged, though his anguished expression belied his casual gesture. "My staying home wouldn't have made a difference. Fern said they were playing outside one moment, and the next Atèn and Zoet were coughing and looking feverish. Yrne didn't fall ill until after midnight."

"No headaches?" It was out of my mouth before I could stop it.

Ianys narrowed his eyes as he shook his head. "Is that what Ninge had?"

No point in keeping that from him, now. "Yes. And a high fever." I wanted to tell him how sorry I was again, but Ianys held his hand up.

"Fern already examined her. Doesn't seem any worse than a summer bug right now."

The wobble in his voice made me swallow any other questions I might have. He was trying to put up a good front, but he was unsure, insecure, on edge. I sent a prayer to Ma'terra for Atèn to not have more than a simple fever. I couldn't bear it if Ianys and his family suffered what Ninge's family was going through. Had it only been this morning that I'd sent her a prayer for Ninge and his family?

"Fern offered to look after her, with both her children ill as well, but Atèn only wanted to be with me. And I've got too much work to stay home." He sighed, eyes fixed on Atèn. "So, I told her she could come with me if she promised to sleep. She said she didn't want to—on top of everything, she's been having nightmares about an old grey-haired elf coming after her—but she drifted off as soon as I'd tucked her in."

"Like father like daughter," I quipped. Ianys had been sick once when we lived together...before... The high fever hadn't stopped him from going out to the forge, though his mentor had been anything but amused when Ianys fainted before he could even greet him.

Ianys beamed, no doubt thinking about a different situation. "That she is." The pride faded from his eyes when Atèn began to cough again. Ianys walked over to the cot and knelt next to her.

"Want me to leave?"

"Why?"

Because Atèn wasn't supposed to know about us? Because I craved to hug him and I couldn't? I sighed. Neither were reasons to leave. Besides, he looked like he could use a distraction. I groped for something to say. "Are your parents enjoying having Fern and her family around?" I regretted my words immediately. Her children had fallen ill as well.

Ianys must have seen something in my eyes, because instead of answering my question, he said, "Zoet and Yrne would have succumbed to the summer bug sooner or later, Kel, whether here or at their new home."

If that was what it was. I took a breath and forced the thought from my mind. No use in making it worse. "Where are they off to?"

"A village close to the sea, at least two moons from here. You know what Fern's like when she's got her mind set on something. I can't believe they're leaving that gorgeous little mountain village for a windy village by the sea." Ianys shook his head, though his expression showed the fondness he had for his older sister. "And when you ask that vowed of hers about it, all Bolder answers is that he's always wanted to swim in the sea."

Bolder, if I remembered correctly, came from the same tribe the guide was born into, just across the mountains. He and Fern had met in a village way up north, where they'd both worked in the same infirmary. Fern as a healer, Bolder as a nurse. They moved from village to village every three or four turns. I should be grateful that Ianys had his roots firmly planted here.

Ianys yawned, and I trailed my fingers across his arm, making certain to keep it out of sight from Atèn, even though her eyes were closed. "Did you sleep at all?"

Ianys shook his head. "She was shivering in my arms all night. But it doesn't matter. I can sleep when she's better."

Taking a step back, I studied him with narrowed eyes. He was sweating and a bit pale, but he wasn't shaking with the effort of keeping the bellows going. His energy hadn't reached its limits yet. "All right. But when she is, you *are* going to sleep."

"Or what? You'll put me in the cells for the day?"

"Don't tempt me."

Ianys laughed. "Get back to me in a couple of days, and I might take you up on that. In the meantime, I could do with some strong tea. Mind making me some while you're here?"

"What you need is an apprentice," I said as I made my way over to his tiny door-less kitchen. I set water to boil, and reached for the goraf without asking Ianys what he wanted.

"Don't you start." Ianys took a large piece of iron and held it above the fire. "My parents have been nagging about searching in other villages, but I'd rather wait. There's a young elf who shows promise right here. He just turned fourteen, and I don't want him to have to go elsewhere because I already accepted an apprentice." He yawned again. "And I can't handle two of them."

"All right. I won't nag." But I'd have to make sure he took that rest.

A knock on the door stalled our conversation. Therdra, Ianys' mother, stood in the open doorway, watching me. Her expression was almost melancholy, a look I remembered from those long-ago days after Ianys had left me when she'd asked me how I fared. I wasn't sure why she was looking at me that way now. I finished making Ianys his tea, and poured Therdra a mug as well. Wishing them both a blessed day, I excused myself to make my rounds.

I'd barely made it outside when Therdra's voice rang out behind me, calling me to wait for her. What could she want from me? Had we been too obvious? I glanced back inside at Ianys, but he seemed as bewildered as I was.

Therdra smiled as she approached me, though the melancholy hadn't quite disappeared from her eyes. "I'm glad you and Ianys are speaking again, Kelnaht." She linked her arm through mine, dragging me with her as she walked along the side of the giant tree forge. She didn't stop until we were out of Ianys' sight, and she wasn't looking at me, either. "When Ianys told us you were no longer together and introduced Naia as his vowed, we didn't know what to think. You two were so in love all those turns ago." She finally lifted her gaze to mine. "What went wrong between you, Kelnaht?"

I blinked as I tried to comprehend what she was asking. At the same time the anger I still felt at Naia threatened to bubble up inside me. Ianys' deceased vowed had forced him to break with me and made him promise not to let me raise Atèn.

I forced my anger down and took a deep breath. "That's not for me to say." I pulled my arm out of hers. I had to get away before I said something I'd regret. "Please, excuse me." I turned around and followed the path into the village.

Nothing could get her question out of my mind. Not even having lunch with Taruif's kind-hearted and soft-spoken mother. Had Ianys not explained the situation to his parents? He loved me, it was in his eyes when he looked at me, but I couldn't help feel that old stab of betrayal again. He'd only told them we'd split up. An afterthought, as if I hadn't mattered. Ianys had only been thinking of Naia.

THE WORRIED EXPRESSIONS I met when I entered the village the next morning were the same as the day before. The scale of the nervous chattering, however, was new. Why were there so many elves hanging around outside the infirmary?

Instead of turning to the person closest to me for information—Kore's father, I assumed—I veered towards Ellon, who was flanked by two dirty-blond, male cloud-elves as wiry in build as Ellon was. All three scattered flour with every step they took, and they carried baskets of what smelled like fresh bread. I waited while Ellon gave the other two directions and sent them off with a quick slap to their arses.

"What's happening?"

Ellon didn't take his eyes off the two elves. "Healer Muros collapsed."

As I opened my mouth to ask him more, the guide and Elder Rynth stepped out of the infirmary, and the elves surrounding them burst into a cacophony of questions. The guide appeared about to collapse, his face as ashen as his hair, and if I didn't get him away from the throng of villagers, the elves would have even more to be concerned about. Muttering an apology, I took bread from Ellon's basket and wormed my way through the crowd.

Amongst questions about Ninge's health—he was hanging on, but still unconscious—Muros collapsing, and Fern and her vowed taking over, the guide didn't even protest when I slid next to him to support him. Elder Rynth shot me a grateful look.

"Report back here as soon as you can," she said and motioned for me to take the guide away.

He didn't utter a word of protest as I grabbed him by his arm and led him away from the chattering elves. Only when we reached his safehold did he manage to find his voice. "I need to be—"

I shut him up with a shake of my head and had him sit in his favourite spot with the bread. I was burning with need to know about the children, but I knew my duty was to stay with him. Belatedly, I thought about pouring us some juice or cleansing ourselves, but when the guide shut his eyes and settled into a more relaxed pose, I decided we could do without. The bread would have to suffice.

As soothing as the safehold was, I found myself watching the guide eat and relax for the first time in days, more than meditating myself. Of course, unlike the guide, I had had a decent sleep.

Because of his hair the colour of ash, his wise appearance, and the authority he wielded, the guide seemed much older than his age. It was easy to forget he was barely five turns older than Taruif. He carried so much responsibility for us all, and it was hard for him to let go, especially when a child was involved. It warmed my heart to see him try, if only for a moment.

I wished I knew what was going on at the infirmary. Solving a crime? That I could handle. This useless waiting, this wondering without having any part in events or being able to help, was nerve-wracking. Still, I could at least make sure the guide had rested.

When the guide re-opened his eyes and fixed his gaze on me, the edge of exhaustion had disappeared from his features.

"So Healer Muros collapsed?" I asked.

The guide took in a sharp breath and nodded. "Healing young Ninge pushed him to his limits."

Far past, if he'd collapsed. There was something in the guide's voice that suggested he wasn't telling me everything. "But Ninge is still with us?"

"He's hanging on, but barely. It's a mess, Kelnaht. Every time Healer Muros heals him, another part of young Ninge's body seems to shut down. And he hasn't woken even once."

"Does he have a chance, with Fern helping?"

That brought the guide up short. He stared at the floor for a long time before answering me. "I don't know. Healer Muros has been unable to find out what is causing young Ninge's organs to shut down. He hasn't had the time. He's been too busy trying to keep him from dying."

"But now he has Fern to help him," I pressed him.

The guide grimaced. "I tried talking him into it yesterday, but he wouldn't hear of it. Said he couldn't allow her in until he ruled out contagion. Which is why none of young Ninge's wider family are allowed back into the infirmary, and his mothers not allowed into his room. I think Muros's exhaustion affected his judgement. He needs to accept help."

I threw him a sharp look. One he waved off. "I'm resting now, aren't I?"

It took a lot of effort not to roll my eyes at him. "I guess merging our energies to support them is out of the question?"

"That depends on what Healer Fern decides. She is in charge now." The guide sighed. "At least as long as Healer Muros is out. But... if there's a risk of contagion, Healer Muros and Apprentice Zelg may well have caught it already. They barely spent a moment away from young Ninge's bed."

The guide was right. It was a mess. "Is there anything I can do?"

"You'll have to ask the elders, but clearing the elves away from the infirmary would be my guess."

It wasn't what I was asking for, but it would at least make me feel useful. "All right."

The guide made to rise, but I shook my head. "I understand your duty, Guide, but if you don't rest now, you'll be of no use to anyone. Sleep. For a little while, at least."

I didn't wait for his agreement, but when I reached the centre and he wasn't following me, I let out a breath and nodded to myself.

All elders were now standing outside the infirmary, speaking to the elves crowding them, but no one was listening. They were too busy shouting questions and demanding answers. I plucked a leaf off a nearby bush, held it between my thumbs and, with the aid of some energy, let loose with a loud, shrill whistle.

Everyone went quiet and turned to me.

"All of you. Go home!"

Murmurs rose up from the crowd, but I shook my head. "You're not helping young Ninge or Healer Muros by hanging around and demanding answers. The healers and elders understand your worries, and they will send news as soon as they have the answers we're all looking for. The best you can all do now is take care of your families fend your children." I wanted to add "and pray", but no doubt Ma'terra had been called upon many times in the past few days already.

I fixed my gaze on the chipped edge of a table as the crowd slowly dispersed and the elves went home, so I didn't have to see the disappointment, the fear, or the anger in their eyes. I wished I had the answers they were looking for, wished I could make promises that Ninge would pull through, that *all* the children would be all right, but the whole tribe knew the outcome was uncertain, and nothing I said would change their belief. Only seeing Ninge healed and playing outside with his brother and friends could do that.

Blessed Ma'terra, please make it so.

Chapter Twenty-One

C ROWD CONTROL, AS the elders called it, was my job for the next couple of days. Despite my request, more villagers turned up at the infirmary. Some sat with Ninge's family at the centre, chatting or playing knobbles, in quiet support. Others came demanding answers, though never the same villagers twice, not after getting a personal reprimand from me which included the promise of a night in the cells if they didn't leave.

Most of the time, I'd be sitting with Ninge's family—Ellon, Kore, and their two apprentices—and playing knobbles with them while we waited for news. In between, both Taruif and I made certain to visit Ianys whenever possible to check how he and Atèn were doing.

Ianys was working a piece of iron with a frown on his face when I walked into the forge. His hair was damp along the edges, clinging to his head. Droplets flew everywhere with every move he made, every shake of his head, and every slam of his hammer. The frown on his face never eased, not even when he nodded at the piece of iron and dipped it in the vat of cold water next to the anvil.

He hadn't heard me come in.

My gaze was pulled to the cot, but Atèn wasn't hidden beneath the blankets today. My heart pounded in my throat as I faced Ianys. But as I opened my mouth to draw his attention, footsteps sounded behind me, and I turned to find Ciper, Naia's mother, with a basket nearing the forge. She regarded me with the same polite but distant smile she always seemed to give me. The one that made me want to scream at her that I had no idea why her daughter had hated me.

Her soft, "Master Kelnaht," didn't seem to disturb Ianys at all, and I returned Ciper's greeting in the same way, even though I wanted to run. For a moment we stood watching each other, and I tried to pretend I had just finished business with Ianys. A habit I couldn't shake, even though we'd openly rekindled our friendship in the past five moons.

Friendship. I had no doubt that if she'd caught one glimpse of my expression while I'd been watching Ianys, she'd know exactly how deep our 'friendship' ran.

The hammering ceased, and I didn't need to turn around to realise Ianys was standing behind me.

"Anything wrong with Atèn? The boys?"

I wanted to reach out to Ianys at the harried tone of his voice, and let out a huge breath when Ciper shook her head. "They're fine. They're resting, and their fevers have dropped a bit already. All three of them." She held up the basket she was holding. "Therdra told me you missed lunch, again. I thought I'd save you some time."

"You didn't have to bring me lunch." Ianys' voice was shaky.

"I know. I thought we could talk for a moment." She glanced at me, a strange, inquisitive expression in her eyes. "But I didn't know you had a visitor."

Ianys looked from Ciper to me, and I tried to shake my head without her noticing. He held my gaze for a moment before turning back to Ciper and smiling at her. "He was asking after Atèn. I have time for a talk, if you want."

As soon as Ciper put the basket on the table, Ianys whispered, "I'll see if I can come by tonight."

I felt the urge to touch him, but resisted...barely. I wanted to talk to Ianys myself, but I wished them both an enjoyable lunch and left.

I hadn't even reached the centre before I bumped into a

stricken Novice Darver.

"Has Ninge—"

Darver shook his head. "No. He's still holding on, but two more children have been brought in. Young Dess fell unconscious on his way to the infirmary, but young Kitai is still awake. Both suffer high fevers and complained of headaches and light hurting their eyes."

"But young Kitai isn't unconscious?"

"No. At least, she wasn't when her father brought her in." Darver clenched his fists. "Oh, Master Kelnaht. What is going on?"

That was the question everyone needed answered, and to which no one had an answer. But with three children this ill, and Muros still healing himself, the healers were bound to need more energy than they had right now. "Where is the guide?"

"Inside. I wanted to be with them, but Healer Fern is sticking to Healer Muros' decision to not let too many people into the infirmary." He took a breath. "And the guide feels it's better if I stay here and be available for parents and children should they need me."

Of course he was inside. Stubborn fool of a guide. He should have rested more, should have let Darver inside with the children, since Darver was the one the children talked to. But even if I'd been there to stop the guide from going in, he would have sneaked past me, somehow. "And the elders?"

"Elder Sotih and Elder Garren are guarding the entrance."

"I'd best get over there and help them." I studied Novice Darver's face. "Where were you off to?"

"I...they're all so loud..."

I put my hand on his shoulder. "Go take some time in the safehold, and then do what the guide told you."

He seemed relieved at being told to get some rest. "Thank you, Master Kelnaht. If anyone needs me..."

"I'll tell them you'll be with them as soon as you can." I was not sending anyone to the safehold, barring an emergency.

"I won't take long."

I resisted telling him to take all the time he needed. At least he was smart enough not to take a path that led through the centre.

By the time I reached the infirmary, all the elders were gathered there. No villagers crowded them, so it seemed they had heeded my words, but the number of elves seated in the centre had nearly doubled. No doubt family of the other children. What had Darver said their names were? Right, Dess and Kitai. Were they friends with Atèn, too?

I took a deep breath. No use thinking about that now; I had other matters to see to. The matter of supporting the healers and nurses, for one. And there was no better time than now, with all the elders in one place.

Elder Sotih stopped my question before I could even ask it. "We've already discussed it, and Healer Fern agrees we can no longer wait for them to find out whether young Ninge is contagious." The way she grimaced, I assumed Muros had objected to their decision. "We've decided to round up some of our strongest elves, those without children, to support the healers in their work."

"I volunteer."

Elder Sotih shook her head. "I'm sorry, Master Kelnaht, but we cannot allow it. I'm sure you understand we can't risk our truth seeker becoming the victim of whatever sickness ails young Ninge."

"But—"

She held up her hand. "Our decision stands, Master Kelnaht. We need you to keep the peace."

I wanted to slam my fist against the wall. I wanted to help, not stand and watch, no matter how logical and reasonable elder Sotih sounded. My heart raced, but I managed to pull myself together and accept her decision. "How is Healer Muros?"

"Working. His energy levels are slowly rebuilding, and one of the nurses is watching over him to make sure he doesn't overexert himself again." She scanned the elves sitting at the centre and lowered her voice before continuing, "Though he claims pushing himself did not cause his collapse. Which is why he is objecting to our decision so vehemently."

"The others are holding up?" I didn't want Ianys having to worry about his sister as well as his daughter.

"They're tired, but the nurses are monitoring their energy levels at all times, and Healer Fern has asked us to set up a thorough cleansing of the infirmary. Which means, Master Kelnaht, that as much as I'd like to keep you informed, we need to get back to work."

There was nothing for me to do but let them do their job while I saw about mine.

I woke in the dark to someone knocking on our door. I wasn't the only one. Ianys went rigid in my arms at the next knock, and on Ianys' other side, Taruif shot up. "Who's that?" he asked as he pulled at the blanket to keep it from sliding off us.

"Master Kelnaht? Master Kelnaht!" a familiar voice yelled outside.

I groaned. "It's Novice Darver. I have to go." I kissed them both, dragged my body out of bed, and dressed. Ianys' panicked expression almost broke my heart, and I wished I could promise him everything would be all right. I couldn't hear anything specific in Darver's voice as he called out again, but my heart clenched at the idea of something happening to Ninge, or any of the children. Taruif and Ianys were both watching me with similar anxious expressions now, and I quickly ran down the stairs, not wanting my last image of our night to be this quiet hopelessness.

Novice Darver leaned heavily against our tree as I opened the door. He looked shattered and pale in the soft light of our lantern. "They tried," he said, tears in his eyes. "They tried so hard, but they couldn't save him."

I glanced towards the stairs and drew the door shut behind

me, trying to prevent Ianys from overhearing. I doubted Novice Darver had come here in the middle of the night only to tell me Ninge had died, and I waited to hear what he needed from me as I rested a hand on his shoulder and mumbled a quiet prayer to Ma'terra to watch over Ninge's essence.

"Healer Fern wants you to..." Darver voice gave. He cleared his throat and tried again. "To process the room as soon as you can."

"Process Ninge's room? Why?"

"Healer Fern needs you to confirm her findings for her. She said if she's right about what she's found, this can't wait till morning."

No time to waste, then. I closed the door, spread my wings, and took off. I'd already crossed the clearing when I realised Darver's flight was anything but smooth. He kept losing height, and it took him a lot of effort to even stay airborne.

I landed. "Come on down. We'll walk."

It seemed all guides showed a measure of stubbornness, because Darver refused and only shook his head—which, of course, made him lose height again. He pleaded with me to fly ahead, but I wasn't going to leave him behind, not as distraught as he was.

I grabbed him by the leg and pulled him down myself. "Shut up and start walking. We can't afford to lose the time."

By the time we reached the infirmary, Darver was ready to collapse, and I made him sit down as soon as we were inside. A nurse immediately came to get me, but not before performing a simple health shield. "A precaution," she said.

The reason became clear the moment I was let into Ninge's room. On one side of the room, Ninge lay on a bed, covered with a thin sheet. At least, I assumed the covered body was his. On the other side, Fern rested with her eyes closed and her cheeks flushed with fever. Nurse Bolder, her vowed, and Muros sat next to her bed. Muros was doing better than the last time I'd seen him, but Bolder showed signs of fever.

Fern opened her eyes when I approached the bed. "Don't

worry, Master Kelnaht. If I'm right, Bolder and I will be fine after some much-needed rest." She glanced at Ninge's bed, and her expression darkened. "But I fear for the children."

"What did you find?"

She raised her eyes to mine. "I have no personal experience with this, but there are tiny dark spots all over his organs. We checked for oermas infection, but while that causes rotting of organs, it has never caused anything close to what we've been healing these past few days. There is only one other thing that could have caused this much damage in such a short time. And if I'm right, we're no longer dealing with just an illness, we're dealing with murder."

Murder? I held my breath and wished for her to not speak the words I feared she was going to utter. If it was murder, then it was...

"Black root poisoning, Master Kelnaht. I think young Ninge died from black root poisoning."

That. If Fern was right, I was going to need a lot more than a nurse's health shield before examining Ninge. Being infected wouldn't kill me, but it would take me out a day, or two, and if this was black root poisoning, we couldn't afford to lose that much time. Not if we wanted to save our children.

By first light the next morning, Ninge's room had been processed and sealed off, Fern and Bolder's fevers were already coming down, and I was exhausted. Only continuous re-shielding had kept Nurse Calea and me from running a fever, but it had come close. Despite taking the time to go through my predecessors' notes at the archives beneath Elders' Court, I had not been able to confirm or rule out black root poisoning. The dark spots Fern had found on Ninge's organs contained no usable traces of black root spores for me to check. It was proof in a way, according to the notes, but not proof enough.

Which was why Taruif, elder Sotih, and I were out in the forest this early, searching for signs of trees infected by black root poisoning.

Taruif wasn't faring much better than I was. Before I hit the books, I'd gone back home to wake Taruif and ask what he knew. I was almost glad to find Ianys had already left. I couldn't tell him about the black root poisoning, not when he was already so worried about his daughter.

I was still trying to get my head around the fact we might have a case of black root poisoning on our hands. There was only one known case in the history of our village—or even our neighbouring villages—and that had happened almost sixty turns ago. Over half the children in the village had died before the cause had been found and the murderer caught.

Black root wasn't a natural tree sickness. Black root was elf-made, forester-made.

While the elders had made it clear they did not suspect Taruif, or Merel, in any way, they insisted elder Sotih should accompany us on our search. It would make it easier to reassure the tribe, should anyone disagree with their opinion.

As Taruif led us to the most obvious places, where the children went to play, he explained black root was easy enough to spot. "Lay the root bare and if it is black as soot, the tree is infected."

After applying shields to avoid infection, the two of us carefully bared the roots of every tree surrounding the first play area, with elder Sotih watching from a distance, but none of those trees were infected. Same with the next play area. Meanwhile, I thought over everything I remembered reading about the long-ago case.

The forester infecting the trees all those turns ago had been an elf named Pendra. According to the notes, everyone in the tribe had known she hadn't been terribly fond of children, but to find out she'd deliberately poisoned the trees to murder them had shaken the whole tribe. Her magic had been harnessed, and she had been banished for life. She would never be able to infect trees again. One less danger to the tribe, to any tribe.

Because of the severity of her crime, Mistress Pendra had also not been given permission for her essence to return after death. But I couldn't help wondering if she could have come back all these turns later, despite being banished. For what? She'd be powerless to infect even the smallest trees with her magic harnessed. But there was no one else I could think of who would do this to our children.

"Kel!"

Taruif's cry went straight through me, his voice full of fear. I ran towards him, my heart pounding, wishing him wrong. Until I saw the root he was bent over.

Bits of the root lay bare, black as soot, looking as though it would crumble to dust at the slightest touch. Which, according to our research, was exactly what would happen. The resulting dust carried spores ready to be inhaled by unsuspecting elves. Their traces were difficult to detect, and, on top of that, the spores left the dying body with the last breath, to be inhaled by the closest elf.

Black root made adults only slightly ill, but it could kill children whose energy hadn't settled yet. Settled energy provided a natural defence, and fought the spores, but a child's wild energy fed the spores, leaving the children without any means of defence. Ninge never had a chance once the spores had dined on his energy.

Taruif's face had gone pale. "Prin, my cousin…her baby is barely three turns old."

I wrapped my arms around him, and we stared at the black root until he had himself back under control.

Continuing our search under Elder Sotih's shocked and watchful eye, we discovered that only two young trees had been affected. But two were enough to kill. Even one would have been enough. Close by, an old oeral tree held a large swing. Whoever did this knew exactly which trees to infect.

Though I was eager to examine the area, Taruif wouldn't let me.

"Not before I've destroyed the black root. And I'll need to consult the notebooks for that. Couldn't find what I was looking for earlier."

No doubt because he'd been sending himself blind going over what he knew about detecting black root poisoning. "Then we need to secure this part of the forest. No one should come here until the trees and the black root are destroyed."

Taruif shuddered. "They summoned a forester from another village to take care of it last time. There should be a report of how to destroy black root."

"Do you know who they summoned?"

Taruif shook his head as he took goshe leaves out of his bag and knelt down to cover the bared roots of the first tree. "I know my mentor took over from them, a few moons after it happened, but I can't remember the name."

I grabbed some goshe leaves of my own and did the same with the second tree. As a visual warning, we wrapped string around a set of trees surrounding the area to make it inaccessible. Once we were done, elder Sotih had us merge our powers to create a repelling spell strong enough to hold off even the murderer. Or so we hoped.

We walked back to the village in silence. We'd been gone for hours, but life in the village was just starting up as we walked into the infirmary. As elder Sotih disappeared into the room where the other elders were staying, Taruif and I sat in the hall.

Taruif was trembling as I wrapped my arms around him. "What if the tribe think *I* did this?"

I pulled him closer. "You've heard the elders. They don't suspect you."

Ever since his sentence reduction this past winter, Taruif had been slowly reconnecting with his family, and the tribe that had pretended he didn't exist for so long. Too long. Everyone greeted Taruif now as he walked past. He visited his mother nearly every day. She dined with us regularly. I wouldn't let him slide back into believing the tribe thought him capable of this... this evil.

I needed to figure out who was responsible for infecting the trees with black root. I sent Ma'terra an apology for wishing for a case of theft to keep me busy. This was not what I'd asked for.

Of course Ma'terra had no hand in this, but I felt better for apologising.

CHAPTER TWENTY-TWO

SIDE BY SIDE, enjoying a mug of goraf tea, Taruif and I sat on the steps of our home and waited for Ianys to arrive. Taruif's eyes were closed, lines of exhaustion etched into his face, and he had a small number of notebooks stacked beside him, which he'd been poring over since he left the infirmary. They'd been written by Taruif's predecessor, spanning almost forty turns between Mistress Pendra's last entry about growing some mushrooms—dated after the first children had fallen victim to black root poisoning—and Taruif's first entry as forester. Taruif's predecessor had dreadful handwriting, and it had been a long time since Taruif had last had to read the books. He was having a hard time with it. Especially since he had yet to find a mention of black root poisoning, despite having spent most of his afternoon in the dreary archives beneath Elders' Court.

Crowd control and discussions with the elders on what needed to be done next had limited my own time to investigate the only known case of black root. When I finally managed to get to the archives, Taruif had been hunched over one of his notebooks, snoring. He'd reluctantly let me drag him out of there, bringing an armful of notebooks home with him, and make him dinner. He had to have been exhausted not to complain about my inferior cooking.

I couldn't help but smile as Taruif slid closer to me and leaned his head on my shoulder. I took his mug before he dropped it, put it down on the steps, and wrapped my arm around him.

"I'm not asleep," Taruif mumbled into my neck.

"You're not drinking, either."

"I've had enough tea, thank you."

I kissed the top of his head and finished my own tea as the sound of footsteps announced Ianys' arrival. At least, I hoped it was Ianys. Neither of us was awake enough for another crisis.

My heart raced, and I tried to shuffle back as Ianys stormed towards us. He grabbed me by my tunic, dragged me up, and pushed me against the tree—putting pressure on my wings— eyes shining with fury and lips trembling. "I can't believe you're sitting here drinking tea while Atèn may be in danger!"

Fern. The elders had been wary of letting the tribe know about the black root poisoning before a cure was found, so he had to have heard it from Fern. She should have known better.

I struggled to stay on my feet and tried to push Ianys off me, but he was too strong, too driven. Taruif clamped his hands around Ianys' wrists and forced him to let go of me. While Taruif pulled Ianys back, I wiggled my wings as I took deep breaths, hoping the pressure hadn't strained them.

"Be reasonable, Ianys." Taruif sounded calmer than he looked. "If he doesn't replenish his energy from time to time, he won't be of use to anyone. Least of all Atèn."

Ianys growled, fists clenched and panting with excess anger. "Then summon help from other tribes."

"And wait days for them to turn up?" I countered, trying not to let his anger rule me, even if my chest ached, and I could still feel the pressure of his knuckles. "The nearest village is over a day's flight away." I didn't want to let him know the elders had decided not to send messengers anywhere, for fear of spreading the black root poisoning.

Ianys deflated, eyes widening as he stared at me. I don't know what he saw, but he sank down on his knees and wrapped his arms around my legs. "I can't lose her, Kel. I can't."

I didn't even realise I was trembling until I ran a hand

through his hair trying to soothe him. I wished I could promise him he wouldn't lose Atèn, but I couldn't. Not when the healers had no idea how to save the children. But I wanted to.

I wanted all the children to be cured, wanted the murderer caught and stripped of their power. And much, much worse. The victims were children, for Ma'terra's sake, innocent children, defenceless against black root poisoning.

"I can't stop thinking about it," Ianys whispered, leaning his forehead against my hip, shivering. "I keep seeing her, drenched in sweat, screaming out her nightmares."

Taruif knelt behind him and rested his cheek against Ianys'. No words could soothe Ianys' fears now, so we didn't utter any. We stayed still and waited for Ianys to stop shivering.

When he finally did, Taruif kissed Ianys' cheek and put his hand on Ianys' shoulder. "Let us take your mind off it," he whispered.

I could almost hear the unspoken, "We could use a distraction as well."

Ianys let go of my legs and turned on Taruif so fast that I couldn't stop him from pushing Taruif to the ground. He jumped up, face contorted in anger. "Take my mind off Atèn? It's that easy for you, isn't it? Forget my daughter, as long as you can have me. But I can't forget. I can't just *take my mind off* her. You have no idea what it's like to sit by her bed while she has nightmares. Or not being with her when she's in pain. She means everything to me, but you barely ask after her. And I'm still here while she is fighting a fever, wondering if she's breathed in poisonous spores!"

Taruif looked up at him, his face showing the same shock I felt. "No. I…I only meant to comfort you."

"That was uncalled for," I told Ianys, but he raised his fists at me instead.

"Don't *you* talk to me."

There was so much anger in his voice, so much despair. I moved towards him, but he swung a fist at me, forcing me to step back.

"Atèn is ill, and all you two can think about is sex, instead of..." His voice broke, and his whole body shook as he panted, anger coming off him in almost tangible waves. "I don't want to see either of you. I have Atèn to think of."

He stomped off, fists clenched by his sides. I was torn between running after him and letting him go.

Taruif shook his head at me. "He won't listen now." It was the pain in his voice more than what he said that made up my mind. We had to let Ianys go.

Taruif was trembling as I helped him up, much as I was. Ianys disappeared through the trees, and we were left staring at nothing.

"I truly didn't mean..." Taruif sagged against me.

I wrapped my arms around him. "I know. And I think he'll know as well, when he thinks about it." When he calmed down. When Atèn was better. "He's worried." Rightly so. We were all worried, but it was too close to home for Ianys. "Come. We need to rest."

But rest would not come. Neither of us could fall asleep. I reached for Taruif's hand as he rolled onto his back for the umpteenth time. He grabbed me back, hard, and rolled into me, clinging to me as I clung to him. And still we couldn't find rest.

In the end, we reached for the only possibility left to calm us.

Taruif devoured more than kissed me, determined to drive all thoughts from our heads. He moaned and squirmed against me as I tightened my hold on his hands, forcing them above our heads.

We fell into some sort of rhythm, right up to the point where I could feel Taruif's muscles tightening, his body stiffening. I pushed hard against him, bursting to come, but I wanted Taruif to take his pleasure first. He was close, trembling with need, his eyes on me, his fingers flexing against mine. He was beautiful when he came, beautiful as he kept bucking against me.

It didn't take much more to send me over. I closed my eyes as we panted and shuddered against each other, sharing butterfly kisses until our heartbeats slowed down.

Afterwards, holding each other close, sheets pulled over ourselves to keep us warm in the middle of the night, our thoughts returned to Ianys.

"He won't leave because of this, will he?" Taruif asked, the worry clear in his voice.

"No," I answered, but I wasn't so sure.

We should have been there for him, with him. Instead we were here, together, while he was with Atèn, alone. I'd never felt guilty about Ianys not being with us before, but I did now. It felt wrong to me, and from the way Taruif was looking at me, tears in his eyes, it was clear he felt the same.

Both Taruif and I slept fitfully, and were up well before sunrise, with our noses in our notebooks. We occupied a corner of our sofa each, notebooks and silence balanced precariously between us. Ianys leaving the way he had didn't sit well with us. But instead of searching him out, talking it out, we'd opted to continue our research. Fighting black root, and finding the murderer would speak louder than any words we could think of.

Not wanting to miss any mention, I re-read the books from about a turn before the incident happened. At moments like this I missed Brem. Missed having someone to help me with time-consuming tasks, though, my new apprentice was supposed to arrive any day now.

At least these notes were legible. Taruif was still trying to decipher his mentor's scribblings. Which made it even more painful when I was the one to find the information he needed. It was in a couple of torn pages folded into one of my notebooks. On the back of the folded pages someone had written: *BR/Mistress Valen/evidence.*

I unfolded the pages, and found everything I thought Taruif needed, written down in clear script by a forester called Valen. I tried to grab Taruif's attention, but he was so absorbed by what he was doing, he didn't hear me the first or even the fifth time. In the end, a firm tug at his trousers made him gaze up at me, blinking.

"What?"

I waved the pages in front of him. "Vorsen grounds is what she used to destroy the infected trees."

"What?" He blinked again. "She who? How do you know?"

"Because her account of the case was folded into my notebooks."

"Whose account?"

"Mistress Valen. The forester the tribe sent for."

Taruif took the pages from me and started reading. "Oh. It says she had passed the forester's test that same moon, but was the only forester available at the time." Taruif didn't take his eyes off the page as he shook his head. "She fell ill the first time she tried to destroy the infected trees because she forgot to shield herself."

He read the rest of the pages in silence, but before I could focus on my own notebook, he spoke up again.

"I think I would have liked to have met her. Feverish or not, she didn't give up. She tried a lot of things before she found out about the vorsen grounds. Though…" Taruif looked up. "I can't believe something as simple as vorsen grounds actually worked."

Vorsen grounds were sweet-tasting seeds, ground to a pulp and mixed with water. It was mostly used to feed babies when they couldn't drink their mother's milk. They were also used for a sweet dessert porridge.

"According to the notes, the vorsen grounds have to be fresh. That means I can't use the dried ones in store." Taruif sighed and refolded the pages. "Guess I'll be hunting down vorsen seeds the rest of the day."

"How long?"

Taruif rose. "They don't grow close, but if I go now, I might make it back before sunset."

"Take Merel with you."

For a moment it seemed Taruif might protest, but then he

nodded. "Will you let the elders know where I'm going? I don't want to waste time."

"As soon as I'm done going through these." I pointed at my notebooks.

Taruif rested his hand on my shoulder and tried for a smile. "I hope it won't be much longer." I wasn't certain whether he meant the notebooks, or us being away from Ianys.

I let out a sigh, but couldn't form the words. Instead I closed my eyes and leaned in to kiss his hand. I dreaded resuming my reading. What if there wasn't a solution? What if more children —Atèn—became sick, or died?

But there had to be an answer. Some of the children had survived last time, so they must have found a cure. I opened my eyes, focussed on the notebook in my hand, and went back to reading.

Ten pages later I had yet to find anything useful. Someone knocked, and I rose with a sigh and opened the door.

It was Novice Darver, looking distraught, though less exhausted. My throat closed, and against hope, I prayed for the children to be all right.

"Oh. You have to come, Master Kelnaht. He's...he's...there's blood everywhere."

"Blood?" I grabbed Darver by the arm. "What happened?"

"He stumbled into the centre covered in blood."

"He who?"

Darver pulled his arm free and gestured towards the village. "Your new apprentice."

Chapter Twenty-Three

"Joren?"

Joren, a stocky, winged stripling, fell to his knees as I reached him, grabbing the bench to steady himself. His short blond hair was matted with blood, his tunic and trousers soaked in it. He was out of breath and his voice croaked as he pleaded, "You have to come help me, Master Kelnaht. I did everything I could, but he was too heavy and cried out every time I tried and—"

I grabbed his shoulders to stop him from talking. "Are you wounded?"

Joren blinked hazy, pale blue eyes at me, then stared at his bloody hands. "Oh. Er... No. It's not mine. It's his." He pointed at Novice Darver. "I told him it wasn't mine. But he's hurt so badly, and I couldn't—"

"Where?" I interrupted him. If this was not his, and someone out there was wounded enough for this much blood to soak into Joren's clothes, we couldn't waste any time.

More blinking. Joren wet a thumb, and raised a shaky arm. He stared at his thumb as it caught the wind, biting his lip, and finally pointed at the path leading past the cells.

"Right. Sit." I turned to Novice Darver. "Can you arrange a cart?"

Darver nodded and walked off while I made some tea for Joren. By the time Novice Darver returned with cart and driver,

Joren's hair was blood-free and clinging wetly to his head. Someone had been kind enough to give him clean clothes, although they were somewhat on the large side. I'd wrapped Joren's bloody clothes in goshe leaves and told Darver to take them to my workshop.

Joren rose, pale and unsteady. I wanted to leave him behind, but he wouldn't hear of it. I could have locked him in the cells, but he deserved better than that. I hoped he'd doze off in the cart, but he stayed awake and alert enough to tell the driver where to go.

"Do you know what happened?" I asked him as we both knelt down next to the victim.

His face was lax and bloodied, and he was covered in a thick cloak that didn't match the colourful clothes peeking out from underneath. It wasn't a familiar face. Even pale, his skin had an undertone of the warm, light brown colour of erst bark.

I rubbed my hands together and held them above the victim's heart and mouth. His heart rate was thready, but he was still breathing, if unsteadily. He was also unconscious.

"No. This is how I found him. His breathing was shallow, and he wasn't reacting when I tried to wake him up."

Where had this elf, this traveller, come from? Couldn't be anywhere near, because no elf like him had ever passed through our village. His hair was a shock of bright red; a strange combination of bound and loose curls, decorated with colourful beads. His face was delicate, with gentle features and long lashes.

"I'm not sure they're male, Joren."

"Oh."

I carefully removed the cape and flinched at the sorry sight of the elf's wings. They were badly torn in a number of places, and there was a gash across his shoulder that bled through loose bindings of blue fabric, not unlike Joren's bloody tunic, pushed beneath the elf's ripped clothing. "You bandaged them?"

Joren nodded. "He—I'm sorry, *they* bled when I tried to pick them up. I took some tunics from my bag to try and stop the bleeding." He bit his lip. "I didn't bring a healing kit with me."

I waved off Joren's excuses. It didn't matter what he'd used to bind the wounds, as long as he knew how. Despite the bloody mess, he hadn't done too badly.

As if the traveller's peculiar hairdo wasn't enough, they were wearing the most curious clothing. Their trousers were more like a collection of different strips of fabric, as colourful as the beads in their hair, bound together at waist and ankles. Their scraped knees peeked through the strips.

Motioning for the driver to come closer with the plank, I told Joren to take the traveller's feet. "Can you shove the plank underneath them when we lift them up?"

The driver nodded and knelt with the plank.

"Watch out for their wings." I warned him.

Another nod, followed by a gruff, "I'm ready."

I knelt down next to the traveller's head. I couldn't fold the wings, so I had to drape them over the traveller, who keened and jerked, no matter how carefully I tried to handle them. "I'm sorry," I whispered as Joren and I tilted and lifted them.

They let out a bloodcurdling scream, but the driver was quick to shove the plank under them and we lowered them before we hurt them too badly. We left their wings draped over them as the driver and I picked up the plank and carried them over to the cart.

The traveller whimpered at even the tiniest movement, despite being unconscious, but stilled once we settled them into the cart. Joren and I sat on either side of the traveller, and we braced ourselves for a difficult ride. The journey back to the village seemed to take a lot longer than the trip out, and I wasn't sure whether to be grateful or worried when the traveller stopped making any sound.

When we carried them into the infirmary, Nurse Yasca was waiting for us. "Bring him in." She led us past the children's rooms and into the last room on the left. The room was dark and the beds were empty.

The driver and I put the cloud elf in the bed, plank and all.

"What happened to him?" Yasca asked.

"I don't know," Joren answered. "I found them like this."

Yasca threw me a puzzled look. "Them?"

"We're not quite sure of their gender," I explained.

"All right. Found them where?"

Joren barely knew the area, so I answered for him "In the fields close to Uriek Pond."

The door opened, and Fern entered the room, holding her hands up to show she'd already cleansed them. Yasca whispered something to her, and stepped out of the way.

"How long since you found them, young Truth Seeker?" No doubt the whole village had heard of Joren's arrival by now.

Joren frowned as he thought about it. "When I arrived the sun stood high." He hung his head. "I know I spent too much time bandaging him, and I haven't even secured the site, but—"

Fern held her hand up to quiet him. "You can argue with your mentor about priorities later. Let's see if we can fix them up."

Eyes wide, Joren nodded and faced me. I shot him a reassuring smile. He had much to learn, but he had done the right thing in taking care of the victim before securing the scene.

Fern moved her hands over the traveller's body and scanned them. "They've lost a lot of blood. The shoulder wound seems to be the worst, but they have some nasty breaks, including their wings." She held her hands over the traveller's neck. "This wasn't an accident, Master Kelnaht. Someone or something choked them." She glanced my way. "You might want to check that out."

Assuming she meant after the healing, I nodded at her.

She glared at me. "Time's wasting, Truth Seeker."

"Don't you want to heal them first?"

"And erase the bruises from around their neck? Just be quick about it, will you?"

I opened my mouth, and closed it again. I'd been too focussed on saving the traveller, not on gathering evidence. With a sigh, I took my bag of herbs and cleansed my hands. Scanning the traveller's neck reminded me of Brem drawing the fingerprints, last time we had a case that involved choking.

Joren was too inexperienced to know what I'd want from him, so I'd have to do it myself, but I did need paper. "Nurse Yasca. Can you get me some paper and a pencil, please?" I asked without looking up from my scanning.

This choking hadn't been done as 'carefully' or 'lovingly' as in the case one and a half turns ago. This had been brutal. And not done with hands. There were no fingerprints at all. The imprints rising to the skin's surface resembled the links of a necklace. But these links were larger than any necklace I'd ever seen, and judging from the dainty and colourful wristbands the traveller wore, it was doubtful the necklace had been theirs.

A piece of paper was held in front of me. I hadn't even heard the door.

"I can do that," Joren piped up next to me. He had rolled up the sleeves of his borrowed tunic and cleansed his hands. He took the paper from Yasca before I could and bent over the elf. The way he held the pencil over the elf's neck, using his thumb to measure the size of the links, was a little clumsy, but it would do.

I moved my hands to the traveller's face and scanned a bruise beneath his right eye. The shape of the bruise resembled a fist. Not a large hand, smaller than mine. "Any breaks in the bone beneath?"

"Not there, no," Fern said, "Not enough force."

It turned out to be the least severe wound they'd suffered. Yasca cut clothing away as I moved my hands, while Joren tried to keep up with the drawing. His work wasn't as detailed and neat as Brem's, but it was usable. I still caught the trembling of his hands, no matter how hard he tried to hide it. This was a tough first day of his apprenticeship. I admired his determination.

The traveller's body—thin, wiry, no breasts—showed many bruises. And most weren't caused by fists like the one on their cheek. They all showed the same pattern as the bruises around their neck. Whatever this chain of links had been, it had been heavy enough to do a lot of damage. But why?

"I'm afraid I can't allow you to turn them over, Master Kelnaht. Not with their wings in this mess. I hope you understand," Fern said as I'd finished scanning. "And with all of us running on limited energy, I can't allow you to stay in the room as I heal them, either."

I nodded. "I know. I do need images of the damage done to their back, though." I turned to Yasca. "I'd like a drawing of where the wounds on their back are. You don't need to draw details, unless something other than this shape shows up."

"I can do that."

"Thank you. How are you on energy, Healer Fern? Really?"

"I'm fine for now. But Yasca will get me back up should I need it. Now, please, leave, so I can heal them."

WE'D BARELY STEPPED outside, when Elder Rynth stopped us.

"Have you seen Master Taruif, Master Kelnaht?"

I could have slapped myself for forgetting to send someone to tell the elders where Taruif was. "He and Apprentice Merel are looking for vorsen seeds," I said, and passed along the information we'd found.

"We'd found a mention of Mistress Valen's solution of vorsen grounds in the elders' archives as well, but only a line or two. We hoped Master Taruif had more information. Good of him to take immediate action."

"He expected to be back before sunset."

"Good. Good," Elder Rynth said, though she seemed preoccupied.

"If that's all, Elder Rynth, I'd like to get my apprentice cleaned up."

She blinked and only then seemed to notice Joren and his dishevelled state. "Yes. Right. Novice Darver reported about that situation earlier." She bowed her head in greeting. "Pleased to meet you, Apprentice Joren. I understand you've had quite the day already. I hope that hasn't put you off moving here?"

"No, Elder."

I had a feeling Joren was too shaken to say anything else. I bade Elder Rynth goodbye for the both of us, and took him home.

Joren seemed relieved to be ordered into the bathroom for a wash, while I took some extra bedding from the chest in the corner and took them downstairs. Our dwelling only had the one bedroom, so I readied the sofa in the living room for Joren. It would have to do for now. I wasn't going to let him sleep in my old dwelling on his own.

Joren was barely sixteen turns old and, from what I'd seen of his overbearing parents when I'd gone out to interview him, not used to living on his own. Though I'd had several families offer to take him in, I liked Novice Darver's suggestion that he would move into my old dwelling above my workshop with Joren and act as his guardian. I was certain the guide had a hand in Darver's offer, but if Joren wanted to give independence a try, living with Novice Darver wasn't a bad choice for a shy but intelligent stripling like Joren. But for tonight, he'd be sleeping here.

When I was done, I set water for tea to boil, and took the stairs to the bedroom. Joren sat on the chair wrapped in the towel.

I frowned. "Didn't you bring any spare clothes?" I asked, and remembered too late that he'd used one of his own tunics to dress the traveller's wounds.

"I don't know where I left my bag," Joren said, sounding embarrassed.

Right. I hadn't seen him with a bag, but I hadn't seen a bag at the crime scene, either. Maybe he'd left it at the centre, the infirmary, or in the cart. "We can search for it tomorrow," I said as I reached into the wardrobe for an old tunic and pair of trousers. I grabbed an extra tunic as well. "To sleep in."

When he came down, he sat on top of the bedding, looking lost. I handed him a mug of goraf tea and settled on the chair closest to him. "Are you all right?"

Joren blew softly into the mug. "I'm fine, Master."

I didn't have a lot of experience in dealing with striplings, but I knew a thing or two about apprentices—well, one apprentice—and Joren was not fine, at all. But he clearly didn't want to talk to me about it, and that meant I'd have to drag Novice Darver out of bed at sunrise to make sure Joren would be fit to join me tomorrow. The last thing I needed was an overwrought stripling. Hoping to take his mind off the ordeal, I asked about his family.

Joren seemed eager to talk. He told me about the games he and his younger brothers played, and about flying with his loving but too-protective father. I let him talk and talk until his eyes drooped and he nearly dropped his mug. It was empty, and had been for some time, but Joren had kept playing with it as he spoke. I took the mug and draped the sheets over him, wishing him a blessed rest.

Too lazy to heat water to rinse the mugs, I spelled them clean and put them away. It was getting dark out, past sunset, and I was anxious for Taruif to return. With a sigh, I slipped out of our dwelling and sat down on the steps, mentally hurrying Taruif along.

Finally a twig snapped, and Taruif appeared through the trees. He wore a weary smile as he slipped into my arms and kissed me. My heart skipped a beat, but I had to stop him when he tried to push me inside.

"We have a visitor."

Taruif glanced toward the bedroom window, a hopeful expression in his face. "Ianys?"

My stomach clenched. I hadn't seen Ianys at all today. "I'm sorry. No. Joren, my apprentice." I told him about the wounded traveller.

"So that's what all that muttering about a new arrival in the infirmary was about. I thought maybe another child had fallen ill."

"I'm not certain this is better. They were severely beaten.

Joren and I are going back to where he found them to secure and process the scene in the morning."

Taruif yawned. "I have to get up early to grind vorsen seeds."

"You found them then?"

A nod. "More than I expected. But it took a long time." And another yawn. "Merel slept in the cart most of the way back."

Right. Time for bed. I took his hand and led Taruif inside, shushing him when he tried to talk and pointing to where Joren was sleeping. Upstairs, I helped him undress, tucked him in, and climbed in with him as soon as I'd shed my own clothes.

Neither of us talked about the Ianys-shaped void in our bed.

Taruif's body was chilled as I plastered myself against him, despite the warm weather. His heartbeat was slow and steady beneath my hand, but his tattooed vines seemed dull in the moonlight. He yawned again and closed his eyes as he drew me even closer.

Chapter Twenty-Four

J OREN AND DARVER hit it off right away when I introduced them, and I left them to talk while I checked in with the elders. They were unavailable, so I went to see how the healers' newest patient was instead. Because they hadn't awoken yet, Nurse Calea was hesitant to let me in, but when I assured her I'd shielded myself, she allowed me a few moments.

I wasn't so much surprised by the guide sitting next to the new patient as by his expression. I couldn't quite decipher it, but it wasn't one I'd seen on him before. Not even a cough from me could drag his attention away from the traveller. I grabbed a chair and set it next to the one the guide was sitting on. Only when I reached out to tap his shoulder did the guide turn towards me.

"Oh, Kelnaht. Did we have an appointment?"

I shook my head. "I came to see how the new patient was doing."

"Not as good as I'd have hoped," came Fern's tired voice from the doorway. She looked far too haggard for this early in the day.

"Are the children all right?" I asked.

"Again, not as good as I'd have hoped. We're fighting and not losing yet, but it's close. We can't keep the poison from spreading." She dragged a chair over and sank down on it. "But about this patient."

Only the traveller's head and the tips of their wings were visible above the sheets. They lay in the middle of a wide bed to keep their wings from hanging off the sides.

"I've managed to heal most their breaks and wounds." Fern let out a breath. "Not their wings, unfortunately, or rather, not their left wing. The right responded well to healing, but the damage to the left one is too extensive. We've splinted it best we could, but it's doubtful it will grow back. If it doesn't, we'll have to amputate."

Amputate? I shuddered, and my wing muscles twitched in sympathy. Even the loss of half a wing would ground the traveller. Their wings might still be strong enough to carry them, but their balance would be skewed, and the tiniest breeze from the wrong direction would have them adrift in the air, or plunging to the ground.

"How long until they regain consciousness?"

"There's no saying right now. They could wake up any time, but I doubt they'll be fully aware before tomorrow." Fern shook her head. "But even then they might not be able to tell you anything about their attack. The choking damaged their vocal cords. I did my best, but it might be a while before they can talk. If ever."

That did not sound good at all.

The guide hovered his hand over the traveller's still body. "Anything on what they were choked with?"

"Not yet. Joren and I will be processing the scene as soon as he's finished talking to Novice Darver."

"Is he all right?" the guide asked.

"He says he's fine. I sent him to Novice Darver to make sure he's up to working."

Fern pushed herself up from the chair. "If you find out anything that might help me in healing my patient, let me know, will you?"

"I will." Though I feared nothing I'd find at the scene would tell me why someone had beaten the traveller this badly.

When Fern left the room, I faced the guide. "Do you have

any idea where they come from?"

"There are a couple of tribes they might belong to, but we can't risk a messenger." The guide put a hand on the sheet when the traveller moaned, moving it in a circular manner, as if he were rubbing the back of the traveller's hand. They quieted down instantly.

"Are you calming them down?"

"Don't tell Healer Fern, but they have nightmares."

"You can sense that?"

The guide shot me a rueful smile. "I can, yes."

"Dare I ask how?"

"They know I'm a guide and their essence is calling to me."

There was something in the guide's expression that made me wonder if he was telling the truth. I narrowed my eyes. "What are you hiding? Do you know them?"

"No. Nothing like that. I promise you, Kelnaht. If I find out who they are, I will tell you."

I still thought he was leaving something out, but I let it go. "Then I'm glad you're here to calm them."

The guide drew in a breath as he continued his rubbing motions. "I know it's not the same, Kelnaht. They weren't designed for cloud elves. But do you think it would work? The wings?"

I couldn't pretend not to know what the guide was talking about. This past winter, a troubled elf named Sorse, bent on stopping the reduction of Taruif's sentence, had kidnapped a stripling. Sorse had been killed by his sister after we'd arrested him, but we'd discovered that he'd been working on artificial wings, created from bone and shanna leaves.

I didn't want to think about Sorse and his hatred of Taruif, but the guide had a point. Perhaps the wings could help the traveller. "We know they work as a whole. Brem tested them time and time again. But I don't know if they can be adapted to fit the traveller." And I wasn't certain about using them at all. I thought I'd made my peace with their existence, their usefulness, but...they'd been created by an elf with nothing but revenge in his heart, and I couldn't see past that.

"Yes. They probably won't work." His eyes were telling me he wished differently, though.

I couldn't imagine not being able to fly again. To soar on a breeze. Maybe it could be made to work; maybe wings made of bone and shanna leaves could help this traveller fly again. *If* they woke up.

As if that was the worst we were dealing with right now. I had a murderer to catch, and children to save. "I'd best go—"

The guide squeezed my hand in a crushing grip and froze for a moment. I put my hand over his, trying to pull free, but his trembling grip was too strong for me.

"What is it?" I asked, but the guide had his eyes closed and didn't even seem to hear me.

The next moment, he slumped into the chair with a pained cry. "I know who attacked them. And old, grey-haired elf. Cold eyes. A female."

His voice sent a shiver down my spine. "Grey hair?" Why did that sound familiar to me?

Ianys? No, not Ianys. Atèn. She had dreamed about an old grey-haired elf coming after her. It couldn't be a coincidence.

I muttered a hasty farewell to the guide and all but ran out of the infirmary to look for Ianys. It didn't even dawn on me to ask how the guide knew what the elf had been dreaming about until I reached the forge. No doubt some secret guide power.

IANYS WAS HAMMERING away at some hot piece of iron when I entered the forge. His tunic stretched across his muscled, sweaty back as he hit the iron again and again. If only I could plaster myself against him and everything would be all right. But it wasn't, and I cleared my throat as I called his name.

At least Atèn wasn't lying in the cot today. An open conversation about her nightmares would be difficult enough without her here.

"Ianys!" He still didn't hear me. Of course he didn't, not with all the hammering going on. But I couldn't wait. Joren should be finished talking to Darver by now, and we had a crime scene to process and an old elf to find.

I moved as close as I dared and called his name again, louder this time. When that didn't help, I waved my arms about to draw his attention as I all but yelled his name.

He started and nearly dropped his hammer. He glared at me as he put it down and checked his work. With an irritated sigh, he put the iron back into the fire. "This had better be important, Kel."

He said Kel, not Kelnaht. Maybe not all was lost between us. "I'm sorry." For interrupting him, for making him feel we weren't worried about Atèn, for everything. "I wouldn't—"

His gaze mellowed for a moment. "I know. What is it?"

"You mentioned Atèn was having nightmares."

Ianys' eyes widened. "*That's* what you're here for? Atèn's nightmares? Why do you need to know?"

"There is a wounded traveller in the infirmary who dreamed about a grey-haired elf." I didn't dare tell him she had attacked the traveller. He was on edge enough. Though, how an old elf had managed to wound anyone so severely was beyond me. Her powers had to be strong.

"A traveller? And you think it's connected?"

"With them and your daughter dreaming about what sounds like the same elf? Yes, I do." It gave me shivers.

He tilted his head and stared at me. Then he huffed and relaxed his stance. "Her nightmares remind me of those stories Mum told us when we were younger. About the wicked ones who preyed on misbehaving children?"

"My mum told me the same ones. But that was about a whole tribe, not one single elf. And they were said to hunt in groups, if they even exist. I'm sure your mother or Mistress Ciper told Atèn the same stories, and I'm sure she knows the difference." Not to mention those elves had nothing to do with black root poisoning. "What do you remember Atèn saying? Did she mention any details?"

Ianys leaned his gloved hands on his anvil and closed his eyes. "She mentioned the grey hair, being scared and running away. She mentioned whispering and being caught. Bony hands grabbing her arm, and cold eyes staring right through her. And that was when she'd wake up." Ianys opened his eyes. "She was screaming and shaking, every single time."

Cold eyes. Another similarity. "How is she?"

He gave me a distant look. "Her fever is down, finally. Last night was the first time she didn't have that blasted nightmare."

"Good to hear." I reached out to caress his cheek, but stopped myself and ran my hand through my hair instead. "Only one more question, then you can go back to work. Did Atèn ever mention seeing the old elf?"

"You mean here? In the village?" His voice took on a panicked note, and I wished I didn't have to ask. "No. No, she hasn't mentioned anything like that. Only her dreams."

"Thank you." I wanted to touch him, to reassure him, but I didn't want him to take it the wrong way, so I merely nodded.

I turned and left, only to freeze when Ianys continued, "She keeps saying she can still hear the old elf's belt clinking."

Ianys' comment about the clinking belt ran through my mind the rest of the morning, while Joren and I searched for his bag—we found it next to a bench in the centre—and as we secured the crime scene. The belt was never far from my thoughts. Could it be the chain used to strangle the traveller?

Most of what we found at the crime scene were traces of blood and scraps of paper. We dug out clumps of bloodied grass from the dry ground—there hadn't been any rain in weeks—and picked up every last scrap, wrapping everything we found in goshe leaves. I had no doubt most of the blood belonged to the traveller. The attacker had taken great care not to leave any evidence.

Unfortunately, the dry weather meant no useful footprints. So I was surprised when Joren discovered drag marks, slightly wider than wheel marks, leading us to a shallow stream. Something had been dragged away from the scene, tearing at grass and weed, and sending up sand dust, leaving spatters of blood in its path. Something that needed cleaning.

The more I stared at the marks, the more certain I became they had been made by the clinking belt Ianys had mentioned. The impression of links we'd found on the traveller's body could fit with a chain belt. Though, why drag it and leave traces instead of carrying it to the stream? Had it been so bloodied the attacker hadn't wanted to soil their hands?

I needed to find that belt. Surely it would bring me closer to finding out who had attacked the traveller, and why.

I kept thinking of Mistress Pendra, who had caused the first black root poisoning. She'd be old enough to fit the description of the grey-haired elf. But it was a ridiculous thought. She might have been capable of wielding a heavy belt to injure a fit young elf, despite her age, but with her powers harnessed she couldn't have infected the trees with black root. Besides, why would she come back to the tribe that had declined to allow her essence to return after death?

I shook myself out of my thoughts and helped Joren pack up the last of the evidence. None of my musing would be of any use unless I found proof. Right now, all I had were traces of blood and scraps of paper that could be the answer to all our questions… or nothing at all.

BACK IN THE workshop, after a thorough cleansing, Joren and I unpacked in silence. I was so caught up in processing the first scraps of paper, that I didn't notice Joren wasn't at my side until I wanted to ask his opinion. Instead he stood at a distance, biting his lip as he furiously scribbled in his notebook. My first instinct was to ask him what he was doing so far away, but I held my tongue as it dawned on me I hadn't invited him closer. I'd been too preoccupied with what we'd found, with the thoughts in my head, to mentor him properly, and I cursed myself. I had to do better. Especially with Joren so eager to learn, despite what he'd gone through the day before.

I knocked on the table. "Come, put your notebook on that empty corner, and scan these scraps." I indicated the ones I'd already worked on, wanting to gauge his insight. He should at least be able to tell they were made from the same materials.

Joren frowned and worried his lip as he concentrated on the scraps. "The pieces contain the same mixture of grass and bast fibres."

"Not bad."

He was hesitant and not quite sure of himself, not unexpected from an apprentice. But when we continued to the blood samples, he was more knowledgeable than I remembered him. "You have been practising."

His cheeks flushed as he nodded. "Yes. Master Hirde allowed me to watch him work when one of his apprentices hurt her leg. Only a couple of days, but it was fun, and he said he wished he could have trained me himself."

"He told me that, too. Would you have preferred that?" Joren hadn't said anything about it when I interviewed him.

"No. Mama would have insisted I stay at home, instead of moving in with Master Hirde, like his apprentices usually do. And I didn't want that."

Ah. He might not have said as much, but I'd read him right, at least.

"Darver… Novice Darver told me about acting as my guardian. He said you approved. I think I'd like that."

Just like that, he seemed more like the stripling I'd met than the one I'd seen the day before. "By all means, you can make arrangements with Novice Darver after we've finished."

He smiled, cheeks still flushed. "Thank you."

"Don't thank me, it was all Novice Darver's idea. Now, we had best get back to work, hadn't we?" Back to the blood samples.

Or, that was the plan, until Elder Morenn entered the workshop without knocking.

"We gathered a search party, Master Kelnaht, flyers only. You can leave at any time."

"A search party?"

"Has no one informed you? I apologise, it's been a busy morning." Elder Morenn took a deep breath and ran a hand through her long hair. "A hunting party found a fox chewing on some remains south towards the Kalan Mountains."

"Remains of what?" Not elven, I hoped.

"Chicken. They don't dwell there, and so far no one has reported any missing."

Which could mean an outsider's presence in the forest. No doubt the elders thought it had something to do with the black root poisoning. It was a flimsy lead at best, but considering the circumstances, one that should be checked out.

Joren and I wrapped up as fast as we could, and ate while I instructed the ten-elf search party. After this past winter, I'd insisted on a small group being trained for searches in case of another abduction—or worse—and the elders had agreed. I still wasn't comfortable with others doing part of my task, but at least they weren't clueless. I created two groups. One, led by me and Joren, would stay low to the ground, zigzagging around the tree trunks—and one, led by an elf named Riak, would fly high above the trees for a broader search.

We scanned the area between the village and where the remains of the chicken had been located and found nothing that betrayed a presence in the forest. Whoever had been out here was good at hiding their tracks. There were no traces on the chicken bones either, which were scraped clean and only showed the marks of fox teeth.

I widened the search, and still we found nothing. Had the chicken bones been a distraction? I kept my thoughts to myself and widened the search again, and again.

While these flights were easier and more comfortable than those I'd had to perform this past winter, the sun was setting, and we couldn't keep this up for much longer. It was time to head home.

"Master Kelnaht!"

I turned mid-flight and veered past a tree to my left and up to bring myself next to Riak.

Riak pointed down at a small clearing scattered with dandelions. "There is something on the ground."

There did seem to be something blinking in the fading sun. "Stay up here. All of you," I called out. "And keep your eyes open. Warn me if you spot anything else."

We were farther from the village than I'd expected. At least a couple of hours on foot. It was also in the opposite direction from where Joren had found the traveller.

Hovering over the clearing, I reached for my pouch and sprinkled herbs over my hands to cleanse them. I took deep breaths and, from another pouch, took the ground vorsen seeds Taruif had given Elder Morenn. She'd said it wasn't an immediate solution, but since it destroyed black root in tree roots, it should get rid of traces of black root on my hands.

As I drew closer, the object turned out to be a wide belt. I scanned my surroundings first. Wouldn't do to be caught unaware. No one near, but judging from the snapped twigs on the ground and the broken ones in the bushes beyond, someone had been here not too long ago. Had they heard us? Seen us?

It was breezy in the clearing, and dandelion seeds whirled around me. I blew them away as I landed next to the belt. It was made from rough leather, and had two leather pouches attached to it with an elaborate iron chain. The shackles resembled the ones around the elf's neck, but these were smaller. Much larger than those of a necklace, though.

I didn't open the pouches, remembering Taruif's warning about the dangers of black root. I couldn't afford to fall ill, even though it wouldn't do me any lasting damage. From reading the notebooks, I knew what to look for, and I kept that in mind as I scanned the belt for strange traces. And there it was. Exactly how the notebooks had described it. A weird tingle at the edge of my core, immediately followed by a sudden energy drain.

My heart thudded as I dropped the belt. I grabbed more vorsen grounds to rub into my hands, and my energy flow tapered off. It was frustrating not to be able to scan deeper without being affected by the black root, but at least this proved the belt belonged to whoever had infected our trees.

I cleansed my hands again, put on my gloves, and kept a tight lid on my energy as I wrapped the belt in a triple layer of goshe leaves. As an extra precaution, I created a shield around it when I was done, and put it in my bag.

I was halfway to rejoining the group when I saw her. She wasn't running, she wasn't hiding, she just stood there and smirked at me. I slammed hard into thin air. My breath whooshed out of me. My wings went limp. And I dropped.

CHAPTER TWENTY-FIVE

IT WAS DARK and blurred when I opened my eyes. I blinked, hoping it would clear my view, so I could see where I was. A door closed, shoes scuffed across the floor, and it smelled familiar. The infirmary. It had to be the infirmary. I hoped I was in the infirmary.

"Taruif?" There was no answer, but there had to be someone in the room. "Joren?"

I blinked against the blurriness again. It didn't help. Even if it had, it was too dark to see properly.

"You blasted dross."

Ianys. His voice was rough, like he'd been crying. I reached out to him, but found only empty air.

"I can't handle this, Kel, but I *had* to see you."

"Don't leave," I whispered, trying to grab him, but the door creaked, and Ianys was gone.

The next time the door opened, my sight was no longer blurry, though my stomach seemed to be turning.

"Kel?"

I let Taruif's voice wash over me as he sat on the edge of the bed, an unfamiliar notebook in his hand. It was good to hear, though not that particular tone. "I…" My throat was sore, dry, "I'm awake. Did you see Ianys?"

"Ianys?"

"Yes." I hadn't dreamed it, had I? "He said he had to see me. I thought maybe you talked to him."

Taruif took my hand and kissed it. "No. I did walk past the forge, but…" He let out a frustrated breath. "I couldn't go in. I don't even know if he was there. The door was closed."

"I'm sorry."

He squeezed my hand. "It's not your fault. Not just your fault. If only we didn't need to sneak around to be with him. If only we could just walk into the forge and make him see sense."

"As soon as I'm out of bed."

That made Taruif snort. "You've been unconscious for over a day. They won't let you go yet."

"A day?"

"Do you remember what happened? All your search party could tell us was that you simply stopped flying and dropped."

"They didn't see her?"

"Her who?" Taruif asked. "They didn't mention anyone. Joren thought he heard someone laugh, but they couldn't find anyone."

She must have hidden herself. I shook my head but that brought about a bout of nausea. I leaned over the edge and emptied my stomach.

Taruif put the notebook away and held me, caressed me, cleaned me, then laid me back on the bed with care. "I suggest you don't move again. You're suffering from severe energy drainage."

"The belt?"

Taruif brushed a hair out of my face. He was stalling. No doubt he thought work was the last thing I should be talking about. "Is that what's wrapped in the goshe leaves? No one dared open them. No. Fern found traces of black root in your nose and mouth. And dandelion seeds."

"The field was full of them."

"Yes. Turns out black root was clinging to the dandelion seeds scattered all around the clearing where you found the belt." Taruif pressed me down when I attempted to sit up. "Merel and I already took care of it. The area should be fine by morning."

I closed my eyes. I'd lost a whole day because I let myself get bested by dandelion seeds. "Anyone else affected?"

"Some suffered fevers, but nothing a bit of rest didn't clear up."

I let out a breath. At least I'd been the only one foolish enough to get caught in the trap. "The trull! She was watching me, you know? The grey-haired elf." I still couldn't help but wonder if it had been Mistress Pendra, even though her powers were harnessed.

"The one Atèn has been dreaming about?"

"Exactly. She stood in the shadow of the trees as I took flight, watching me with an arrogant smile on her face. She wasn't even trying to run. It was as if she'd been waiting for us. And then I slammed into something, and I just…dropped."

"I can't believe you managed to fly at all with that amount of black root in your system," Taruif said. "Though it could be that the vorsen seeds Fern found in your gloves hid the effects, until your energy dropped without a warning."

"Where is Joren?"

"With Novice Darver. I offered him the sofa again, but he'd already agreed to spend the night at Novice Darver's. You can be proud of him, even if he chatters almost as much as Merel does. He saw your fall and shouted to your group to catch you before you hit the ground, though you did knock yourself into some rather unbendy branches."

"It's a good thing I can't feel the bruises right now," I muttered. I didn't look forward to feeling them later.

"You don't have bruises, Kel. Fern healed them. Though, she was griping about silly elves eating away her energy when she had children to save."

The children! "How are they? How is Atèn?"

Taruif said nothing, but his expression changed instantly.

"No." Please, no.

"Young Dess didn't make it. He died before sunset." Taruif closed his mouth. Opened it, and closed it again with a shake of his head.

"What else?"

Taruif's voice was barely more than a whisper. "Two more children were brought in today. Not Atèn."

Another child dead, two more ill, and here I was, wasting precious time because I was too stupid to not recognise a trap.

"At least you now *know* the grey-haired elf is still here to catch," Taruif added.

True. But it didn't make me feel much better. I should have caught her already. Should have seen the trap. What if I'd exposed Joren to the black root?

This wasn't helping. Joren's magic wasn't wild like a child's. He'd have been sick, but he would have made it. I swallowed against the lump in my throat. Unlike Ninge and Dess, and the children the healers were still fighting hard to save. "Any word on when I can leave?"

As if he'd heard me, Bolder arrived and examined me. "Your fever's finally down. You can go as soon as you can move without vomiting or getting nauseous."

Considering my reaction to shaking my head... "Guess I'm staying the night, then."

"It gives me time to tell you about our mission to rid the infected trees of black root," Taruif said as he took my hand.

"Tell me at least something went right."

"I'd expected having to wait hours, days maybe, but as soon as we'd dumped a bucket of ground vorsen seeds onto them, the roots began to shrivel. It put me off vorsen porridge. At least for a while. There's something in those seeds that attacks the black root dust and destroys it completely. Instantly. They'd done the same to your hands, just..." Taruif sighed.

"I didn't shield my nose and mouth."

"Yes."

"Can the vorsen grounds be used to heal the children?"

Taruif's expression didn't fill me with hope. "They don't know yet. Rubbing the grounds into their skin doesn't seem to be working. They're now trying to strain the grounds."

Long after Taruif left, I lay awake, mulling about what to do next, until darkness finally claimed me.

As soon as I was back on my feet—without the room spinning around me—I was back in the air as well. While in bed, I'd had plenty of time to prepare a plan of attack. Not that I'd needed much time. All three locations had been in or around clearings: the traveller, the chicken bones, the belt—assuming the cases were related. As long as the grey-haired elf was watching us and focussing on clearings, it shouldn't be too hard to get at her…if I forgot about the black root poisoning for a moment. It wasn't a perfect plan, but with the time constraint, it would have to do. I knew this forest. All I needed was to not fall into her traps again, and I'd have her.

We made our way through the forest as silently as possible, sticking low to the ground, checking ahead before crossing open spaces, and keeping an eye out for anything that moved, barring rabbits. A couple of those jumping out from underneath bushes had spooked us already.

Hours later, we'd found nothing. No traps, no bones, no fires. Nothing to betray the old elf's presence anywhere. Still, we weren't about to give up. She had to be somewhere, and I was going to find her. I *needed* to find her to save the children.

I slowed as something moved at the next clearing, and motioned for the others to stop. In this heat, we all looked ridiculous with our gloves on and masks over our mouths and noses. In times like these, having the guide's ability to put an elf to sleep would have come in handy. If I could do that, I could have left Joren and the flyers at the village, and I'd feel more comfortable.

At my sign, Joren motioned all the elves to take their positions. I drifted ahead, and hoped it wouldn't be another rabbit. Approach and capture. Seemed simple enough, if I discounted the effects of the black root poisoning. But would it work in practice? How much black root was she carrying? Why wasn't she affected by it?

Cackling echoed around me before I could see her, but she *was* there. I almost froze hearing that laugh, and could imagine Joren being spooked by it. It sounded...evil. Pure evil. Then I saw her. She stood with her back towards me, hidden in the shadows of a tree. I raised my hand to give the sign.

But then a scream rang out, coming from somewhere to the right of the grey-haired elf. The cackling stopped and the elf started to turn around. If I didn't act now, she was going to see us, and my careful planning would blow up in smoke.

Without giving it a second thought, I all but threw myself at her, hands out in front of me, scanning, rope ready to bind her. Her grey hair was long and hung down her back in loose strands. Her voice grated as she spoke words in an ancient language few elves still knew.

I threw the rope before the old elf could move away. Muttering the binding spell, I pulled the rope tight, clamping her hands to her body.

She dropped something, a cloth bundle. It burst open, and dust flew up at me in a breeze, at both of us. Despite the gloves, despite having my mouth and nose covered, my energy dropped. Still, I didn't let go of the rope. I couldn't let her get away now.

She struggled, pulled at me, but I held on with all I had. My grip weakened as my energy drained. My hands cramped, and the rope slipped.

As one my group landed beside us. One of them grabbed my shoulder to steady me, and another took hold of the rope. Joren took the lead and rambled the lines I'd taught him about apprehending and being allowed to request a conversation with the guide, or her own guide, if he were willing to travel for her. And all through this, the old elf cackled and murmured in the ancient language.

Unable to stay upright, I sagged against the elf behind me. Someone rubbed vorsen grounds across my face and mask, ridding it off the black root she had tried to infect me with.

I let myself be lowered to the ground. I'd done what I'd come for. We had her.

Despite us gagging her, the old elf never stopped her muttering as we marched her through the forest to the village.

A cool hand pressed against my forehead. "You're burning up."

"I'll be fine, Joren. Did you send word to the guide?" At least I thought I'd ordered Joren to send word. One of the flyers was a messenger, after all. I couldn't quite remember, though.

"The guide and the elders, yes."

"Good." I closed my eyes and was promptly jerked upright again.

"You need to keep your eyes open, Master." Joren took me by my arm.

I blinked, too tired to protest, too tired to shake myself loose from his or Riak's hold on me.

The old elf walked in front of me, two elves on either side, holding on to the rope I'd tied her with. They were barely more than shapes in front of me. But those shapes and the endless muttering reminded me of something, something I couldn't place.

It was hard to keep my eyes open or pay attention to where I was going. A low hanging branch slapped hard against my shin. I cried out, and suddenly it dawned on me. "Stop. We have to stop. They might need our help."

The group looked to Joren, and Joren bit his lip. "Who, Master?"

"There was a scream right before I caught her."

Joren's expression only turned more puzzled. I hadn't imagined it, had I?

"Master, we—"

"Don't argue. Take two flyers and go back. Now."

Joren opened his mouth to object, but just then a scream rang out from behind us. He let go of me and bowed his head. "Of course, Master." He took flight, followed by two of the others.

I sagged against Riak. At least I hadn't imagined it. Steadying myself with Riak's help, I shook off my exhaustion and focussed on the old elf. She was still muttering, but there was something off about the way she was holding herself. As if she was preparing for something.

"Pay attention!" I shouted at the elves watching her, but it was too late.

The old elf jerked hard at the rope, causing both her keepers to lose their balance and let go of her. She was off in an instant, her bound hands held out in front of her. One of the elves sank to the ground, clutching his ankle, while the other, Ugard, scrambled after her. I hoped he'd catch her, but I feared what she'd do to him if he did. This wasn't his job. Unsteady on my feet, I pushed away from Riak and took flight. I wasn't going to let her hurt anyone again.

Following them through the trees, I was glad to see Ugard advance on the old elf. But as he reached for her, she threw something at him. I couldn't see what it was, but it hit Ugard in the face. He lost his balance, and fell.

It was up to me now. My exhaustion was slowing me down, but I knew I could catch her again if I pushed myself a little harder, a little further. Especially since she couldn't use her arms with the binding spell I'd put on the rope. I picked up speed. My wings held, with only the barest sting of pain. The rest of my body was complaining far more. I didn't give in. I couldn't give in. Not with being this close to capturing a murderer. I thought of the children lying in the infirmary, and pushed myself to fly faster and give more.

As I passed Ugard and gained on the old elf, the pounding of wings beating against the air came from behind me. It gave me the boost I needed.

The old elf stumbled. She caught herself and kept running, but it was clear she too was tiring. All I had to do was grab the rope and hold on until the rest caught up. I could do it. I stretched out my arms and dove at her, ready to grab anything I could get hold of. Just a bit more…

I hit the ground with my left shoulder and pressed my lips together to keep from crying out, but I had the edge of her tunic in my hands. The old elf went down as well. I reached for the rope as she fell. She kicked at me, screaming through her gag, and hit me in the chest. I gasped for breath, but managed a firm hold on the rope. As soon as she moved both feet together, I let go of the tunic and grabbed at her ankle, ignoring the pain that shot through my shoulder. My energy was low, but I managed enough of a binding spell to glue her legs together, making it harder for her to move them.

By the time the rest of my group reached me, the old elf had stopped screaming and gone back to muttering, occasionally kicking out to hit me in the chest. Nothing as painful as that first kick, but I was sure the bruise would be impressive.

I sat up as Riak took the rope from me, woozy and in pain— my shoulder hurt more than my chest. I wished we had a cart, because I doubted I could make it back to the village in this state. Someone helped me lean against a tree and gave me water from a flask. I thanked whoever it was; my vision had gone back to that tired blurriness. "Is Joren back yet?"

"Not yet, Master Kelnaht."

I hoped I hadn't made a mistake sending Joren after the screamer. I closed my eyes.

"You're not sleeping, are you?"

The guide's voice jolted me out of my sleep and I shot up, crying out as I jarred my shoulder.

"What are you doing here?" I glared at him. It wasn't his fault, but he apologised nevertheless.

"Apprentice Joren sent for reinforcements."

Cheeky apprentice. "Did you bring a cart?"

The guide was about to say something, but I shushed him

before he could reply, realising I couldn't hear the old elf. I blinked and focussed on where she'd been… where she was still lying.

"I subdued her," the guide said. "Her muttering made your flyers nervous."

Of course it did. "Joren?"

"Here, Master." Joren knelt next to me. He seemed all right.

"Did you find whoever was screaming?"

"I did, a female elf. She's distressed, but not hurt."

"Good." I made to get up, but neither the guide nor Joren would let me.

"Apprentice Joren told me she tried to infect you with black root again," the guide said. "How are you feeling?"

"I'm fine. I was rubbed down with vorsen grounds after we caught her."

A hand touched my forehead. "He was burning up earlier," Joren told the guide. "But he doesn't seem to be running a fever now. Master Riak said he hurt his shoulder."

"Best get him on the cart," the guide said.

I struggled to get up again. "I can—"

But I couldn't. A strange warmth settled over me, and all I could do was close my eyes and give in to it.

Chapter Twenty-Six

M Y SHOULDERS DIDN'T burn or throb when I rolled them, and there was no twinge or sting in my chest when I stretched myself. I was tired, though, and my wing tendons were sore. I had better take it easy flying for a while…again. Which would be inconvenient, but manageable.

Leaning against the wall in the corridor, I stared through the barred window in the door at the old elf sitting in the cell.

Not any old elf. Pendra.

She seemed too fragile, too *old* to be able to do what she had done, not to mention that her powers had been harnessed. She shouldn't be able to use them.

"Are you certain this is Mistress Pendra?"

Elder Morenn leaned against the wall opposite the cell, a pained expression in her eyes. She didn't look at Pendra at all. "Mistress Geine had to be sedated after she recognised her propped up in the cart as we drove through the village. She has never forgotten the face of the elf who killed her child." She stepped forward. "And she wasn't the only one. Many of our older elves recognised her, followed us here, tried to drag her from the cart. They threw rocks at her."

I put my hand on her shoulder. She trembled beneath my touch.

"I apologise for not being there to stop them."

"It's not your fault, Master Kelnaht. They were angry, and

rightly so."

I had no doubt. How much pain must they have felt, recognising her, seeing her? How much pain was she still causing? "Her powers were harnessed. How could she have done this?"

Elder Morenn gave me a wry smile. "That is what we want you to find out. She was carrying bundles of black root in a number of hidden pockets when the nurses cleaned, cleansed, and shielded her."

Pendra had not stopped muttering in the forest, but she was eerily quiet now, staring at the wall. Her bound hands were resting on the table in front of her, and her feet had been tied to the chair legs. She seemed immobilised. But I had no doubt she was still dangerous. I shuddered at the thought of going inside her mind.

"Has she slept at all?"

Elder Morenn shook her head. "We laid her down at first, but she became agitated when the guide's spell wore off. She kept pushing herself off the bedding, and we were forced to tie her to the chair."

"Why don't you want me to interview her yet?"

"The reason for that is waiting for you in the first cell."

There was someone in the first cell? How had I missed it? I frowned as I pushed myself off the wall and walked over to the first cell. Curled up on the bedding lay a wisp of an elf, face hidden by a heap of bound and loose curls of golden blond hair, decorated with colourful beads—similar to the traveller. "Who is that?"

Elder Morenn joined me, sounding concerned as she asked, "You do remember the screaming you sent Apprentice Joren to investigate, don't you?"

I blinked, and tried to straighten the thoughts in my head. "This is the screamer?"

"Yes. And a feisty one, too. Feisty and scared at the same time. And a good pair of lungs for screaming. She made Apprentice Zelg quite nervous when he examined her."

A female. "Was she injured?"

"Some scratches and bruises from running through the forest barefoot. She carried traces of black root as well, but not enough to infect anyone. One of the nurses cleansed her."

The female stirred, but didn't seem to be waking up yet.

"Healing sleep? Or natural sleep?" I asked.

"Natural. The moment Apprentice Zelg was done and we closed the cell door, she quieted and fell asleep. She hasn't woken since. She must have been exhausted."

"Is there anything else I need to know before I interview her?"

"Her name is Leni, she calls herself a herbalist." Elder Morenn narrowed her eyes at the sleeping Leni. "And her magic was harnessed."

Harnessed. Interesting. Not as innocent as she seemed in her sleep. We didn't have herbalists in our village. Our nurses usually dealt with potions and creams for aches and pains.

"She also seems to know the traveller, and was demanding to see them." Elder Morenn lowered her voice. "We denied any knowledge of them. For all we know, she was the one who attacked them."

There was something in her voice. "You're not certain."

"No." Elder Morenn took a breath. "She claimed they're called Uruf, and they both belong to the same tribe. Of course, we won't know the truth until they wake up."

Or until the guide found out through the connection he had with the traveller. "Has someone told the guide?"

"He knows." She turned to me. "Could she have been capable of inflicting the traveller's wounds?"

"I'll let you know as soon as I find out." I favoured Pendra as the attacker, but it was possible this elf had something to do with it.

"If you don't mind, Master, I'd like to rest before joining my colleagues. It's been a long night."

"Of course, Elder. I won't take up more of your time."

She nodded at me and went outside. Only then did it dawn

on me that I had no idea who'd be sitting in on the interviews. I was about to call Elder Morenn back when the guide appeared on the path. He stopped to talk to her for a moment, and then came to join me at the cells. "You look much better than you did when we found you."

I narrowed my eyes at him and crossed my arms, trying not to comment on the shadows beneath his own eyes. "You subdued me." My thoughts were muddled, but I remembered the warm sensation that dragged me into slumber.

"You gave me no choice. If I hadn't you would have aggravated your injuries even further than you already had, and you were too close to tapping into your reserves."

I closed my eyes. He was right. Of course he was. But that didn't mean I had to like it. "Please tell me you weren't up all night."

He put a hand on my arm and smiled. "Elder Rynth commanded me to rest the moment both our...guests...were taken care of."

"You weren't in the infirmary when they released me." I'd checked in on the traveller, and the guide's chair had been empty.

"I spent the night in my own bed. Healer Fern kicked me out."

I liked Ianys' sister more and more. My heart clenched. I longed to talk to Ianys. "When I spoke to Nurse Yasca this morning she said the children were hanging on. And so were the healers. Taruif and the nurses were still working on straining the vorsen grounds. They hope to try it out later today."

"Yes. Elder Morenn told me."

And the new arrival, Leni, was still asleep. "How long should I give her?" I asked as I glanced at her. "I can't wait forever."

The guide tilted his head. "She's awake. She just doesn't want you to know," he said, louder than he'd spoken before, obviously wanting her to hear him.

And indeed, she moved and peeked out from beneath her curls.

The guide smiled warmly at her. "Good morning, Mistress Leni."

Her skin was the warm colour of erst bark, the same as the traveller's. She was wearing a simple tunic, probably given to her by a nurse or the elders, but the colourful trousers she wore underneath were similar to the traveller's.

We entered the cell and invited her to sit opposite us. She flinched, and there was nothing of the feistiness Elder Morenn had mentioned.

Interviewing her was a slow process. Elder Morenn had neglected to mention how easily Leni cried. Hiccoughs and tears every couple of words, and what she did say was barely audible.

I found myself repeating questions in rotation, hoping with each repetition her answers would become clearer, while the guide tried to make her feel at ease.

When Elder Garren and Joren interrupted the interview to bring us lunch, I was still going over the same questions. Joren complimented me on how much better I looked, as he set the basket of bread on the table. I let him rattle on in the hope it might soothe Leni's nerves.

It seemed to have worked, because after lunch, young Leni—who had turned twenty some six moons ago—seemed much more contained.

"Why was your energy harnessed?"

For once, she didn't seem on the brink of crying, but merely swallowed and faced away from us. I took a breath, and prayed to Ma'terra she would stay this way.

"I...I thought I knew better than my mentor. I mixed the wrong herbs." A tear splashed on the table. "If he hadn't realised..." She glanced at the guide, then raised herself up to face me. "It was a family. They'd eaten bad fish for dinner and became ill, very ill... I could have killed them."

I gave her a moment to wipe her tears. "You were banished?"

Her eyes widened. "No!" She slapped a hand to her mouth and blushed. "I apologise. No. Nor shunned. It was just a mistake."

"But they did harness your energy."

"Yes. For two turns."

"If you're not banished, what are you doing here? Were you sent here?"

She shook her head. "I needed some time to myself, and I...I thought she was lonely, you see. And she...but...if... she was lying."

This didn't make much more sense than her teary and hiccoughed answers before. "Who was lying?"

"Mistress Pendra."

"I asked permission for a three-moon leavement—personal time to trek around and become used to being harnessed," Leni said with barely any sniffling. "I couldn't face them, you see. My parents, and the family I nearly killed. It was too hard."

She seemed awfully young, but I understood. To make a mistake like that and then be around the ones you loved, knowing what you had done, was hard. I'd seen how much it had affected Taruif, and Jarda, who had been shunned this past winter for taking her brother's life.

"It wasn't too bad. I could still pick herbs, and Master Oen had taught me some creams I could make without having to infuse energy. Simple recipes, but they kept me busy." She shrugged. "I planned to sell them in the next village. But then I met Mistress Pendra."

Pendra had had all the appearance of an old elf in the forest on her own. No wonder Leni had wanted to help her.

"I thought she was lonely, but no matter how often I tried to talk to her, she kept her distance and never talked back to me. She only glared at me, stern, the way Master Oen did when I'd done something wrong. So I left her alone."

Yet, some time later, she ran into Pendra again. "It was after I'd sold my creams in the next village. I didn't know what to think of her, but travelling together is better than being alone, you know?" Leni worried the hem of her tunic. "I know now that I was wrong, but then… I never should have left home."

I gave her a moment to gather her thoughts, and turned to the guide. He nodded, his expression softer than it had been before, which only strengthened my conviction that Leni hadn't been the one to attack the traveller, Uruf.

"During the moons we travelled together, Mistress Pendra became friendlier to me. She was very interested in my creams and potions. It was all she ever talked to me about…and, fool as I was, I showed her all I'd been taught, made her some potions, too. Not just to sell, either." Leni swallowed. "But I only had three moons of leavement, and I needed to go home." She clenched her fists even tighter.

"She wouldn't let me. At first she convinced me to travel to the next village with her. Persuaded me I could sell some of my creams for food and then go back home." Leni looked up. "She was right, you know? We didn't have much food, so, it was only logical. But when I talked about going home after I'd sold my creams, she…she grabbed me and told me I had to stay with her. She needed me to make potions for her. I waited for night, waited for her to sleep, and left." She rubbed her arm.

"But she wasn't asleep. She came after me, and twisted my arm. She threatened to break it if I tried to leave…"

She was quiet for so long, I wondered if I should say something, but the guide put his hand on my arm and shook his head.

Leni, still rubbing her arm, staring without seeing us. There was so much fear in her eyes that I couldn't help but reach out. She flinched away from my touch, but only for a moment. Her tentative smile was disarming as she put her hand into mine. She took a breath, and continued her tale.

"I tried again and again, but she always knew, and in the end, I stopped trying. As long as I made the potions she wanted, she left me mostly alone. And then the mumbling started." Leni shuddered. "I didn't know what it meant, but the closer we got to your village, the more she mumbled. Whatever she was mumbling about didn't make sense. The words weren't...right."

Tears dripped on the table as she told us what finally made her run from Pendra. "Uruf appeared. They saw me and waved. Mistress Pendra was convinced Uruf had come to warn your village about her. But I don't think anyone in my village even knew about her." She shivered. "Mistress Pendra threw one of her belts at him. I'd seen her kill animals with it, but... I keep seeing Uruf fall out of the sky, their wings torn, blood running down their arms. And she kept beating at Uruf when he was on the ground."

"You think Uruf was looking for you?"

Leni nodded. "I was supposed to be home moons ago. Maybe someone from my tribe had seen me going in this direction. Or maybe my parents sent messengers to several villages?"

It was possible. "Why didn't you come to us?"

She pulled her hand out of mine. "You're her tribe!"

And after travelling with Pendra, how could she know who to trust? "But you trust us now?"

"She's in a cell. I heard what the old elves screamed at her." She put her head on the table, which muted her voice, but we could still hear her as she added, "Did she really kill their children?"

And siblings, and... so many innocent lives lost. I swallowed against the lump in my throat. "Yes. And we think she's done it again."

"I didn't know." Her voice was barely more than a whisper.

I didn't think so.

"Can you tell us which potions and creams Mistress Pendra was interested in?" the guide asked, suddenly.

"Healing potion, mostly used to treat nausea. And a potion for burns and bruises. Neither is very potent without infusing energy, I'm afraid." Leni shrugged. "I thought she needed them because travelling tired her out."

I doubted that was it. Could this be related to the black root?

I shoved my chair back. "Thank you for your cooperation, Mistress Leni—"

"Can I see Uruf? Please? They *are* here, aren't they? I need to know they're all right," Leni pleaded.

The guide rose, and gestured for me to follow. Leni's wide eyes were still begging us as I closed the door behind me, and followed the guide outside.

"What is it?"

"You're wondering about the potions, aren't you?"

He caught onto that, had he? "We need to figure out what Mistress Pendra needed those potions for. Maybe one of the nurses can examine them for us."

"Apprentice Joren didn't find any of her belongings. But she could tell one of the nurses the ingredients, certainly." The guide seemed to stare right through me. "And maybe, while I take her to the infirmary, she could be allowed some time with Uruf."

The name rolled off his tongue so easily, so…familiar, it seemed. "You knew their name?"

"No. But I'm glad to know now."

If I didn't know better, I'd say the guide was blushing. But he couldn't be, could he? Not over a traveller he didn't even know.

"All right. Take Mistress Leni to the infirmary. And she can see our traveller after she speaks with the nurses, but only in your presence."

Chapter Twenty-Seven

"Mistress Pendra's system is shutting down," Apprentice Zelg said as he cleansed his hands. Nurse Calea stood behind him, doing the same. "Much slower than the children's because her magic isn't wild. But she has exposed herself to the black root in such a severe manner that the poison has started to infect her."

"How long does she have left?"

Zelg's expression turned dark. "Longer than the children."

I felt the same way. At least we had a chance to find out how to cure the children. I shuddered to think of Pendra dying before they were healed. "Thank you, Apprentice Zelg."

He inclined his head and made his way back to the infirmary.

The guide appeared next to me. Had he been standing here all along?

"She needed Mistress Leni's potions to keep her on her feet until…"

He didn't need to finish his sentence for me to understand. "It seems that way." The guide was pale, too pale. "Are you certain you are fit to join me? You could have Darver sit in."

The guide shook his head. "I have dealt with plenty of prisoners during my turns as a guide. Darver is not equipped for this. I won't risk her taking advantage of his inexperience."

Neither would I, though I wasn't convinced the guide was as

prepared as he claimed to be. Not that *I* was.

"Where is Mistress Leni?"

"Still with Uruf. Elder Layt is watching over her."

We waited for Elder Garren, who had insisted he sit in. I took a deep breath. The elders had made it clear I was to use my powers and go into her mind, despite her poor health. But she wasn't going to get any better, and our priority was the children.

Elder Garren was to be present, for our protection. Of course, that meant I'd have to do whatever he told me to do. It was no longer my interrogation, it was the elders'.

Elder Garren seemed as harried as Elder Morenn had earlier, but his expression was severe, determined, and I didn't even dare ask if he was ready. We entered the cell, and the guide sat next to me, across from Pendra, and bade her a polite good morning.

Pendra stayed quiet, looking at something over our shoulders, avoiding eye contact. Elder Garren didn't sit down. He leaned back against the wall, and nodded at me to begin.

For the next hour I asked questions, going over them at least three times, but no matter what I asked, or how I insisted or prodded, Pendra refused to answer any of them. She kept staring at the wall behind us.

I told her the consequences of keeping her silence, more than once, each time giving her time to nod or shake her head, to rage, even. But there was nothing. I had no choice but to go into her mind.

I breathed deeply as I cleansed my hands with herbs, but nothing could take away the dread of having to do this. It was the worst part of my job, to be so close to someone's essence, to see or experience what they experienced. But we needed to know if there was any chance of curing the children.

There was no reaction from Pendra when I activated my energy flow and moved my hands apart. I took one more deep breath, two, willing my hands not to shake as I pushed my palms forward and directed my energy towards her.

It was dark in her mind, almost too dark to find even a

single memory strand, but I pushed on, and the darkness lifted. Several strands appeared in front of me, but which one did I need? I focussed on the children, on healing them. One lit up. It didn't seem recent, but I was drawn to it, nevertheless. I grabbed hold, and sank into Pendra's past.

I stood in front of the elders, not the elders I knew, but I recognised the inside of Elders' Court. This part was always disorienting. It was like I was Pendra. I could experience what she had experienced, and I could sense her emotions, her thoughts, but I couldn't hear her voice.

One of the elders rose. "Banishment. You'll be escorted out of the village in two days and not allowed to return, not even when it is time for your essence to leave this existence."

The fierce anger in the elder's voice did not shake Pendra. I —she—was numb. No. Dead. She was dead already. She died the moment they harnessed her energy. How could she function without it? There was nothing left for her to do, to live for, if she couldn't tend to her trees. Not even the summer blooms that were about to flower.

"You murdered our children," the elder continued, "You introduced a poison into our tribe and endangered their lives, our future. You are no longer part of us. We banish you. You will never again be a forester, never possess any powers again."

As if being forced to heal the rotting children hadn't drained my—Pendra's—energy completely. I shuddered. Though I couldn't hear her curse the guide for forcing her to heal the children, I could feel her anger. Her frustration as well. She wanted to know how deep the guide's powers went, wanted to be as powerful as he was. Then they would never be able to harness her power.

Her anger almost consumed me when she realised she would never be able to tend to her gardens again, and her whole being cried out for revenge.

With a gasp, I rose up from Pendra's memories and shuddered. Her sorrow, though genuine, seemed to only be about losing her energy, her connection with her plants. She felt no remorse for what she had done. None at all.

"Are you all right?" the guide asked, though he refrained from touching me.

I nodded. At least I'd seen one useful fact in that memory. She'd been forced to heal the children by the guide. There had been nothing about that in the archives, and guides didn't keep notes, so I doubted the previous one had left a written account of the incident.

Pendra *could* heal the children, if the vorsen extract didn't work. And so far it hadn't. It had slowed down the poison's destruction of the organs, leaving Fern and Muros more time to recuperate between their attempts to heal the children. But that was only a respite, and only as long as no other children fell ill.

"I'm going back in again," I told the guide as I took some deep breaths to centre myself and prepare myself for re-entrance.

I didn't return to the same strand. I needed to go further back, to see how she had healed the children. Or how the guide back then had forced her.

I too sometimes wondered how deep the guide's powers went, but I had never doubted his goodness. I knew him. He was my friend, and he would do anything to save the children. That included using his powers to force Pendra to heal them... if I could find out how.

I concentrated on strands that were older than the one I'd followed before, and grabbed onto one that lingered close.

I—Pendra—was tending to new growth. They had been neglected, and she felt their craving for attention. Was this what Taruif experienced when he tended to his trees? Plants seeking for attention? Snippets of conversations I couldn't quite follow, but sensed nonetheless?

All around, there were other sounds as well. Village sounds. The sounds of playing that made me—Pendra—cringe. She abhorred their screeching as they passed her, trampling the grass while they threw a ball at each other. No care for the plants squashed by the falling ball.

Anguished cries rose up from the growth in front of me, and I—Pendra—let her hands fall to her side before she could cause more hurt. The rush of rising anger overwhelmed her, and she ran down the path. Anger at the children…at herself, as she almost destroyed one of the blooms.

I pulled out again, leaning hard on the table. So much anger directed at children was difficult to grasp. They were only playing, laughing. I took a deep breath and latched onto another thread.

Her anger lingered, but another emotion surfaced as the image cleared. A sense of…joy. Pendra was giggling.

In front of her stood a small potted plant on the counter, a miniature tree. Pendra mumbled soothing words to it as she scraped away the soil to bare its roots, words of apology for making it ill, words of promise to fix it, soon.

My stomach turned as the roots became visible. They were black as soot. It couldn't be. But as Pendra shook the pot and black dust drifted through the room, there was no doubt in my mind. This had to be black root.

Pendra coughed as the black root dust tickled her throat. She held on to the counter as her energy dipped, and laughed. She laughed. Her mind was filled with excitement, anticipation, and a sickening joy.

Outside children laughed. She put her hands over her ears. To her it was the same racket, day in, day out. All she wanted was for those monsters to shut up.

"They're just lively." It was what the guide had told her when she'd complained. But Pendra couldn't see it that way. To her they were a pest that had to be controlled. Or annihilated.

It was hard not to vomit as I left the strand behind. I never knew what I'd find when I dug into an elf's mind, but I hadn't come across a sense of evil so strong before. I wasn't certain I wanted to know more. How could she inflict so much pain without feeling any remorse?

Anger welled up in me, and I shoved my chair back and clenched my fists. The room seemed to fall in on me as I tried to breathe. The air was too thick. It was too much.

"I need a break," I rasped out as I rose and stumbled out of the room.

NEITHER THE GUIDE nor Elder Garren came after me, and I was glad of it. I didn't want to explain what I was feeling, what I'd seen, even though they'd probably heard much of what I'd experienced. I tended to relay my findings out loud while inside an elf's mind.

I leaned back against the wall, clenching and unclenching my fists, hoping that would stop them from trembling. A soft breeze provided the air I needed to breathe, though it did little to blow away the cobwebs of haunting thoughts and lingering feelings.

I gazed out over the village. It was too quiet. There were too few children playing outside, and not enough voices to drown out the sound of the leaves fluttering in the wind. This eerie lack of noise was enough to remind me what I was here for. Pendra had caused this unnatural quietness in our village, and it was up to me to get the truth out of her.

My hands still shook as I shook herbs out of the pouch and rubbed them into my hands to cleanse them—more for my own comfort than because I actually needed it. I wanted to wash away her sickening joy.

I was about to go inside, when Taruif came running down the path. He stopped in front of me, leaning his hands on his knees as he panted.

"Ianys," he breathed out and coughed.

No. Not this, not now. Please, not now. I dragged Taruif into my arms. "It's Atèn, isn't it?"

Taruif raised his head to touch his forehead against mine. His eyes shone with tears. "They just brought her in. His parents are with him, but..." Taruif's voice gave out, and he closed his eyes. "He looked devastated, Kel. He can't lose her. I don't want to lose either of them."

I held on to him and a strange calm came over me. "Go to him. Watch over him, even if he won't speak to you. Let him know we're there for him. I'll be there as soon as I can."

Taruif took a step back and glared at the cells. "Is she talking?"

I snorted before I could stop myself. "Talking isn't the right word, but I'll find out how to fix it. I have to."

The smallest tug, and I was in Taruif's arms. "Be careful," was all he said. Then he let go of me and ran into the village.

A sense of calm spread through my body as I watched him leave. And by the time I walked back into the cell, my hands had finally stopped trembling.

The guide glanced at me as I sat, a sad expression in his eyes, and asked if I was all right.

"I'm fine," I told him, knowing he wouldn't believe me. "Let's get this over with."

When I glanced at Pendra, there was no impassivity in her gaze any more, but a wild seething anger. I wasn't afraid of her anger. All I feared was what her evil would cost Ianys if I couldn't find what I was looking for.

After a deep breath, I dove back in, trying hard not to let my own anger or my repulsion rule. It was difficult to work out which strands I needed to grab hold of. I took my time trying to untangle them by refining my search. And when at last I found it, I didn't hesitate, but pushed into it.

Pain. As if my head was bursting. As if someone was squeezing my brain and trying to force my energy out of me. Out of Pendra. I knew that. But the pain made it harder to separate my feelings from Pendra's. No words were spoken, but the intention was clear. Pendra had to heal the children. That was what the pressure was telling her. She didn't want to. She didn't care about these pests with no regard for nature. Their screeching had hurt her ears for long enough.

The pressure became heavier, more forceful. It was hard to

resist, but Pendra tried. How could he do this to her? The village needed her. Pendra was their only forester, the only one who could coax their trees into becoming their precious dwellings. They were supposed to be... I—she—gasped at a sharp pinching pain at the base of her skull.

She pushed against the invading pressure. She was not going to let him win.

"You hurt the children, Mistress Pendra. You hurt innocent elves who don't deserve to suffer." The voice was unfamiliar, but it had to be the guide —then, not now.

She pushed harder. He'd said that before, when he asked her to help him save the children the first time. And every time after that. As if she should care about the little pests.

Pendra fought and fought. She thought she could hold out, but the pressure was relentless, and it had only one goal: to make her heal the children, to force her to reverse the damage the black root poisoning had done. They needed her energy infused into the vorsen seeds, because the children's energy shielded the traces of black root against the vorsen seeds. Only Pendra's energy could break through the shield because she had created the black root.

Pendra's screams echoed through me as I sensed the guide break through her defences. She couldn't hold on to her energy, couldn't stop the guide from draining her. I sagged into my chair as I extracted myself from her mind, exhausted, as if my own energy was being drained. Pendra's screams pierced the room.

My vision blurred for a moment. Two pairs of hands helped me up and dragged me out of the cell. They sat me on the bench outside. I leaned my head back and closed my eyes.

"I'll do it," the guide said.

"No," I said, while at the same time Elder Garren said, "But her energy was harnessed. There might not be enough this time."

"Then I'll merge mine—"

"No!" I would find another way. He was too weak, too tired, too overworked.

The guide glared at me. "It is not your decision, Master

Kelnaht. I'm the only one who can do it. You said it yourself when you were inside her mind."

I wished I hadn't.

Chapter Twenty-Eight

ATÈN WAS EVEN paler than she had been at the forge, barring the unnatural blush of fever. She lay so still. My throat closed at the thought she wasn't breathing. But she was. All the victims were still hanging on, even Kitai, though her prognosis wasn't good. The black root was progressing too fast.

Voices reached me, and I turned my head. Not from inside the infirmary, from the outside. Ianys. I moved away from the children and hurried towards the noise. Fern stopped me before I could open the door.

"You have to calm him down or take him away from here."

"Ianys?"

"He wants to see Atèn, and he's not going away until we let him. But we can't. You know we can't."

"I know." The parents were no longer allowed inside. None of the nurses and healers, nor the elders, had enough energy to spare to keep shielding all those who went inside. We could allow none but those who needed to be here.

I could easily shield myself, and even so I had only been allowed in to check up on Leni and Uruf, who were at the far side of the infirmary. Leni hadn't left Uruf's side since she'd been allowed to see them. Since she was a herbalist, Muros had deemed her knowledgeable enough to look after Uruf while the healers focussed on the children, and the elders had concurred. Leni had seemed happy to be with Uruf, and it took her mind off

Pendra, off the children. Though she'd had no idea what Pendra had been doing, she felt guilty for helping in any way.

The noise outside became louder, and I could clearly hear Ianys above others. "You want me to put him in the cells?"

"No. Just talk to him, Kelnaht. He'll listen to you."

To me? My heart skipped a beat. Did she know about us? No, how could she? She only meant because I was the truth seeker. "I'll do my best." I was certain Ianys wouldn't listen at all, but I had to try, for Fern, and everyone trying so hard to save our children.

The moment I opened the door, Ianys practically flung himself at me, and it took everything I had to push him back out the door, so Fern could lock it behind me. "Either you calm down, or I send you home." I glared at him to make certain he knew I was talking to him as the truth seeker, not as his lover or friend, if he even still saw me as one or the other.

Unfortunately, Ianys wouldn't calm down at all. My presence only made him angrier, and it was hard to pretend to be untouched by his rage.

"Twice-blasted dross!" he screamed as he swung his fists, but I whispered a quick spell, and his hands were clamped together.

Ianys stomped and cursed me loudly, red with rage. I muttered another spell and gagged him. It wasn't the best idea, but he was agitating the other elves. If all these elves started to push their way inside, no one could stop them in time. The healers and nurses needed all their energy to keep the children alive.

"Go home," I shouted. "All of you. Let the healers and nurses work in peace. You're not saving your children's lives by hounding them."

I didn't wait for them to acknowledge me. As calm and as loud as I could, I told Ianys I would not stand for him to cause a riot, and dragged him through the crowds. Instead of going to the cells, however, I pushed him along the path to the forge. It would be much quieter there. And I wanted him nowhere near Pendra.

We were halfway when I sensed someone following us. I stopped, ignoring Ianys' angry attempts to tear himself loose, and looked over my shoulder.

It was Taruif, who gave me a sad, wry smile as he caught up and walked with us. When we reached the forge, I pushed Ianys inside, closed the door, and sank to the floor. Taruif sank next to me and pulled me to him. He was trembling, but shook his head when I opened my mouth. We sat in silence while the door banged into our backs as Ianys pushed against it from the inside, again and again. I took a deep breath and closed my eyes.

"You're going to have to let him out at some point."

"I will. I just…" I didn't need to explain how Ianys' pain hit me, with Taruif's eyes reflecting my feelings back at me. "I can't face him right now. He has a right to be angry. We're working as hard as we can, but I couldn't stop Atèn from falling ill, and I'm not sure we can save them at all."

"He has a right to be angry, I agree. At Pendra, and maybe at us. But not at you as the truth seeker. Not at the healers or the elders."

"I can't let him get close to Pendra, either. Not now." I was too afraid Ianys would try to kill her and get himself taken away from Atèn.

Taruif leaned his head against mine and kissed my forehead. "So, how long are you going to let him do this?"

"This" being ramming himself against the door, which creaked, but held. It should, since the door to the forge was double the thickness of a regular door. It was lined with silver bark, treated to stop fire leaking through.

"Until he tires."

"Do you have that much time?"

I shrugged. "If I don't, he'll have to wait for me to come back."

Ianys didn't usually tire easily, but the fear surging through him—fear of Atèn becoming ill, falling unconscious—must have taken a lot out of him. Atèn meant everything to him. The knocks against the door became less powerful and less frequent faster than I'd expected. Still, wrapped in Taruif's arms, I didn't check on Ianys immediately after he'd ceased ramming himself into the door. I left him to cool off a little longer before I finally rose and opened the door.

Sunk to his knees, Ianys seethed and panted behind his invisible gag. His face was red, his teary eyes spitting fire at me. But he didn't lunge at me.

I took a step, but didn't release the gag spell, or loosen his bindings. Instead I knelt in front of him. "I understand your anger, Ianys." My hand trembled as I reached out to him. "I've been inside her mind. She…I don't understand how she could hurt our children like that. She…" I shook my head. I couldn't tell Ianys how deep her hate for children ran. "But there is a chance we can save the children, save Atèn. I know you feel I haven't done enough. But what about Fern? Her own children might be next. Don't you think she works hard enough?"

Ianys' eyes widened. He hadn't even thought about that, had he?

"Even if you're angry at me, you must understand why I had to take you away from the infirmary. Fern can't concentrate on healing the children if she has to watch for elves bursting in. There are only three healers, Ianys." And Zelg wasn't even a full healer yet.

Tears dripped down Ianys' cheeks. He tried to say something, but my spell wouldn't let him. I muttered the release spell.

"…stand." Ianys blinked, surprised I let him speak. He cleared his throat and straightened his back as he looked at me. "I'm sorry." He moved toward me on his knees.

I stepped back, my heart pounding. This was too much like that night.

Ianys blanched and sat back. Maybe he remembered it as well. "I'm so sorry. I shouldn't have exploded like that. I was wrong." He turned to Taruif. "You meant well, but…" He trailed off, awkwardly gesturing with his bound hands.

Taruif gave Ianys a shaky nod, but he didn't come closer.

Instead he stayed in the doorway, shoulders hunched. I understood how he felt. Ianys had been so angry that night. But now his expression, though sad, was full of remorse.

"Truly," Ianys continued, "I'm not angry at you. I..." He shook his head. "I was never angry at you. It just... You two looked so happy together, sitting on those steps, and I felt like I was intruding. I threw you away, Kel. And you, Taruif. You were finally free, and here I was, holding you back because of a promise." Ianys closed his eyes and hung his head. "With Atèn being ill, and thinking maybe you'd be better off without me, something snapped, and I got so angry." He looked up, fresh tears in his eyes. "I said things I shouldn't have said. It wasn't your fault."

I couldn't let him beg any longer. I pulled him to his feet and wrapped my arms around him as I muttered the spell to unbind him. He leaned against me, his face wet with tears. After a moment of hesitation, Taruif joined us, putting his arms around us both, his breath shaky as he muttered words to soothe Ianys.

Ianys whispered, "Seeing her in so much pain breaks my heart. I can't lose her. I can't."

"We're close, Ianys." But I couldn't promise him we could save Atèn. No matter how much I wanted to. "Let Taruif take you home, or to your parents, and pray to Ma'terra. Fern needs all the help she can get."

THE DOOR TO the cells was open, but there was no one in the corridor. No voices or murmurs, either. Not even Pendra's incessant muttering. I ran for her cell.

Pendra leaned askew in her chair, her eyes closed, but her mouth was set in a scream. I shielded myself, and threw the door open. Both the guide and elder Sotih lay prone in front of two steaming buckets, both half-filled with what I assumed was the vorsen extract—a more or less clear liquid.

"You thrice-cursed fool!" My knees buckled, and I sank down next to the guide. "You couldn't wait, could you? You had to risk your life."

I wanted to shake him. He was barely breathing. I reached for his wrist and felt a sluggish pulse. I thanked Ma'terra.

Pendra seemed in the same state as the guide, while Elder Sotih turned out to be merely sleeping, and snoring. Had the guide done that? How could he have been so irresponsible?

I couldn't send for the healers; they were overloaded as it was. I couldn't send for anyone without alerting the whole tribe. The guide would have told me to save the children, first. I could almost imagine the vague proverb he'd use, too. I'd been missing his sayings of late.

With reluctance, I moved the guide into a more comfortable position and rested his head on a sheet I took from the supply closet. I brushed a strand of hair out of his face, and checked his heartbeat again. "I should have known you'd do anything for those children." The slow beat didn't reassure me I was doing the right thing, but he would kill me if I saved him over the children.

Elder Sotih seemed comfortable enough, and there wasn't much I could do for Pendra, or was willing to.

Taking a shaky breath, I grabbed the steaming buckets. "I hope it was worth it." Closing the door behind me and forcing myself to leave them was one of the hardest things I'd ever had to do, and my heart raced as I walked through the village.

Some of the elves gathered in the centre, keeping their distance from the infirmary for a change, turned towards me as I approached, but no one said or asked anything.

Bolder seemed surprised to see me, but let me in and closed the door behind me without a word. I handed him the buckets.

"We've been looking all over for these. Where did you find them?" he asked. "And why are they steaming?"

"From the cells. I hope the steam means that this might just save our children."

He gaped at me for a moment, and took the buckets into the

room where the children lay. I didn't follow him. My shield might still work, but I didn't want to impose.

Both Fern and Muros appeared in the corridor barely a moment later.

"I thought the elders wanted to wait," Muros said.

I had no idea what the elders had decided, since I'd been busy calming Ianys down. "I don't know what happened. I found all three unconscious."

"All three who?"

"The guide, Elder Sotih, and Mistress Pendra."

"Do they need healing?"

"They can wait." At least, I hoped they could. "Children first." As the guide would have wanted.

Muros narrowed his eyes at me. I could tell he wanted to ask more questions, but he nodded and went back into the room.

"Bolder will cleanse you, and then you can come in and help us. I don't want to lose time fetching the elders, and we could use the extra hands with Zelg and Yasca taking some rest," Fern said, and followed Muros.

I let Bolder perform the cleansing and shielding spells, so I could enter the room. My eyes immediately went to Atèn. She was still so pale. "What do I need to do?"

Bolder ladled vorsen pulp into a bowl, poured some of the steaming extract over it, and handed it to me. "Hold this, and follow Healer Muros."

Calea folded back the sheet and bared one of the children. I wanted to look away, but couldn't. I needed to pay attention to what Muros was doing, so I could be where he needed me.

He cleansed his hands and dipped both into the mildly steaming vorsen, taking out a generous amount that he spread across the child's skin. I couldn't remember the child's name, but found myself praying to Ma'terra for his life, for all their lives.

I followed him as he did the same for another child, and thanked Ma'terra that Fern and Bolder were on the other side of the room, caring for Atèn. I didn't think I could handle seeing her like this. Calea made certain the children were wrapped in sheets after they'd been rubbed with the vorsen pulp.

After all the children were rubbed in gloop and wrapped, Bolder poured extract into cups. The extract had stopped steaming and changed colour. The clear colour it had been before had changed into a murky grey, like clouds captured in water. I hoped it was a good sign.

My stomach turned as Bolder poured a little into one of the children's mouths, while Fern moved her hands up and down the child's throat, then lower and lower, as if dragging the extract through the child's body. I had to look away.

"It needs to be done, Master Kelnaht. I know it looks horrid, but they won't remember this," Calea said as she took the bowl away from me and handed me a cup of extract. "Please hand this to Healer Muros."

I nearly froze as she moved towards Atèn. She put her into a sitting position, and sat behind Atèn, so she could support her. It *had* to happen, I reminded myself as I handed over the cup. I tried not to look at Atèn, not wanting this image to overshadow the one I had of a happily skipping child with Ianys' green eyes. Yet I couldn't look away as Muros moved his hands across her throat. I had to be imagining the tension in Atèn's body releasing, but it was the one thing I could hold on to, the one thing comforting me as Muros worked the vorsen extract into her. My thoughts were with Ianys, as I held the bowl and prayed this would work. It needed to work.

After the last child had been fed the extract, Calea and Bolder didn't stop pouring extract into cup after cup after cup. They stoppered the cups immediately after pouring.

"They're done," I said, but Calea shook her head. "Not until all the children in the village have been given the extract."

"But…" I closed my mouth at Calea's glare.

"We can't wait until we know if it works."

I nodded. She was right. "Is there a cart I can load these on to?"

"Bolder and Calea can take care of that," Fern interrupted, leaning heavily against the table behind her. "You need to take us to the cells."

"Maybe I should wake Apprentice Zelg."

"We sent him off just before you arrived," Muros said, rolling his neck, "The two of us may be exhausted, but we're cleansed and shielded, and have enough reserve between the two of us. Take us to the cells."

The crowd reared back as I opened the door and led the healers out. Questions were thrown at us from all sides, and some elves followed us all the way to the cells, but neither Fern nor Muros replied to them. I locked the door behind us, preventing anyone from coming in.

I barely dared to go inside the last cell, afraid we'd left it too late. Fern and Muros had no such qualms. I leaned against the door, staring at the floor in front of me, my heart pounding as I waited.

"The guide is still breathing," Fern said

My knees buckled, and I had to grab the door to stay upright.

"Elder Sotih is fast asleep," Muros looked up at me. "The guide's work, I presume?"

I nodded. "Tha—" My voice gave, and I cleared my throat. "That was my first thought. I'm assuming he didn't want Elder Sotih to stop him."

Muros took a vial out of his bag and held it under Elder Sotih's nose, who coughed, and slowly seemed to come out of her slumber. "Hmm. Yes. I'm inclined to side with the guide."

The moment Fern moved her hands over the guide's core, he cried out in pain. And so did Pendra.

"Stop!" I called out, but Fern shook her head.

"It's not affecting me. Let me try again."

There was no reaction when she moved her hands across the rest of the guide's body, but when she came close to his core, both the guide and Pendra again cried out.

Muros joined her and hovered his hands over the guide, close to Fern's. "He hasn't just tapped into his reserves, he's completely wiped them out."

Suppressing the urge to curse the guide, I asked, "Are they still connected?"

"I don't know," Fern admitted. "But we can't heal him until we know what the effect is on both of them."

"I could go into her mind again." I had never before gone into someone who was unconscious, but I didn't think I had a choice. "But I'll need to get—"

"Whatever you need to do, Master Kelnaht," Elder Sotih interrupted. "You have my blessing.

Chapter Twenty-Nine

I WASN'T EAGER to dig around in Pendra's mind again, but I had no choice. I needed to find out what happened, so the healers could fix our guide.

They'd placed him on a bed next to Uruf at my request. Whatever the link was between those two, I hoped Uruf's presence might help the guide.

I used the first cell to calm and cleanse myself. Muttering a prayer to Ma'terra, I sprinkled herbs across my hands and rubbed them in. It was hard to keep my breathing even and my anger at bay. By the time I finally felt ready to dive into Pendra's mind, all the elders had come to her cell.

"We decided it would be best if we join you," Elder Sotih said as I sat on a stool next to her. "In case you need us. And to support you."

Elders Morenn and Garren dragged chairs to sit behind me and placed their hands on my shoulders and my lower back. I waited until the first awkward tingles of their energy merging with mine had passed, then pushed into Pendra. The boost merging gave me made it easier to gain access, but I still struggled to find my way. It was as though most of her brain had shut down.

The strands were muted, more difficult to distinguish. I searched for any evidence she was still connected to the guide, strands that would lead out of her body, but found nothing. I did find her last moments with the guide, by grabbing hold of the one strand that shone brighter than all others.

Barely a breath later, I found myself—Pendra—staring at the guide sitting next to me.

The guide seemed fearless, showing nothing but his usual kind self, though he looked unusually serious as he tried to convince Pendra to save the children, to heal them and let them be.

"Don't punish the tribe for what happened in the past. They don't deserve to suffer. They shouldn't have to pay for your mistakes."

Pendra growled, and her body tensed as if poised for attack. "They stripped me of my power!"

"No, Mistress Pendra," the guide replied "*You* threw away your power by abusing it. Only you bear that responsibility. These children have done nothing to you. Nor have their parents."

His words started a whirlwind of emotions in in Pendra. She'd heard it all before, but it wasn't what she wanted to hear. She wanted her powers back, she wanted to hear the plants talk to her, wanted to feel them blossom again.

The guide touched Pendra's cheek, his hand hot against her skin as he studied her face, her eyes. She reared back. She didn't want him to touch her.

The guide's expression never changed, and he didn't step back, which only made her angrier. Why did he not cower before her? Why did he look at her as though he cared? No one cared she could never tend her gardens again. All they cared about was getting their precious pests back.

"I can force you, you know."

I—Pendra—laughed. Force *her*? Of course—

It stung. Something cheerful, something persistent, that wouldn't take no for an answer. The pressure built the more she tried to resist it, and her hands opened without her consent. She tried to stop it, but her energy still flowed towards her hands, ready to obey an order she hadn't given.

Her energy wasn't the only energy flowing through her now. I could feel the difference between Pendra's and the guide's. His energy carried a cheerful persistence that invaded Pendra's whole being and made her head spin. She wanted it out. She couldn't do anything to stop what he was doing, but was going to make him pay for it.

I thought my heart stopped as Pendra forced every last bit of her energy into the guide. She couldn't stop their energies mixing or losing some of her own, but that wasn't what she was focussing on. If she could push even the tiniest bit of her infected energy into the guide's body, she might just be his undoing.

I couldn't watch this. It had already happened, and I couldn't stop her—I was only an observer of her memories—but I'd never wanted it more than now.

Pain hit me, hard. Not my pain, not even Pendra's. I sensed the guide's presence leaving Pendra. But whose pain was it?

That sense of cheer still flowed through Pendra, and I knew. Because the guide's energy flowed through both of them now. In Pendra's drive to hurt the guide, she'd hurt herself as well. His energy had absorbed the last bit of energy the way Pendra had wanted it to. His energy was infected with black root the way hers was. But not just inside him. No. The energy he'd forced into her was infected as well, giving the black root more to feed on. It latched onto the new energy as it would wild energy, and it hurt.

Gasping for breath, I pulled out before Pendra could retreat into herself. Her heart slowed as I sank down in my chair, and the realisation hit me. The black root had infected what little energy she still carried in her core back then, and that infection had seeped into her body. Not enough to kill her at once, but to slowly eat through her until her body was all poison.

That her energy had been harnessed had not mattered in the end. Her blood had been all Pendra had needed to infect the trees.

She had fought it, kept herself alive to return here, take her revenge, and to send her essence home, even if she'd been denied permission. She had come here to die.

It was like the black root festering inside her was directly connected with the anger she carried. I shuddered.

"Are you all right, Master Kelnaht?"

I took deep breaths and turned to Elder Sotih. "Yes. But she's not doing so well. Her essence is slipping."

"It won't be long. I know. We sensed it through you. Go tell the healers what you found."

On shaky legs, I left the cells, leaving the elders with Pendra, and took flight. The centre was almost deserted when I landed. The nurses would be distributing the vorsen extract by now. Maybe most of the elves had gone home to be with their children.

Ianys stood at the edge of the centre, with his parents. He looked pale in this light, and his stance betrayed how tense he was. I ached to pull him in my arms, but if he saw me, he didn't acknowledge it, though Therdra gave me a friendly nod.

I slipped into the infirmary and searched for a healer. If any of them were still awake. Fern stood in the corridor next to the guide's room. She leaned against the wall, her eyes closed.

"Shouldn't you be resting?" I asked her.

She snorted. "Tried that. I keep waking up. Besides, someone has to watch the guide. He's not doing well."

"How are your energy levels?"

"Why?" She narrowed her eyes at me.

"The guide needs to be treated with vorsen the same way the children were."

"He's not…" Fern pushed herself away from the wall. "But he is, isn't he? Connecting to that trull infected him. Is that what you're saying?"

"All her energy, little as it was, merged with his. She was infected with black root, and now he is, too."

Fern shook her head. "It shouldn't be possible. He's an adult."

"And so is she. An adult with barely an energy core to speak of, where the black root festered for many, many turns, weakening her. This is not the black root it was all those turns ago, this is something...evolved. And if it can kill her, even as slowly as it has been, it can kill the guide."

"I probably have enough energy to go through this one more time."

"If not, I have some to spare."

With help from Bolder, we undressed the guide and rubbed vorsen pulp into his skin. We wrapped him into the sheets—though it was more difficult than wrapping the children. None of them were cloud elves. We had to leave his wings outside the wrapping, so they could breathe. At the same time, we had to make certain the vorsen pulp at the base of his wings was covered and warm.

I settled behind him, no doubt smearing pulp into my clothes as I leaned him against me. Fern draped one last sheet over him to cover his shoulders, and mine as well. As Bolder poured the extract into the guide's mouth, Fern helped him swallow it and guided it down his throat, his chest, and into his stomach, with each sip Bolder gave him. Like Atèn, the guide seemed to relax more and more as Fern worked to get the extract into him.

Finally, they both stepped back, Fern leaning heavily against Bolder. "All we can do now is wait."

I woke up to Taruif slipping into our bed, plastering his chilly body against mine. I shivered. "You're cold."

Taruif snorted. "Good morning, sleepyhead. About time you woke up."

About time? I opened up my eyes. The sun was brighter than I'd expected. I yawned. "How long did I sleep?"

"It's nearly lunch time. Merel and I already finished our rounds. I sent her home to tend her own garden."

"Lunch time? Why didn't you wake me?"

Taruif raised an eyebrow. "There was no waking you. Besides, the elders told me to let you sleep."

"When did the elders tell you? Did they need me?" I made to rise, but Taruif stopped me and wrapped himself around me.

"Stay. Last night, remember? I told you I met Elder Garren before coming home."

My mind was foggy, but he was right. He *had* told me. He had also told me Pendra had died not long after we had treated the guide with vorsen. "No news then?"

Taruif shook his head. "Not from the infirmary. Healer Muros went in when Merel and I started our rounds. The centre is filled with elves again, though. There were even children playing."

"That's good news, right?" Of course it meant nothing. Those children might not even have been ill. I chose to see it as a sign of hope, though. "Did you see Ianys?"

Taruif shook his head. "I went by the forge, on my way here, but he wasn't there."

I rubbed my cheek against his. "He's probably at the centre. Maybe we should go there, too."

Taruif turned my head to his and kissed me, bristle pricking my skin. He tasted of goraf tea and smelled of freshly cut grass. When he let me go, he sat up and grabbed something from the night table. It was a notebook. It looked familiar. He ran his fingers across the spine, a thoughtful expression in his eyes.

"What is it? Did you find something else?"

"Not about black root. Or anything to do with Pendra, or the children." Taruif opened the notebook, carefully separating the pages and pushing them flat. "I just thought you should see it."

He handed the notebook to me hesitantly, as if he wasn't sure I should see it. I looked at him for a long time, trying to figure out what was going on, but he only shook his head, and pointed at the notebook.

"Just read it, Kel. You'll understand."

I read the passage he pointed at, stared at Taruif, and read it again, and again. "What is Mother's writing doing in your notebooks?"

"It's not my book or my mentor's, it's your mother's. She writes about her work, and you. I don't know why this was in my stack. I'm not even sure why it was in the archive."

Could I read more? *Should* I read more? Finding this felt intimate enough, even if it was only a note that she'd moved in with her mates, Doek...and Ciper. I knew she'd been in a triad, but with Naia's parents?

"You can curse me for reading it, or asking you this, but do you think Naia's feelings towards you have something to do with her parents loving your mother?"

I had no idea why Naia had disliked me. "You're assuming she knew. Could be she just didn't believe in triads." Still, it seemed too much of a coincidence.

"Could be."

"What are you thinking?"

"That Doek and Ciper might know why Naia disliked you."

"If they knew, don't you think Ianys would, too?" All he'd known was that Naia didn't want to share him with me.

Taruif shook his head. "Ianys wouldn't want to say anything to them related to the promise."

That reminded me of Therdra's comment when she saw me at the forge. I told Taruif about that meeting. "I don't think Therdra knows about the promise. She asked me what happened between us."

"See. He's not even talking to his own parents. Why would he talk to Naia's?"

He had a point. "Just...try not to get him into trouble." My stomach rumbled. Time to get up. "Want to have lunch at the centre? Or stay here?"

From the amused shake of his head, it was obvious Taruif knew I wanted to find out for myself how the children were doing, and soon we were on our way to the centre.

As we filled our plates with bread and cold meat, Ianys and Naia's parents approached the centre from the opposite direction. Ianys seemed as exhausted as he had been last time I'd seen him. Had he even slept?

We sat at a table not far from them, wanting Ianys to know we were there for him. Taruif put his hand over mine. "He was up well after midnight. I hope Atèn is all right."

So did I.

Seded, Taruif's mother, sat across from us and placed a hand over ours. "Good to see you rested, Kelnaht."

"Thank you, Seded."

Taruif gestured at the food laid out in front of us with his free hand. "Have lunch with us, Mother."

"I already shared lunch with your aunt, thank you, but I could do with some tea."

"Tea it is." Taruif walked to the cauldron, and came back with three steaming cups.

"No news?" Seded asked.

I shook my head.

"Those poor children. One of the nurses gave Prin's little one something to drink last night, or so I heard. She'd been crying all afternoon. Poor Prin was afraid she was turning worse. But it seems her fever didn't rise, and she calmed down enough to fall asleep. She slept right through the night."

That sounded hopeful, at least.

Suddenly silence fell over the centre. We all turned toward the infirmary, where Muros stood in the doorway. He seemed more rested than I'd seen him in days, and he was smiling.

"All children in the infirmary are showing improvement. Their fevers are slowly coming down, and there has been no further organ failure during the night."

The whole centre burst out in massive cheering. Taruif wrapped an arm around me and breathed shakily into my hair. I squeezed his knee, and let out a breath myself. The children would live.

Muros motioned for silence. "One of our patients has woken up." He seemed to search the crowd, and my heart nearly stopped when he pointed at Ianys and said, "Your daughter wants to see you, Master Ianys."

Time slowed. I rose when Ianys did and smiled at him, even though he had his back to me as he listened to Muros. But then he turned, and beamed at us. Warm tingles flowed through me. It was so good to see him happy.

In the next moment, his lips were pressed against mine, his arms wrapped around me, and every sound in the centre faded. Part of me knew this shouldn't happen. Ianys would never risk losing Atèn this way. He wasn't thinking. I should stop him. But the other part of me couldn't get enough of Ianys' warm body against mine, and I wanted to hold on to him for as long as I could.

Something shattered in me when Ianys let me go. One moment there was love in his eyes, the next a stricken, shocked expression took its place, as if he couldn't believe what he'd done. He swallowed hard as he backed away from me. I didn't know what to say, what to do, as he walked right past me, past his own family—and Naia's—and followed Muros into the infirmary. And I was left to deal with the aftermath.

Too many eyes were staring at me. Too many words— questions?—that didn't make any sense. All I could do was try to catch my breath as I stared at the closed infirmary door, and pray to Ma'terra that Ianys hadn't just gained his daughter back, only to lose her.

A hand on my hip settled my thoughts, if only for a moment. I let Taruif pull me to him, let him lead me away from the centre and those staring eyes. He had Ma'terra's patience as he took me home. His words barely registered, but the love in his voice did, even if Ianys' stricken expression was still on my mind.

Taruif carried me upstairs, undressed me, and tucked me in. With too many thoughts running through my head, I lay in his embrace, wetting his chest with tears that wouldn't stop falling. His whispered words of love filled but half my heart. Something was missing, and I was afraid I might never get it back. *We* might never get it back. Taruif might not be shedding tears, but the possessive way in which he held me, and the way his heart pounded, were telling enough. He was as scared as I was.

I snuffled into his chest.

"He'll be back, Kelnaht," Taruif said, but a tremble in his voice betrayed his fear.

"What if they take Atèn away from him?" I couldn't live with myself if that happened.

"Then we fight for him. We'll petition the elders." He ran a shaky hand through my hair and placed a kiss on the top of my head. "Whatever happens, we'll be here for him."

I tried to hold on to that hope, to the resolute tone of Taruif's voice, even if deep inside I didn't think Ianys would come back to us if he couldn't have Atèn.

Chapter Thirty

A KNOCK ON the door startled me awake. It had been afternoon when Taruif and I had returned home, but the shadows on the wall clearly indicated a morning sun. Taruif was gone, and my eyes were swollen from crying. How long had I slept?

Another knock.

I hoisted myself out of bed with a sigh, wriggled into a sleeveless tunic with my wings folded, and stepped into my trousers. I was still doing up the string as I walked barefoot down the stairs. If someone needed me in a hurry, there were boots by the door I could slip on.

Blinking against the bright sunlight, I opened the door…and nearly closed it again.

Standing in the dew-wet grass were Ciper, her vowed, Doek, and a subdued—if glaring—Ianys. Taruif appeared from somewhere behind them, wearing a pair of light trousers and a short-sleeved tunic, and smiled at me. "You'd better let them in."

My hands trembling, and my voice not much better, I bade them welcome, and stepped back to let them enter. "What brings you here this morning? Is Atèn all right?"

"Atèn is fine, Master Kelnaht. A little weak, but without fever," Ciper said. She carried a bundle of cloth with her. "But we would like a moment of your time."

Ianys mumbled something about not wanting to be here, but

Doek told him to be quiet. His voice was dark, but there was no trace of menace in it, only impatience.

I hoped my hands weren't trembling too much as Taruif pulled me to him. I didn't know either of them very well. They were my mother's age, and I knew Doek was a potter, but that was all.

"I'll make some tea," Taruif said. "Why don't you sit down and listen to what they have to say."

I could barely breathe. All I could do was hope it wasn't about taking Atèn away from Ianys. "You talked to them?"

"I had to. Our secret is out in the open now anyway. And they were glad I came to them."

"But…"

"Just listen to them. All right?"

"All right." Though, I wasn't looking forward to the conversation, and I wasn't about to face them without Taruif. So, I waited until he finished making tea, and followed him.

Doek and Ciper sat on the sofa, Ianys between them looking like a storm about to happen. He was not looking at any of us as Taruif poured everyone goraf tea.

We sat opposite them, my trembling hands in Taruif's warm ones, and waited.

Ciper fiddled with the cloth while Doek blew in his tea cup. Neither seemed eager to start this conversation. I wasn't either, but this waiting didn't help.

"What did you want to see me about, Mistress Ciper, Master Doek?" I said, trying not to think about the kiss.

"It seems a situation has arisen that we might have easily solved, had we been aware of the problem, and had we not been…misguided in our beliefs." Ciper's smile was wry as she caressed the cloth-covered bundle resting on her knees. "But, first things first. Master Taruif told us how he found your mother's note about the triad Doek and I once formed with her."

I nodded. "Mother only mentioned a triad once, and she never told me her who her mates had been. She mostly talked about Father."

"I'm not surprised. She loved him very much. We were thrilled when they met. They fitted well together. She was a beautiful elf, your mother."

I glanced at Ianys. He seemed surprised. I guessed he hadn't known, either.

"We parted on good terms. We stayed close friends, and visited each other regularly, with your father as well." Her smile turned sympathetic. "Until your father passed away. Your mother wasn't coping and withdrew from friends more and more. And then she passed, too."

As if Ianys wasn't squashed between them, Doek reached out and put his hand on Ciper's, resting on the cloth bundle.

"We kept an eye on you, as much as we could. You were always polite, but you barely knew us by then."

I leaned into Taruif, and he wrapped an arm around me. I had no idea. I barely even remembered Father. I'd been very young when he passed. "Why are you telling me this?"

Ciper looked at Doek, who gave her an encouraging nod. "Master Taruif told us you were concerned Naia's dislike of you stemmed from our relationship with your mother. But, like you, she was too young to remember our triad. Unfortunately, that brings me to the next part. When Naia started seeing Ianys, we didn't know about your relationship with him. Therdra was very unhappy when Ianys cut off all contact with you, Master Kelnaht. She kept hoping the three of you would work it out. But... I have to admit I was relieved. Naia..." Ciper swallowed and caressed the cloth again. "I don't know how to say this without blemishing my daughter's essence, but until this morning, we believed you resented her intruding on your relationship with Ianys."

I blinked. Oh, I resented her all right, for the promise she'd had Ianys make. But back then? "I didn't know he was seeing her until after he left me." I couldn't help the bitterness, and I threw an apologetic glance at Ianys that he didn't see because he was looking at his lap. "I never even talked to her." We never crossed paths, either.

Ciper nodded at Ianys with a sad little smile. "Yes, after some prodding, Ianys told us how he chose not to tell you."

Ianys seemed torn between anger and shame. He avoided looking at any of us.

Carefully, Ciper unwrapped the cloth, revealing a thick bound notebook. Next to her, Ianys gasped. Doek clasped a hand on Ianys' shoulder, and whispered something in his ear. Ianys turned his head away from the item Ciper was revealing.

"Naia kept a journal since she was little. Ianys brought it to us…after she passed away. He didn't want to be tempted to read it." She opened the journal at a seemingly random page.

"We could never bring ourselves to read it. But after yesterday's display, and Master Taruif's visit this morning, we wondered if reading Naia's journal would help us understand what had happened."

She stayed silent for a long time, staring at the cloth, and only drinking because Doek handed her a cup. When she looked up at him, it was as if Ianys didn't exist. There was so much love between them, it made my throat clog up. Doek took the cup from Ciper's hand when she finished it, and urged her to go on.

She put her hand on the page with a sad smile and turned to Ianys. "We don't mean to cause you pain, but I can't do this without reading passages to you."

Ianys frowned. "I'm not—" He tried to get up, but Doek wouldn't let him.

"You need to hear this, Ianys," he said.

Ianys pressed his lips together and sat back, but his hands were shaking.

Ciper turned to me. "She was afraid you would take your hatred for her out on Atèn." She lowered her gaze to the journal, and read, "He hates me for taking Ianys from him, for not letting him be part of our relationship. I can see it in his eyes when he passes us. How could I let him raise my child with hate in his heart? Maybe he won't allow her to remember me. He might be cruel to her and take his feelings towards me out on her. Atèn is too precious for that. And Ianys loves me. He loves Atèn. They are so alike. If I make him promise to keep Atèn from Kelnaht, he'll do it. Like he promised to leave Kelnaht when I became pregnant. I'll make him promise, so Atèn won't suffer."

I couldn't speak, couldn't breathe. How could she think I would do such a thing when she didn't even know me? Though I *had* hated her, I felt sick that she had seen it so clearly and drawn such a terrible conclusion.

Ianys went pale, and Doek let go of him. Ianys leaned his elbows on his knees. "Why didn't she tell me?"

Ciper put a hand on top of Ianys' arm. "Because you still loved him. Over and over she writes how much guilty she felt to have forced you away from the other elf you loved, because she couldn't bear sharing you with him."

"I loved *her*, too."

I couldn't stand how broken Ianys sounded.

"We know you did. And you were always good to her." Doek pulled Ianys into an awkward hug. "I'm sorry. If only she'd come to us with her fears, we could have helped her, and she wouldn't have asked so much of you. We hope, in time, you can forgive her."

Ianys' hands were folded in his lap, knuckles turning white as he clenched them tight. He didn't speak or raise his head, but he nodded.

"We mean it, Ianys." Ciper closed the journal. Both she and Doek rested their hands on Ianys' folded ones. "She should not have made you promise. We know this won't give either of you back the turns you lost, but we, as Naia's elders, relieve you of that promise."

Taruif let out a breath, and tightened his arm around me. I could barely believe what I was hearing. After all we'd been through, these simple words almost seemed too good to be true. But they were spoken, and repeated when Ianys didn't seem to have heard the first time.

Even after Naia's parents left, Ianys sat frozen on the sofa, though I could tell he was breaking apart. It was in the way his eyes radiated pain, even if he wasn't looking at us. It was in the way he trembled as he hunched in on himself and clenched his hands hard.

"He needs you," Taruif whispered in my ear, his hand hot against my back.

There had been times, before we got back together, that I'd wished I could hurt him the way he was hurting now, but all I cared about was helping him. Loving him.

I climbed over the table and sat next to him. He trembled as I wrapped my arms around him and pulled him against me. For a long time, he was unresponsive, in his own world, but I held him through the stiffness, murmuring how much I loved him, had always loved him.

The trembling turned into shudders as he started crying, his hands grabbing at my tunic. When Taruif joined us, adding his warmth to our embrace, Ianys truly let go, his body slowly relaxing into our touch as he sobbed.

Nothing needed saying after his tears dried up, not even when we took him upstairs, tucked him into bed between the two of us, and held him in the aftermath.

IT WAS DARK outside when I woke to a hand sliding down my hip. I opened my eyes to find Ianys studying me with intent. Behind Ianys, Taruif was softly snoring.

"I'm so sorry," he whispered as he rubbed circles across my hipbone. "I panicked. I wasn't thinking. But I should not have left you standing alone. I'm sorry."

I raised my hand toward his cheek and brushed lips against his. It had hurt, yes, but in a way I was glad it happened. Without, we might never have found out the truth, and Ianys might never have been free.

Free. Ianys was free. My heart thumped. It hadn't quite sunk in that he was at last released from his promise. Free to be with us. "What are you going to do now?"

Ianys frowned. "Talk," he finally said. "To the guide, my parents... to Atèn." He trailed his hand up my side until he could rest it on top of my chest. "I'm worried what she'll think. It's been the two of us for so long. What if she doesn't like you? Or Taruif? What if she—"

I quieted him with a kiss. "You worry too much. You've got Ciper and Doek's blessing. And if Atèn doesn't like us…" I hoped she would. "We'll figure something out. Remember Prin? Taruif's niece who lives with her two vowed in those two connected trees?"

"But they *want* to live apart. I want us all to be together."

"Then we'd best hope Atèn won't mind moving in with us." I sent a prayer to Ma'terra. We could use a bit of help.

"I'd be happy just to have her with me again," Ianys whispered, a touch of sadness creeping into his voice. "I thought I was losing her, Kel."

"I know. But she's getting better, Ianys. They all are." Including the guide, I hoped, and our traveller, Uruf. If only we could have saved all the children.

We were quiet for a long time, Taruif's gentle snoring the only sound in the room. No matter how hard I tried to clear my head, flashes of thoughts ran through my mind, about the guide, the children, even Pendra. My legs twitched, and my wings itched. I didn't want to leave the bed, leave my mates, but my restlessness would only disturb them.

But as I moved to rise, Ianys' hand clamped hard on my hip. "Don't go, please."

My heart raced at the heat in Ianys' expression. "I need…"

He brushed his lips against mine. "I can make you fly."

Behind Ianys, Taruif stirred and blinked at me across Ianys' shoulder. "What are you two whispering about?" Then he blinked again, and his expression went serious. He looked from me to Ianys, who nodded at Taruif, and back.

The look passing between them was so familiar, tears welled up in my eyes. Ianys was truly back with us.

Ianys winked at me. "I'm going to make him fly." Then he

took hold of me and threw Taruif a beaming smile as he rolled us over, so I was in the middle. "Care to give me a hand?"

Taruif snorted. "Who said anything about hands?" He handed Ianys the opened bowl of oil, and dipped his fingers in.

I expected him to slick me, but instead he plastered himself against me, mindful of my folded wings, and slid his hardening, oiled cock between my thighs.

"No hands. See?" He belied his words by brushing oiled fingers across my chest and nipples, making me shiver and moan.

"Good?" Ianys asked as he trailed slippery fingers down my hip and slicked both our cocks. He was quick to swallow my stuttered "yes" with a kiss.

Taruif's tongue in my neck drove me mad as he rocked against me with tiny thrusts, pushing my cock into Ianys'. I shivered...and then Ianys pushed back. There was no slow teasing, just an endless assault of pleasure. And it was exactly what I needed. As I grabbed Ianys' shoulders, the flashes of thoughts drifted off before I could wallow in them. They were chased away by a pinch here, a caress there, and the rhythmic back and forth of their warm, sweaty bodies, taking me higher and higher. Being pinned between them, enjoying the heat of their bodies against mine, was the best place I could be.

Taruif shifted, angling himself so his cock brushed the skin behind my balls. I gasped and trembled, but Ianys swallowed my moans as he rocked his cock into mine with fierce, shallow thrusts. The loss of rhythm between them disorientated me as much as it excited me. I craved to move, tried to chase their thrusts, but being stuck between them forced me to surrender to their flow, erratic as it was.

Though Ianys in the middle was fast becoming our favourite position, because he hated being teased the most—something both Taruif and I had turned out to enjoy—this loss of control was exhilarating, freeing.

Our gasps and outcries filled the spaces between slide and touch, until Taruif reached his peak. Shivers travelled down my spine as he moaned his release in my ear, and shot against my balls.

The scent of his climax permeated the room, egging us on. Ianys' movements became even more erratic, harsher, too. I held on to his shoulders and lost myself in his rhythm and his kisses.

Taruif was still moving, as well, pushing me into Ianys with every thrust, and brushing his lips across my cheek. His fingers were trailing a hot path down my chest and stomach. I shivered as he took us both in hand, and jacked us off. Ianys reclaimed my mouth in a desperate kiss, but a keening sound still escaped as he froze and came all over me, which set me off. I came with a cry, my muscles tensing and releasing, and tensing and releasing, over and over.

Our harsh breathing was the only thing that could be heard for a long time after.

I'd missed this. I'd missed the three of us being together. I missed the easiness with which we fitted against each other, no matter what the combination. With Ianys free, I'd never have to miss this again.

We lay together, a tangled, sweaty mess. I started when one of them slid a hand across my side, but the hand quickly settled on my hip.

"Sorry," Taruif mumbled from behind me. He kissed the back of my head.

One of us really needed to get up to fetch something to clean ourselves, but none of us had the energy. Taruif pulled at a sheet with his feet, and together we managed to drag it up. Sunrise was still a while away, and I dreaded to think about ripping hairs out of my chest, or balls, as we untangled ourselves after we woke.

Then it dawned on me that Ianys would still be here when we woke. He had no reason to leave before sunrise. He didn't have to hide any more. *We* didn't have to hide anymore.

I smiled. What were a few hairs between us, when Ianys was staying for breakfast?

Chapter Thirty-One

The sun stood high in the sky, as Novice Darver led the procession out of the village and to the burning grounds. With every step, more voices joined his strong, clear voice as he sang the Prayer of the Dead. There were so many elves standing along the edges of the path, it seemed as if the whole tribe had turned up.

Behind him, Dess and Ninge's families followed, side-by-side, pulling carts on which the children had been laid out, wrapped in cloths and furs. Only their faces were visible.

A multitude of blooms were placed onto the carts as they passed the crowd. Kore, Ellon, and their apprentices flanked the carts, picking up the children who couldn't reach, and helping them place their blooms.

It was the children's voices joining in the Prayer of the Dead that broke my heart, and I couldn't help but turn my head to see how the guide was doing.

Far too pale, and not fit enough to walk on his own, the guide sat on the cart Taruif and I were pulling, grief written all over his face. Next to him, Uruf the messenger sat propped up against him in a similar state—they'd only woken up two days ago—their damaged left wing limply draped over the edge of the cart. At least the healers hadn't amputated it…yet.

Neither elf was well enough for any strenuous activity, yet neither could be persuaded not to attend. Worse, it had taken a stern talking to by the elders to convince the guide Darver was more than ready to do his duty. Needless to say, he wasn't pleased.

I was just happy he had pulled through.

Nevertheless, he insisted on joining the procession even if he wasn't leading it. And, in the end, Taruif and I had volunteered to cart him around. I didn't quite understand why Uruf was here, but the guide seemed happy to have him close. He said it was the link, but it was clearly more than that. The guide had been very close-lipped, but there was something in his eyes that gave his feelings away. I was curious, and I hoped he'd tell me about it, one day.

Leni walked next to the cart, quiet and teary, holding Uruf's hand. She had offered to work for our tribe as penance, even though her powers were harnessed and we asked no penance of her. Muros had been interested in her gift for making working creams even without her powers, however, and had offered her a position at the infirmary. She was staying with one of the nurses, and both she and the guide had barely left Uruf's side.

When the procession reached the burning grounds, the Prayer of the Dead echoed all around us. The carts were placed near the pyres, and from around the grounds, more children appeared to place blooms on the carts. From amongst the crowd, Atèn appeared, cheeks wet with tears, dragging Ianys with her. She placed a small bundle of blooms on Ninge's cart, and did the same for Dess.

When Ianys picked her up, he whispered to Atèn, and when she nodded, he threw us a small smile and walked towards us. He put Atèn on the cart, and gave her a kiss on her forehead.

"I told her this would be more comfortable than sitting on my back," he said as he hugged both of us, and leaned against the cart, close to Atèn.

Atèn wasn't at all interested in her papa hugging us. She didn't even glance away from the pyre when I moved closer to Ianys and took hold of his hand. But it made Ianys smile.

On my other side, Taruif leaned in and wrapped an arm

around me.

Slowly the crowd parted, creating a circle around the pyres. The voices around us faded, and torches were lit when Ninge and Dess were placed on the pyres, blooms and all.

The elders stood behind Novice Darver as he sang the Prayer once more. He had his wings spread, and held his hands in front of him, forming bowls. Silence fell upon us. Even the children attending were quiet.

"Both families," Novice Darver said, "have chosen to say their goodbyes in private. Let us give them a moment."

I closed my eyes, and prayed to Ma'terra to watch over the children, not only those we had lost, but those we had been fortunate to keep as well. Taruif murmured his own prayer. With my free hand, I reached for his, resting on my shoulder, and squeezed.

When I opened my eyes, Novice Darver approached Dess and Ninge's families, bowing his head to each one of them. They bowed back and readied the torches.

A cry rang out, and Ninge's younger brother ran at Darver, who knelt nearly as gracefully as the guide and gathered the young elf in his arms. They stayed huddled together for what seemed like a long time, though it couldn't have been more than a moment.

Finally, Novice Darver rose, settling the child on his hips, and spoke, "Instead of our usual conclusion, Iwar would like to sing his own prayer."

Iwar shook in Darver's arms when the pyres were lit, gazing at the fire. But then his young voice rang out into the silence, thin and shaky, but sincere. He prayed for his brother to watch over him as he followed his path without his guidance, his jokes, his teasing, and his tricks. His voice grew stronger with every line. It was a familiar children's prayer, and after the first verse, some of the children—including Atèn—started singing along with him.

None of the adults joined in. Instead we all listened to the children singing their final goodbyes to Ninge and Dess, who would be sorely missed. Standing between the elves I loved, I blinked away tears when the prayer was done and Iwar rested his head on Darver's shoulder.

IN THE LONG days after the burning ceremony, life in the village was slow to resume. The sense of fear, of shock, hadn't quite left us. More than usual, elves would gather at the centre for a meal or a chat. Often Kore's elves could be found fluttering about with baskets of bread, though, according to Ellon, Kore wasn't baking more than she should. And many an elf could be found heading to the guide's safehold for guidance at any time of the day. As could I, when neither my mates nor a flight could clear my head of Pendra's memories.

No one was lingering outside when I approached the safehold. The guide and Uruf were sitting on the grass in front. The guide's soft, melodious voice washed over me, as he talked to Uruf. There were pauses in the conversation, since talking was still difficult for Uruf with the damage done to their throat, but that didn't stop the guide. When the guide wasn't talking, he sat with his head tilted, as if listening to something only he could hear.

It became more and more obvious that there was something going on between those two, something beyond the bond between an elf and their guide—even if our guide technically wasn't their guide—and I was waiting for the guide to open up to me. Still, if it made the guide smile like he was now, and looking more relaxed than he had been in weeks, then I was all for it.

Uruf's broken left wing hung awkwardly behind them. The healers had done all they could to mend it, and had advised Uruf to not fold it unless they could without any pain. The guide and I had only spoken briefly about using Sorse's design to 'fix' Uruf's wing, so they could at least fly again. Nothing could be done until Uruf's wings had healed completely, though. Not to mention that we needed to find a bone carver willing and able to recreate Sorse's work.

"Master Kelnaht." The guide rose. "Come in."

"I didn't mean to interrupt."

"Nonsense. We have an appointment. You're not interrupting." He nodded to Uruf, who smiled at both of us, and motioned for me to go inside.

I was too restless to sit. "I'd rather take a walk, if that's all right."

No questions, yet, no tilted head. He merely changed direction and led me to a path going around the village.

Neither of us spoke for the first few moments, but the guide kept sneaking glances at me as we walked. "Did you have a nightmare again?"

"They're not…" They were mere flashes of memories I couldn't seem to stop invading my mind. The guide knew this, yet he persisted in calling them nightmares. It was useless trying to change his mind. "Yes. Though not as intense. But none last night or the night before."

"Good." He waved at an elf hanging clothes, a wee one sitting at her feet.

"But that's not what's occupying your mind now."

I snorted. Anyone could have figured that one out, with Solstice approaching.

"Ah. Yes. But why are you nervous?"

"I don't know." There was nothing to be nervous about. Not about claiming Ianys. If anything, I was looking forward to it. It had been a long time coming. Or maybe I did know. "I'm not looking forward to changing dwellings. I've only just moved in."

"I've heard young Atèn is excited about getting a new bedroom."

True. When we were with her that was all she would talk about. "She's been helping Taruif pick a tree, too. But Taruif has his eyes on twin trees not far from the forge."

The guide nodded. "I know which ones he means. They

would suit him nicely. And Ianys. Being close to work and family."

More importantly, they weren't smack in the middle of the village. "I'm just not looking forward to leaving our home."

"Hmm. Remember what I said about puddles?"

I shoved my hands into my pockets. Of course I remembered. Those words had stayed with me all through last turn. "Avoiding them won't make my path easier to travel."

"Exactly." The guide stopped and laid his hand on my shoulder. "Taking responsibility for Atèn, raising a child, is a big responsibility, but no one is expecting you to be perfect."

I shouldn't have been surprised he understood. "I don't want to mess up."

"Every parent messes up. It's how they learn. But neither Ianys nor any of Atèn's grandparents will mind helping you and Taruif adjust."

"They've been very welcoming to us already."

The guide smiled and resumed walking, leaving me to follow. "Ianys' happiness is as important to them as Atèn's."

He wasn't wrong. Besides, Ianys' happiness was important to us, as well.

At the far edge of the village, Jarda sat against the bark of her dwelling, restringing her bow. The guide waved at her, and she waved back with a wistful expression in her eyes.

"How is she holding up?"

"She's had a very difficult couple of weeks. Her eldest fell ill right after young Atèn was taken to the infirmary."

And being shunned, Jarda wouldn't have been allowed to see her. "Is she all right now?"

The guide nodded. "She's seen the girls playing outside. She knows they're all right."

"You would have let her see her daughter, wouldn't you?" It wasn't really a question. The guide knew how to make things like that happen. It wasn't his job to uphold our laws, he was here to help us forge our path, support us through good and the bad, as he had the three of us. And I was more than grateful to him for that.

The guide only smiled at me, but didn't answer my question. His silence *was* the answer, even if he did change the subject as we took a sharp left onto the path back to the safehold.

"How is Apprentice Joren settling in after the black root?"

After the black root. It was almost as if the elders had forbidden us to speak of Pendra. Her name hadn't been mentioned by anyone since the burning ceremony. Not even at her own burial. A burial, not a burning, and certainly not a ceremony. She had been banished, and as such deserved no courtesy but a simple grave in the forest, far outside the village.

At least I was the only one haunted by Pendra's lingering memories. Though there was something in Leni's eyes that made me think she hadn't moved on, either.

"Joren is enjoying exploring his talents without anything serious happening." And learning fast. My new apprentice was like a sponge, the way he soaked up knowledge.

"If it could last through the summer, that would be nice."

"Or next turn." I'd had enough of murderers and abductors for a while.

The guide cupped his hands and gazed at the sky. "May blessed Ma'terra grant us such a reprieve."

Taking a deep breath, I sent her my own prayer to add to the guide's.

When we returned to the safehold, Uruf was still sitting on the grass with a book in their lap. The guide stopped before we reached him and faced me. "Thank Taruif for the lovely tree he found for Uruf, will you?"

"Uruf?" So that was what Taruif had been up to. Sneaky forester mine.

"Yes. They needed a place to stay when Healer Muros dismissed them from the infirmary."

"They're not staying with you until they go home?"

The guide opened his mouth, then closed it again and shook his head.

"Is something wrong?" Had I misunderstood the way he was

watching Uruf?

"No. It's…" He worried the hem of his tunic. "They need to be their own elf. I don't want them to feel…indebted to me if they're staying."

"Staying permanently?"

The guide shrugged, but I doubted he was as nonchalant about it as he tried to seem. "For a while, at least. Until we've tried the wings, though they don't know about that, until Healer Muros gives them the all clear. Until…" The guide worried the bottom of his tunic. "Until we figure out where to go from here."

So, there *was* more to it. "You want them to stay."

"Only if they want to."

I wrapped the guide into a tight hug. "I hope they do."

The guide took a shaky breath. "So do I."

"Master?"

I faced Joren, turning too fast, and the guide had to grab me to keep me from stumbling.

"I'm sorry, Master." Joren flushed. "I didn't mean to startle you."

I straightened myself. "That's all right. Did you need something?"

"There's been a fight. A bet on a game of knobbles gone wrong. I locked them in the cells, but I can't get them to calm down."

The guide caught my eye and we both laughed. So much for a reprieve.

TARUIF AND I walked the path to the Solstice Circle hand in hand, accompanied by the muffled sounds of elves enjoying the last rays of sunshine in the village. Taruif wore braided, black leather bands around his wrists, but had foregone the one around his neck. He'd put on his favourite dark green trousers, with a simple black short-sleeved tunic on top of it. I wore a braided wristband as well—a gift from Taruif—and a simple, light-brown tunic over darker trousers.

I'd offered to braid Taruif's hair, but he'd insisted on wearing it loose, as I was. It tickled my bare arm as we walked, making me shiver despite the lack of a breeze. This summer promised to be a hot one. I hoped it would be a tranquil one.

As we approached the Circle, we could hear the crackling of the fire, though it had been kept small, so as not to add too much heat to the already warm night. On the other side of the fire, Ianys sat, eyes on the fire, droplets of sweat dripping from his furrowed brows, and knuckles white where he was clutching the bench.

I wanted to go to him, but Taruif held my hand and led me around the fire, showing our status and intention to the other participants. None of them paid us much attention, though one or two did glance at Ianys, who ignored their curiosity.

It was strange to see him this vulnerable. Out here in the open, at least. I'd expected him to be brash and tough in his approach. Instead, he didn't look up when we passed him, or even when we sat next to him on the bench. He stoically stared into the fire.

Gazing at the fire quickly became old. I bounced my knees and swallowed against my dry throat as I exchanged a glance with Taruif. Should we wait for him to acknowledge us? Or should we take the initiative?

Taruif shook his head. "Patience," he mouthed.

I had patience, though I wasn't certain giving Ianys time would help him. I placed my hands on the bench, willing them not to shake. My left hand touched Ianys' right, only barely, but enough to show him we had his back.

Elves came and went at the Solstice circle. Some shared vows that were accepted with hugs and kisses. Others left without so much as a word, and my heart clenched in sympathy. There had been a time when both Taruif and I had suffered the same.

Not until there were but a few elves left did Ianys finally

unclench his hands from the bench. He reached out for us, and took our hands, bringing them to his mouth to kiss them, one by one. Still staring at the fire, he rested our hands in his lap and said, "I have great responsibilities, but my path ahead is as foggy and blurred as the path behind me." He took a shaky breath and squeezed our hands. "I can't promise a path without puddles or pits, but I've travelled on my own for too long. Will you catch me when I stumble?"

Tears welled up in my eyes as I sank to my knees in front of the bench and rested my head on our clasped hands. I'd promised myself I wasn't going to do this. It was all in the past. But now the words were said, memories of waiting for him to vow himself to me—waiting in vain—flooded my mind. Today, I could finally let go.

Warmth enveloped me as Taruif joined me on the ground and wrapped his free arm around me. My mates. The two of them. Mine. I straightened and leaned against Taruif so I could look Ianys in the eye. I was no doubt a mess with reddened eyes and tears drying on my cheeks, but I didn't care. Though tense, and blinking some tears away of his own, Ianys was beautiful in the firelight.

"Whether puddles or pits, I will gladly share your responsibilities and catch you when you stumble."

Taruif tightened his hold on me. "I will catch you, will help clear the fog from your path, and share in your responsibilities."

"You are ours, and we are yours," we concluded together, the way we'd agreed before walking here.

Tension flowed from Ianys as he relaxed his posture, and he threw us a brittle smile. "I am yours, and you are mine."

His voice cracked on 'mine', and he raised his hands to draw us close. We rose, Taruif far more gracefully than I, and pulled Ianys to his feet into an awkward hug with our hands trapped between our bodies. Awkward as it was, we were reluctant to let go, and held on until the fire became too warm, and it was time to go home.

Bursting with joy, I walked hand in hand with Ianys and

Taruif into the village. I couldn't stop myself from smiling. Less than two turns ago, I'd thought the three of us would always have to hide our love for one another.

Now, there was no promise nor shunning to keep us apart.

No more secrecy.

We were free.

"WHERE ARE YOU taking me?"

Uruf's voice lost its strength on the last word. More than two moons since the attack, they were slowly recovering from what Muros called voice fatigue. Their bright red curls were pinned up, and they were wearing similar brightly coloured clothes to the ones we'd found them in—thanks to their brothers bringing them some of their belongings.

Though we'd made most of the journey by cart, their face showed exertion from the short walk, and they were slowly losing patience with us.

The guide—looking much healthier after his moon-long forced rest—put a hand on Uruf's arm and smiled. "It's not much longer."

Uruf huffed. "You just don't want to tell me."

"It'll ruin the surprise."

"A surprise in the middle of the forest?"

"Yes."

Trailing behind them, I tried not to laugh. In truth, the guide was more than a little nervous about Uruf not liking what we had for them. Not to mention that we wouldn't know if it worked until Uruf tried it out.

Uruf's broken left wing had not healed the way Muros had hoped, and he'd been forced to amputate the top half to keep a bone infection from spreading to the rest of Uruf's wings. They were now finally able to fold them without pain, but with a wing and a half, they would never be able to fly.

As we neared the cave, Fyash, the young bone carver the guide had approached for the task with the elders' permission, was waiting for us. She was fiddling with her carving knife, and seemed as nervous as the guide. Behind her stood Elder Layt, who'd insisted on overseeing the work.

"Good day, Mistress Fyash, Elder Layt. I hope you haven't been waiting long?"

Fyash shook her head, her cheeks pink. "Not at all."

Elder Layt merely inclined his head.

The cave's opening was at least two elves high, but narrow, and one by one we entered. Inside there were two chambers. A smaller entrance, from which the second chamber was barely visible.

Fyash disappeared into the second chamber with Elder Layt, but the guide held us back. Or rather, held Uruf back. I followed Fyash, and left the guide to explain the surprise to Uruf.

Even though I'd seen her design two days ago, the delicacy of her work still impressed me.

When we'd first shown Fyash Sorse's wings, she'd been overwhelmed by the task granted her. She'd almost refused, because Sorse's talent had been immense, and Fyash didn't think she'd be able to do his work justice. But we'd convinced her to give it a try. It had taken her over a moon to create it. The secrecy had been a heavy burden for her, and both the guide and I had visited her regularly while she worked. The result was simply beautiful.

Fyash trembled when I squeezed her shoulder. "You've done well, Mistress Fyash. Don't doubt that."

She took a shaky breath. "What if it doesn't work?"

There was no time to answer as the guide led Uruf into the chamber.

Uruf's eyes were drawn by the wing—little more than half a wing—laid out on a sturdy table. There were tears in their eyes, and in the guide's as well, as they approached. "This is beautiful."

I smiled at Fyash, who blushed at the compliment.

"I can't promise it will work, but it should be light enough to carry, and when attached, it—" Fyash shook her head. "We'll get to that, later."

Uruf's smile was brittle when they looked at Fyash. "Even if it doesn't work, I'm grateful you gave it a try." They ran a hand over the wing. "I've never seen bone cut as fine as this."

I couldn't stop myself from glancing to the far corner of the chamber, where Sorse's wings were hidden beneath sheets, ready to be shown to Jarda if this experiment worked. The guide had insisted she had a right to be told, and the elders had reluctantly agreed. Maybe, turns from now, the tribe would be told of Sorse's work, but, for now, it would remain a secret.

"How does it work?" Uruf asked.

Fyash pointed to thin leather strips attached to the wings on several sides. "We bind these to your stem and wing bones, and bind the excess shanna leaves to the bottom of your wing to reduce air leakage."

Uruf tilted their head, studying the design, then spread their wings to look at their damaged left wing. They turned to the guide. "You measured my wings?"

The guide nodded, not looking at Uruf at all.

"When I slept?"

Another nod.

Uruf regarded the guide, their smile less brittle than before. "All right. Let's try it, before I lose my nerve."

With the bone carved so fine, the wing was light and seemed fragile, but shanna leaves were some of the sturdiest leaves in the forests. Tests had shown it could withstand a harsh wind easily. I held the wing in place, while Fyash tied the strips, one by one. She checked with Uruf before and after tying each one, making sure she wasn't hurting them. The guide studied Uruf's face to be certain they weren't hiding any pain. When Fyash was finally done, I let go of the wing and stood back.

Across from us, the guide was still watching Uruf's face, his expression anxious, and his hands hidden in the sleeves of his cloak.

Uruf moved their wings in slow flaps, testing it. "It feels weird. Like something is pulling on my wing."

It stayed firmly attached, though, and swayed seamlessly with every motion Uruf's wings made. We stepped back as their movements became firmer, wider.

"I think I could get used to that feeling." Uruf walked over to the guide and took his hands. "Thank you."

"Not until you've flown. Besides, it's not me you need to thank. It's Mistress Fyash who spent over a moon of free time creating it for you."

"I'm sure it'll work." Uruf inclined his head at Fyash. "Thank you, Mistress."

They turned sideways and carefully stepped through to the smaller chamber, and repeated the sideways walk until they were outside. They gazed up at the sky, let out a slow breath, and started flapping their wings.

The new wing stayed firmly attached as they picked up speed and tested the endurance. Only when they seemed certain the wing would hold did they lift off.

I muttered a quick prayer to Ma'terra as their feet left the ground, and I could hear the guide doing the same.

Uruf rose above our heads, but then they lost their balance, and fell. We ran to catch them, but they landed with barely a stumble.

The guide took Uruf's hands in his, mumbling something we couldn't hear. Uruf laughed, pulled the guide closer, and flapped their wings, once more. "Thank you. Thank you all. It'll take some getting used to, but you gave me back my flight."

I'd been all for this experiment from the beginning, but its success still left me with a bittersweet aftertaste. I would never quite forget the elf who had created the flawless wings Uruf's was based on. He had been so full of revenge, of hate.

Yet, how could I not smile when Uruf jumped into the air again, and flew circles around the guide?

Acknowledgements

A big thanks to:

My critters throughout all three acts for helping me iron out the kinks: Act One—Cleon, Jordan, JRose, and Kaje; Act Two—Jennifer, Lor, Lou, and Kaje; Act Three—Ceri, Imke, Keelan, Larissa, Mieke, and Tami,

Tam for the inspiration for Kore and her lovers in Act Three,

Simoné, for the gorgeous cover art that really makes Kelnaht, Taruif, and Ianys shine. And for Taruif's beautiful tree,

KJ Charles, for all her editing, but especially for the developmental edits for Act Three. You rock!

Tami Veldura, for the proofreading, the blurbs, and catching those stray issues,

Jarsto, Dorinde, and Jasper, for being there when I need you,

My husband and kids, for their faith and support.

About the Author

Blaine D. Arden is a purple-haired, forty-something author of queer romance mixed with fantasy, mystery, and magic who sings her way through life in platform boots.

Born and raised in Zutphen, the Netherlands, Blaine spent many hours of her sheltered youth reading, day dreaming, making up stories and acting them out with her Barbies. After seeing the film *"An Early Frost"* as a teen in the mid-eighties, an idealistic Blaine wanted to do away with the negativity surrounding homosexuality and strove to show the world how beautiful love between men could be. *Our difference is our strength*, is Blaine's motto, and her stories are often set in worlds where gender fluidity and sexual diversity are accepted as is.

When not writing or reading, Blaine has singing lessons and hopes to be in a band someday. Supporting Blaine in pursuing her dreams and all matters regarding household, kids, and cairn terrier, is her long-suffering husband for over twenty years.

Blaine is an EPIC Award winning author and has been published by Storm Moon Press, Less Than Three Press, and Wilde City Press. Her scifi romance *"Aliens, Smith and Jones"* received an Honourable Mention in the Best Gay Sci-Fi/Fantasy category of the Rainbow Awards 2012.

For more information about Blaine and her books, visit her website: http://blainedarden.com

Also by Blaine D. Arden

A Time Traveller's Valentine (short)
Click Your Heels (short)
The Fifth Son (novella)
Aliens, Smith and Jones (novel)

<u>Tales of the Forest Series</u>
Oren's Right
The Forester (Forester Triad Act One – single release)
Lost and Found (Forester Triad Act Two – single release)
Full Circle (Forester Triad Act Three – single release)

<u>Freebies</u> (available on Blaine's website)
Color Me
The Storyteller
Slippery When Wet
An Invitation to Love

Oren's Right
A Tales of the Forest Short

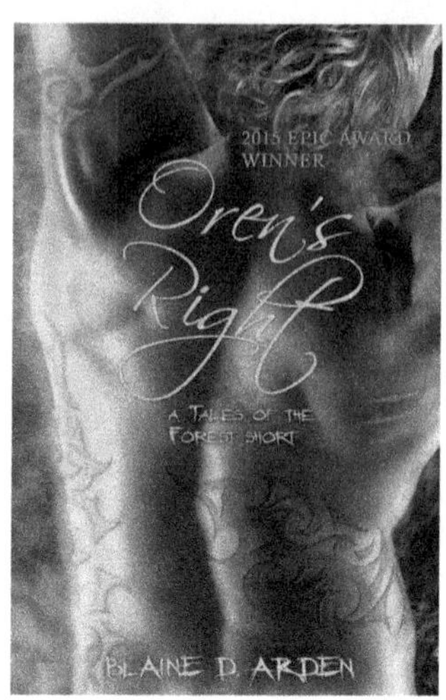

Following his principles will break two hearts.

Forester Veld loses a piece of himself to mute baker Oren when they first meet, but Oren is vowed to Haram. When Haram is killed, Veld denies his heart to respect the mourning period. It's the right thing to do.

During Haram's funeral, Oren proudly bares the brands that show the nature of their love; Haram owned him, heart and body. The elves pity Oren and think he's broken.

Veld has no intention of dishonouring Haram's memory, but his death may not have been an accident. Only a forester can learn what the trees have seen. However, Oren's independence is threatened, and if Veld does not offer what Oren needs, Oren may never be his to claim.

THE FIFTH SON

A PRINCE WITHOUT POWER

In a land where magic is commonplace, Prince Llyskel has none. He can't command spells, he has never been taught to fight, and as the fifth son of the King, he will never rule. Everyone believes he's a weakling, most of all himself.

Powerlessness is Llyskel's problem—and his pleasure. In his secret fantasies, the prince dreams of nothing more than finding himself helpless at another man's hands… particularly the hands of Captain Ariv of the Guards.

Then Ariv makes Llyskel's dream a reality, and as the powerless prince surrenders to the soldier's desire, he finds his own true strength at last. But a web of royal politics is closing around Llyskel, threatening to tear him from his lover, and it will take all his newfound courage to escape…